The Marsh Man

Mark Vivian was educated at Bedford School and the City University where he obtained an honours degree in psychology in 1984. Raised in Luton, he now lives with his long-term partner Gill and dog Layla near the Dorset coast. A sports enthusiast, his participation in recent years has been curbed by back problems although he still plays regular football. Mark has taught psychology, and also English to foreign students. Amongst other jobs, he has worked for Stockport County football club. More recently he has been writing many freelance features for glossy magazines, most of which concern locations to explore in France. There, the Vendée is an area particularly close to his heart. His other main interests include palaeontology, nature and forensic sciences.

The Marsh Man

Mark Vivian

The Marsh Man

Olympia Publishers

www.olympiapublishers.com
OLYMPIA PAPERBACK EDITION
Copyright © Mark Vivian 2009

The right of Mark Vivian to be identified as author of
this work has been asserted in accordance with sections 77 and 78 of the
Copyright, Designs and Patents Act 1988.

A CIP catalogue record for this title is
available from the British Library.

ISBN: 978-1-84897-028-1

This is a work of fiction.
Names, characters, places and incidents originate from the writer's
imagination. Any resemblance to actual persons, living or dead, is purely
coincidental.

Olympia Publishers is part of Ashwell Publishing Ltd.

First Published in 2009

Olympia Publishers
60 Cannon Street
London
EC4N 6NP

Printed in Great Britain

Dedication

For Gill – my partner, protector, and inspiration. Special thanks
to a truly wonderful friend, JMT, for all his support and
wisdom, to the artist Jacqui Sieger for her magnificent cover
painting, and to readers Rob, Ralph, Julie and Michael for their
kind and generous help.
Last, and by no means least, in memory of dear and brave
Thomas Mastandrea – a too brief but brilliant sparkle of light in
the lives of all who knew him.

PART I

Bedlam

1

They may be the only mortals capable of grasping reality, but not even a single Nuddite will ever know what had happened on those marshes, Percival Nudd reminded himself, sitting, arms folded, in front of a physician for the insane. He anticipated being questioned about a matter he would refuse to discuss, and braced himself. He attempted to hone his wits razor-sharp, but the strop wouldn't deliver. Nudd recognised the alarming pattern. Despite being fully conscious, he had scant control as a bad dream became that familiar nightmare flinging him right back to 19 October 1883 – and it arrived in a rush. The sound of thundering hooves galloped around Nudd's head. Louder and louder the tormenting racket intensified. Nudd began panting. His heartbeat accelerated and he felt the blood drain from his stomach walls. Nudd grimaced and finally, finally after grappling with his gasps, he regained some composure by repossessing his breathing. As he established these rhythms and clung on to them, so the sound of the hooves faded, liberating Nudd to cope with the physician.

Cognizant of his patients, the physician appreciated that this one was sane enough to realise that he probably wouldn't be allowed to walk out of Bedlam yet. Perhaps not, as Nudd was only too aware, until he revealed something of the secret that had radically altered the course of his life. So far the defiant Mr Nudd had yielded only morsels about a pitiless location but nothing of the event. This secret was too personal, too terrible, and perhaps too shameful for Nudd to divulge. In truth, itself an unstable element of Nudd's psyche, this was something beyond even *his* comprehension. He was determined to keep it locked away in his head and his diary. Nobody else had the right to investigate it. Anybody else, Nudd always reassured himself, would be gravely imperilled by meddling. In any case, only God can explain the inexplicable – Him and, distressingly, the Devil.

Percival Nudd carefully considered the physician. He saw a taller man – not unlike his his own physique – with tidy, combed-across hair fixed with a sheen by an application of beeswax pomade that had finally replaced the lard and petroleum jelly concoction. This hair, and especially the toothbrush moustache mounted only above the middle section of the upper lip, had a red tinge most discernable in strong light. When standing, the physician's gracile physique became more apparent. Nudd saw an uncomplicated man with many years of expertise in his chosen profession. Right now, decided Nudd, he knows neither with whom nor with what he is dealing.

"Religious mania, Mr Nudd, is indeed an unfortunate affliction," began the doctor softly, his words partially supporting Nudd's opinion. The physician smiled. A visit to the physicians' room might intimidate many, were it not for Dr Norton's usual knack of putting patients at their ease. He continued.

"The good tidings are, that in our experience, this nervous disorder can eventually disappear altogether with time and applied diligence. Even better, Mr Nudd, in our opinion here at Bethlem, you are a significant distance down the path to a full recovery. No longer restricted to the gentlemen's airing enclosure behind the hospital, you are now granted permission to exercise at the front – just so long as you continue to inform staff at all times of your whereabouts. Additionally Dr Kenelm Strange, as you will recollect, had considered treating you with a course of moral therapy. He has since agreed to defer this. The prognosis is favourable, Mr Nudd, and confirming the opinion of the Physician Superintendant when you first arrived here for this admission, we totally concur that you are *not* an incurable," he added with an invigorated smile of encouragement. Nudd cautiously returned the gesture. Step by step, Nudd recognised the need to remain calm and to say the right things, and at the right time.

"This, doctor, *is* good news. I do feel that I am almost ready to return to my Emily," he agreed. The physician was no fool, and he took the opportunity to tax Nudd's ability to respond strategically.

"Ah yes. Your wife. It is a little unfortunate that she is still reluctant to visit you here."

"I'm afraid that Emily is of a rather timid disposition," Nudd explained. Momentarily he visualised his wife dutifully making the effort to smile politely while serving refreshments to his followers – before slipping back out of sight with a grimace. "In her letters she states that she is most eagerly awaiting my return."

"Of course. I'm sure she is, Mr Nudd. But on the subject of your visitors, I am a little concerned about the frequent visits you receive from a Mrs Harriet Porter and a Mr Joshua Broad that have been brought to my attention. I fear that their contact with you is – one could say – less than gainful in view of your problems."

Nudd, reacting with a weak smile, was irked. He may well have recently been suffering from another bout of melancholia – if they insist. He may well have crashed too far down into the clogging gloom like a grub languishing under the winter soil. With the sort of problems with which he alone had to contend, altogether different from the medical variety preoccupying the physicians, it was, he reckoned, to be expected.

Nudd responded calmly.

"This really need not be of concern, doctor. Not anymore. I believe that I am sufficiently cured and now strong enough in character not to allow my followers to adversely influence either my behaviour or my notions. The melancholia has loosened its grip, and I can clearly see the folly of my ways."

"Forthright and lucid words, Mr Nudd. This is encouraging, although I still harbour some significant reservations about your two friends," said Dr Norton, recalling a selection of unflattering comments he'd heard about the peculiar twosome he'd only glimpsed. Norton neither laughed nor rolled his eyes. Nudd stroked his finger down one of the trimmed side-whiskers that reached his jawline. Queen Victoria's eyes, from her portrait on the wall, watched both men closely.

"I understand why, naturally," he said.

"Understanding why is not necessarily removing the problem."

"These are two loyal friends who have stood by my side during the bleakest of times," Nudd resumed at pace, "and whilst plenty have turned the other way to avoid me. It would scarcely be honourable to discard them now. In any case, as I have recently explained in a letter to Mrs Nudd, my intentions are to seek a quiet life devoted to my family and to God. And when I speak of my devotion to God, I mean to say that I intend only to lead the modest life of a good Christian: daily prayers, following the Commandments, reading the Gospels, and attending church. Everything else I have already cast aside. So long as I can find suitable labour, or so long as the funds continue to arrive from my anonymous French benefactor, this is a path from which I will not be led astray," Nudd said.

"Is this French benefactor a follower or, perhaps, a friend of your church?"

"Ah! I am unable to tell you, doctor. I don't know myself, although the offerings predate the founding of the Nuddite Church. I have an inkling about the identity of the benefactor. My guess is that it is a wealthy family of aristocrats. That is all I can suggest. God, for His reasons, has declined to answer my questions although one might reasonably conclude that these sums of money are answers to but some of my prayers. These funds are much needed since donations from my Nuddite followers have drastically declined. The latter will surely cease altogether now that I have cast all aside."

"But," contested the physician, pointing with his eyes up and down Percival Nudd's person, "you haven't quite cast everything aside, have you?"

Nudd initially remained mute. His expanding eyes indicated an amassing of emotion. With pressure mounting they popped from their sockets and Nudd's face distorted. Words spewed out like a deluge from the mouth of a gargoyle perched high on the edge of a cathedral roof.

"Sobriety is fast replacing the departing confusion that has afflicted me and so disturbed my moods," Nudd spurted, "although it would be careless of me not to affirm that I am not a lunatic and have never been so. Sometimes a mortal, beckoned by God to undertake a special mission on His behalf, will inevitably collapse periodically under the great burden of responsibility and knowledge he has to carry. This is not a sound reason to lock away a man inside a lunatic asylum, even acknowledging that my burden has, at times, been troublesome to endure. Thomas Huxley, by contrast, until his recent death, I am told, had been questioning the very existence of God. This was a man, a disciple of the diabolical Darwin, who claimed that he could not know of God's existence. This was a man who was in urgent need of having his obscene, his bizarre mental affliction subjected to unrelenting therapy in this very institution. But he walked about on the outside at liberty whilst his insanity festered and his blasphemous ideas were allowed to poison the minds of the vulnerable. God, in His wisdom, ultimately opted to silence him permanently. The Reverend Nudd is a living martyr. Even Jesus…"

Dr Norton smiled awkwardly, nodded, and put his monocle to his right eye. He glanced over at his cricket bat, one of his collection of four, propped against the far wall. Just for a moment he felt he needed it. But not to hit Nudd over the head as, he knew, a number of patients on the Reverend's ward would feel tempted to do.

"Yes. Let me look again at my notes," he said quietly, inspecting some papers with interest. Nudd dropped his head into his hands.

"I'm so sorry, doctor," Nudd sighed after pulling his face back up. "I apologise profusely for my outburst. Please, please just try to understand the enormous frustrations I have to tolerate, and the enormity of the decisions I must confront."

"Oh! I do. I am not without sympathy for your predicament, Mr Nudd. Far from it. Now then," the physician continued, "a more important issue, possibly critical, concerns what exactly took place a while ago on those French marshes. Now that your strength has revived, as I've just witnessed, perhaps you could finally reveal to me something of this secret. I fear that if we are never to know of these events, then there persists the difficulty of attempting to treat your affliction partially blindfolded, so to speak. What occurred on that trip was obviously a seminal moment in your life. I dare say it is the key to unravelling the origins of your problems. Perhaps if you do not wish to discuss these matters in person, you could permit me to read your journal recordings of these events."

As Dr Norton spoke his patient's composure visibly disintegrated. The sound of the hooves hammering the ground had returned. Worse still, Nudd felt himself on the back of the horse. With his splayed legs binding to the flanks of the animal, and his body pinned forward, he gripped the reins and spurred the horse onwards through the darkness. And despite the caresses of dawn, this was the blackest conceivable darkness that had visited the marshes. The horse half stumbled. It recovered its footing, snorting violently. It lurched several times and almost toppled over. Like an octopus affixed on a swell-borne boulder, Nudd was wrapping himself over the horse in a tight grip. His legs still pincered the animal's belly, his elbows impaled its shoulders, his ribcage grated the withers, and Nudd felt the damp, stringy mane slapping his face. They thundered onwards, like a train at full tilt along the rickety tracks of an abandoned tunnel, devoid of that distant dot of light signaling the ordeal's end. On and on they fled, man and steed, without looking back. The condensing vapour of their combined breath was trailing in their wake like a long, eerie tail.

Dr Norton was dismayed by Nudd's terrors. They had been dictating his life and threatened to tyrannise his destiny. Norton pressed on.

"And after all this time," the physician added, "we still haven't resolved your debilitating phobic problems. I am unaware of any progress whatsoever," he pointed out, though realising he may as well have been talking to an empty chair. He raised his monocle to glance down at a letter written by Nudd's family physician, a Dr Reginald Russell:

...his aversion to watercourses remains obdurate, if little more than an inconvenience since he very rarely encounters them. His fear of horses, by contrast, can result in incapacity of considerable consequence. For example, the patient confines himself inside his house. This confinement may last for weeks on end during the worst periods. These typically occur once melancholia has taken a strong hold. Mr Nudd's wife reports to me that on occasions when this problem is acute she tries to encourage her husband to escort her on brief strolls. In response he is roused from inertia in the first instance, behaving with the incoherence and excitement of an agitated neurotic. Wild expressions and gestures accompany unintelligible rantings. Following several minutes of these outbursts he withdraws back into his condition of melancholy. During Mr Nudd's manic phases these phobias are tempered by his generally chaotic state of mind. Delusions of possessing extraordinary powers, lack of sleep and nourishment, and euphoria are characteristic. Fifteen years ago Mr Nudd returned from France a completely different man from the one

who had sailed from these shores a month earlier. The pathological patterns have persisted since then. Accordingly I suggest a prognosis offering little prospect of permanent restoration of stability.With your greater experience of such disorders you may have reason to disagree. In my opinion…

Dr Norton attempted eye contact with Mr Nudd.

"I feel we are groping around a labyrinth. Unnecessarily. The key to unlocking the door, to gain entry to the chamber of answers, lies inside your journal," he explained, but his patient's head was deafened to these words by the clamour of galloping horses.

Nudd had to put a stop to this. The only way to escape from the flashback was to seize the present by addressing the physician – and then preventing him from conjuring up this piece of the past.

"Forgive me, doctor. I will not discuss the events of the Breton Marshes with anybody, neither will I sanction access to my diary. Absolutely not. I wish to avoid discussing your request any further. Please respect my wishes. Please respect that this is a secret that cannot be shared with any other mortal. I shall not waver, so whilst I implore you, I nonetheless shall not submit. So do not ask again, doctor. Emphatically I say no. And perhaps this should be the end of our session because at once I am feeling nauseous and weak."

"Forgive my lack of understanding, Mr Nudd, but why do you constantly remind yourself, if I am not mistaken, of the events that trouble you so overwhelmingly?" asked the physician, nodding with raised eyebrows towards some words embroidered onto his patient's tunic.

"Yes, doctor, these are heavy words that the Reverend Nudd wears painfully like the stigmata etched onto the body of Saint Francis of Assisi. You are not wrong about their origins. But you fail to comprehend that it is my solemn duty to bear these words. I have learnt to stiffen my upper lip and to associate them as applicable exclusively to the tribulations of others. For that is their purpose. It is

God, doctor, who has decreed that the Reverend Nudd wears these words at all times wherever he treads in His kingdom. It is only well-meaning but naive and – forgive me – interfering people like you who attempt to direct my mind back to the Breton Marshes and foment the turmoil. I must, therefore, take leave of you."

"Presently, Mr Nudd. But before you take leave of this room," heeded Dr Norton, "please permit me to add some words of caution. While not wishing to dishearten you, or in any way challenge your progress, I feel the need to suggest that a return home to your wife is a premature notion at this time. I also harbour reservations that you are ready to embark upon the simple way of life you have just described. You have a change of clothing – raiment of more modest and conventional appearance that Mrs Nudd has sent in a package. Perhaps when the time arrives for you to decide to discard your current attire, and, er, notwithstanding God's decree that you've just mentioned, we can then appraise the conviction of your progress with more confidence. Perhaps additionally when you decide to reveal to us the events of the marshes, we can be similarly empowered."

A third flush of sweat oozed through Nudd's skin. Globules formed above his eyes before running down his face and dripping onto his lap. His intestines writhed, and he felt his heart pumping overloaded blood through the veins of his muscle fibres. His mind tripped backwards as he found himself on that horse again. Now he was galloping away from the village, but not towards those marshes. Absolutely not. He didn't look back as he heard the roars of fury – possibly even the wallop of a club – fading behind him until all that remained was the rumble of hooves and the thudding of his heart. These vivid memories had to be jettisoned. Nudd had to escape either from the physicians' room or well away from the conversation's path.

"I said *not* the marshes. Thank you, doctor. *Not* the marshes." Nudd paused and swallowed some deep breaths. "Gravity – yes, *gravity. This*, doctor," he exhaled, "I am prepared to discuss with you."

"What about gravity?" Norton asked.

"Can you explain gravity, doctor? Can you tell me what it is and how it functions?"

"Goodness me, Mr Nudd. I'm a physician – not a physical scientist. No of course I can't."

"Well did you know that two Americans have demonstrated that there is no ether? The stuff doesn't exist?"

"Yes. Actually I do recall reading about that. Problematic for our understanding of light waves."

"Well if there is no ether that means there is nothing to convey the force of gravity either. Nothing at all in the manner, for instance, that a conductor conveys electricity or a body of water conveys waves. Absolutely nothing."

"Mr Nudd. Why are we discussing gravity?"

"Because the only solution possible is that God has created a supernatural one. Gravity, Dr Norton, is supernatural."

"You may well be correct in your assertion. Alternatively it may be that we are still awaiting a very clever scientist to demonstrate something that we don't yet know about gravity – or light. I'm still unclear why we are discussing this subject. How does it relate to your problems? Is this a topic chosen to avoid discussing your problems?"

"Dr Norton, I had long suspected that there was no ether between celestial bodies. The confirmation of this was God's way of preparing me for a very special relationship with Him, whether you like it or not. It was a sign."

"Mr Nudd, I am aware that many people who consider they have special relationships with God are convinced they've received just such signs," said Norton. He smiled at his patient for a moment. Then, like a pair of index fingers pointing at Nudd, his eyes pushed forward. With the calm tone of reason Norton continued.

"The vast majority, however, do not ever require the sort of assistance offered by a hospital like Bethlem. I'm afraid that we need to shift from something about gravity to something of gravitas. I am more interested in discussing your diary than the workings of gravity."

"I said *not* the diary. That means *not* the diary. The Reverend Nudd bids you good day," spluttered the patient, standing up in a bizarre costume that inflated the lean frame of a forty-eight-year-old man. This costume might have been some brash fool's idea of a warlock's garb to impress at a fancy dress ball. It was, however, the holiest of vestments of The Nuddite Church. A flowing white robe with purple and gold trims cascaded down from the shoulders. A black tunic displayed an embroidered portrait over the chest section: the faces of Mr Nudd and his wife. Words inscribed beneath proposed, *'Enter the wilderness alone and confront the Devil',* and black flannel trousers and fraying shoes completed the combination. With his robe sweeping the floor behind him, Mr Nudd stepped robotically out of the room with staccato movements. He paused only to pull open the door. Jerking along a corridor towards the gallery that accessed his room, Mr Nudd was intercepted by the florid mass of Mrs Porter – accompanied a pace back by the negligible Mr Broad. She cradled Nudd in her arms and tugged him down to splash kisses upon his forehead. A person unknown, certainly to Percival Nudd, had been awaiting him like a leopard in the shadows near the physicians' room. His ears were pricked, and his eyes rarely missed a thing nor said a thing. Lurking behind at a discreet distance, and gripping his green cloth cap to his waistcoat, this man with rust-coloured hair crept after the self-styled reverend and his entourage. He was awaiting the right opportunity.

2

Two men, sartorially splendid in their sumptuous jackets and top hats, were overdressed in the heat. They were ambling slowly together in the South London oasis of St George's Fields. The senior gentleman was more conservative in dress. The younger man was wearing his new frock coat. It was dark and elegant, tailored with expertise, sporting giant lapels, divided by a neat seam around the waist, and dropping the skirting to his knees. The lawns, surrendering yellow stains to the fierce sun, extended towards the clutter of Lambeth's other world in the distance. The busy borough wouldn't reveal another such haven of greenery until, heading towards Lambeth Bridge to cross the Thames, Lambeth Palace offered a grander plot. Trees and shrubs at St George's Field's, solitary or clumped, struggled to suck up enough moisture to nourish their curling leaves. The two men were engrossed in conversation that shunted them along the pathways leading further away from the colossal stately building. Long wings of four storeys, accommodating the female patients on the left and men on the right, stretched out like open arms from a sturdy body. From this central mass rose a high dome – a cupola like the top of a peeping shaven head – that caught the eye a fraction after the grand portico of classical pillars. Beyond the rear walls of this great behemoth, two smaller buildings originally containing the dangerous lunatics labelled criminally insane had long been demolished, and their human contents dispatched to Broadmoor. It was the notorious basement wards that both the sane and the insane feared. Down below, the attendants were a different breed: more restrainers than nurses. Out beyond the extravagant facade the lazy currents of warm air conveyed butterflies and bees across lawns towards the colours of shrubbery blooms.

Sharing these capacious grounds with the two well-dressed men, other people roamed or sat on benches as they pleased, chatting excitedly or seeking solitude. Two small gatherings were earnestly engaged in games of croquet. Plenty of these *others* were lunatics trapped in their own unusual versions of the world. The remainder were typically either attendants or visitors chaperoning a selection of the afflicted. Inside the magnificent edifice many more wandered the corridors or sat in the wards of mock tea-room character, the doors to patients' rooms decluttering one side of the elongated galleries. The decor in these galleries was as cheerful as funds could afford. Plants, paintings, caged birds, comfortable furniture, busts and statues improved the ambience. Even pets – dogs of *good boy* behaviour – were permitted to roam the galleries and curl up by their owners' beds at night. These owners and their fellow patients were an assortment of human shapes and faces that busied themselves with useful activities. The fit and able women assisted with housekeeping, and the men pumped in water supplies or manipulated needle and thread for general tailoring and repairs. Withdrawn into stifling inertia were the less than fit and able. Elsewhere, hidden within spartan rooms below ground level, the more conspicuously troubled were shackled either by restraining contraptions or by their frozen minds. The two men strolling through the grounds of their workplace were specialist physicians. All about them a myriad of birds flocked amongst the foliage. This was St Mary of Bethlem, a lunatic asylum more commonly known as Bedlam.

The young student doctor, comparatively sturdier in stature, was asking his colleague about his plans for the evening. He was keen to engage his senior colleague with manifest enthusiasm.

"*The Grand Duke,* no less? I didn't know that your wife enjoys operettas. I do believe I sympathise with you on that, my dear fellow. I applaud your fine taste. I too would prefer a string quartet to Gilbert and Sullivan, but we must indulge the ladies. We must pander to their wishes. I confess to also being partial to a lively bit of music hall entertainment from time to time. Cast my eye over the latest batch of Marie Lloyds," said Dr Kenelm Maxwell Strange, his glazed, staring eyes fashioning a leer while his ajar mouth, creeping up at the corners, evoked interpretations with either ambiguity or unease. Dr Strange's overall face posed riddles. His thinning fair hair, short and crimped, and tangled side-whiskers made him look older than he was – despite the absence of a beard or moustache. Of standard height with broad bones and slack, under-exercised muscles, he might have been an athlete had he been so inclined. The two men walked on. After waiting unsuccessfully for a prompt Dr Strange elaborated.

"Consider something yet earthier: a crawl through the bowels of Whitechapel with a plentiful flow of ale and high spirits. It does no harm, my good fellow, to see how the other half live from time to time – and believe me there are some extraordinary sights to behold. Trust me."

"You probably have a good point, Dr Strange," accepted Dr Thomas Norton. A flying insect with dangling legs bit him on the back of his neck. "But the experience sounds altogether too raucous for my constitution. I tend to avoid locations where drunken high spirits are liable to erupt into fights," he added and brushed the insect away.

"Have you never attended an organised bare-knuckle fight, doctor?" asked Strange, and the two men halted once more. "Never witnessed two solid men stood thumping the daylights out of each other until one keels over, and all for a purse of a few silver coins?"

"No."

"It is primeval, at once grotesque and somehow admirable. It is fascinating. Have you never watched vicious dogs set against each other in a pit?"

"No. It doesn't sound particularly appealing to me."

"Trust me." said Strange. "Observing the performance of the spectators around the pit is arguably more enthralling than the gruesome events inside it."

"I dare say. Er, quite likely. As you know, I'm a keen cricketer," said Norton reinitiating the perambulation. Norton was often teased by colleagues for keeping one of his bats in the physicians' room. He found it useful to practise shots when thinking through his patients' problems. He also kept one where he lodged at the hospital with his wife above the administration block; another at his Sunday house in Clapham, inherited when his father had died, where he and his wife sometimes received guests, and which was their intended destination should and when Norton retire; and the fourth bat permanently inhabited his canvas cricket kit bag, extracted before Norton strode out to the crease and replaced after his dismissal. Did he sufficiently understand a patient's problems? Is the therapy working? Does it need amending, and to what? Is a patient fit to be discharged? Or worse, should a patient be transferred down into the basement? Even worse still, is the patient an incurable who might have to be transferred to a county asylum? Or Broadmoor? When such dilemmas required careful consideration, Norton would pick up one of his three practise bats and repeatedly go through the motions of defensive shots. As he gradually got to grips with the problem, his strokes became more attacking. Once he was confident that he was arriving at the best solution, so his attacking shots attained maximum expansion with high follow-through or a two hundred degrees swivel.

As if with the curtailed flourish of a controlled cover drive, Norton added,

"The contest between bat and ball, rather than between dog and dog, suits me admirably."

"The point of team sports like cricket has so far eluded me, Dr Norton. I developed a disliking for such activities at school –

especially football. Recently however, I confess, I attended a football match in East London. Clapton Orient against Luton, if I recollect accurately."

"They make excellent hats in Luton, especially the boaters. Is their team any good at association football?" asked Norton who always heard and appreciated the birdsongs.

"I didn't really notice," answered Strange. "I wasn't even sure who won. Truth be told, the lure was less the muddy spectacle and more the fascinating behaviour of the spectators. Crammed in shoulder to shoulder, and cheering, cursing, abusive and bellicose, they were a whole lot filthier than the quagmire of a pitch. It was like being amongst primitive warring tribes of boot-tanned natives. Not an altogether pleasant experience. But as I had anticipated, examining these base people whipped to a frenzy was of greater interest than the sight of twenty-two men kicking around an inflated pig's bladder, as well as flesh, out of each other. No. I do them an injustice. They were kicking around a lump of wet leather. I fancy your sport, cricket, is a more dignified affair – but I fear with less coarse spectators an even duller event for my liking. Not having properly played the game, however, perhaps I'm not best placed to comment on its virtues."

"As a matter of fact," resumed Norton, "I'm playing in my next match two weeks hence for The Royal College of Physicians against the Gentlemen of Hampstead. Anyway, music and cricket: they are my two passions away from work. Although, er, I can see your point, especially in our chosen profession, of the benefits of dipping into darker elements of our society. I suspect you are made of stronger stuff than me, Dr Strange."

"Forgive me, Dr Norton, but despite the high regard in which I hold you – indeed you are more than a mentor to me – dare I suggest that I am more ambitious? Take our patient Mr Nudd, for example. This is a man whom I wish to understand so much better. In fact I'm resolutely determined to do so," said Strange. The physicians momentarily stopped again. The leer returned to Strange's face. He put on his spectacles and continued.

"I know that you also naturally share this desire – but for limited purposes. You, my eminent colleague, desire this for but one goal: to help restore the patient back to permanent sanity. I, however, have two goals in this instance. Of course the primary aim is to help the patient – and to this end our efforts have to an extent been rewarded. But it is additionally my intention to better understand the processes by which an unequivocally unremarkable man like Nudd reinvents himself as a guru who can attract a substantial following. There seems to be a clear link with insanity, but is it insanity that creates the guru, or does the guru inevitably succumb to insanity? Do the corrupt attain power, or is it power that corrupts? It is fast becoming an established fact that most religious gurus undergo a period of severe melancholy and self-doubt before embarking upon their new lives. A bout of insanity, perhaps, misleads the would-be guru into believing that he had been spiritually enlightened. You are obviously familiar with these premises."

"Of course, Dr Strange. And general mania and melancholy often converts into *religious* mania. But where, precisely, is this, or indeed. Percival Nudd, leading you?"

"*This* is my opportunity to unravel some of the mysteries, and to demonstrate a definitive pattern as yet unparalleled in our knowledge. Establish all the possible relevant facts about Mr Nudd, present a paper, and consequently establish my reputation – as a by-product, naturally."

"Oh! So am I to understand that you have either completed or abandoned your comparative research into the syphilitic and the undiseased brain?"

"Put to one side for now," answered Strange, replacing his spectacles inside a jacket pocket. "Others evidently have vastly superior resources at their disposal to establish the link between advanced syphilis and general paresis of the insane. I was reading an article about this in *The Lancet* only the other day. Nothing special."

"So how do you propose to delve deeper into Mr Nudd's past to uncover what you require?" inquired Norton, as he halted by a beak-chattering tree that provided welcome shade from the sun's onslaught. He disregarded the swirling cloud of midges a few feet away, and faced his colleague.

"I'm not advocating any form of radical treatment akin to torture. Certainly not, my dear fellow. Although a week in a basement ward might encourage our Mr Nudd to be less intractable with his personal disclosures."

Norton raised an eyebrow.

"We eschew the practice of coercion here as you know, Dr Strange," he said.

"Of course. Although the word I had in mind was *persuasion*. We disapprove of physical restraint yet we still shackle some patients. Such tight confinement leaves the capable patient with little to do but ponder."

"Sadly, as you point out, we still do – but only in acute circumstances hardly applicable to Mr Nudd."

"I suppose one could argue that Mr Nudd scrapes into the category of gentleman lunatics."

"I think, Dr Strange, we moved on a good while ago from deciding that social class determines who is fit and proper, on the now thankfully rare occasions, to be secured in fetters," said Norton. "Remind me to lend you my copy of John Conolly's book on the subject."

Dr Strange opened his mouth as if to respond but, with it remaining poised, refrained for a laboured moment.

"I'll return to my original point," he eventually said.

"I was rather hoping you wouldn't. But you have my attention."

"Thank you, my dear fellow. We know Nudd is believed to have written a diary account of his experiences in France, and that these would probably log the catalyst for the metamorphosis from Mister to Reverend Nudd. More than likely Mr Nudd experienced what he perceives to be some sort of divine revelation. His diary account of the events triggering his subsequent religious mania probably represents what amounts to the Book of Revelation to Percival Nudd. But is this scripture nothing less than the rambling delusions of a sick mind? Or alternatively does it record how calamitous misperceptions can divert a sane mind to lunacy? Looking further down the line, and beyond this current stage of Nudd's life, can the egotistical type ever revert back to the normal personality?"

Norton's eyes meandered away aimlessly while he weighed his response carefully. A magpie's arrival emptied the tree of other birds. Norton returned to Strange's leer.

"These are interesting questions, granted. If you are referring strictly to Mr Nudd, I hesitate to describe him as egoistical. Whilst most gurus undoubtedly suffer from this type of personality, Nudd is somewhat atypical. His bubble is too fragile. After a phase of inflation it bursts and he collapses into melancholia. Dr Strange, I am familiar with the notions you raise, and with the apparent existence of this journal. Alas, I have not come remotely close to persuading him to allow me to view it. Should the case have been otherwise I would be only too delighted for you to subject it to your scrutiny."

"Nudd's obstinacy need not prove a barrier, Dr Norton. I intend to get my hands on his diary. There are ways of persuading people. The Reverend Nudd, as he calls himself, believes he is almost fit to return home."

"And I've told him that this is a little premature," interjected Dr Norton. "Though not impossible. When our chaplain recently attempted discourse with him, Mr Nudd, ever aloof, scoffed that he possessed far more knowledge than a mere hospital chaplain. If you recall, when our chaplain first attempted befriending him less than three months earlier, Mr Nudd stated that he possessed more knowledge than any other living soul on this Earth. This, Dr Strange, represents progress, don't you think?"

"A little, I concur. But what if he was told that it was exceedingly premature? That we couldn't be confident about his prognosis unless we knew more about the aetiology of his problems. That a certain diary would be absolutely vital in furnishing us with the information we need to set in motion his cure and release. Moreover, he could be made aware his release would be conditional on handing over his diary."

The chattering magpie clambered closer along a branch. It squawked violently, and Dr Norton felt tempted to do the same.

"Dr Strange, I have to protest that I'm not happy about where this path is leading us. Let me also furnish you with some words of advice that I hope will be taken in good spirit and serve you well," cautioned Norton, rubbing the stinging lump rising from his neck. "You are a student, a clinical assistant. You greatly impress me with your hunger for knowledge. I am, though, slightly concerned that you are over-zealous in your efforts to realise ambition. Might I suggest that you take a little more time to develop a more robust understanding of our profession? Theory is no adequate substitute for sound practical experience. Experience accumulated over a protracted period acquainted with a diversity of patients. Attempting at such an early stage to make a name for oneself may ultimately do one's reputation, profession and patients a disservice. A case of more haste, less speed. Perhaps applicable to both you *and* Mr Nudd."

Dr Strange, putting his spectacles back on, reacted with a leer, exaggerated by pulling his mouth wider. Norton changed the subject.

"Goodness me. The humidity is rising. By Jove! I do believe we are presently due a thunderstorm."

He removed his gentleman's hat and fanned his face with his spare hand. He looked up at the sky, and then let his eyes float around and settle briefly on the portico. Norton had seen near there, without actually noticing, a pair of men uninvolved in the hospital's routines. Others present in the grounds may have noticed them but not heard their conversation, like that between the two physicians, of a private nature:

"Excuse me," whined a voice, "but sometimes you call me an idiot, and sometimes you say I'm no idiot. I'm wondering, pardon me for asking, if you're thinking most of the time whether I'm an idiot or not."

"Even if ya were an idiot," an Irish accent responded, "dat's a foine question and not at all idiotic. Da power of yer moind brings a smoile to me face. And predictably you are totally correct: yes, I *am* tinking most o' da toime. Only a complete idiot would be after tinking dat I'd recruit a complete idiot for such a voitally important mission."

"Oh! That's alright then. Thank you very much. Lufflee! Oh dear. I think I've got a sudden problem and might need to be excused soon."

"Eaten sometin' nasty, have ya?"

"Oh no. Only Mrs Porter's prune cake. It's delicious."

"Prunes, eh? Dem droid ploms – like what da French gentlemen and ladies from Paris eat? I always knew you were hoighly sophisticated from da moment I first clapped me oyes on ya."

"Chinamen eat them too, I think. Maybe not dried. And also Japanmen. From the Orient. Not the Orient Are where the three kings came from but further and outer Orient."

"I know where da Orient is. *Orient Are.* Do ya have anyting solid in yer head or is it all runny loike a pauper's gruel?"

"I don't really know. I had some gruel yesterday but I think it must have passed through by now. Mrs Porter doesn't like gruel. Once I was with Mrs Porter and we were buying some plums. There was a

Chinaman in the shop. He might have been Japanmanese. Mrs Porter said he was a Chinaman from Japan. This man said that they were very nice, the prums. I said they are *plums*, and he said, yes, that's right, prums. So I asked him what they call a plum in Japan. He said prum."

"Prum, indeed. Are you takin' me for some koind of idiot? Is dis some tomfoolery game wit me?

"Oh no. Oh dear."

"No? Well do ya know how a leprechaun pronounces da word plom? Well?"

"Plum?"

"Troy again."

"Prum?"

"Again, for the love o' the Blessed Mother."

"Plom?"

"I tink you are takin' me for a complete fool. Playing wit da moind of a senior police officer – someone o' my rank. And it's *Detective Inspector*."

"No, Detective Inspector. Honest. Oh dear."

"Are you honestly tinking dat an idiot would be after hoirin' you for such an important mission? If so, would dat den make us both a pair o' idiots? Who do ya tink moight be da bigger idiot? You or me? Leprechauns, indeed. You'll be tellin' me next ya actually seen one."

"Oh dear. I need to be excused now, Detective Inspector. It's getting most urgent."

"Is it? Stand up straight when I'm talkin' to ya, and prick yer ears sharpish."

Away across the lawns and overhanging the physicians, the magpie squawked again then flew away. Dr Strange ignored both the bird and his senior colleague's weather prediction. He roped back Norton's attention with a sharp tug.

"And to be frank I anticipated your response, which is neither offensive nor unappreciated. However, the difference between us, excepting your seniority and vastly greater experience, is that you are preoccupied solely with the welfare of every individual patient – a noble if not impossible task considering our scarcity and their abundance. Consider that, doctor. We have nearly two hundred and fifty patients here, two physicians including yourself to support the Physician Superintendant, and three Clinical Assistants including myself. One can hardly include the stewards and nurses in this particular equation."

"Which is why, Dr Strange, and not dismissing the importance of individual contributions, it is vital that you understand the necessity of working as a team member no matter how small the size of the team," said Norton.

"Of course, my dear fellow. Though this neglects my point. Consider your strategy – the team strategy, if you like. I, on the other hand, am of the opinion that to better understand a few broken minds we can make advances to better mend a thousand. And I do not apologise for my lofty ambitions. Returning to our enigmatic friend Nudd, let me impress my point. In Vienna, Sigmund Freud, I am informed, is working on a book describing how dreams can unravel the mysteries of hysteria and other diseased behaviours. It is some way short of publication into the public domain. Yet I have already obtained a great deal of Freud's drafts. There are ways. If you will forgive my impertinence, dear fellow, for all your very fine qualities it is apparent to me that you lack ruthlessness. You possess intellect, application, and the worthiest of intentions. You may tell yourself that you are satisfied with your life, which to a large extent may be true. But in this world it is dog eat dog, and you have been content to wait politely for the scraps when you could have been gorging on feasts. It's dog eat dog – and our friend Nudd is an imbecile whose impertinence is impeding better men from helping both him and others. I will get my hands on his diary. One way or another."

3

The impending night reeked of sulphur. Veils of blackness were descending to extinguish the boroughs. In the East End of London the evening was grimy. A thick filthy haze and, way higher above the rooftops, a membrane of cloud obscured the moon. Close to the slums, within foraging range of the marauding rats, the drinking streets of Whitechapel were lively with self-destruction. The glow of street lamps attracted the moths and illuminated the human forms passing by. These were mainly pleasure-seekers, the escapees from drudgery, or the great granddaughters of *Gin Alley*, desperate to hustle a few extra pennies to feed their vices, their families, or both. A pestilence rented its flesh so that filthy beds in turn could be rented for the night. Across these beds, the length and breadth of the stain and debris-deposited linen was stalked by fierce bedbugs that mobilised in the murk. From every direction they crawled mechanically towards warm human flesh into which they could jab their twin hypodermic snouts to suck out poisoned blood. Their calling-cards were welts that sometimes turned from the burning red into a septic green. There were few safe havens, indoors or otherwise. Supplementary light spilled out of the taverns, along with drunks, brawling men, squabbling women, and transient couples seeking a dark alleyway.

"No, Frenchie. Not tonight. I'm here on other business." insisted Dr Strange inside the Marquis of Bute as he shrugged off the woman who, clasping his shoulders, had pounced on him.

"Ah. But monsieur. For one shilling I can put a very big smile on your face," the woman pleaded, sliding her arms fully around the man.

Her Anglo-Saxon features misrepresented Gallic origins that identified themselves when her French accent trickled from her lips. Her eyelashes fluttered above irresistible brown eyes with the gloss of chestnuts, her beige ringlets were thrown backwards from beneath her fancy bonnet, its dyed brown feathers exceeding the top like giant autumnal ferns soaring above a round plateau. "*Meme* bigger than the last time," promised this woman. Strange barely noticed her floral dress of tans and yellows that engulfed her creamy flesh and frothed down from her shoulders to her ankles, only contracting in a tight spasm around her waist. Partially unwrapped to hint at the contents, her dress covered all except the glaring picture frame section below her neck exhibiting generous twin portions of succulence. Strange dismissed her.

"Get *off* me will you, woman. Didn't you hear me the first time? You do understand English, for God's sake. I said I'm not interested tonight."

"You a very miserable boy tonight. So why you come here? You really want try some English mutton not as sweet as Frenchie? Ah! Oui. Je comprends. You are looking for your *very, very* nice friend Monsieur Garbett?"

"As a matter of fact I am. And he's not particularly nice – nor is he a friend. And nor, as far as you are concerned, do I know him. Is that clear? But if you *have* seen him tonight, perhaps you could do me the courtesy of telling me where I might find him."

"And then you come back to Frenchie for some *ooh la la*?"

"That depends on whether or not I find *mister* Garbett, and whether he's in the mood to do some business with me. Then, and *only* then, I *might* be in the mood to do some business with you," Strange informed the woman, whilst looking around the crowded saloon. It was a staggering, singing, groping, shouting, shrieking, cackling, and quaffing confusion. "In any case," he continued after a roving squint, "it's Thursday. So in *your* case, it's not very likely."

"So, is Thursday. Why is a problem?"

"You reacquaint yourself with the dolly-tub and mangle every Monday don't you?" asked Strange. "So you insist."

"Ah! Oui! The wash-house. Every Mondays. And the douche bath."

"That means you are still relatively fresh on Tuesdays, needing to drench yourself with extra perfume by Wednesdays, and becoming distinctly stale by Thursdays."

"Huh! Is not normally a problem for you. The Saturday two week ago was not a problem for you. And I can tell you *monsieur le medecin* I wash away the smell of mens every day after *travail*."

"Well any day of the week is a problem," said Strange, interrupted by somebody's coughing fit nearby, "any day is a problem when I'm only interested in finding Mr Garbett. I'll revisit the question I politely posed a while back: have you seen him?"

"*D'accord*. I think I saw Monsieur Garbett in the Nag's Head," recollected Frenchie. "Come back see me after," she called out to the shut ears of the physician who was already pushing his way out and back onto the street.

Within the tarnished redbrick walls of the Nag's Head, only marginally less boisterous than the Marquis of Bute, Garbett was spotted at a table in the far corner accompanied by his wobbly paunch, his facial stubble that never quite became a beard, and by two other seedy-looking rogues with their tankards of ale. Strange braced himself in preparation for conflict with Garbett's ferocious odours. Personal hygiene was not something that many people regarded as a daily priority, even when they did not lack the means to deal with it. And Garbett was one of the worst offenders Dr Strange had ever encountered. He didn't blend in well with the general stench of vile air. No. The industrial fumes, the raw sewage that clotted the Thames and slurped back past the overwhelmed pumping stations, the remaining open sewers, all the choking cess-pits, and the excrement that was still carted away during the night to be dumped elsewhere, all of these rancid manifestations of London's entrails cowed in the presence of Mr Garbett. Unmuzzled, his smell forced most people in an already unsavoury environment to snatch their noses away. For, unlike Frenchie, neither Mr Garbett nor his clothes were ever seen inside a wash-house. As this man became aware that he was being approached, he muttered something to his companions. The thug Bert Tordiman and the rogue sometimes known as Old Sparky both promptly decamped to another table. Garbett rose to engage with Dr Strange.

"In need of a few more severed 'eads are we?" he whispered into the doctor's ear through festering dental ruins. "Fresh from the morgue, or fresh from wherever I can find 'em. Eh? Nice and dead, a corpse's head. 'Ow many do yer want this time?" Strange stood back. He raised up his hand to gesture Garbett to stop. He replied in a low voice.

"I don't want any heads. I've dissected more than enough brains for the time being, thank you, and the last one you procured was diseased and therefore useless for my purposes. I've a rather different proposition for you this time. But nothing at all beyond the scope of your usual type of enterprise. Am I mistaken," asked Strange, clenching his nostrils, "or are we in the year 1858?"

"Eh? Don't fink you woz born then, sir. Right now weez in 1898, ain't it?"

"So it has seemed for most of the year – though not at this very moment. Never mind," continued Strange with a snigger, deactivated when struck by the head-butting stare of the huge thug who had been sitting with Garbett. The older little man with baggy trousers and hooped shirt, Strange checked, was looking elsewhere. Strange considered nodding courteously at the thug, changed his mind, and resumed the business on his agenda.

"You are, are you not, an accomplished house burglar, Mr Garbett?"

"One of the best, sir. For the right reward or fee. The *very* best, sir. For the right fee that includes the price of a recce, guv. For the right fee. 'Specially from a toff all-square-rigged like yerself, sir. Not forgetting me expenses, like," said Garbett who had leant down to scratch some flea bites above both ankles. "There's the specialist kifers I'll be wanting 'cause each burglary is different and ya need to make sure ya got the right tools, like. Maybe need a snakesman to get through a small gap. And I know just the very cocksparrah, sir – though the boy he don't come cheap. Maybe need a cracksman if we're dealing wiv a safe. What's the wheeze wiv 1857 about?" he asked, and Strange shrugged his shoulders and wrinkled his lips.

After a short while, the time it took Strange to brief and negotiate with Garbett whilst tipping down half his pint of ale, he was back on the street again. He gulped at the sulphur-saturated London air that swathed his face like a stale towel the instant he wrenched open the door. Though the thug was best avoided, Garbett's unfriendly stench was more inhospitable than ever. Strange had never seen him in a change of clothing, and he smelled as though he spent much of his time ferreting about and sleeping amongst summer rubbish dumps or underground sewers. Quite possibly, some of the time he did, Strange reckoned. There were plenty of people in London who made a living picking their way through such locations, falling asleep on the job, and indifferently disseminating the repulsive kisses of muck wherever else they went about their daily business. Old Sparky was another example. Travelling up and down the country's highways, he duped, pilfered and contaminated. A small man with grey hair of wire wool straightened under his exhausted hat, his usual ploy was to pose as a tradesman and then disappear with a hefty upfront payment for materials after barely beginning the agreed work. His odour was terrible, but it was his voice, steeped in Lancashire drawl, that was unforgettable, above all else, to his victims and associates. Many southerners struggled with his accent to grasp what Mr Sparks had said – a problem exacerbated by a voice easily mistaken for a heavy-duty iron chain being dragged across cobblestones. When protesting his innocence about a crime he'd probably committed, a squealing piglet was collared to the end of the chain. Mostly he had over the years managed to position himself tens of miles ahead of the police and clients he'd conned. When in London, Old Sparky would supplement his deceptions by selling stolen goods to Garbett on the cheap before swiftly removing his stench and vagabond clan elsewhere. The thug Billy Tordiman was equally dishonest but operated very differently. Originally raised in Devon by a grandmother, he pimped off his retarded common-law wife who he threw out to work on the streets around Spitalfields. Tordiman was known to definitely deal in scrap metal and builders' supplies. Whatever else he engaged in was open to much muttered speculation. Back and forth with his horse and cart, in and out of his yard, he sent shivers down spines aplenty. Banging and crashing about late at night he kept even the inebriated awake. Few dared, however, to complain about his nocturnal activities. Tordiman rarely wore a hat. He preferred to fully display his head – a huge shaven lump that might have been hewn from an elephant's thighbone – and to intimidate by pacing up and down the road with lumbering strides while staring at an unfortunate. Sometimes he carried his sledgehammer. Tordiman's reputation for beating unconscious those brave enough to challenge his behaviour was heeded by the majority. This was another specimen who failed to observe the basics of personal hygiene, though not to the extent of Garbett. The reprobate who had just boasted of his housebreaking skills passed on *useful information* to Tordiman because he was better an appeased ally than potential enemy.

To escape Garbett's clinging presence Strange had almost catapulted himself out onto the street's flagstones, and the woman known as Frenchie was waiting there to catch him.

"You seen Monsieur Garbett? You want to spend a little time with Frenchie now, cheri?"

"Right now? Yes, I probably would," agreed Dr Strange pushing out his words with irritation despite the comfort of her perfume. "But it's not going to happen because this evening has already been too expensive after my meeting with Mr Garbett. For such a straightforward task, something that's second nature to a brigand like him, he drives a hard bargain. Goodnight."

A very different female voice crashed into Dr Strange's ears.

"I'll show you a good time, mister. An' all for the price of a couple of gins," yelled the emaciated young Irish woman who had been squatting by the tavern wall. She struggled upright on thin, unsteady legs like a just born fawn, dripping urine onto the pavement. After giving her wet knickers a quick wipe of the hand, she stumbled between Strange and Frenchie, then collapsed against the young doctor's torso. She managed to steady herself, slopping her arms around the physician as much to support herself as to ensnare a customer. Strange turned his creased face away, but the Irish woman began clumsily smearing kisses across the side of his face, suspending her assault only to repeat her offer.

"I'm a naughty, girty dirl and I'm all yours," she slurred.

Strange twisted his neck to dodge her kisses and the accompanying mixed vapours of stale clothes, cheap perfume, and liquor. They clung to his flesh and burrowed up his nostrils like gaseous parasites.

"I'll sh-show you a gery vood time, darlin'. No. I'm mean a very good one. Yes. The best good."

"Get *off*, will you. You nearly knocked my hat from my head," Strange barked, and prised away the woman's arms so brusquely that she almost keeled over backwards.

"I know thish woman you're with," slurred the Irish woman, taking a while to regain some balance. "She's a French whore and she'll, she'll, she'll give you, she'll give, yes, a dose you of the Prench fox. The French, the French pox. Fuck me. Everybody's a bastard and I'm wall wet." she persisted. But Strange totally ignored her. He pulled out a handkerchief to wipe down his face, cast aside his arm, and then flicked the cloth onto a paving slab. Strange addressed Frenchie instead.

"I'm sure there'll be another occasion when your Gallic charms will be able to tempt me. Maybe as a modest way of celebrating if Mr Garbett delivers successfully," he concluded, striding away only to pause to manufacture a smile and tap the brim of his hat.

"Wait, monsieur. Please wait," implored the woman, trotting after the doctor with one hand hitching up her dress for ease of movement. "Why you spend time with Monsieur Garbett? Why you pay him money? So you say is not my business but I tell you he is a *bad* man. Is not for me to ask about your businesses but he is very bad man for doing the businesses. His odour is terrible and I think this come directly from his rotten heart."

"Yes," agreed Strange, continuing on his way without even glancing at his pursuer. "My affairs, Frenchie, are not your business."

"But monsieur. Perhaps I can find you better mens than Monsieur Garbett for doing the businesses."

"Credit to you, as it's on this occasion due. But I doubt you can." Strange dismissed her.

"No wait. You a very educated man and me is just a common woman. But you don't know everything. I know things about Garbett that are very, very bad."

"What exactly do you know about him that I don't, then?" asked Strange, finally stopping and turning to face Frenchie. Further behind Cathy was retching down on her knees.

"His name is not Garbett," answered Frenchie. "This, I think, is maybe a name of one of his sad mistresses. He don't use his real name. You want know why?"

"Come on then, tell me."

"He a deserter from the British army. You want know his real name?"

"A deserter, eh? So who is he really, then?"

"Ah! No, monsieur. You want know his real name but you don't want to help Frenchie who need to find rent money to pay for a room to sleep in every nights with my childrens also."

"I should have known this was coming," Strange scoffed with a chuckle. "And there was me thinking that you were actually a half-human dollymop when in truth you're a bonafide harlot. Credit retracted."

"Very easy for you to make judgement, monsieur. Life is sometimes very hard. I came here from Paris as a dancer taking many monies home to my poor father. Then I marry an Englishman and then he die from the cholera. Then they say I am too old to continue as a dancer. They say I am an artichoke – sweet enough inside but with wrinkles on the outside . But not sweet enough because the mens want to watch young girls dancing. Huh, I am only thirty-two when they say this to me. This is three years ago. So what do I do? Can you explain me? My poor husband he leave me no money, only three beautiful childrens. Three boys. I don't have the English malady of taking gin and opium. I don't smoke tobacco. And because of this I still look young. Not like some of the women here who are five years younger than me but look like twenty years older. Like that drunken Wexford Cathy woman a moment ago. She is a tragedy. She has only about twenty-five years but she already look like she has already

43

forty-five. She has earned some money tonight but she only buy *alcool* with this. She will, poor sad woman, probably sleep in a gutter tonight. And me? What happened? Sometimes I find job as seamstress but often there is no *travail*. So I work the Haymarket all dressed up nice. Then this is not so good because the men go there to find young girls. Many young girls. People tell me they changed the law for the age of consenting to sixteen years. And what happen? Even more and more girls much younger than this working there. So now I come here. But non. Is not *agréable*. But, monsieur, I have to pay to feed my three childrens, and for weekly lodgings. I don't want ever to have to pay for a night in a dirty netherskens. And, monsieur, I will never send my childrens onto the streets like that Mary Halfpenny who instruct her childs to thieve and pick the pockets. She do this every time she is sick with the fever again and again. For me, not this. Life can be hard."

"Have you finished? I didn't ask for the story of your life. It doesn't interest me. Nor do most of the whores who throng these taverns and streets with their clapped out carcasses, their rotting gums and noses, and with breath of mercury and alcohol that could fell a polar bear from ten paces. Frankly, when I want a good time, as you rightly recognise, there is a plentiful supply of fresh young daisies aged thirteen or fourteen willing to satisfy me at a penny a time. If I turn to *you*, admittedly with acceptable hygiene and sobriety, and equipped with the knowledge of pleasuring men, then for a reasonable price you interest me exclusively for such pleasures – up to the point when I pull my slacks back up. This, therefore, does not include listening to the story of your life nor any other type of social encounter," said the doctor through his leer. He scrutinised the woman for a few seconds but maintained his tone. "This is normally without exception. However, Frenchie, I'm not totally without pity for the lower organisms that infest our society. Here's sixpence. Now tell me more about Mr Garbett."

"One shilling and for this I tell you everything I know."

As Strange was on the verge of responding, Wexford Cathy's voice tore through the dense atmosphere, her faint Irish lilt exaggerated by intoxication and rage.

"Think she's better than me do ya, you stinkin' piece of rotting pig's arse hidn' under a posh gent's hat?"

Frenchie looked back to see Wexford Cathy propping herself up against a water trough, and retching to offload her vomit into it. She missed the target, splattering the pavement and part of her dress. Frenchie winced then refocused on Strange.

"A tanner is all that's on offer," he insisted, having again ignored the wretched desperation of Wexford Cathy. "And that's generous because you're forgetting one small matter. I could have you apprehended and charged for withholding evidence about one of Her Majesty's deserters. You could be hanged," Strange added, with a sly grin as he targeted Frenchie's eyes that, with the extra two inches of elevation from her boot heels, were almost at the same level as his own.

"And so could you also be hanged for not reporting what you now knowing about Monsieur Garbett," Frenchie retorted. Strange leered into her face, reached into his breast pocket for his spectacles and planted them across his eyes. He moved his face towards Frenchie's and his lips gradually parted before erupting into a volley of laughter. He half composed himself.

"Mr who? I am a physician. Of good breeding stock and educated at Harrow School," he cackled before continuing. "You are a common whore who works the taverns and streets of Whitechapel. You're not even English. Not even British. I think we know which one of us would be believed by the authorities. Don't we?"

"Don't flatter yourself, monsieur. I only prefer business with mens like you because *au minimum* you wash and change your clothes a few times in the week – not like most mens here, like the stinking

Monsieur Garbett. I don't think you more handsome. I know you are *not* a lot better. Just cleaner with profit of better education. Yes, I take sixpence, and so I tell you about this Garbett man whose real name is Benjamin Barrow. But I am not telling this to a gentleman."

"And since you are not a lady, and since you don't consider me better than the filthy sewer rats like Garbett, how do I know that you will be telling me the truth for my sixpence?"

"It is what I know, monsieur. And you know I always do my business *honêtement* and to provide the satisfaction. And Monsieur Garbett? *Alors*, people say too many things when they have drunken too much. But he don't say this to me. Agh! Never is he my customer. But anyway, some place somewhere, somebody will recognise a person who try to pretend to be another one. Sixpence is good for some food. It start to rain now. A tempest I think. I tell you fast about Monsieur Garbett, and then *bonne nuit*."

Frenchie was not wrong about Garbett. After a few tours in the dusty heat of Egypt Benjamin Barrow opted not to return to barracks from formal leave. Barrow had slipped away having first paid an unauthorised visit to a munitions store. The missing quantities of .303 rifle cartridges and the new cordite explosives were only discovered after Barrow had failed to report back for duty. The rumours had been circulating about another campaign in the Sudan, eventually to culminate in a new war four months later in 1896. This was not something in which Barrow wanted to participate. Also hovering was the threat of being sent to the Northwest Frontier for those endless skirmishes with the fierce hill tribesmen who refused to yield to the arrogant might of the Empire. Benjamin Barrow had swallowed enough foolhardy commands of Eton-educated commanding officers. He decided to turn his back on the hardship, heat, blistered feet, diarrhoea, fever, injury, and possibly far worse for the pecuniary gratitude that could be scavenged from a London rubbish bin. The world had many pleasures to offer, attainable through one's own enterprise. It just needed liberating. He had heard many times that considerable fortune was to be made in New York, whatever the nature of the business. So instead of rejoining his infantry regiment, he paid for his passage across the Atlantic where he installed himself as Paddy O'Halloran. Twenty months later he had reappeared in England, residing in London under yet another name, and just far enough away from his home patch of Chatham to slash the risk of being recognised by those who had known one Benjamin Barrow.

4

So here was "Freddie Garbett", a wanted man on both sides of the Atlantic, slowly tugging a little cart past the tall terraced houses along a Pimlico road. The cart, advertising 'KNIVES SHARPENED' in big letters on both sides, was released into a static position two doors away from number 35, the address of Percival Nudd. On this door a large bronze plaque was affixed, and the semi-literate Garbett carefully scanned the words until he was confident he had correctly identified every one. Through screwed eyes he read the inscription: *'HOLY WORLD PALACE OF THE NUDDITE CHURCH'*. And beneath this he registered *'His Holiness The Reverend P. C. I. Nudd'*. It certainly doesn't look like much of a palace, he pondered. But there has to be contents inside worth far more than a stupid diary. He may as well help himself to the palace treasures, when the time comes to break inside and half-inch the diary. In any case, this would better resemble a regular sort of burglary. A standard job instead of the blatant targeting of one specific item. Indeed, this was a job with considerable potential for a glut of bonuses, concluded Garbett, as he poked his tongue through his mouth to lick his lips. Greatly encouraged, the noxious vagabond hovered nearby for over an hour during which time he attracted the buzz of flies and a modicum of trade. Though gratefully receiving these pennies, his primary preoccupation was the reconnaissance of the Nudd domicile and its surroundings. This task was assisted by a week-old copy of *The Pall Mall Gazette* in which Garbett pretended to be engrossed. The street was generally quiet. A handful of horse-drawn carriages and carts, plus a few individuals, had passed by. It offered a mixed bag of prospects. On the one hand there would be few witnesses to a break-in. On the other, a stranger would be rendered all the more conspicuous. This place was a different kettle of fish from his Whitechapel turf. Over there few people bothered to lock their doors. Mostly because they didn't possess any hard assets worth stealing. Here, he would probably have to break a window. Garbett decided to drag his cart around to a parallel street beyond the rear of the Nudd house. There he learned that discreet access would be more viable through an alleyway, and then over several garden walls before slipping down into the Nudds' garden. This way he would be able to gain entry in the near darkness of about four in the morning, and away from the eyes of any unlikely soul passing the front. Before returning back to his original position by number 39, Garbett knocked on the doors of each house whose garden he would need to traverse, asking any occupants if they had knives requiring sharpening. At each door he listened carefully for the barking of dogs. Garbett smiled on his way back. The absence of dogs augured well. Mrs Nudd and her children were the only other obstacle to overcome.

Inside a Bedlam cavity Dr Strange was intercepted by his senior colleague as he emerged from a gallery ward. His facial muscles glinted the hint of steel.

"Hello, there. Been to visit the Reverend?" Norton asked him.

"You mean Mr Percival Nudd?" laughed Strange dismissively. "Not especially. We exchanged a few words, but in the course of doing the rounds."

"Well I'm glad I've bumped into you because what you were saying the other day has set me thinking," said Norton – without being dishonest. "I'm fascinated by your exploration of Whitechapel's evening activities. Your point about the education derived from investigating humanity's seamier strata may well be valid."

Dr Strange's face relaxed a touch, and his mouth slackened ajar before he responded. "I'm heartened, nay, honoured, that you are beginning to see things my way. There's a glut of cranks, villains and wretches to observe both by watching and engaging in conversation. Learn the anatomy of the flawed human mind."

"Just so long as curiosity doesn't actually kill the cat. I just might venture to Whitechapel to have a look for myself."

"Good for you. Best not to mention it to Mrs Norton, though."

"Why ever not?" asked Norton, as the pair drifted towards the physicians' room.

"Some things are best kept exclusively between reliable friends and colleagues. Tell Mrs Norton and she'll react badly. Dealing with a spouse is like dealing with anybody, really. Don't give them what they don't want. She certainly won't want to hear of you visiting Whitechapel. Trust me."

"I see what you mean," agreed Norton with a tone of encouragement. "No. My wife won't in all probability like it. She does worry. Do you ever feel in danger when you are there?"

"*Feel* in danger? I recognise that there are some perils. It always helps to have a cool head. It helps to be adaptable and have the capacity to manufacture effective responses according to the circumstances."

"How interesting," Norton remarked, as they entered the physicians' room. Realising he had raised an eyebrow he dropped it.

"It's purely about awareness and playing the game. It's about keeping one's wits to outwit others. Trust me."

"Actually I was commenting on your assertion that you don't feel danger."

"And for my part, dear fellow, I find it fascinating that we encounter such extreme displays of emotion or *feeling* inside this institution. These people *don't* have calm heads. It's simply because, I presume, they are deranged."

"Now *that's* also interesting. I wonder. I'll offer you a choice. Number one: I'm impressed by your ability to keep your wits. Number two: I've a little voice in my head encouraging me not to tell my wife if I visit Whitechapel. So, have your wits revealed the option uppermost in my mind, or do you detect any dishonesty in either statement?" Norton asked.

Strange pulled out his spectacles and fitted them slowly in place.

"I'm not really sure I know what you want me to say."

"I'll make it simpler. Did you detect any dishonesty in my two statements?"

Strange considered his answer. He had been able to sustain, through his leer, eye contact at all times. Norton, however, had begun to falter – and they both knew it.

"The bit, probably, about not telling your wife."

"Spot on. Were you able to feel the dishonesty in my voice? And did it bother you?"

"Yes, I detected some symptoms. I also know you to be very straightforward. It's all about detection. Feeling doesn't really enter into it. In the same way it hasn't escaped my notice that we haven't had a conversation of this nature before."

"No. It's illuminating, and I'm wondering if you have some advantages over me when appraising our patients," said Norton, half twitching his eyes away.

"So tell me, dear fellow, do you detect any dishonesty in what I've been saying?"

"I'm not sure, Dr Strange, that I have your detection capabilities. There were moments, however, when, er, I felt uncomfortable with what we both said. Do you, perchance, detect – or even feel – that I'm not genuinely keen on visiting Whitechapel?"

"I didn't straight away. But I detect it now."

"Interesting."

"Do you ever detect any dishonesty when I'm speaking to you?" asked Dr Strange slowly.

Dr Norton glanced across the room at his cricket bat. If he had commenced this session with assuredness, maybe even a bold dash of panache, he was now batting with caution. Though not without a modicum of control.

"Usually no. I don't," he said. "It's true, however, that on occasions I feel a discomforting sense that I might have tasted the flavour of deception. And although it's true that I'm not too enamoured with the prospects of a Whitechapel junket, I still reckon it might be useful. I'm just unsure about telling my wife. And if I didn't, I'd probably still feel the need afterwards to reveal the truth and apologise."

"Maybe a visit wouldn't be such a good idea when a steady head is requisite to allow your intellect, rather than your heart, to assert control. You have a first-rate mind, Dr Norton, but dare I suggest, my dear fellow, that you also *feel* too much? At least you will probably never have to apologise for being caught doing something behind Mrs Norton's back."

"Well it's not a pleasant experience."

"Being caught out is merely an inconvenience. You shouldn't allow it to become anything more."

"No. I mean it's not a pleasant experience to discover that a cherished one has breached your trust."

Garbett had already expended too much of his time on his reconnoitre. There were other business opportunities to exploit. He decided upon one final throw of the dice for now to see what turned up, and he began approaching number 35 to knock on the door. But he hesitated and then stepped back. He had become aware that a slight, dark-haired woman carrying a small leather travelling case was heading, face lowered under her bonnet, at pace towards the *same* door. Garbett turned to her elfin features and pinched the peak of his hat with a smile betraying his missing and rotting teeth.

"Good day to you, Madame. Gideon Johnson at yer service," he introduced himself.

"Might I offer me services to a lady as elegant as yourself," he continued, concealing the fact that he deemed this woman's attire to be more fitting of a senior servant such as a housekeeper than the lady of such a house. "Sharpening knives is me business, Madame. Do yer lot for a deuce. For a penny more I'll return in a month and do the lot again. The whole lot. Only thruppence to sharpen 'em twice. Tell yer what, for a fine lady such as yourself I might be persuaded to…."

"Monsieur," interrupted the woman. "I am a visitor to this house," she declared with an unmistakeable French accent. "I have no knives for you to sharpen. *Merci*," she said, and then rapped the doorknocker urgently. Garbett retreated further back to wait outside number 37 next door. He observed the portal of Nudd's palace opening. A more impressively dressed lady beckoned the French woman inside, and then quickly pulled the door shut without even a glance beyond her guest. Garbett continued to wait, doing his best to conceal his surveillance from behind his newspaper. Nearly an hour later the door opened again.

Garbett called his senses to muster, and focused them on the doorway. As the French woman departed, Garbett strained to hear her say,

"Thank you, Madame. The stew was very good. The gateau was excellent. I return in one month on the three of September."

With quick bird-like footsteps she sped away. Garbett picked up his cart and shunted it after her.

"Oi! Madame. Oi! Giss an honest trader a moment, will yer?" he pursued her. "Oi, French lady. Madame! I ain't no scabby dog gonna bite yer," he spluttered, having almost caught up with the woman's brisk legs. She stopped and turned to face Garbett.

"Excuse me. Monsieur. I have a train to take. Please permit me to continue."

"I was only wondrin' if you knew whever the lady of the 'ouse what you was just visiting has any knives need sharpenin'."

"Monsieur, you have to ask this lady. Not me."

"No. Tell yer the truth, Madame, and forgive me manner, only I was wondrin' summit else. Whever you might like to take some refreshments with me. Before you catch yer Mary Blaine, like. See if I can't whet yer appetite if you ain't got no knives need whetting. It's thirsty work this. Standing 'round and pushin' me cart about in this weather. I would be right pleased if you'd do me the honour of yer company, Madame. No flash house nor nuffink like that. Only a right proper and respectable establishment. One fit for a lady. Like yerself."

"Monsieur, I thank you for the very encharming invitation. I just had very nice refreshments and unfortunately I am pressed to take my train. First, you know, I must to walk for a bit and then must to take the tram. After the tram I must to take a train to Charing Cross and then to take the train to London Bridge, and another train there to Folkestone. This is very, very many to do and I am very pressed. Thank you," she replied, and began on her way again before being halted yet again by words Garbett shouted at her.

"I couldn't help overhearin' that you be coming back 'ere in a month. P'raps next time you could do me the honour of letting me escort you somewhere special to take a *lady*. Not just some pot of coffee neither. A bite to eat all plump and sweet. For the finest lady the finest treat. Served cold or 'ot, pick of the lot."

The French woman, ten yards ahead of Garbett, paused to listen. Without looking back she then hurried off at an even quicker pace. Soon she was fifty yards away, and not long after was nearer a hundred when she crossed the road and veered around a corner. Garbett stopped to watch. Tapping this woman further when she next returns might be invaluable before attempting a break-in, he told himself. Can't be too careful. That physician toff will have to wait a while.

5

"Dr Norton!" shrieked Mrs Porter over three weeks after Garbett's reconnaissance mission. Her words ricocheted violently around the physicians' room that was situated below the cupola and directly behind the hallway leading to the portico.

"Dr Norton. Just how, tell me, can the Reverend Nudd fulfil his Holy mission on behalf of God when he is incarcerated here? If you don't sanction the discharge of his Holiness the Reverend Nudd from this institution, I will invoke the Lunacy Law to obtain his release."

"She will, you know. She will. She's a marvellous woman. She will, you know, added the nodding Mr Broad, with his insipid voice.

"Madame, compose yourself please," Norton calmly requested and smiled at Mrs Porter. He did wonder why she hadn't mentioned invoking God's assistance. "And please sit yourself down, Mrs Porter. I understand well that your intentions are honourable. I do not hesitate to accept that you speak in the belief that this would be the best course of action. Alas, while I am not at liberty to discuss either Mr Nudd's illness or his residence here with you, I am disposed to inform you that we shall allow Mr Nudd to return home when he is ready to do so. As yet, we are of the firm opinion, this moment has not arrived," Norton explained.

The woman was evidently not pacified. The corset, fighting an impossible battle to contain her swelling girth, for the time being held firm. It also strangled her ability to breathe easily. A mite higher, her bosoms jiggled up and down indignantly like shaking fists. Her burgeoning plumpness helped betray the fact that the residue of all those long, comfortable decades had cost Mrs Porter her prime: the undulations of flesh against fabric were partially obscured by the dress that flopped down in expanding frilly layers, and bundled up into a mound over her rump. The bustle, secured over the back of Harriet Porter's petticoat, and stuffed hard with horsehair like an over-pumped rugger ball, exaggerated her already copious posterior to such an extent that the chair upon which she was now uncomfortably perched had barely the room to accommodate her. Though still keen to enhance certain curves, and groping for youthfulness, Mrs Porter had lost sight of the mark where *shapely* and *fashionable* had become unfortunately confused. She had learnt to offset the spherical metamorphosis of her stomach and hips by elongating her body with ever lengthening heels. Underneath her lank straight and naturally blonde hair, dropping to her shoulders and topped by a circular congealment of plumage that resembled the mutilated carcass of a parrot, the true colour of her mood was unable to clearly reveal itself on her facial canvas. The make-up smothered her flesh like butter generously applied to cold toast, blusher smeared blobs over her cheeks, and waxy red lipstick perverted a mouth that had a large painted mole dabbed near the left corner. In her youth she would have certainly caught the eye of plenty of men – but turned the heads of few. Now she presented a cruel parody of a middle-aged woman even more desperate than ever to attract the attention of men. In her blazing pomp she would not have looked out of place amongst an itinerant freak show. Likewise her companion, Mr Broad. This man, though, was less animated – at times to inertia. Nor was he prone to the expressions of a passionate woman. He spent much of his time basking in Mrs Porter's company gazing wide-eyed at her. Mr Broad lacked any kind of stature. On the rare occasions when his flabby frame wasn't slumping and allowing his paunch to overspill towards his knees, he still did not quite reach the same height as Mrs Porter elevated on her highest heels. His round billycock hat, a permanent fixture even indoors, engulfed most of his messy hair. His facial flesh was unkind, a spattering of pink blotches erupting into flaking skin. His small eyes shrank even further behind the thick lenses of his spectacles that sat on a stunted and upturned nose. The skin problems, combined with his dull attire and lacklustre manner contrived to make him look substantially older than his true age. Little about either his physical features or his character offered any redemption. Lethargy – and the company of Mrs Porter – was the only way forward that comforted Mr Broad, and this man was as flaccid in appearance as his feeble voice. Dr Norton, whilst experienced enough to note that appearance could often disclose something of the personality, and the influences shaping that, was not judgemental. He noted how Mrs Porter presented herself, but the thrust of his interest was with her concerns. She was still indignant.

"You completely fail to grasp that the Reverend Nudd is anything *but* insane," ranted the woman, clutching a locket hanging from her neck identical to the pendant Mr Broad was wearing. "He carries a great burden," she added, then prised herself from the chair to stand up, straightened herself, and puffed out her chest. "God needs him, the world needs him, and I need him. He cannot properly conduct his ministry and proceed with his great mission while held here in Bedlam and treated like a lunatic."

"Rest assured, Mrs Porter, that nobody here to my knowledge is treating Mr Nudd like, to use your label, a lunatic. Though it must be stressed that two independent physicians certified him as in need of medical intervention when we received him. And the Committee of Hospital Governors confirmed his admission a few days later. Please accept that we grant Mr Nudd the utmost respect and compassion as he recovers his strength after a difficult period of his life. If you really want to do something useful on his behalf, something you may not have considered so, might I suggest that furnishing me with a bit of information about the Nuddite Church would be helpful. This is not to pry, I emphasise, but there are many mysterious gaps in our knowledge of Mr Nudd. The sooner we can better understand him – these burdens, for example, that he has to bear – the sooner we can manipulate his therapy with greater precision and allow him to return home. It is difficult to know how to help Mr Nudd shoulder these burdens if we are unfamiliar with their precise nature and origins."

"Very well, doctor. I suppose I *could* be persuaded in the circumstances. So what do you wish to know?" asked Mrs Porter, and Mr Broad, ever willing to be her chivalrous beau, clasped her hand.

"What, for example drew yourself to the Nuddite church. What drew you to Mr Nudd?"

"Oh! Glory be! I'm almost too ashamed to tell you," Mrs Porter exclaimed. Mr Broad turned to gaze into her eyes and reassure her, and Mrs Porter shrugged away his hand.

"You don't have to tell him anything you don't want to," he whined, "But you've got nothing at all to be ashamed about, Mrs Porter. You are truly a marvellous lady."

"Your companion is correct in that you are under no obligation whatsoever to divulge anything if you deem it too personal. Or indeed anything at all. Perhaps you could merely disclose some details with which you feel comfortable," Dr Norton added softly with a gentle smile. "Why don't you sit down." he gestured, nodding towards the discarded chair. A hiatus ensued, terminated when Mr Broad offered Mrs Porter a clean handkerchief that she snatched from his fingers to dab at her brow. She sat down.

"Please. Why don't you also take a chair, Mr Broad," suggested Norton. But Mr Broad, as if tethered to his female companion by an invisible leash, remained standing beside her instead of pulling up another chair. Dr Norton waited calmly.

"I was, I was a fallen woman, doctor. I was a sinner of sorts. Though not without reason, you understand," the woman eventually began quietly, her eyes dropping into her lap. "My husband was a very, very, very dear man – distinguished, educated, generous, and not without pecuniary means. He had been a successful merchant importing tea and coffee from the colonies. Alas, he was nearly twice my age. And, I regret with shame, I grew to be bored with my life. We didn't have any children, you see. We did try in the early days but we were not blessed with success for reasons that God alone knows. You see if there had been children my time would have been better occupied. At length I considered answering some of the many newspaper advertisements offering children for adoption along with a modest fee. My husband wasn't so keen, feeling that at his more advanced stage of life the arrival of a baby might upset his routines. And you will know, doctor, this so often gives rise to bowel irregularity. Yes, boredom is a terrible affliction, doctor. Quite ghastly. It generates many ideas to counter it, schemes to seek and obtain some excitement. Satan is only too aware of such opportunities. Oh dear! I think I'm becoming tearful," she announced as her voice quivered. She momentarily raised the handkerchief she was still clutching to her eyes, dropped it to her nose, blew into it, and without even glancing at him handed the sticky white cloth back to Mr Broad.

Dr Norton intervened.

"Mrs Porter, if this is too painful for you to recount, I will not press you to continue."

"I'll be fine. I just need to compose myself," she sniffed.

"She'll be fine once she has composed herself," echoed Mr Broad. "I think I'll sit down now because my legs are aching something terrible, but I'll be right beside you, Mrs Porter," he added. Then he dragged a chair next to his Venus and sank into it like, as so often at home, a pig in its wallow.

Mrs Porter ignored him. She straightened her back, thrust forward her bust, and took a deep breath.

"One morning," she continued, "when I was out and about to buy some groceries, I had a blackout. I fainted. Mr Broad here, who I didn't know from Adam, happened to be passing by and rushed to my assistance. By the way, he prefers to be known as Mr J Kenyon Broad. Anyway, he comforted me, whilst I administered the smelling salts that I always carry, supporting me from collapsing and helping me up most gallantly. He also picked up my groceries that had spilled everywhere. This is how we first met. We developed a spiritual friendship, plutonic you understand, but it soon became abundantly clear that Mr Broad wanted rather more. Not being particularly partial to Mr Broad's variety of masculinity – as he has long known – we discovered that we could both obtain pleasure from... Oh dear. I need to recompose myself," explained Mrs Porter, and paused to allow her rapid breathing to settle down. "You understand, doctor, that some activities can be intimate without fully extending to adultery. I'm not referring to Mr Broad here. Prepossessing is not a word I would use to describe him. However he does possess a few singular qualities. He is a Nuddite and a loyal escort. Oh dear! I think I mentioned adultery, though not complete adultery, you understand. Far from it."

Dr Norton again intervened.

"Mrs Porter, please understand that I will neither press nor expect you to continue."

"Thank you, doctor. You are most kind. I would even use the word *soothing*. The benefits that Catholics derive from the confessional is becoming apparent. Anyway I have asked God for His forgiveness, and He has forgiven me. He has also elevated me to an exalted position where I stand at the side of the Reverend Nudd and lead the Reverend's great mission of salvation in his temporary absence. I think I'm rather brave, doctor."

"Mrs Porter is wonderfully brave," Mr Broad commented.

"Yes, Mr Broad, the physician knows," Mrs Porter uttered brusquely. "I *am* able to continue," she said, and took another deep breath. She announced, "Mr Broad likes to be disciplined by a lady. To a limited extent I enjoyed, such was the overwhelming tedium of my life, to administer this discipline. This is not adultery, doctor, but a form of moral therapy in the same way that you administer a variety of them to your patients, you understand. Mr Broad was in need of some discipline to correct his unfortunate habit of charming the spitting cobra."

"Goodness! That sounds highly dangerous," said Norton. "I had no idea Mr Broad partakes in such dangerous leisure activities."

"Perilous. I keep telling him that he'll end up insane, locked away in an asylum like this. It corrupts the soul, you understand. You should know this, doctor – being a physician of the mind. And the bible strictly forbids this sort of behaviour."

"I think you've lost me, Mrs Porter. My knowledge of snake-charming must be very limited. Are we not talking about a snake enticed out of its basket before an audience with music piped by the charmer?" asked Norton, glancing with increasing but hidden doubt at Mr Broad who had remained passive except for the odd fit of sniffling.

"Oh! Really, Dr Norton," scoffed Mrs Porter. "Mr Broad's *solitary vice*."

"Ah! I see. Yes, indeed. But it's not appropriate to discuss Mr Broad's business like this. Not at all. Er, you had been mentioning administering discipline. We don't need to know why you felt Mr Broad needed this. But if you don't wish to continue…"

"I'll courageously continue. Satan knew that I was vulnerable and put temptation right in front of me. Alas matters spiralled out of control. I was like a runaway carriage with Satan holding the reins and lashing the horses to drive them ever faster. Lashing is not an inapt word to use, doctor. I knew that I was merely relieving my boredom by providing a service to needy men like Mr Broad, and before long I had established a little business of ill repute, using Mr Broad's house for discretion, and charging modest fees for my services. My list of clientele grew, and… Oh dear! On some occasions, when I found a client to be desirable, I succumbed to partaking in some less benign sins of the flesh. Although I should stress that I hesitate to describe them as adulterous, you understand."

An open-eyed Mr Broad, who now had a green lump hanging from a nostril, stirred to nod his support. The lump fell onto the cusp of his upper lip.

"She's certainly not nor ever was a wanton woman," he said. "Mrs Porter is a marvellous lady. Like aristocracy. And I've never known her to break wind. Not once."

"Thank you, Mr Broad," snapped Mrs Porter. "But I am engaged in a discussion with Dr Norton and I'm quite capable of managing it without assistance. Nor do I wish to be reminded that *you* have an especially unsavoury flatulence problem. To cut to the quick, doctor, after ten months my shameful activities were discovered. It was an act of God's benevolence. The police came and put a stop to them. My husband inevitably learned about them and stood by me like the dear, dear man he was. He used his influence and connections with some senior police officers and a local magistrate to ensure that the whole affair was swiftly buried without a prosecution in a court of law. Whether or not Mr Broad here seeks his titillation elsewhere I know not. I haven't asked because I don't wish to know, although I expect he would tell me if I did ask. I have far more glorious responsibilities now, you see, than assisting a lonely and unfortunate man to find some comfort in his proclivities. Oh! Woe is me. My dear and loyal husband – I think the shame and distress was too much for him. He passed away from pneumonia during the night not long after. Satan, you understand, is quick to take hold of the vulnerable and lead them astray. My head was in tatters. I was distraught. *Godfrey's Cordial* calmed my nerves during this time, and helped me to sleep better at night. It's the laudanum, you understand, in a palatable syrup – and may I personally recommend it to you, doctor, as something you might like to administer here to the more distressed of your patients.

Though my biggest recommendation to anybody, troubled or not, is to join the Nuddite Church. The Reverend Nudd, you see, put me back on a righteous path after another encounter...."

"Your recommendations are noted. Now, Mrs Porter. Forgive me for appearing to be harsh, for I am not without sympathy and I have witnessed many times the havoc that boredom can wreak on behaviour. And I should also reiterate, insist, that any personal issues relating to your platonic companion Mr Broad should be his business to disclose or otherwise. But permit me please to ask a question, one intriguing me somewhat persistently whilst I was listening. I'm interested to know whether you feel you can take any personal responsibility for your own behaviour? Or is it always, for example, a function of Satan – or alternatively of a sort of saviour like Mr Nudd?"

"Of course we have responsibilities, to both God and to ourselves, to fellow Nuddites, to our families and to our neighbours. But you clearly underestimate the scheming powers of Satan."

"And what of the powers of Mr Nudd?"

"Well, Mr Broad was already a Nuddite. Even if not fully committed at that stage. After my husband's funeral I had descended to my lowest ebb. For a while I even spurned Mr Broad's hand of friendship. He wrote me a letter suggesting that I try finding new purpose and salvation at The Holy Palace of the Church World of Nudd. So I attended a prayer meeting and, as I was saying, had another encounter – this time with the Reverend Nudd himself. We prayed for ourselves and each other; we prayed for the soul of Thomas Henry Huxley; for the souls of the Menecks – those who do not believe in a God at all; and we prayed for the souls of the Nonnudds – those who have faith but have yet to see that the only complete way to reach God and salvation is through the Nuddite Church. In particular everybody – the congregation of around thirty or fifty, probably as many as a hundred – prayed for me that evening, and during the course of one evening shortly after the Reverend Nudd absolved me of all my sins and welcomed me into the fold. I found solace, became a regular attender, and marvelled at the words of wisdom spoken by the Reverend Nudd. The Reverend is an extraordinary man, blessed with astonishing gifts which included the wisdom to recognise mine. At a Nuddite meeting only a month or so before he was transported away to this ghastly place, the Reverend honoured us by sharing some of his deeds. He told me about the occasion when he was attacked by a pride of tigers up in the Himalayas. These are mountains rising to the middle of central Asia, you understand, higher than the Alps, and ruled by the Queen as part of the Raj. It was an *extraordinary* event. Unarmed without so much as a humble stick with which to poke them in the eyes, the Reverend was able at once to placate these ghastly man-eating beasts when they were on the point of leaping upon him to gobble him up. Yes, all he used – in addition to his exceptional courage and the counsel of God – were his eyes and some miraculous hand signals. Before he knew it the vicious brutes were lying on their backs as tame as pussycats while the Reverend scratched their bellies. There's no place for tigers in a civilised world, doctor. There's no reference to them in the Garden of Eden. They deserve to be shot. Every last one of them."

"That *is* extraordinary. I had no idea that tigers hunted in packs."

"Well you wouldn't, doctor, would you? With all due respect, such knowledge is likely to be in the domain of only the truly enlightened – the Nuddites."

"I hadn't realised either that Mr Nudd had ever travelled to the Himalayas."

"Ah. Only in a manner of speaking. It was in a dream, you understand, that he travelled there and tamed the tigers. But as the Reverend explained, it was through this dream that God was able to personally communicate with the Reverend his special gift of being able to completely tame a pride of hungry tigers. That is no ordinary talent, doctor."

"Quite," Norton responded, raising his eyebrow. "A talent that no doubt will chance one day to be most useful to Mr Nudd. Moving on from these deeds and talents, I'd like to...."

"There's so much more," Mrs Porter persisted. "Did you know that he can run the mile in less than seven seconds?"

"Unsurprisingly, I didn't."

"He also revealed that just before bed he runs all the way to Oxford and back, and that he has now thrice climbed the north face of the Eiger mountain using only his bare hands and unshod feet. Oh! I nearly forgot to mention that he can now levitate to a height of twenty-nine feet and seven and a half inches by flapping his hands and concentrating his mind."

"In dreams?" asked Norton.

"No. When fully awake just as you and I are right now. He has a special knowledge of gravity, between The Reverend and his Maker, you understand. You may be a septical, doctor, but you don't truly know the Reverend Nudd. Neither, of course, doctor, have you ever seen him commanding the dais and preaching in full flow. He explains how God contacts him through electronic impulses, sending him messages and divine secrets down lightning bolts during storms. Did you know, doctor, that God can communicate with chosen individuals by using lightning rather like a telephone line or telegram wire? No. But now you are better informed!" Mrs Porter revealed with glee. She reminisced further, her eyes now fully fastened on to Dr Norton's, and her bust bouncing up and down. She relived those first few months when she proved herself worthy of being a fully confirmed Nuddite, and she shared these recollections with Dr Norton. She revealed how exceptional prayer had been devoted to a patch of turf in the rear garden of the palace to prepare it for a special purpose. She enthused about her role in raising donations from the other Nuddites to purchase the materials necessary for erecting a holy chapel there, and she boasted about the size of her own, though unspecified, "particularly substantial" donation. Her eyes rolled around her face in rapture as she described the moment when she became fully confirmed, and received the locket, secured around her neck by the hands of the Reverend Nudd, that contained an image – printed from an engraving – of the faces of Reverend Nudd and his wife Emily. She congratulated herself on organising Mr Broad's full Nuddite confirmation, and she complained about the contents of the locket.

"It is an honour and a blessing to carry the Reverend's image against my body. But having to dangle an image of that woman below my neck is another matter altogether I can tell you, doctor. Perhaps one day in the future this hideous blasphemy will be remedied. It will be perhaps my image next to the Reverend's."

"Possibly, Mrs Porter, possibly. So was this chapel ever built?" inquired Dr Norton.

"Of course, and mostly from the finest imported white marble, doctor. Although it is not a chapel of conventional size or structure. It is much more impressive than that. It is very small, you understand, and one cannot enter within it. Its appearance resembles more a spindly pyramid like a colossal white spike rising from the ground. Inside is a cavity – a chamber, if you like – the size of a standard picnic hamper. This cavity stores protective energy which is why the holy structure is known as the *PE Chapel*. As I have already described to you, doctor, it resembles a small pyramid that is elongated upwards. We stand in a tight circle praying, with congregation members having to take it in turns because its size only permits a dozen at a time to form a tight circle around it. Sometimes we dance around linked hand to hand. In this way, you understand, our prayers in the form of electronic energy are absorbified for storage within the cavity. It is very scientific – and with all due respect, doctor, of a scientific progress probably beyond your capacity. But there's more. Because the PE Chapel points upwards to a height of precisely fourteen feet and three inches, it can additionally receive instructions from God during thunderstorms. The PE Chapel then conveys the energy back out to whomever needs protection from malign influences. It is truly the most amazing device I have ever set my eyes upon."

"Fascinating, Mrs Porter. Is this protective energy visible to the eye? Can it be seen in some form leaving the chapel to, er, shroud a selected individual with protection?"

"Do you know it's interesting that you should ask that, doctor. Although I haven't witnessed this myself, according to the Reverend Nudd it floats out like a tiny luminous ball about the size of a large cooking apple. He refers to it as benevolent ball lightning."

"This is indeed most interesting. More importantly, I hope this information will enhance our therapeutic efforts with Mr Nudd. Tell me, Mrs Porter, I am interested to know of the role that *Mrs* Nudd plays in any of the proceedings." the doctor asked.

"Oh! Goodness. Very little actually. Although she does rather inadequately attempt to tend to our needs by providing us all with some cake and muffins during our meetings. The refreshments are satisfactory, but I must say that my cakes receive absolutely all the compliments on the occasions I bring them. No. I am doing *her* a disservice. As the Reverend Nudd explains, she is dutiful, she is his rock, apparently, and she is the devoted mother of his two children, young Percy and Amelia, even if she is unremarkable in appearance to the discerning eye. I dread to imagine how she looks first thing in the morning but I shouldn't be cruel," said Mrs Porter, straightening her face and hardening her voice. Mr Broad, whose green lump had been wiped onto his cheek where it was drying like glue, suddenly piped up.

"Very true. Emily, Mrs Nudd, is a very fine lady and a supportive wife and a devoted mother. Just like Mrs Porter said. Mrs Porter is on a different level altogether, though. An angel, doctor, and an angel from heaven in mortal form. She needs to be wrapped up in cotton wool. And she bakes a much better cake than Mrs Nudd. My advice to you, Dr Norton, is that if there is a Mrs Norton or you have a lady friend, then you should wrap her up in cotton wool," he added, and Dr Norton acknowledged Mr Broad's contribution with a smile before addressing Mrs Porter once again.

6

Not far from Dr Norton's conversation with Mrs Porter, Mr Percival Nudd was lying on a bed in a side room off one of the long ward galleries. Flat on his back, his eyes facing the ceiling, Mr Nudd was still fuming that the same steward had once again suggested that he undertake some chores to assist with the running of the hospital.

"When will you irksome people comprehend that I have far weightier preoccupations?" Nudd had dismissed him. "Now please leave me alone so I can give them my full and pressing consideration. Thank you." It wasn't long before he shut his eyes and rolled over onto one side. Elsewhere Mr Nudd's wife, Emily, was already preparing the early evening meal. Slim, elfin, dark-haired and blue-eyed, appealing without the features of classical beauty, she looked to have aged little since her wedding day except for permanent anxiety that lined her forehead and radiated like spokes from the corners of her eyes. With her husband absent, she had only two other mouths to feed. The days of preparing a lavish dish like 'Raised Game Pie' from *Mrs Agnes Marshall's Cookery Book* was, for the time being, an exercise of the past. The housekeeping budget no longer extended to purchasing a variety of meats – and certainly not game like venison, pheasant and quail. Other ingredients such as pâté de fois gras were out of the question, and because simple button mushrooms were now only a rare treat, truffles were completely out of the question. Lining one margin of a wooden tabletop was an assortment of metal tins and glass or earthenware storage jars. Arranged neatly on the other side were diverse metal baking moulds and implements that included Mrs

Nudd's prized whisk. She was preparing a raised pie using the coldwater crust technique. Its contents were to be humble pork, carrots and leek. These meals would always be sufficiently large to feed an extra mouth, should her husband suddenly return home unexpectedly. Rock cakes were also on the day's cooking agenda. These, along with scotch short cakes and scones, helped to satisfy the children. Sweet dessert jelly had become a weekly treat, and baking grand cakes, no longer easily affordable, was still undertaken for the Nuddite prayer meetings. In her husband's absence this was a gesture of support. In truth, she yearned for him to find a more conventional vocation to preoccupy his daytime hours, free up the evenings for family activities, and bring in something resembling a steady income. Emily had earlier completed sweeping the floors and sliding the duster across most of the surfaces. The entire house had been cleaned over the previous day and a half with the exception of her husband's throne room. She only ever entered this to serve refreshments during the meetings, and to clean up at their conclusions. At all other times the door remained locked, and visiting this room in any case was very low in Mrs Nudd's hierarchy of interests. She occasionally lost concentration when performing her chores. Her hands dithered whilst preparing a paste for her pie as her mind drifted out of the house and beyond London. She envisaged herself, in the company of her children and her husband, sitting at the dinner table of a little cottage, her husband ravenously devouring his food with a big smile whilst describing, between mouthfuls, his day at work. She suddenly realised that she was gazing through the window into the back garden, and directly at the PE Chapel. She screwed up her eyes and jerked them back inside the kitchen. Emily Nudd's thoughts frequently wandered away from her present circumstances. However, as she constantly reminded herself, when, as an eighteen-year-old she had stood at the altar in her wedding dress, she had promised to honour and obey, through sickness and in health, the man called Percival Conrad

Ignatius Nudd. She had written to her parents with such pride to inform them that Percival was taking theological training. She had written with such disappointment when Percival had dropped out before formal ordination into the Anglican Church. Establishing the Nuddite Church had left a permanent sigh seeping from Emily's mouth. She pulled open a cabinet drawer and removed a pile of letters. She sifted through what was mostly an assortment of demands from creditors that had begun dropping on her doormat like autumn leaves portending a bleak winter. She had witnessed the Nuddite congregations recede to a trickle – a reversal of fortunes preceding her husband's latest institutionalisation. Nuddite donations had been drying up even quicker. The only reliable source of income had been the monthly sums of money brought to the house, of French origin but explanation unknown. Emily would not ask the courteous French courier for more and she was, God knew, less than happy to accept the generous sums handed over by the woman. Emily replaced the letters inside the drawer, retaining just one – a letter recently arrived from her husband. She quickly re-read Percival's intricate scrawl – almost gothic in design like much of the contemporary architecture, though the extent was determined by the elevation of his mood. Emily Nudd pulled a face as she read her husband's letter. He was claiming that the hospital physicians had finally seen the light and come to realise that he was indeed undertaking a most special and Holy mission. Percival went on to claim that the physicians were now solely concerned that he would soon be fit to return home in the strongest of health to resume executing the duties that God had bestowed upon him. Emily's facial expression worsened. She could have been sucking on a ferociously sour lemon. She marched into the little scullery towards a large bin, but paused before turning back into the kitchen. Emily tore up the letter into small shreds and flung them into the stove fire. Her thoughts darted back once more. All those years ago at her wedding ceremony she would not have believed for a single moment that her life would unfold like this.

As Mrs Nudd switched her attention back to the evolution of her pie, somebody else had thoughts of her husband, amongst a select few others, in his mind as he traversed a section of London that led towards St Mary of Bethlem hospital. Currently a resident of Shoreditch, he was sporadically on the lookout for lodgings in another borough with a denser Irish population. The unrelenting influx of East European Jews had saturated such a large clump to the east of the city that they had now begun displacing the British and Irish inhabitants of Shoreditch. Relocation wasn't a priority yet. In any case he rarely stayed too long at any address lest his face became too familiar or because business summoned him back to Dublin, New York, or Boston. Wherever he slept and worked he preferred to be as conspicuous as a hunched tiger in grassy scrubland. This man, with his short, rust-coloured hair and green cap to match his eyes, randomly varied his route to the hospital in South London. Walking towards Shoreditch, however, was Mr Garbett. He had crawled out of his temporary digs near Brick Lane clutching a canvas bag secured to his body by the shoulder straps that crossed over his neck. Inside, the small publications were carefully wrapped to hide their illicit nature. There were some deliveries to be made in Shoreditch, and from there his intermittent courier activities extended into Islington. Mr Garbett glanced across at the rubble-cluttered gap where the slum block known as the Marketside Rookery had been recently demolished. A handful of rag-clad urchins were clambering among the debris. Garbett cleared his throat and spat onto the pavement. He wouldn't be spending any further nights inside *that* rookery. As he continued on his way he noticed Wexford Cathy creeping awkwardly out of a grocery shop with an apple in her hand. Her grey face was barely alive, her eyes bloodshot and surrounded by the darkness that was devouring her fast. Garbett didn't know it, but Wexford Cathy was an escapee from an institution in Ireland. After a friend of her father had violated her body when she was lean, freckled, and barely thirteen years old, she had been dragged screaming to a moral correction establishment run by the Magdalene Sisters. It hadn't mattered that Cathy had done all that a young girl could manage to fight off her abuser. It seems that the only mistake she had made was to tell her mother about the incident. The nuns would ensure that she slaved away throughout the long days for them, repeating her prayers, and taking brutal beatings for the stated purpose of converting her to God and a worthy life. These nuns were not sisters of mercy. They showed Cathy no compassion of any form. Some of them even molested her body with drooling lips, and pulled her head by her hair in-between their legs to force the girl to pleasure them. These experiences, though unpleasant in the extreme, wreaked less damage to Cathy than the general brutality of the regime, the obscene hypocrisy of the nuns, and their unrelenting insistence that Cathy was nothing other than a disgusting sinner. After two and a half years she finally grabbed a rare opportunity to escape. She headed across the sea after paying for her passage by selling her crucifix and a quick sample of her flesh to a sailor at the Dublin docks. Her family had all but disowned her, and so she had sought a new life in London. Here she was free to do as she pleased and go wherever she decided. But she could never shake off the damage already so brutally inflicted. Poverty tightened the shackles. Her basic skills of cleaning, laundry, and elementary cooking that had been drilled into her by the nuns were of scant use. And if the demand for domestic servants and chambermaids had been rising, as London and its wealth inflated like a balloon, the numbers of the needy had accelerated faster. For all of the bloated middle- and educated-class employers, far too many girls possessed only these skills. So now, as the nuns had regularly reminded her, Cathy was "nuttin' but a dirty little harlot".

Garbett knew nothing of this. Nor, unlike Frenchie, would he have cared. Frenchie had more than once begged Cathy to return to her family in Ireland. On the last occasion the young woman had told Frenchie that she had been orphaned at the age of thirteen. For Mr Garbett, Wexford Cathy was simply a gin-soaked, opium-bludgeoned whore whose circumstances were so desperate that she could be persuaded for a throwaway fee to pose in some of the little publications that he disseminated around nooks of London. The best bit, for Garbett, was that for introducing them to the photographer, he would take a bigger cut of commission than women like Cathy would be paid. There was plenty of money to be made for men like Garbett in this trade. In Shoreditch alone he had six deliveries to make this week. Mr Wood, the respectable family man and coal merchant was the first client to visit. There was also Mr Cohen, Major Herbert, Mr Karpov, Mr Milosz, and of course the insatiable Miss Pringle, a former girls' schoolmistress. All of them, of course, were strict church attenders, and a lucrative ratio of them – Miss Pringle included – could occasionally be persuaded by Mr Garbett to be introduced to an inpecunious female for discreet pleasures. Even Garbett recognised the double standards of the times. But for Mr Garbett, the only implication of this was the fattened opportunity to earn more commission. He walked onwards towards Shoreditch where he would make his first delivery in the coalmerchant's private office.

The rust-haired man, if he had passed Mr Garbett walking in the opposite direction along the pavement, would not have seen him. On his seat, whatever the mode of transport, he rarely looked through the windows to watch the world reversing by. He tended to sit impassively with his eyes facing ahead. On this occasion he had opted to catch a ride on an omnibus into the city district, and then taken the City and South London Railway from King William Street to

Stockwell. This underground line was relatively new and made use of electric traction. Beneath his green cap the faintest of sniggers crossed the man's unyielding face in the blink of an eye. Down in the subterranean transport system he had been momentarily thinking about the Necropolis line – the underground train that had been transporting the dead to a suburban cemetery for nearly half a century since a spate of cholera epidemics had over-burdened the morgues and cemeteries inside the metropolis. The man visualised a particular corpse on board, rattling south through the dark tunnel. He didn't linger long on this thought, nor on other potential distractions. The nature of his work required a calm mind with tight focus. As the hydraulic lift pulled him and some other passengers back up to street level, he briefly considered the link between the name of this underground's coaches with his destination. These coaches, with generously cushioned seating but bereft of any windows at all, were known by the monicker "padded cells". Back up on street level this man now turned his attention to negotiating the relatively short distance to St George's Fields and the hospital that, like the train, inevitably contained some padded cells somewhere below ground level.

7

Back inside the physicians' room, Dr Norton was still persisting with Mrs Porter in the tiring hope that she might provide some additional information helpful to Mr Nudd's treatment.

"Is there anything else you would care to tell me that you, er, estimate to be of assistance? I'm expecting a colleague at any moment. So anything at all disclosed with brevity, since I do need to attend to other business here forthwith?" Norton asked.

"It should never be forgotten that flagellation is far from the worst of sins. Some men are healthier of spirit following discipline. Our children likewise. And never forget that some Christians have believed that, far from being a sin, the act of self-flagellation purges the body and soul," said Mrs Porter before addressing Mr Broad without even a glance.

"Medication time. I need my medicine."

Mr Broad pulled a flask from his coat pocket, unscrewed the lid, and passed it over to Mrs Porter who snatched it from his hand. She gulped down some shots of the contents, and returned the flask to her companion. Norton couldn't hide his surprise.

"Forgive me, but I thought the Nuddites preached temperance, Mrs Porter."

"Most certainly we do, doctor. But this is strictly medicinal, you understand. As a physician you should be well aware of the medicinal benefit of Scotchman's whisky."

"Quite. So I've heard. The medicinal properties of whisky, and also the purging of sin through flagellation."

"Have you tried them, doctor?" asked Mrs Porter.

"You should, you know," added Mr Broad.

"I sometimes imbibe a small dram of whisky. But I'm thinking about Mr Nudd. Trying hard to. Anything else you could divulge that might assist us to help *him*?"

"There's one other issue I'd like to broach with you, doctor. I am thoroughly dismayed not to have yet received an invitation to grace with my presence one of the Bethlem balls. I wonder if you could remedy this oversight. And I am certainly concerned that, should the Reverend attend one of your balls, he might be enchanted by one of the many ladies present, and tempted, you understand, to take her into his confidence. I am not implying that the Reverend is in any way weak, but without my presence there is a risk of this occurring, and, you see, he has no better nor more worthy confidante than myself."

"Rest assured, Mrs Porter, that Mr Nudd will not be permitted to attend one of our balls unless he agrees to wear clothing more suitable for such a function. To date, he has declined this opportunity. For the very same reason he was denied permission to attend the patients' outing to Kew last week, and to Greenwich before that. Now then. Has anything else occurred to you that might help us to help Mr Nudd?"

"You know, doctor, I think I might be able to help you and all of your patients."

"Really?" asked Norton. "What are you proposing?"

"A cake. One like no other. The baking mixture will include prunes and walnuts. The prunes will calm the nerves by cleaning all the poisons out of the system that are likely to cause irritation to body, mind and soul. This is particularly germinal to the intestines and bowels, you understand. The walnuts, being firm but nutritious, fortify the brain. This, as you know well doctor, will help prevent moral weakness which is a major cause of lunacy."

"That's all very interesting, er, no doubt, er, very tasty, but…"

"I shall patent this cake but give you my assurances now that Bethlem Hospital will be the very first lunatic hospital privileged to use my cake as a therapy."

"Very thoughtful," said Norton trying to smile. "But I must insist we return at the moment to specifically helping Mr Nudd. If there is anything at all that has occurred to you, please tell me."

But before Mrs Porter had the opportunity to probe her mind, the turn of the door handle interrupted her thoughts and Dr Strange walked into the room.

"Forgive me for disturbing you, Dr Norton. I wasn't expecting you to have company at this moment," he apologised.

"That's quite alright, doctor," said Dr Norton, and he introduced his colleague to Nudd's companions. Dr Strange reached for Mrs Porter's hand and kissed it.

"Delighted to be acquainted with you at last, my dear lady," he gushed. "I am instantly enchanted. And naturally I'm pleased to make your acquaintance also, Mr Broad."

"Goodness me," remarked Mrs Porter, swirling her eyes back at Dr Norton. "What a handsome young colleague you have."

Dr Strange whispered loudly to the senior physician. "I merely wanted to ask you if you were in agreement that we proceed with the cold shower therapy for a particular elderly female patient."

"Of course. Miss K. We'll discuss that in a moment. Mrs Porter, Mr Broad, thank you very much for your time. It has been most enlightening and very much appreciated. But if you'll excuse Dr Strange and myself, we have something to discuss privately. Dr Strange, Mrs Porter has been telling me about Mr Nudd's church. I am sure, since you are also concerned with Mr Nudd's progress, that you will no doubt be in equal measure grateful for Mrs Porter's disclosures."

"Mrs Porter. Your reputation of grace and inspiration precedes you," Strange halted her as she stood up to depart with Mr Broad.

"Have you been so admirable as to reveal the contents of Mr Nudd's diaries pertaining to his trip to the Breton Marshes in France?"

"I'm afraid that I haven't. I neither know what the contents are, nor would I betray the Reverend Nudd if I did so."

"Infinitely more admirable than disclosure, dear lady. I have ascertained in a jiffy that it's true that not only do you possess the feminine qualities of Aphrodite, but also the virtues of a saint. And I understand from the Reverend Nudd that in his absence you are leading his prayer meetings. It must be so reassuring to him that he has a loyal follower like you with both the leadership and wisdom to do this. I might even be interested in attending myself."

"Ooh! Would you really, doctor? Though I hasten to admit that it is the Reverend Nudd – when he is back to his imperious self at full flow – who is the very special one to guide and inspire you. In any case your presence might cause me some unease. I wouldn't be at my very best if too self-conscious," twittered Mrs Porter, and Mr Broad instantly intervened with words of encouragement that plodded despite their slavish conviction.

"You do yourself an injustice, Mrs Porter. You're a truly marvellous prayer leader. The very best – except for the Reverend Nudd."

Dr Strange continued to court Mrs Porter's favour.

"I suspect your companion knows you well – including all your great talents, dear lady. Who knows? Your prayer leadership might provide the inspiration behind the conversion of another soul to the Nuddite Church," he said, his bulging eyes drawing in bulging eyes while furrows of concern drifted across Norton's brow.

The previous evening returned, for a moment, to Mrs Porter's mind. She revisited the garden at the Nudd residence, she heard the chanting, the comments of flattery, and she saw nine other followers of Nudd linked by outstretched arms circling the PE Chapel. She nearly laughed aloud as she saw Mr Broad break the circle by stumbling as the remaining Nuddites began to spin together around the pyramid with sideways strides. She felt a hot flush of excitement as she saw the followers listening to her every word and praying at her promptings. She felt a twinge of irritation when she saw Emily Nudd glancing down from an upstairs window. Most of all she wallowed in images of herself, wearing her long, loose, silky white dress, and with the mock diamond tiara that Mr Broad had bought her to crown her head. Just for a split second her images vaulted forward in time as she imagined herself back in the garden, and from there inside the house. In the spartan Holy room she was sitting on the Reverend's throne chair. She witnessed herself repositioned on the dais, preaching to hundreds of Nuddites crammed into the room and all jostling to get a better view of her as she spoke. At her side, even holding her hand in these fanciful images, stood Dr Strange. Mr Broad didn't exist at all in these thoughts – and only when she watched herself asking the Nuddites to pray for the Reverend Nudd was a potential blunder averted. No, the Reverend wasn't forgotten.

Dr Strange's voice jolted Mrs Porter's mind back to the present.

"So where and when do these meetings take place, dear lady? The doors are surely open to allcomers. I need precise details of the prayer meeting venue."

"You know, doctor, I think I really would after all be gratified by your presence at my prayer meetings. They are held every Monday, Wednesday and Friday evenings from seven o'clock until nine at the Holy World Palace of the Nuddite Church in Victoria – practically in Belgravia although rather more in Pimlico, you understand. Except not a week on Friday because Mrs Nudd will be visiting her mother in St Albans for three nights and so there will be nobody to let us in and serve the cake and muffins. Though I hasten to add that I was willing to bring the fruits of my own labour – cakes that are far more popular than the dry efforts Mrs Nudd serves up. Would you like to write down the address, doctor?"

"I don't believe that I need to concern myself with that now, dear lady. We'll have it here and I'd only need to request it from one of our clerks. It is with deep regret that I won't be able to attend for a few weeks due to other commitments, but I certainly hope that our paths cross in the meantime. Very soon, preferably. Very soon."

"Oh! I do hope so."

"Now, unfortunately, Dr Norton and myself have some confidential business requiring our attention. Until next time, dear lady. Until next time, Mr Broad. On second thoughts, would you care to wait outside for a few minutes? I would be honoured, nay thrilled, to make a future engagement to harvest the fruits of a more substantial conversation with you. Grant a humble young physician, please, the privilege of arranging to spend a little more time in your exceptional company."

"Dr Strange, of course Mr Broad and myself will be awaiting you. How could I possibly decline your request?" squealed Mrs Porter. She flung back her head and her smile almost burst her face as she bounced out of the room pursued by Mr Broad. After the door shut, Dr Norton emitted a short sigh of unease from his rumpled face.

He sat down and gestured Strange to do likewise. He flicked his eyebrows up a couple of times and met Strange's eyes firmly.

"That was quite a performance with Mrs Porter," he began with a steady voice of authority. "I feel obliged out of seniority as well as concern for you to express my distaste for your conversation with Mrs Porter."

"But I must protest, my good man, that it is all to the benefit of our patient, Mr Nudd."

"No. I don't accept that. I believe that in your misguided – reckless, even – determination to establish an eminent reputation for yourself, you are attempting to exploit Mrs Porter for the eliciting of information. It concerns me that this is more for the benefit of writing a case study paper you recently expounded to me. In short, this is for your benefit only. Your impetuosity needs to be curbed."

"But my dear fellow, you misconstrued....'"

"No." Dr Norton interrupted decisively. "Do me the courtesy of listening to what I have to say. I am giving you very sound advice. Whether you adopt it is a matter that only you can decide. I can only hope you do. But first I can and will insist that you listen. It would be entirely remiss of you to devote too much of your energy on the one patient. And that's despite sympathising with your curiosity about Mr Nudd. You know only too well that we have hundreds who require our attention."

"You have to admit that a man as thoroughly dull as Percival Nudd becomes a fascinating enigma when he is able to found his own church and inspire such loyalty. Sometimes I wonder if his hold over his followers is based solely on the mystique created from his experience in the Breton marshes – an episode about which nobody else knows practically anything at all," Strange pointed out.

"Furthermore," stressed Norton, "your proposed paper on the aetiology of the guru's mental states is a splendid idea – but not yet. And you may be right about Mr Nudd's mystique being significant. But has it occurred to you that this could be accidental? Rather than to engender mystique, he may be keeping his experiences to himself as a consequence of the sheer terror of his recollections. Or even some onerous guilt? As for Mr Nudd's ability to inspire such loyalty in his followers, take a closer look at them and note their own personal problems with lack of direction or self-worth. Note also that the Nuddite congregation, never large, is shrinking fast."

"I see what you mean."

"You have much to learn," Norton continued, "about psychological medicine generally, Dr Strange. It would be both to your and also your patients' advantage to equip yourself as thoroughly as possible with the whole range of complicated afflictions that we encounter here. And the therapeutic practices likewise. Addressing your comment about Mr Nudd being dull is a case in point. We have only observed the melancholy. We have neither seen the stable Nudd nor indeed the manic Nudd that precedes the crashing of his mood. This is the second occasion I have known this particular version of Mr Nudd. He spent some time with us fourteen years ago, shortly after returning from France, and just before his transformation that eventually led to founding his Nuddite Church. Read my notes on his case history again. This is a man who wanted to be a scientist but was deprived of the opportunity to enter mainstream academic study at Oxford or Cambridge universities despite being a studious grammar school boy. And because, in all likelihood, he was deemed to be *merely* the son of a modest apothecary. This is a highly frustrated individual – and perhaps resentful one – who resorted to dabbling around the outer fringes of pioneering science after being briefly apprenticed to his father. Deep down he is not a happy soul, but he found some sort of role and status for himself by becoming a guru. Granted, something significant occurred during a trip to France that diverted him towards a religious odyssey. Granted, it was significant enough to be a catalyst for psychological instability. And granted, I wish we knew what occurred because it would jolly well help if we are to provide an enduring cure that doesn't see him ever returning here for a third time. But whatever happened in France, his fundamental and unfulfilled ambitions alone are sufficient to upset his equilibrium. I urge you to take note of the overall picture, Dr Strange, even if some parts are missing. Like a jigsaw puzzle, we might have to make do with pieces at our disposal. The trick, Dr Strange, is to accumulate enough knowledge about individual case histories, the most fitting therapies to help our patients, and learn how to get to know the specific person without any presuppositions. This doesn't happen overnight. Consider also that being in the position to help some of these people is a rare honour. You are classified as a student for the obvious reason that it is exactly what you are."

Norton paused. Strange pulled out his spectacles, his mouth ajar, and placed them in front of his fixed stare at Norton. The senior physician continued after a moment's reflection.

"Of course the process of learning is unending. I will still be sizeably bereft of the necessary knowledge to help every single one of our patients on the very eve of my retirement. But for now you have a great deal to learn in a relatively short space of time. I hope I have made myself clear, Dr Strange, and that you will heed my counsel."

Meanwhile, on a bench near the physicians' room, Mrs Porter sat preening herself, adjusting and readjusting the green feathers on the top of her head. They now resembled the remains of an exploded parrot. Mr Broad sat glumly next to her. Five minutes later the conversation between the two physicians still hadn't yet run its course.

"Yes, Dr Norton," agreed Strange. "You have made your point. It is pertinent, and a product of considerable experience. It shall be observed. Thank you."

"Excellent! Now then, I believe you wanted to discuss another matter with me. Miss Kimbel?"

"Yes. I advocate something altogether shorter and sharper than a thorough course of moral therapy. Cold showers, perhaps, or maybe some electric shocks?"

"I would most definitely recommend neither," Norton instantly responded. "On what grounds do you consider any of your suggestions to be beneficial to her?"

"All that woman ever does is to sit knitting throughout the day without the least inclination to communicate. She refuses to cooperate with daily routines like laundry, bed-making, washing-up or any other household chores expected of our female patients – even more impertinent since she's a voluntary boarder here exempt from paying fees. And on top of that the woman continues to be devoid of any courtesy or respect. She's even worse than Nudd. He contributes little and only has time for his grotesque pair of visiting sycophants."

"Can we focus on Miss Kimbel, please?" Norton requested.

"Of course, Dr Norton. Yes, this woman is yet worse I tell you. You must surely agree, my dear fellow, that such behaviour is not only socially unacceptable but also symptomatic of a mind corrupted to a condition of obstinate insanity. My suggestion is that you have her certified as insane, then we can re-admit her, and force upon her a range of therapies from which she would not be at liberty to walk away."

"I would not countenance such a measure. And as for her behaviour being unacceptable I beg to differ, Dr Strange. Have you not read the notes made on her admission here?"

"Well I might have done. I expect I must have. As we've acknowledged we are overrun with patients and consequently struggling with a mountain of paperwork," answered Strange through his teeth.

"All the more reason not to dwell disproportionately on Mr Nudd and your lone research."

"Yes, I do recall reading Miss Kimbel's notes," said Strange.

"In that case I suggest you re-read them and think again. Miss Kimbel has suffered a terrible ordeal. She was brutally assaulted in her home during the process of being robbed of her most precious possessions. She spent two weeks in St George's Hospital recovering, then another two at Atkinson Morley's. She is sixty-seven years old, poor lady. She may have recovered physically from her terrifying ordeal, but not psychologically."

"Of course not. How shortsighted of me."

"Very shortsighted, as you concede. And those psychological scars take longer to heal," Norton persevered, as if unconvinced he had spelt out enough. "She recognised her assailants – two young men who are neighbours. One of them, despite coming from a quite well-to-do family, keeps bad company. Alibis were fabricated for both of Miss Kimbel's assailants to protect them from our dubious justice system. Other neighbours who could have testified on behalf of Miss Kimbel were also persuaded to say nothing. So there was no justice for Miss Kimbel. And it is hardly surprising that for the moment she has lost her inclination to show much respect or courtesy towards others. I would advocate that in the first instance she receives as much comfort and consideration as we can afford her. Then we must help her with utmost sensitivity to regain some of her ability to firstly integrate here, and then secondly to fit back into our troubled society."

"I am indebted to you, Dr Norton, once again. I shall henceforth appraise our patients with more rigour."

"Excellent! Now if I recall there are two people awaiting you in the corridor. It would not do to keep them tarrying for too long – nor our patients. And it would certainly not do to forget what we agreed a few minutes ago. Mrs Porter, it seems, also has a propensity for psychological instability. She is a lost soul desperate for a purpose in a life. Equally she is a lonely woman desperate to be desirable to men."

"My dear fellow, your observations are faultless."

As if uninterrupted Norton calmly continued, looking Dr Strange straight in the eyes.

"The Cartesian proof of existence *cogito, ergum sum*, or *I think therefore I am,* is insufficient for Mrs Porter. *I am important and adored by men, therefore I am* is her requirement, and I would not like to learn that her vulnerability has been exploited. Good day, for now, Dr Strange."

"Of course not, Dr Norton," Strange replied as he stood up, removed his spectacles, brushed down his frock coat, straightened his waistcoat and necktie, and groomed his wispy hair with his fingers. "Good day to you, and thank you again," he uttered, and took leave of Norton to find Percival Nudd's two friends sitting patiently just along the corridor.

8

Dr Strange thudded around like a raging lumberjack in the corner of the saloon bar. He threw down his hat onto the cruddy floorboards and took a kick at the table leg. The beer from two pint tankards sloshed miniature foaming waves across the table surface, from which Strange snatched some volumes bound in leather, and tossed them across to Garbett.

"Deary me. Tantrums, tantrums," scoffed a nearby woman with a luridly decorated face, and a stomach as overloaded as her bust and rear. "I know what you need to calm you down, loverboy. Come over here and let Aunty Dolly work her magic," she suggested. Strange declined with a contemptuous glower. Although far worse customarily flared up in the pub, he was attracting a bit of attention. Strange probed the mass of clientele, maggots writhing in an open sore, and satisfied himself that the shaven-headed thug was absent. He addressed Aunt Dolly.

"Mind your own wretched business," Strange hissed, viciously scratching through his hair and into his scalp. He snatched up his hat and turned back to Garbett.

"Outside, now," he commanded. "I need some air – even the East End's vilest vapours will suffice. And what I have to say, you will most certainly agree, would be far better away from a flea-pit tavern full with flapping ears."

Strange barged his way out of the Nag's Head. Garbett gathered up the five leather-bound volumes and followed him out into the drizzle.

"Give them to me," Strange instructed at a quieter spot, grabbing the tomes back from Garbett. "*This* is the diary of Percival Conrad bleeding Ignatius Nudd for the year 1879; this one for 1880; this one for 1881; this one for 1882; and this one for the year 1884. These are all completely, totally, and utterly useless to me. What was the specification for this task? Tell me. What was it?" he demanded, slapping the diaries back into Garbett's clutches.

"To purloin the diary for the year 1883, sir. But it weren't there, honest, guv. It weren't wiv these lot. I searched 'igh and low, like. It weren't there. These years was the closest. Ain't they no good?"

"No they damn well aren't, and I've already paid you half the fee plus some expenses for absolutely nothing."

"Yeah. Well on that subject, 'ow 'bout paying me the other 'arf. I done me best. Best I could for yer, sir."

"My! You don't lack gall, you impertinent charlatan. Pay you for what? And in any case, didn't you help yourself to plenty of other valuables there for the taking?" Strange asked. He attempted to assert his authority by thrusting his face closer to Garbett's. A gust of wind, despite rinsing them with the specks of rain, launched Garbett's odours at Strange. He recoiled.

"Well," began Garbett, "' you said in the briefing that it had to look like a general sorta burglary. Not just for them diaries. So I done that, natural, Dr Maxwell. Just 'elped meself to a few worfless baubles. Blimey, I just want me other 'arf that's due me now."

Strange untwisted his handkerchief then wiped his face clean.

"Do you indeed?" he contested, baring his teeth while rain dripped from the brim of his hat.

"Yeah. That's right, Dr Maxwell. And if I don't get it I'll see to it that you'll never find nobody again. Nobody round these parts willing to do any business wiv you again."

"I hope you are not threatening me, Mr Garbett – or whatever your real name might be. I *insist* that you return to the Nudd domicile and stage another burglary. Search again, man. And this time do a more thorough job. Get me the correct diary, and you will get the rest of your fee. I cannot ask certain people too many questions, so you'll just have to find out for yourself the most suitable moment to break in next time. Is that clear?"

"Now 'old onto yer horses, Dr Maxwell. First orf, what's wiv the bit about whatever my *real* name might be? Eh? Garbett's me name, ain't it? So don't you be going all queer on me."

"As you say, Mr *Garbett*. As you say," said Strange, composing himself, but not yet relinquishing his leer.

"Second, sir, that ain't such a good idea. Not doin' anuver burglary. Not so quick after the last one. It 'elped last time because of the pea-souper. The fog come down particular thick. Makin' orf I was as visible as a harem of naked dancing girls to a blind beggar. Anyhow I took all the best bits. You know, the silver goblets and the silver cigarette case. And them silver-plated candlestick 'olders. I took the cream of the jewellery. The bleedin' lot."

"Just a few worthless baubles, indeed."

"Orwight. Orwight. It were a bit better than that. I 'old me 'ands up. Orwight, a lot better. And yeah, there was this bronze statuette about a foot high. Most peculiar it was. Like one of them pop'lar classical arrangements wiv a hero slaying that arf-bull and arf-man creature. A mining-sore, or somefink. Only it weren't that Greek or Roman geezer doin' the slaying. It were some strange fellow wiv a long flowin' cape. He 'ad a sort of picture engraved on his chest, and thin little side-whiskers running straight down his face. Most peculiar. Give me the creeps. And it were in this dark room. With the drapes closed. It were locked so that interested me to get in. Know what I mean? Pick the lock. Have like a sniff around. And even more peculiar."

"Ha, ha, ha, ha, ha, ha, ha, ha!" suddenly roared Strange in a fit of uncontrollable mirth.

"Yeah. Funny ain't it," Garbett agreed. "Like I were just sayin', guv, even more peculiar there was this great big armchair. All fancy curling shapes carved of finest wood, like. It 'ad a big comfortable cushioned seat wiv a velvet covering. On the back part, facing towards ya like when ya look at the chair, there was this great big picture. I fink it were porcelain. Maybe enamel. Were inlaid into the wood, and it were the same geezer what was slaying the bull creature. Only wiv the colours and all that ya could see his robe thing proper. It were white and gold and purple. And the picture on his chest were a man and a woman. The man wiv the woman was 'im. So I reckon. So I sit meself on this chair. It were like a throne. But I got me a creepy feeling about this geezer. You know, like he were watching me. Like he might 'ave special powers of wizardry. So I threw the chair over. It were a right mess. The bleedin' porcelain picture went and fell out and smashed on the floor."

"Ha, ha, ha, ha, ha, ha! Ha, ha, ha, ha, ha!" Strange erupted again before instantly stiffening his face.

"That's all very interesting, and would be all the more amusing, Mr Garbett, if you hadn't accepted a handsome sum of money only to fail your task. There must, *surely,* be more that you could gratefully loot if you went back in search of the missing diary. Porcelain perhaps? Plenty to fill your mucky boots, I've no doubt. Maybe those worthless baubles you could sell to those whores in the taverns before they drink away their squalid earnings."

"Yeah. But ya see, Dr Maxwell, there weren't too much cheap bits. Not even to decorate a Judy's lodgings. Not worf the risk. But there were some proper stuff left. Plenty of nice porcelain plates. Some figurines and vases and the like – there were even bits of Bow china I recognised. I ain't no expert, though. And there was this vase wiv Chinese pictures on it that I knocked onta the floor. It smashed up proper. But ya see, sir, it ain't no good. Trouble, is porcelain breaks too easy after you've bagged it in the sack and made yer run for it. Try scarpering fast over brick walls an all wiv a sack of a score of porcelain objects. You've got yerself five score when ya tip the stuff out. Probly only a handful of small bits worf takin'. Nuffink to quarter fill a swag bag. Just a few cheap morsels to shove in me gropus. Ain't worfit."

These words failed to thaw the iced glaze of Strange's eyes. Garbett persevered while Strange scratched around the top of his head several times, bunching his fingers upwards to examine under the nails.

"But I do 'appen to know somefink that might interest ya, guv. That 'ouse receives a visitor, it does. It's a lady from France. Comes all the way over wiv her stink of garlic. That and her other dirty French 'abits, she does. Stays for 'bout an hour. Then disappears orf again. Quite nice she is mind you, sir. Even if she is French. Wouldn't mind getting better acquainted, if ya know what I mean. Put old Nebuchadnezzar out to grass. Anyhow, I happen to know *she's* returning. Yeah. In a few weeks' time. Peculiar, eh? What do ya reckon, sir?" he asked.

Strange spread his eyes around the street without actually looking at anything. He scratched his scalp again as his eyes passed across the bricks of Whitechapel. Only the very new buildings, like the long overdue wash-house in the early stages of erection, were prominently red. The less new had already altered to a muddy maroon, and most of the even older buildings were blackened with soot. The complete set would only appear uniform at the dregs of a Whitechapel dusk. In daylight the stark architecture and disintegrating fixtures were overbearing to all but the anaesthetised, steeped like sloeberries in gin, or smoked in an opium haze like kippers. Everywhere presented brickwork in rows, in walls and in rectangular blocks. Rotting, rectangular wooden doors were surrounded by rectangular windows with panes fitted in rectangular lattice frames. Occasionally, to soften the edges, some windows and doors were arched at the top. They were all as good as pointless anyway. The panes were rarely washed. If one could see out beyond the coating of grime, the endemic fogs suffocated the light and hid the rectangles within rectangles. Less restricted vision accessed slimmer rectangles, the shutters and the shop plaques, that were secured across the rectangular bricks. Here, inevitably, paint flaked away and cast iron rusted. Weeds took their chance to root into cracks, and the hardiest mosses and lichens clung lugubriously onto the coarse bricks. Even during the brightest daylight Strange paid scant attention to such details. His mind was otherwise occupied as right now. He nodded and turned his eyes to Garbett.

"It is indeed peculiar, and it might also be too hasty, as you point out, to break in again," he calmly mulled over the options while his eye deviations accelerated for a few seconds. Strange, through his leer, then stared directly into Garbett's eyes.

"How could any woman resist old Nebuchadnezzar while visiting London in 1858?"

"Whah? Yer on about 1858 again, Doctor Maxwell. I tell ya it's 1898. You know it is. They says 1858 were the year what they called the *Great Stink*. 'Ere in London, if I ain't mistaken."

"Is that so? What an extraordinary coincidence because the air around here seems to have become significantly fouler. Of course it is 1898, and what woman wouldn't succumb to your charms, Mr Garbett? A rare treat indeed. It's a known fact that if one sufficiently pleasures a woman, he could even get her to commit murder on his behalf. Just one thing though, I suggest – no, I *insist* – that you don't try too hard to tempt her with the fruits of your loin. Some hospitable persuasion will suffice, and old Nebuchadnezzar will have to remain indoors to bide his time," Strange continued with another scratch and a violent shake of his head. "It's a fact, I happen to know, that, and unlike the forthright women of these isles, their French counterparts are quite averse to being rushed into carnal delectation. Not even when drunk on the strongest of liquor. For now a more gentle approach is essential."

"Praps I might, like, get her to tell me a fing or two. Then report back to ya here or in the Bedlam gardens. The usual place. When the job's done."

"Indeed. Perhaps you could," agreed Strange as he dug out a soft scab from under a fingernail that he'd scratched off his scalp. "I'm very much hoping so. She might just prove useful. Although after you've accomplished the task I'd prefer to meet you *here*. Yes, stay away from the asylum for now, Mr Garbett. Scrub up and don't frighten away the French woman with the prospects of Nebuchadnezzar rearing his unsavoury head. And dispose of those useless diaries. Burn the bloody things."

9

Strange had shorn away his locks, which were now resurfacing with the faintest residue of growth and the texture of suede. Mrs Porter was bursting with a compulsion to remove his hat and rub the top of his head with her restless fingers. Strange kept his hat firmly on his head with a smile, concealing the hard scabs that ribbed his scalp. A disappointed Mrs Porter was urgently ushered by the trainee physician away from the columns of the Bedlam portico, and down the steps into the hospital grounds. At all times Mr Broad was just to one side of his otherwise elusive goddess, though inevitably at least half a pace behind her. After progressing with preliminary small talk along a pathway, Dr Strange linked his arm with Mrs Porter's. The sun had almost climbed to its zenith, and the remaining moisture deposited by another thunderstorm during the dark hours of the morning had already perished in the aggressive heat. A residual haze lingered nearer the river. It thickened in shade and odour towards the East End, gravitating towards the ghostly sweatshops and unswept warehouses, of which plenty were discarded carapaces. Sometimes the East End had the greyness and stink of an unprepared corpse in urgent need of disposal by incineration. At this time it looked gravely infirm, but slowly recovering a tinge of colour. Bethlem gardens were only a couple of miles away – they might as well have been a couple of thousand.

The unlikely threesome passed a group of chattering ladies playing croquet to their left and, a little further on, an assembly of men assiduously playing bowls to their right. Strange, painfully contorting his facial muscles to manufacture an array of exaggerated smiles or to dilate his eyes, gripped the Nuddite woman's attention. Mr Broad's attention, however, had been already diverted by the rust-haired man who had on occasions shadowed Percival Nudd. Mr Broad had seen him light up a cigarette at the foot of the steps beneath the portico, and then, significantly, replace one hand against his hip. After a few minutes Mr Broad had selected his excuse.

"Excuse me everybody, I have a requirement for a quick visit to the gentlemen's room," he apologised to the couple who barely noticed. Then he plodded over to the wiry rust-haired man still nonchalantly puffing on his cigarette. His green cap hugged the hair that resembled coir matting. His face of sharp angles, tight skin and a small pointed nose, like his overall features of bone and snapping sinew, indicated a high strength to size ratio. His alert green eyes also issued a warning. They flickered, searched, and impaled. They seldom exhibited a semblance of emotion. He pulled out a photograph from his jacket pocket and held it under Mr Broad's nose for a few seconds.

Back on the path a grinning Dr Strange was feeding Mrs Porter with another ladle full of flattery.

"The Nuddites, and the Reverend Nudd in particular, have truly been blessed by your devotion, dear lady. That I, a young man so naive in the workings of God and His world, could only benefit from your many qualities."

"Oh! The bliss. I cannot cope with the bliss. You so tantalise a passionate woman," swooned Mrs Porter, closing her eyes as her head listed. Without the support of the physician she would have crumpled to the ground.

"Thank you. Thank you," she gasped, pausing to pant like an exhausted dog before continuing. "Thank you so very kindly, doctor, for saving me from the perils of a heavy fall. Oh! You are equipped with such strong arms for holding upright a stricken lady. I have a propensity for blacking-out from time to time. It must be due to the intense heat, you understand."

"Do not concern yourself, dear lady. It was my great privilege to be at hand to assist you. I almost feel embarrassed by my good fortune to be sharing some moments with you. And on the subject of assistance, as I've been informed, in your conversation with my esteemed colleague you will undoubtedly prove to have done the Reverend Nudd a service of tumultuous significance. We can hardly thank you enough. You merit unparalleled credit, and when the Reverend Nudd is of sound enough mind – or to be more accurate, of replenished vigour – he will undoubtedly be scarcely able to personally thank you enough. Irrespective of the fact that the Nuddite Church may not be of Catholic denomination, I foresee you being celebrated as the first Nuddite to be canonized," Strange continued, drawing closer to Mrs Porter's ear. By this point Mr Broad had come scurrying back to join them as fast as his wheezing breath and hurting legs could shift him.

"Oh dear. I'm feeling faint again, doctor. My knees are weakening," sighed the woman, with Strange's words fluttering around her head. The physician, with his arm clasped tightly around Mrs Porter's bulging waist, and Mr Broad, re-established at half a step to the rear, guided her to a nearby bench and sat her down. As Mr Broad attempted to take control and brush Dr Strange to one side, he inadvertently knocked off his own spectacles. His hat followed, flipped onto the lawn. Strange then placed himself next to Mrs Porter, while Mr Broad, still puffing like perished bellows, squatted down to rescue his billycock. After inserting his head back into his hat, he lowered himself onto all fours to grope around for his spectacles. Mrs Porter payed no attention at all to Mr Broad's fumbling efforts. Nor did Strange. Instead, with his arm still around her, he seized the moment to further encourage the woman.

"You know you could be of even greater assistance to the Reverend Nudd."

"I wish I could be, doctor. We need to have him resurrected back to his former self: a man of inspiration and leadership, a man of great wisdom and energy."

"Absolutely. I couldn't agree more, dear lady. And despite his melancholia, these qualities you mention are still very evident. His current difficulties, after bouts of intense activity, and all the while having to absorb the sins of his followers…"

"The sins of the entire world, doctor."

"Indeed, after absorbing the sins of the world, it is not unusual for such a great individual to plummet into the abyss of melancholy. It's as if all his energy has rushed out at once and the store, so to speak, has suddenly run dry. Hence his problems which inevitably result in some confusion. The flames of frustration are whipped up into a raging conflagration. The Reverend Nudd knows that he is a great leader of men, and a crucial emissary of God. Yet unfortunately he has temporarily lost his strength to undertake his vocation. We cannot permit his burning frustration to roast him alive. This is why we need, as a matter of urgency, to see as far into his mind as is possible."

"As far as the Almighty will allow," said Mrs Porter.

"Absolutely. We must become acquainted with him with intimacy second only to God. Only in this way can we proceed with courses of therapy that will ensure that the Reverend Nudd can continue his great work without further lengthy interruptions when he, so to speak, runs dry," said Dr Strange, as Mr Broad rummaged around by his feet. "The Nuddite church, I have been reliably informed, must prosper and reach out to every soul on the Earth. And clearly as the Reverend Nudd's deputy, the importance of your role in tandem with the Reverend's cannot be underestimated. It is imperative that his energy is never again sapped dry. Nor that his frustration destroys him. Your role could be critical, dear lady."

"A most eloquent and thorough explanation, doctor. And such clarity of foresight. You are quite brilliant," declared Mrs Porter at the moment when Mr Broad staggered upright with spectacles in his hand.

"You are too kind, dear lady," smiled Strange, as Mr Broad adopted a standing position to their rear behind the bench. "But let me reiterate. It is clear to me that you urgently need the restoration of the Reverend Nudd to his former self. You need him back at the helm, don't you?"

"We *all* do, doctor. As you have just so rightly pointed out. And you might be persuaded to attend our prayer meetings when the Reverend Nudd has returned. You might even, as I've previously suggested, like to attend whilst he is still absent. It is I, doctor, yes, Mrs Harriet Porter, who is currently conducting prayer meetings. It is such a burden, you understand, such a terrible burden – and the numbers attending have been dwindling. I acknowledge that it is an exalted blessing to stand in for the Reverend, and though I say so myself it is not without reward when I have the congregation in my thrall – and their comments that are so complimentary. Forgive me, I'm blushing. But despite these considerable rewards I do lack some of the necessary knowledge. But with your support..."

· "Yes, yes. That might be possible. Dr Kenelm Maxwell Strange at your service, dear lady. Although currently I have extremely limited spare time with my duties here and my interminable studies," said Dr Strange. But before he was able to continue, the conversation was interrupted by hysterical and high-pitched giggling from a male throat a few yards behind the bench. They all looked round to see a yellow-flowering, bushy shrub from where the noise emanated. Suddenly a young male, perhaps in his mid-twenties, tall and slim, sprang upright from behind the bush like a jack from its box. He flung out his arm to point at Dr Strange.

"You," he shrieked. "You, you, you, and you," he fired, pointing rigidly at the doctor. Mr Broad, visibly shaken, leapt awkwardly away from this volley to secure a safer position at the front of the bench jammed against Mrs Porter. For the second time since tumbling out of bed his billycock, rolling around on the path, had became parted from his head. The skinny young man hadn't finished.

"The rat ate the cat and the cat ate the bat. So the emperor sent it to hell, pell mell, pall mall, minnie pannie, aunt Annie," he screamed, and then skipped away bursting into further fits of giggling.

"As I was about to say," recommenced Strange, "it's an alluring possibility that I might be able to attend your prayer meetings, Mrs Porter. I apologise for the interruption just then. That lunatic shouldn't have been allowed to roam out here at the front. Whoever let him slip out will be reeling after I've imparted a strong word or two. To return to important issues, I fail to comprehend why the congregation should dwindle so much under your temporary leadership. It doesn't make sense."

"Yes," interjected Mr Broad after tentatively treading back to the rear of Mrs Porter, "She's marvellous. She really is. It's not Mrs Porter's fault that the numbers have fallen. It's probably all down to that other business."

"And what, might I ask, is this other business?" Strange resumed to Mrs Porter after throwing a half glance at her escort.

"Oh! A most unfortunate business. The Reverend Nudd and I persuaded most of the followers to donate some money to refurbish the Palace. With more befitting ornamentation, you understand – including a throne."

"The Palace?"

"Yes, the home of the Nudd family and the holy place of worship. As I was saying, the Reverend Nudd decided to invest much of this money in an overseas investment in the belief that it would double in no time. The promises were irresistible. Unfortunately the enterprise collapsed and the entire investment was lost. Terrible, truly terrible, doctor, and some of the Nuddites became disillusioned and left the Church. But it wasn't the Reverend's fault, you understand. The problem, as he explained, was that the Prayer Energy Chapel had not yet been completed and was thus unable to protect the investment. And some say, the Reverend included, that it was a test, by divine intervention, of the Church's strength to remain steadfast at a time of loss and disappointment," Mrs Porter sighed, her voice briefly fading before reinvigoration.

"Foul play is also a possibility," she suggested. "Mrs Emily Nudd may have been involved. Poor *plain* Emily. She is not cursed with disagreeable features, you understand, but even when wearing her make-up she is quite unremarkable in appearance. No, I don't trust that wife of his."

Before Mrs Porter could elaborate, everybody's attention was caught by a huge man shaking violently as he staggered towards and then past the trio along the path. This was John "Big Jack" Collins, a former heavyweight bare-knuckle fighter who had spent the last years of his career as a fairground boxer.

"A tragic case," commented Strange while the disintegrating bruiser was still within earshot. "He was admitted here a month ago but we shall have to move him on. He's an incurable. He'll probably end up in a county asylum with the paupers. Formerly a top pugilist but I fear he received too many blows to the head and is now afflicted by irreversible damage to his brain. I saw him fight only a year ago at a travelling fair. What a sight. A clean-shaven, polished head with a moustache like bicycle handlebars. Fifty-seven years old and yet harder to knock down than a lofty citadel protecting a king and his fortune. Indeed, once as strong as a bull elephant, he's now nothing more than a blithering, twitching idiot. Appallingly cruel fortune."

"A county asylum? Heaven forbid. The poor man. I've heard of syphilis destroying the most manly of men, but this too is a veritable travesty," said Mrs Porter.

"You were talking about a disastrous investment, Mrs Porter. You mentioned a chapel."

"Yes. If only God had favoured our investment like he had favoured the investments Mr Broad's father made many years ago. His investments like alchemy turned copper into silver and ultimately into gold – although it took a great many years. Mr Broad is still living off the dividends from his father's investments now. Although I do think that he needs to find himself a job. I keep telling him he'll spend all the money and end up in the workhouse. In any case regular employment would be healthier for him. He's become too portly, and it would improve his complexion and skin disorders, don't you think?"

"Without a doubt."

"You see, he sits in his favourite chair for long periods during daytime with the curtains drawn closed while he indulges in his solitary vice. Shutting out the daylight like this isn't good for his skin – nor all the sweaty excitement. Don't you agree?"

"Without a doubt," agreed Strange as he briefly turned to peer at Mr Broad. "A barrel full of sludge. Forgive me, Mr Broad, Mrs Porter. I didn't mean to say that. Heaven forbid you thought I was commenting on Mr Broad. Sort of slipped out. I think it was the words *skin disorder.* I always associate them with a barrel of sludge and I've no idea why. Just one of those funny idiosyncrasies. Ha, ha! Perhaps it's the thought of inserting someone with flaking skin inside a barrel of vinegar overnight to cure the problem. Just consider for a moment the acidic molarity being too potent, and discovering the next day not the patient but a concentrate of sludge. Ha, ha, ha. There again with some patients one might not even notice the difference. Ha, ha, ha, ha, ha! Perhaps steeping but only one part of a male patient's anatomy in vinegar might cure several problems at once. But I cannot think which part off the top of my head. Ha, ha, ha, ha, ha! My dear Mrs Porter, I am speaking only in jest. Though best not to utter the words *skin disorders* again."

"Oh! What a hilarious wag you are, doctor," laughed Mrs Porter. "You do make me laugh. I did think you were commenting on Mr Broad just for a moment."

"Heaven forbid! I believe that *you* were doing that, dear lady, and working your way through a long list," Strange sniggered.

"Quite right. How clever you are. Had I yet mentioned Mr Broad's bowels? No. And then Mr Broad is also cursed, you see, by bowel and bladder difficulties – and flatulence. We've even prayed to God that he restore these body parts to better health but I fear that in His supreme wisdom he has better things to do with the protective energy than to ameliorate Mr Broad's toilet troubles."

"Good grief! That astonishes me. How well you must understand the Almighty. But enough of bowels, skin disorders and barrels of sludge for now. Returning to this chapel you mentioned...." prompted Strange.

"The chapel. I've explained this to Dr Norton. It's a solid marble structure that we energise with our prayers, and this energy is then dispensed by God protectively – to a recipient He deems suitable. Do you know that I haven't yet been invited to one of the hospital's monthly balls?"

"I didn't, dear lady. What a bewildering impropriety. I've no doubt you will be invited to grace us with your presence soon. I shall have a word in the ear of the organiser. To return to all you've just revealed, I'm still astonished that the congregation should wane when the prayer meetings are led by somebody as remarkable as yourself. It genuinely is a grave matter of expedience that the Reverend Nudd resumes his leadership, with one Mrs Porter by his side, as you know only too well. This is where *you* can make *all* the difference. For example, do you know anything of the events – and I can't emphasise the importance of this enough – do you know what occurred on Mister, I mean, the Reverend Nudd's trip to France in 1883? I know that my colleague has been pestering the Reverend Nudd quite frightfully for his diaries that record these events, but I really don't believe that we have the right to read them. It is the Reverend Nudd's unequivocal right not to hand them over and we must respect this."

"You are so right, doctor."

"Indeed. But for us to learn *something* of these events would with certainty be in the Reverend's best interests. And yours, too. I can feel God awaiting your crucial intervention here, Mrs Porter – and ignoring every other aspect of every other activity of His entire Kingdom as He awaits your decisive and glorious contribution."

"Oh doctor! I do believe you could persuade me to tell you anything. I've already laid bare some of my soul and most shameful secrets to Dr Norton. Though my secrets weren't really shameful, you understand. Not terribly. But for you, however, I could strip myself totally naked with complete abandon. And I am aware, you understand, that you are absolutely correct about the invaluable assistance I could provide on behalf of the Reverend Nudd. Alas, there is little I can tell you. Although I do recall one particular occasion when the Reverend was preaching to us. There was simply insufficient space to accommodate all of us in his throne room so we stood, shoulder to shoulder, breast to back, in the pouring rain outside in the Palace garden. I recall that the Reverend told us that the Devil comes in many guises to wreak havoc amongst us. He mentioned that the Devil had appeared to him as the *Marsh Man,* whatever that is. When some of us asked him to elaborate, His Holiness the Reverend replied that this Marsh Man was the most terrible manifestation of evil that one could imagine – even worse than the diabolical creations of the most dreadful nightmares. The sort that one awakens from shouting aloud in terror, you understand. He even said that being trapped in the cave of the Cyclops would be a lesser horror than being marooned in the marshes with this ungodly phantom. Mercifully he wouldn't elaborate further. We Nuddites do appreciate, you see, that this was one of those seminal moments. John the Baptist, Jesus Christ, and lately the Reverend Nudd to name but a few – all the great prophets had their experiences in the wilderness that helped to shape their destinies. So, on the occasion when the Reverend revealed something of this, he then said that instead of a chapel on the marshes – where Satan himself lurks both in the nearby terrain *as well* as in the heads of the people of the chapel, whatever that means – he would afford us a chaste chapel at his Holy World Palace. Hence the raising of funds was initiated. I remember the sermon vividly. It was intense. It was powerful and frightening, doctor. My knees weakened and my bosoms shook. Mr Broad firmly gripped my hand. Oh dear! His hand was rather sweaty. It reminded me of holding a fillet of wet fish. And the sermon also went some way to explaining what we refer to as the *Final Solution*. Just before the battle of Armageddon, you understand, and the Reverend Nudd will notify us when it is imminent, each and every one of us Nuddites must seek a wild and lonely place to confront the Devil alone. We must not flinch. We must stand firm. After we have compelled Satan to retreat and concede defeat in the face of our fortitude, then and only then will we be given access to ultimate enlightenment. Let me explain matters another way. The Reverend once told us a parable. I don't recall the story now because it was so very long and awfully complicated, you understand. But I'll never forget what The Reverend said at its conclusion: beware the toad dressed as a man – for beneath its finest garments shall be found warty and poisonous skin. And beware the man dressed as a toad – for he shall be found concealing himself in dark holes, and spurning roast mutton in favour of eating flies."

"What a fascinating proverb, and unfathomably profound to all except the Nuddites. I am impressed. So only then, as you were elucidating, after repelling Satan, you become a Gnostic?" asked Strange.

"A Gnostic? Erm, a Gnostic. Oh yes. Of course. That as well, I expect. As I was explaining, we shall be equipped to survive the final battle, you see. You can read something about it in the Book of Revelation. And as sole survivors the new world shall be inherited by the Nuddite order. I recall a Mr William Blunt asking the Reverend if the marshes would be a suitable location for the ghastly encounter. And he replied like a man possessed that there was no better place. No better place, doctor. I profess, come the time, that I won't be looking forward to this. Anyway, some of the Nuddites persisted in begging the Reverend to reveal more of his own encounter. To no avail, and I was rather relieved. He explained that it was especially personal, and that it was an episode he would now rather avoid contemplating, and that if he was ever summoned to recount it, then God alone had this privilege. The moment was gloriously intense, doctor, and that is all I can tell you. I am bereft of further details. My cup has run dry. I have furnished you with every last drop of milk from my bosoms, doctor. I presume that when you talk of a trip to France, we are referring to the same episode," Mrs Porter checked.

Mr Broad had also been checking: looking over his shoulder from time to time in case any more lunatics were hiding in the bushes. In the main he had stood behind wearing an insipid smile. Occasionally his mouth churned, distorting his lips, and creating the impression to anyone who might have watched that he was trying to dislodge an uncertain tasting toffee from his teeth.

"The very same trip, undoubtedly," answered Strange. "Your presumptions are inspired, dear lady. The *very* same," repeated the doctor as he heard distant bell chimes blown into St Georges Fields from a church tower. He paused and then pulled out his pocket watch from inside his frock coat.

"Well I never," he continued. "Have we been in conversation for so long already? An hour of your company flashes past in a second. Alas, I am neglecting my patients. There is much work to be done striving to free the demons from these poor people afflicted with troubled minds. We do our very best here, dear lady. My primary colleague, Dr Norton, is away from the hospital for a couple of hours on some unspecified business. Hence my duties have even weightier responsibility today," Strange added. He knew that his senior colleague was up to something to be hidden from him. That, or he had some mischievous secrets of his own to be hidden from everybody. Norton, Strange knew, was not a man comfortable in the company of deception. At least Strange had the chance to profit from his absence.

Norton handed a shilling over to the haggard, painted woman in the Whitechapel public house. She had introduced herself as Nellie. Nearly an hour earlier at a similar establishment just down the road he had paid another woman thruppence but they hadn't strayed from the rickety, sticky table. In between, Dr Norton had also spoken to several other women, buying the occasional drink for their company, but not handing over any cash. One of them had almost fallen on top of him. She was probably aged no more than thirty-five years, Norton recognised, despite looking nearer seventy. He also recognised all the symptoms of *phossy jaw* – the yellow skin, and, after losing her bonnet into Norton's lap, the missing hair from her scalp, for a start. No amount of make-up was able to hide the dark green and pustular flesh that rotted around the gnarling bone of her mandible. The phosphorus, from all those years of slave-labour making matches, had planted its seeds of doom. They had germinated aplenty. Alcohol was accelerating this poor woman's death. But alcohol, as Norton accepted wistfully, was all she could afford – selling herself for a mere penny a go in backstreet gutters to the broken men who slept there – to subdue her mental and physical pains. He wished he could help her but knew she had already fallen too far to cling to anyone's outstretched finger tips. Norton wondered if he should take a more active role in campaigning against the exploitation of poor workers – in particular those who ingested dangerous chemicals in the course of their labour. He knew, though, that he had his work cut out at Bethlem and, in any case, he was hurriedly visiting Whitechapel for an entirely unrelated and specific purpose. Norton politely invited haggard, painted Nellie to sit down. This woman had long since become separated from her husband. She had taken to drink, and he had beaten her. He had beaten her and she had taken to even more drink. She had abandoned her husband and two surviving children, and had chosen a life on the streets to the alternative hell of the workhouse. The Nellie woman sat down and then stood straight back up. She insisted that she thoroughly satisfy Norton with any need he selected, that she was the very person with whom he should become acquainted – but only for a fee. Norton pointed out that he had already paid her after declining the offer of a drink. Nellie explained that Norton had so far only paid her for a spot of company that didn't include conversation or any other services. Norton raised an eyebrow up his perplexed face. He agreed on the transaction, handed the woman some additional cash, and she beckoned him to follow her out. A stout woman who had been keeping a keen eye on proceedings sauntered over and whispered into Norton's ear that he ought not to flash his wallet about so conspicuously. She added that he shouldn't let his wallet stick out of his pocket unless he wanted it to go walkabout. Norton thanked her then turned his attention again to Nellie. She was irritated.

"Mind yer own bleedin' business, will yer," she berated the stout woman who had advised the physician. "Now push off. Not you, sweetheart. You come with me," she encouraged Norton.

He smiled back uncomfortably and clumsily gestured, brolly in hand, hat under his other armpit, for her to pause. Nellie responded by grabbing Dr Norton, her fingers biting like grappling hooks, and towed him, his eyebrows raised, outside and into the nearest rookery slum.

"I'm sure, Mrs Porter, that for now you'll benefit far more from the exclusive company of your worthy gentleman companion, Mr Broad, than from further conversation with me," said Dr Strange, and pressed his hand on Mrs Porter's next to him on the bench.

"Mr Broad is indeed a friend, but only a companion and nothing more, you understand," Mrs Porter reacted quickly. "I have been truly exhilarated by your presence, doctor," she added, as Dr Strange stood up, kissing her outstretched hand as he sprouted, unfurling, into his stance.

"Oh yes! Mrs Porter is a marvellous friend, Dr Strange. The best I have ever had," confirmed Mr Broad, delaying the physician's exit. "Did you know that it was my fortieth birthday last week and Mrs Porter took me out for a look around Gamages department store, followed by a celebratory luncheon at a pie shop?"

"No. As a matter of fact I knew nothing about your birthday, sir. Astonishingly, nothing at all. Most generous of the lady to buy you luncheon. Such benevolence!"

"Well actually, being a gentleman, it was I who paid for our pies and ale, but it was Mrs Porter's idea and she accompanied me. And I bought her some new enamel buttons in Gamages. It was lufflee."

"I didn't think," intervened Mrs Porter "that Peter Jones or Liberty were quite the right sort of places for Mr Broad. Rather too exclusive, and Regent Street is rather too grand. He might have felt dreadfully ill at ease, you understand. Not to mention the embarrassment caused when his flatulence runs amok inside a busy store."

"Mrs Porter never ever breaks wind because she's a lady."

"Thank you, Mr Broad, Dr Strange will already know that. I prefer, doctor, to visit the more exclusive stores on my own."

"So did Mrs Porter buy you a gift for your birthday? Bake you a cake? A gingerbread biscuit perhaps?" inquired Strange, having smiled at Mrs Porter before turning his attention back to the chaotic eyes of Mr Broad. Below the billycock they were blinking and squinting through his spectacles. Three inches lower, a congealed lump of phlegm was still attached to Mr Broad's chin.

"Ooh, no. I am very partial to biscuits, and especially the wonderful cakes Mrs Porter bakes, but it was better than that. She gave me a pair of her late husband's socks to wear. Very comfy they are. Lufflee."

"And don't you be a naughty young doctor and go forgetting to come along to my prayer meetings so you can fortify me with moral support," Mrs Porter reminded Strange.

"I *fully* understand your desire for moral support, Mrs Porter. This has become *abundantly* clear," Strange chuckled, "And it has also become evident why you follow the teachings so zealously of a man who encountered Satan in the guise of a marsh man near a chapel. Are you aware that the truly greatest of prophets and holy men since the establishment of Christianity have had similar encounters on marshland near chapels? That these are the key forms of wilderness that unlock the door to the greatest wisdom mortals can achieve? And that inevitably a burden of such terrifying intensity and universal responsibility usually causes the odd period of melancholia? Marshland and chapels, Mrs Porter – it is the classic combination. You *are* absolutely certain that this encounter occurred near a chapel, aren't you?"

"Oh yes. The chapel on the marshes. How extraordinary! Such erudition. Oh! You are so knowledgeable, doctor."

"It's nothing. A trifle. It's all there in the textbooks that a privileged few of us are permitted to study, and it's also there in the secret writings of the ancients hidden under the crypt of Westminster Abbey – although the Archbishop did request that I keep this information to myself, so naturally I'd prefer your exquisite self, dear lady, and also Mr Broad of course, to refrain from disclosing this to anyone. I am obliged to forbid it."

"Oh, doctor! You can rely totally on myself and Mr Broad. How marvellous! How marvellous you are. We shall charge-up the PE Chapel and I will take the liberty of asking the Almighty to bathe you, dear doctor, in protective energy. If you see any ball lightning approaching, have no fear. It has been sent by God with *my* blessing. Mine, you understand. Satan will give you a wide berth, and you will be at liberty to continue your marvellous work with the lunatics safe in the knowledge that no harm will befall you."

"How very kind. And with *your* blessing. And with regard to the Reverend Nudd, how extraordinarily helpful you are, dear lady. Your disclosures will prove indispensable. Your details are priceless – should a small visit to Pimlico be arranged. It has been a pleasure." Strange smirked, and Mrs Porter wriggled with self-satisfaction.

"It certainly has, doctor. And I really must bake you one of my delicious cakes. I find good quality cake so comforting. Are you familiar with the intricate skills of cake-baking, doctor?"

"Absolutely, and bread also. My mother has expertise with the baking tin – I often helped her during a school exeat – though I hasten to add that my mother is probably a novice in comparison with you."

"My cake-baking talents are renowned far and wide, doctor. Although, can you imagine this, Mrs Nudd, the silly woman, once accused me of attempting to poison the Reverend. Me, Mrs Harriet Porter, attempt to poison a man – nay a demigod – who I worship? The Reverend Nudd, you understand, has been my salvation. On this embarrassing occasion the Nuddites had all been voraciously tucking into a cake I had taken to a prayer meeting at The Holy World Nuddite Palace. The Reverend began perspiring heavily, twitching, fidgeting and scratching. Then he began talking in tongues. It was marvellous to behold. But Emily, the poor, foolish woman, summoned a physician who diagnosed St Anthony's fire. That's ergosis, doctor."

"Ergosis?" Strange queried.

"Oh! Silly me. Giddy goat! I meant to say *ergotaria*. Caused by the ergot fungus infecting the flour. Have you heard of this, doctor?"

"Yes, of course, dear lady, I am familiar with ergot contamination. I've been a keen student of botany since my schooldays – although I doubt my knowledge is on a par with yours."

"Thank you, kind sir. You are so modest."

"Indeed my father, it was initially deduced, died after a short illness similar to the gangrenous and generally more severe type of ergotism," Dr Strange continued with a sombre tone. "He had just returned home from foreign pastures when he perished. Ultimately it was agreed that he had succumbed to some obscure foreign malady, but in the remote event that our rye-flour had been somehow infected I naturally destroyed the remainder of our batch. And I thoroughly scrubbed clean our baking tins and implements. It was unlikely, but I couldn't take the risk of my mother – or myself, for that matter – becoming similarly poisoned. The eventual diagnosis proved this to be unnecessary but at the time I wasn't prepared to allow risks to my mother's health."

"My dear Dr Strange. How ghastly for you. You poor young man. How simply dreadful for you. And of course for your mother. And, for your father. No. Not forgetting your father. How noble of you to think only of protecting your mother. How marvellous. My deepest condolences. My… How appallingly… Yes. Well, as you can imagine, to continue with the ado at The Holy World Nuddite Palace, we Nuddites corrected this physician and pointed out that the Reverend was merely being touched by the Holy Spirit and that this behaviour was only to be expected. This physician's visit was an abominable interruption to the prayer meeting, you understand, and to the Reverend's miraculous display," protested Mrs Porter before placating herself with entirely different thoughts. "Perhaps I could entice you around to my home for some tea and cake sometime. For tea and cake, you understand. To sample my expertise. I mean to say that a brilliant man with your responsibilities needs to be properly looked after and well nourished. It's been such a pleasure, doctor, and don't forget that I'm still awaiting an invitation to the Bethlem ball."

"The pleasure and benefit have been all mine, dear lady, I can assure you. I have been poised to leave you for several minutes now. My needy patients cannot be neglected any longer. And I must familiarise myself with a recently patented electro-magnetic machine I'm informally putting to the test on several suitable patients. For some time here these devices have been regarded as contrivances of quackery. I, however, am optimistic of their unrecognised value in the relief of certain nervous disorders."

"How marvellous, doctor. How clever you are. An electric contrivance magnetising and quacking machine. Marvellous!" Mrs Porter interjected. Doctor Strange tilted his hat above his smile.

"Perhaps on another occasion I can explain the benefits of the electromechanical massaging device used to treat female hysteria. It's a fascinating insertion in our body of therapeutic knowledge, and slotting perfectly and vibrantly, amongst all our therapies, into place."

"Oh! I see. I imagine."

"I would expect a woman of your learning to imagine so vividly," said Strange.

"Of course I can. Though I shall look forward to… I expect. Yes. Though I sincerely hope, doctor, that your lady patients don't appreciate the experience overly. Nor especially the handsome young physician applying the device, you understand."

"Have no concerns, dear lady. The prosaic physicians here are reluctant to use these devices. Good day to you, Mrs Porter. I have most important work that cannot wait a moment longer. Good day to you Mr Broad," bade Strange, and after only having distanced himself by a dozen or so yards, he heard Mr Broad's whiney voice.

"I feel it is my duty to tell you, Mrs Porter, that I don't like that gentleman very much. He seems too familiar with you already and yet, unlike me, he hardly knows you."

"Do I sense a touch of jealousy? Are you prickling? Your conduct isn't becoming. It's a sin, Mr Broad, a veritable sin that does you no favours. And as far as I'm concerned he can become even more familiar with me – considerably so. The dashing, charming young man. Dare I confess to it but I think I might be in love again," Strange could hear the woman respond. He stopped and pulled out his timepiece, pretended to inspect it and listened further as Mr Broad responded.

"You always keep falling in love with someone new. But you never manage to fall in love with me. Pardon me for saying but these romances don't last. Most don't even begin. It's as if you are seeking the Holy Grail when all you really need to do is take a better look at that somebody who is always by your side."

"But I have, believe me. And the chaste passions of my agitated heart are no business of yours, Mr Broad."

"I only put your interests first, and I hope you won't mind me saying also that I don't like coming here with so many lunatics roaming around. They make me nervous. They could be dangerous but *I'll* always be here to protect you. You should remember that," Mr Broad could be heard complaining. "And I remember reading as a schoolboy that these lunatics are murderingly dangerous. They pretend to be all normal and friendly, then suddenly cut peoples' throats out and then jump on the corpses reciting psalm twenty-three, the Lord's my shepherd I'll not want."

The long taut grin across the physician's face pulled even wider. He moved on, accelerating his stride. An object like a small, feathered torpedo streaked past Dr Strange, horizontal to the ground, and into the dense foliage of a tree. Sparrows blasted out in all directions before re-forming into a flock that soared high over the wall and away from St George's Fields. The sparrowhawk, its wings open, parachuted onto the lawn with a desperately squealing sparrow gripped in its talons. Within a few seconds calm had returned, swiftly ruptured by the voice of Mrs Porter.

"Be quiet will you, Mr Broad," she scolded, before turning her attention to the bolting physician. "Yoohoo, doctor!" she yelled. "Don't forget I've promised you a cake."

Strange almost paused but didn't look back.

"Spineless imbecile," he muttered through his teeth to himself as he lengthened his quick strides. "Ridiculous woman."

10

Lurking near the Nudds' address, equipped with the knife-sharpening cart that he had once again procured, Garbett was waiting to pounce on the French lady who had visited the house a month earlier. It was one o'clock in the afternoon. The air was belatedly hotting-up. Garbett had been prowling there since ten-thirty, and was expecting her arrival at any minute if she kept her appointments to a regular time. He shoved the cart up and down, his vigilance disturbed on the odd occasion when he did some trade. Just after a quarter past one his patience was rewarded. Garbett noticed the French woman, he ascertained from increasingly oblique glances, hurrying towards the Nuddite Palace. He immediately wandered a little further away to avoid fuelling the impression that he was doing anything other than going about his legitimate daily business. He pushed the cart slowly away, then stopped, crouched down, and pretended to be inspecting a wheel from a favourable position for spying on his target. His tongue dropped out of his mouth. She dashed closer at almost a canter. Garbett saw that beneath the bonnet it was unmistakably her: his initial identification had been accurate, and the woman disappeared so swiftly inside the Nuddite palace after rapping the door that she might have been sucked in by a vortex. This was the cue for Garbett to wander back past and reposition his cart a few doors further up the road. The woman would now have to pass him on her way back.

Garbett sat tight for about three quarters of an hour, keeping one eye at all times furtively alerted to movement of the Nudds' front door. Early on during the wait a short but intense rain shower soaked his clothes, unprecedentedly washed for this occasion, although it had necessitated the emphatic counsel of Dr Strange to instigate this radical measure. In the latter minutes a smokey fog had begun to blur all visible edges of more than a stone's throw away. The Nudd door opened and, after a few words that were too distant from Garbett to be discerned, the French woman turned right and hurried towards Garbett's pitch with her head down.

"Good day to you, again, Madame. We met once before. What a nice surprise to see you again, ain't it?" he bellowed with cheerful theatrics, touching the peak of his cap as the woman quickened her step even faster to pass him. Garbett picked up his cart by the handles and propelled it in pursuit.

"Oi!" he yelled. "I'm only being friendly. What's yer problem, eh?" he spluttered. Garbett briefly dropped his cart, coughed violently, and spat onto the pavement. He waited until the woman had turned the corner, grabbed the cart handles and then ran after her. On reaching the corner he saw that he was not far behind, and he eased down to the steady but brisk walking pace of his prey, maintaining a distance of about twenty yards behind. He was reminded of his time in the army, trotting, sweating and panting for maybe as much as half a mile across the dusty ground to help wheel a big gun into position. He discarded the cart. The target now would be altogether easier to subdue. Bystanders or passers-by evoked possible enemy soldiers. There weren't many people around, and although the fog was starting to thicken like corn-starch, there was too much human presence to snaffle her yet. An automobile chugged past at about twice Garbett's speed. It was such a rare sight that he couldn't prevent himself watching it for a few seconds. He switched his attention back to the French woman. Her travelling case swung about awkwardly from her right hand, impeding her balance and the rhythm of movement. She didn't look back once, but Garbett knew that she sensed him unrelentingly behind her. Perhaps, he guessed, she might throw herself off course in a spontaneous attempt to lose him. The woman scuttled across the road, sidestepping first a cyclist and then a pile of omnibus-horse manure that was about be scooped up by two men and slung into a cart. Garbett followed, violently cursing his tiring legs. Then the woman, as Garbett had anticipated, suddenly veered right. Garbett knew plenty of useful nooks and crannies from Spitalfields to Limehouse – but none around here. He hadn't made preparations to investigate any dark alleys that disappeared into seclusion off the initial phase of the French courier's route back. He had believed he could beguile her into sharing his company and sharing some of Nudd's secrets. And why not? Garbett hadn't asked himself this question until the point moments earlier when the woman fled from his advances. Garbett was accustomed to finding willing female company in Whitechapel. There, unlike this French woman, his easy company consisted either of the permanently intoxicated, or the desperate and ancient crones. Had Garbett considered why, it might have occurred to him that barter provided the explanation. Garbett obtained some basic sexual gratification in exchange for either money or for something that could be drunk, eaten, worn or sold. He cursed the French woman and followed her up the narrow street with high brick walls concealing some works courtyards. She had just made a serious mistake, turning up a dead end. With a final spurt Garbett ambushed her. She heard Garbett's approach and tried to outrun him before realising she had nowhere to go. Garbett grabbed the French woman with his hand over her mouth and dragged her a few paces further until a dingy alleyway off the far end presented itself as a suitable hole for secreting her. Having bundled her only just inside, a tiny lair barely afforded by the congestion of abandoned junk, Garbett gripped her like a vice. The bonnet was knocked askew, the ribbon strings cut into the woman's jaw. While Garbett held tight, regaining some of his rancid breath that scattered exposed tresses like gusts of wind, the woman attempted to swing her case into her assailant. It wasn't heavy, but she couldn't extend her arm into a wide enough arc to wield it with any force. After bouncing off Garbett the case dropped from her fingers to the ground. Still breathing heavily, Garbett loosened his hand from the woman's mouth to allow her to inhale a couple of large gulps of air. Then he slapped it shut again with the palm of his hand and felt jets of air blasting from her nostrils across his knuckles.

"I ain't too taken with your French manners, darling. And don't you go thinking' about screamin'. Or it'll be the last fing you do. Understand?" Garbett spat. "And there was me hoping to take ya to a nice little table. For a nice lil bite to eat and some friendly chitchat. Now tell us, bitch, who you are and what's the nature of yer business."

"I only come like a friend of Monsieur and Madame Nudd. I come to make delivery from special friend of Monsieur and Madame. I am servant of their friend. They send me because I speak English," she gasped. Garbett felt her heartbeat reverberating through her taut flesh like a cello string plucked at a high tempo. He smelt the roses of her perfume become contaminated by the odours of fear.

Garbett resumed his interrogation.

"And what kind of delivery is that?"

"I cannot say. I do not know, Monsieur. I come from France with a package. It is a letter I think."

"Ain't they never heard of no postage stamps in France? I think yer telling' me pork pies, darling'. I think yer lying."

"*Honettêment*, Monsieur, I do not know."

"Orwight, you little scratch an itch, I've got anuver little question for ya. And if you don't tell me the truth I'll throttle yer dainty little neck. I'm a trained soldier, sweetpie. I've killed many times, I warn ya," snarled Garbett, yanking his hand down from her mouth and around her throat. "Do you know about a place in some French marshes where there is a chapel? Breton or somefink. "

"Monsieur, please, I begging you I must take a train. I must get to London Bridge station. I am just a servant and I know nothing. *Rien*," the woman pleaded.

"Plenty of trains. You can catch a Mary Blaine after. After I'm done wiv ya. That's if yer a good girl. If ya answer me questions proper," replied Garbett, through quivering lips and exposed, rotting teeth.

"But Monsieur, I have to get a train soon because I have to travel on a steamboat from Folkestone. Please, Monsieur. I do not know nothing," she tried once more.

"First tell me about the chapel."

"Probably thousand chapels there, in Bretagne, Monsieur."

"Yeah. Probly is. What about a town or a village? Place called Chapel on the Marsh or somefink like that? Ever 'eard of it?"

"Yes, Monsieur. La Chapelle-sur-le-Marais. En *Vendée*, Marais Breton. In the *Vendée*. Not in Bretagne. *Aussi* not la Chapelle-des-Marais. Is sur-le-Marais."

"Good girl. Slow down. That's better, darlin'. What about it? What do you know about this place?" Garbett demanded.

"I know this is a bad place. I heard them say. I do not know more," she moaned.

"Say the name again. Say it," Garbett commanded. "Say it slow."

"La... Cha – pelle... sur... le... Ma – rais. La Chapelle-sur-le-Marais."

"You gotta know more 'bout this place. Tell me."

"I do not, Monsieur. I did not go there. Never."

And before having the chance to reiterate this, her scrunched eyes burst open and shot at a sharp diagonal towards the just visible corner of the street entrance.

"Look, I think someone is there," she cried. Garbett stepped back and flung his head sideways. He witnessed a tall, well-dressed man standing twenty paces away, unveiled menancingly by the fog.

Garbett was instantly intimidated by the figure. He stood staring back at Garbett with furious eyes as black as the darkest of nights in Africa with the enemy and razor-fanged predators lurking nearby. An elegant moustache tapered away like swallow wings from the top of his upper lip. Dressed in luxurious clothing underneath a cape, his imposing frame would make the most ferocious of lions cower. A fashionable high hat, with its narrow brim curled up at the sides, held thick black locks in place, and added to his monumentally allotted height.

"Blimey. Who the bleedin' hell? I don't need to tangle wiv that – I don't need no bleeding detective neither," Garbett muttered. He released the woman, flinging her away as he rapidly scanned the alleyway. He spotted a solid wooden gate, lower than the high brickwork, and fled to it. He frantically jumped up a few times unsuccessfully until a splinter spiked his palm and he hung from the top by his fingertips. He paused for a second to take a deep breath, and then with the extra impetus of desperation, he hoisted himself up and clambered over.

11

Out of the grand entrance and down the steps from the portico pranced Percival Nudd. A giant moth just emerged from its chrysalis, his robe fluttered and billowed further outwards as Nudd loosened his movements and the early autumn breeze lifted his inflating robe away from his back. The rust-haired man, known to Mr Broad, and sitting on a bench fifty yards away, rotated his face towards this conspicuous sight. He slowly stood up, now following Nudd only with his green eyes. His target moved one way, then stopped, retreated, and changed direction again. Nudd found a vacant bench on which he carefully seated himself, pulling up his robe from beneath his hips and piling it onto his lap. Percival Nudd too had been looking out for somebody. Then Nudd peered down a pathway, bided his time, stood up, and stepped forward to greet Mrs Porter and Mr Broad. The rust-haired man, monitoring events closely, waited until Nudd was on the point of being embraced by Mrs Porter. Then he made a decisive move. He darted into the channel almost directly behind Nudd, and the instant he perceived that Mr Broad had noticed him he lit a cigarette and then swivelled away into a position of static nonchalance near the portico. Mr Broad shook Mr Nudd's hand with the characteristic firmness of a wilting lettuce leaf. After retrieving his podgy fingers and flexing them, he made his apologies to be excused for an excursion to the gentlemen's room.

"Constipated again, Mr Broad?" complained Mrs Porter, before turning back to Nudd. "Oh, Reverend, Mr Broad's bowel and bladder difficulties never seem to abate. Run along then, Mr Broad," she shouted after her companion who was struggling to attain a moderate trot. Mr Broad, however, did not require the facilities of a toilet. Instead he re-routed to the rust-haired man who ushered him behind some bushes towards the male-occupied right-hand corner of one of the great asylum's wings.

"Any news yet, Mr Broad?" inquired the Irishman as he dropped his cigarette butt onto the ground and crushed it under his shoe.

"No, I'm so sorry. I haven't seen anyone like the man in the photograph, but I have been searching all over just like you asked me. Honest, Detective Inspector Noyall."

"Dat's a shame. A real shame to be sure. Are you certain you're keepin' your oiyes peeled now, Mr Broad?" asked the man, whose own eyes stared with the precision of a rifle's viewfinder. Two other characteristics spoke volumes: these eyes were empty of any hint of emotion, and they could glance from side to side and then back again quicker than a blink. A third characteristic was more ominous: these eyes could impale like a spear through a roasted chicken.

"Oh, yes," enthused Mr Broad. "Without a doubt. I've been looking ever so hard like you asked me. But I reckon you'll still be very pleased with me. It just so happens I have some other information that might be of great interest to Scotland Yard."

"And what moight dat be, then?"

"It's about the burglary at The Holy World Palace of the Nuddite Church in Belgravia. I have a suspect for you."

"At da where? Da Holy what?" asked Noyall with a trace of a shrug.

"The Holy World Palace of the Nuddite Church."

"Where is dis place? Belgravia, you say?"

"Well, actually it's more Victoria. Pimlico, probably – actually. Haven't you heard about it?"

"Mr Broad, we have to deal wit hundreds of burglaries every day. Som of my lower rankin' colleagues will be dealing wit dat. My detective work is far more important, don't you know. Wait a moment. A burglary at da Holy Woirld Palace Church in Victoria? Do you tink it was the man in da photograph I showed you who was responsible for dis heinous crime?"

"Oh I don't think so, Detective Inspector. I have very good reason to suspect a physician. One working here at Bedlam who wants to get his hands on the Reverend Nudd's sacred diaries."

"Wait a minute, will you. The Reverend Nudd, you say. Dis is your friend here wit da crazy costume? I know da one." Noyall laughed. "If I can't foind you, all I have to do is spot da man in da crazy fancy-dress costume and he'll probably lead me to you, so he will. You were telling' me about his doiaries."

"Yes. The man you – or rather your lower-ranking colleagues – are looking for is none other than a certain Dr Norton. I'm sure of it."

"And why would dat be, Mr Broad?"

"Because I know he wants very badly to get his hands on the Holy Nuddite diaries. Very badly. I heard him say it with his own lips."

"Say it wit his *own* lips, did he? Now dat's remarkable, Mr Broad. Tell me more."

"Yes. You see he's very enthusiastic about reading them. Dr Strange told Mrs Porter that Dr Norton reckons they're worth more than their weight in gold," added Mr Broad excitedly. "I always knew I should have been a detective like you, Detective Inspector Noyall."

"And so you should, Mr Broad. First-rate work. But loike I told you before, I'm only interested in the fella in da picture. I want you to keep looking' out for him. Gold, eh? Dat's not entoirely wittout interest. But loike I told ya, you mustn't on no account ask nobody no questions to arouse deir suspicions. And don't you go forgettin' dat you must never ask for me or try contacting me at da Yard. Dis is voitally important. It's a big case, you see. It's so big dat it's shrouded in secrecy – even from most of me colleagues, Mr Broad. Are ya payin' heed now?" asked the rust-haired man as Mr Broad ducked and retreated, flapping his hand at a bee that was buzzing near his face.

Noyall raised his voice.

"Come back here, man."

"Ooo. That's lucky. I think it's gone gone now," spluttered Mr Broad while the bee crawled along the rim of his billycock.

"Hold still, will ya," instructed Noyall. With the knuckles of his left hand he then swiped the bee onto the path, knocking Mr Broad's billycock with it, and firmly trod the insect into the dirt.

"Now let's get back to business and to da man in da photograph, shall we?"

"Pardon me for asking, but are you absolutely sure that this man has been seen here?" Broad queried, picking up his hat.

"What koind of a question is dat, Mr Broad. Of course I'm sure. At least I'm sure dat one of da patients here is sure he's seen him. A fella who goes by da name of Albert Potts. He wrote to the New York Police department shortly after arroivin' here to say dat he'd seen dis other fella twoice. Twoice on da same day – the day of da Derby horse race at Epsom. Da man in da picture, near top dog of a gang he was dat had poisoned and robbed our Mr Potts of his valuables in a New York doive. After recoverin' well enough to travel dis Mr Potts journeyed back home to England. Da whole experience gave him a nasty froight, and he's in dis asylum wit his consequent nervous problems now. It's what a nasty froight can do to a person, and don't you go forgettin' dat now, Mr Broad. But dat doesn't mean he's mistaken. The New York police are after wantin' da man in da photograph. They informed us here at da Yard – and we also have our own reasons for wantin' him."

"But if I see him here isn't it best that I convey a message to you directly at Scotland Yard?" asked Mr Broad.

"Most definitely not, Mr Broad – loike I keep tellin' you. Why do you tink an Irishman loike me has been recruited to work for da Yard, along wit me Irish colleagues Detective O'Boyle and Detective O'Hara?" Noyall asked in turn. He lit another cigarette, inhaled slowly, and scrutinised Mr Broad. Then he continued.

"It's because *we* are capable of mixin' wit da people involved in da Republican movement, Mr Broad. Recruited we were when da Fenians started deir bombing campaigns afresh. Haven't you worked it out yet – a man as moighty clever as you? The Fenians are an American-based organoisation, and dis man we're after apprehendin' is more dan just a robber who once operated in New York. He's hoighly dangerous. Tink about it, Mr Broad. Do you see da connection now?"

"Oh! Heavens above! Highly dangerous. So the man in the photograph works for the Republican bombers."

"To be sure I can tell dat I'm not dealin' wit no idiot when I'm dealin' wit you, Mr Broad. And don't you know dat he was raisin' funds for the organoisation by robbin' welty people loike our Mr Potts? I believe he set up some crooked rat-baitin' rings in parts of Manhattan. Den he opens a doive along da Bowery wit da notorious Mickey Malley. You know da toiype of establishment, Mr Broad? Da clientele, mostly sailors and foreign visitors, are lured inside wit da promise of cheap liquor and wanton women. Do ya loike wanton women yourself, Mr Broad? A man of action and a ravenous wolf, eh, Mr Broad, what wit yer irresistible way wit da ladies, the hot, red blood surgin' through yer veins, da twinkle in yer oiye, and wit yer foine hat? So you'll be after understandin' da workins of dis little deception. So once insoide da doive, ya see, dese people loike Mr Potts are given drinks spoiked wit some nasty poison so dey can be robbed and dumped outside. A nasty but hoighly profitable little organoisation, Mr Broad."

"And so he was robbing people in New York to raise funds for the Republicans," repeated Mr Broad, with astonishment wrought from the mouth of a grim face.

"Totally correct, Mr Broad. After havin' deir drinks spoiked wit chloral hoydrate, dat special little ingredient favoured by da operators of da worst doives from New York to Chicago. Loike ya telled me, you're quoite da detective, aren't ya now?" remarked Noyall. Mr Broad reacted by nodding his face, now expanded into a smug smile. Noyall quickly straightened it with his serious tone.

"And so you'll understand, Mr Joshua Broad, why you must never ever try to contact me at da Yard. I'll come to *you*."

"I see. Oh dear! What a thoroughly disagreeable business," Mr Broad's voice weakened before suddenly perking up. "But what about Dr Norton? Are you going to report him to your colleagues so they can arrest him for burglary?"

"All in good toime. All in good toime. Don't you go frettin' yourself about dat now."

"And what if I don't ever see this dangerous Fenian man? What about if my detective work only helps to convict Dr Norton on the other matter, the diary theft? Will I still receive my payment and a special medal from the Queen like you told me before?"

Noyall threw his cigarette butt onto the path. His eyes never moved away from the glasses below Mr Broad's billycock.

"Mr Broad, you're here almost every day wit dat circus clown of a woman. You're oideal. You're neider a lunatic nor physician nor attendant nor nothin' loike dat. You're especially and particularly not a feeble-moinded. But you are here nearly every day, and you have da makins of a top detective to be sure. If dat man returns there is a good chance you'll see him. I need to know what he does and who he talks to loike I already telled ya. Don't go forgetting neider dat despoite what I just telled you, dis man speaks loike a Cukney. He don't have no Irish voice. Not all Republican sympathisers do, you know. And don't forget also dat he is reputed to stink real awful. Da notorious Mickey Malley persuaded him to scrub up a little when dey was runnin' deir doive, but I suspect he's lapsed back into his filty, rotten habits. It seems dat he's no grasp of elementary hoygene whatsoever. To be sure he smells a lot worse dan you do, Mr Broad, and his stench koind of lingers loike a cat's droppins stuck up ya nose, you know. Ever had a lump o' cat's droppins up ya nose? No? Pig's mess? No? Are ya sure you ain't, now? No? Want me to stick some up dere, Mr Broad, so you don't go after forgettin' how bad dis Fenian stinks? No? Well don't you go forgettin' any a dis, now. Everyting I told ya. I know I can leave dis in yer very capable hands wit your supremely talented detective abilities. All in good toime wit respect to the doctor physician fella. Ya know who I'm after. Look for dis man, do what you have to, and then you'll get what's comin' to you, Mr Broad. Her Majesty the Queen Victoria herself will be trilled wit you, rest assured. She moight even knoight you. Just tink – Sir Joshua Broad," said Noyall, and little bubbles of excitement frothed out of the corners of Mr Broad's mouth.

"Mrs Porter, that's my widowed lady friend, she might even consider marrying me if I were to be knighted," Mr Broad considered gleefully.

"Your lady friend? Marry you? Too roight she moight. Good day to ya, now."

"Lufflee! How lufflee! And a very good day to you, Detective Inspector Noyall," responded Mr Broad. He patted his flabby chest with a sensation of personal triumph, and two items slipped out from the concealment within his jacket. They dropped onto the path by the still smouldering cigarette butt. Noyall pounced too swiftly for the sluggish Mr Broad and grabbed them first. Noyall flicked through a small booklet before reading aloud the words printed on the cover: *"'MR HORACE DIMPLE'S OBSCENE CHASTISEMENT. Mr Dimple is flogged on his naked posterior after being caught peeping at Lady Bontemp's enjoyment of her Sapphic maids. Fully illustrated photographically inside'.* Well, well, Mr Broad. Hoighly illegal printed material, I tink. And what's dis now?" Noyall turned his attention to the other item, a letter sealed within its envelope. "Posted from Broighton and addressed to a Lady Lavinia Lash."

Mr Broad's mouth opened and sweat trickled down his face. His blinking eyes faded from Noyall's view as his spectacles misted up.

"Yes, it's for a friend of mine, an acquaintance actually – sent in error to my address, would you believe. I've yet to give it to her. I'm not really sure if I ought to because she doesn't go by that name any longer. "

"I tink you must, Mr Broad. It's illegal, don't you know, to take possession of anudder person's proivate post. Sent to your address, eh? Lavinia Lash, eh? You pass on dis letter, now, and I'll pretend I haven't seen any of dese tings," said Noyall gravely as he handed them over. A crimson-faced Mr Broad removed his spectacles to wipe off the moisture but was interrupted by Noyall.

"On da strict condition, dat is," the rust-haired man warned, "dat you search dis place loike a hungry vulture for da man in da photograph. You'd best not let me down or you'll have more dan a severe lashing comin' to you, I can promise you, Mr Broad. Off wit you, now."

On his way back to rejoin Mrs Porter and Percival Nudd, Mr Broad screwed up his eyes behind his thick spectacle lenses that he constantly adjusted along his nose, scanning the hospital grounds from one extreme to the other. He returned to the side of Mrs Porter whose vivacity had fled during his absence. Mr Broad hadn't seen her looking this glum since she had heard the news of the Reverend's admission to the hospital. Despite, through a tepid smile, Nudd's repeated insistance that he was a long way from reaching any decisions, Mrs Porter's face sagged. Mr Broad's face, however, still burned with embarrassment.

12

Almost a week later an excitable Mrs Porter stepped carefully out of her house on the rapier heels of her special boots that she had not worn for a while. A long black dress, puffed up around her shoulders and arm sleeves, unfolded down to just below her ankles. A red cummerbund was tied around her waist. It was secured as tightly as her girth permitted without over-prominently squeezing up the two rolls of fleshy excesses protruding either side of the sash. One item Mrs Porter had discarded for the day was her Nuddite locket, although she fully intended to wear it on arriving back home. She adjusted her little circular red hat decorated with a huge black bow. Satisfied, she then set forth, smoothing down her hair that had been cropped and stained blonder for the occasion. Gripping the straps of her cavernous lady's bag Mrs Porter travelled down to Brighton by train on a third-class return ticket. With the carriages, pulled vigorously by the huffing, grunting locomotive grinding along the tracks, Mrs Porter's bulging posterior supplemented the seat's niggardly padding to provide a comfier ride. Mrs Porter's pulse was racing. She needed to divert her thoughts, she realised, shaking back her hair with a tic so violent it almost dislodged her hat and ricked her neck. Mrs Porter straightened her hat before sliding her fingers through the mouth of her bag. After some circumspect delving she extracted a small library of reading material. A variety of penny illustrated papers, providing graphic accounts of the latest crimes and subsequent trials, had been selected to occupy her mind. She perused them for a while, but then with a sigh she tossed aside her copy of *The Illustrated Police Budget.*

She had been unable to stop her imagination drawing a sketch of her own likeness in the dock. Even worse, the title for the publication had been rewritten. In her agitated premonitions she now read a terrifying header: *The Scandalous Mrs Porter's Lewd Shame*. She grabbed at her copy of *The Lady's Pictorial* and, having to make do without her medicinal flask always carried by Mr Broad, eventually found calm amongst its pages.

Mrs Porter had avoided informing Mr Broad of her excursion. She expected that he would mope about at his home, eating biscuits and falling asleep in his favourite chair. After spending two hours at the home of a retired army officer, Major Garfield Hardy-Fisk, Mrs Porter began the journey home. She dispensed with the half-used return ticket. Instead she travelled back in a first class carriage with a glow of contentment shining on her face and rippling through her body. Sharing her compartment with a serving army officer, one Captain Lambert Dixie, Mrs Porter began breathing heavily as she quickly found herself attracted to this splendid-looking man a decade or so younger than herself. Captain Dixie, who had given a good account of himself on the school playing fields – but somewhat less so in the classrooms – was in search of some of the capital's gambling dens where his reputation for indulging in "blackguardly business" was as yet unestablished. Back at his officers' mess few were prepared to play cards or roll the dice with this man. Anyone either caught or suspected of cheating at the tables was, within his regiment, labelled a "Dixie". Had she known about any of this, Harriet Porter would not have cared an iota. Shortly after pulling out of Brighton station, her lurid newspapers forgotten in her bag, she succumbed to an irresistible urge to flirt with this man. On Captain Dixie's part the attraction was less than mutual, and he attempted to fend off Mrs Porter's advances with curt smiles. Without neglecting his manners, he inserted his head deep into his daily newspaper at every available opportunity. Halfway to London he politely excused himself of Mrs Porter's flustered company and disappeared elsewhere. He only returned as the train approached the suburbs of London. Captain Dixie's mood, however, had altered from courteous indifference to dark annoyance, demonstrated at the outset of his return by the way he first slammed the compartment door shut and then thudded onto his seat with his arms folded. His swelling lower lip was oozing blood from a nick, and from time to time he rubbed his shins as flashes of pain warped his face. After pulling into the terminus at London, Captain Dixie bade Mrs Porter good day and then dashed out of the train. Striding behind along the platform, Mrs Porter heard a young woman cry out "That's him", and saw a policeman launch into a chase after Captain Dixie who tried to run through the crowds and out of the station. Captain Dixie swerved, sidestepped and bore through like the accomplished rugger player he had been in the recent past. The young woman hitched up her skirt to join the pursuit, and threaded herself through the startled crowds in the wake of the captain and the bobby.

"Just what has that unpleasant man been up to?" Mrs Porter asked herself. "Yes, I think I did see that girl on the platform at Brighton. A third-class traveller – and as common as the mud and dog-mess that Mr Broad is always forgetting to wipe from his boots." Mrs Porter watched aghast. Confined within her tubular dress, and tottering on her treacherous heels like a circus novice on stilts, she abandoned the idea of following on foot. Craning her neck she followed with her bemused eyes from a lengthening distance until Captain Dixie and his pursuers had vanished from view. The shrill sound of the bobby's whistle evaporated. Mrs Porter shook her head.

"I say! I say!" she yelled at anyone whose attention she caught. "That man, the one being chased out of the station. He's a thorough cad. He's an absolute rotter. He's a bounder, you understand. I say!"

13

While Mrs Porter was experiencing mixed emotions during her little outing to Brighton, Mr Broad was contemplating using the bathtub for the first time since his mother had died. It had been six years. Mr Broad inspected the bathtub. First he would have to shift all the coal into temporary storage. Then he would have to scrub the bathtub clean before decanting hot water inside so he could use it. Mr Broad frowned and returned to his chair. After over an hour of sporadic consideration, and despite the fact that Mrs Porter was forever threatening to drag him by an ear to the nearest bath-house for a once monthly, he decided just after midday to do something else. Something, he reasoned, to make even better use of his time. He would embark on some solo detective work at Bedlam on behalf of Detective Inspector Noyall. He felt it was the least he could do for the security of the nation, he told himself, trying hard to distance his memory of Noyall's discovery of his pornographic publication. Whenever he recalled that incident his face reddened and broke out in flushes of sweat.

Over at St George's Fields, Mr Broad randomly plodded the paths a while before deciding that he would pay a visit to the Reverend Nudd. It was the first occasion he had gone there alone, and without Noyall's or Mrs Porter's reassuring presence he felt more vulnerable to being accosted by a dangerous lunatic. If this wasn't bad enough, Mr Broad feared making a devastating discovery – although curiously this risk had been a motivational factor for his presence at

Bedlam where the lunatics roamed. To his enormous sense of relief very few people had been enticed outside now that the weather had become less hospitable. On entering the male gallery, Mr Broad thought he could see Mr Nudd sitting reading a book. A lean hound with a twitching nose trotted across to Mr Broad, sniffed up his leg and into his crotch. The damp, brown nose, like a quivering lump of aspic, dallied there before pulling out with an explosive sneeze. The hound bounded away and crawled under a chair. Mr Broad, wary of dogs, felt it probably safe to venture slightly further down the long rectangular room to obtain a better look. That man certainly resembled the Reverend, but if so he had discarded his robe and Holy vestment in favour of an unassuming civilian suit. Having crept to within about ten yards Mr Broad stopped in astonishment. He had only ever seen the Reverend Nudd clad in his important Nuddite apparel. Just how should he address him and what else could he say? For a moment matters became worse when the Reverend seemed to look across at him. But as Mr Broad attempted to fashion a smile on his face and pick up his hand to offer an apologetic wave, the Reverend dismissively switched his eyes back into the pages of his book. Nudd angled his head away and pulled the book closer to his face. Mr Broad stood on the spot wondering what to do next. He scratched his cheek. Perhaps it wasn't the Reverend after all. But then again it probably was. The lean hound barked from under the chair. Mr Broad could see that its eyes, a few inches above the floor, were watching him. The dog bared its teeth and Mr Broad gratefully accepted this as a cue to depart to the sanctuary of the gardens – as long as there weren't any dangerous lunatics at large. This was the first time that he had seen the Reverend Nudd dressed like a mere mortal of no particular distinction. Mr Broad arrived at a startling conclusion: the Reverend really had looked quite ordinary – actually just like anyone else. By disrobing and changing into conventional attire he had also shed his mighty aura. Oh dear, thought Mr Broad as he descended the steps to the gardens. Oh dear, oh dear, oh dear! Mrs Porter must be informed the instant she can be found. It's true she enjoys a bit of healthy gossip, but this is altogether more sensational, he thought. Yet Mrs Porter had told him she wouldn't be seeing him on this day. First she had too many domestic duties to carry out, and then after offering his assistance she had given him the different excuse that she had to leave London for the day to see a long-lost relative on a private matter. And might Mrs Porter's evasiveness have something to do with the Reverend Nudd adopting the highly convincing disguise of an ordinary person, Mr Broad wondered. This was a better outcome than the other possibility that might explain her furtive absence – and filled him with dread. Best not think about it. Best to stick to the job, he told himself. Dwell instead upon the prospects of a knighthood.

The leaves continued to fall and add to the protean mosaics on the lawns. Only the berry-studded shrubs and the emerald conifers resisted being parted from their finery. A handful of trees were already stripped to the bone, and four now displayed the mistletoe baubles that had only weeks earlier lurked unseen amongst the rustling foliage. Down the bark and onto the turf, the discerning eye of the fungi enthusiast would revel in the prolific diversity. The less informed might notice the odd sprouting toadstools. Some flimsy and others plump, plenty had already succumbed to hungry insects and opportunistic bacteria. Imploding like weeping ulcers, and nourishing colonies of white slime, the distinctive mushroom aromas had metamorphosised into a pungent stink. Mr Broad was also discernable out here.

He had placed himself on a bench that afforded a sweeping view of the hospital's front, as well as a good portion of the gardens. His eyes drifted around from beneath the brim of his billycock and through the twin, bulbous, glass chunks of his spectacles. He sat there for over an hour, hoping for a glimpse of the man in the photograph, and hoping that scary lunatics would keep their distance. The daylight lost its strength as a vast sheet of cloud crawled overhead. When the first wet specks sprinkled the air Mr Broad, after wiping the persistent moisture from his face, selected the option of temporary refuge inside the hospital building. Trudging in the direction of the portico, with the teasing rain still refraining from falling aggressively, an impulse drew his curiosity towards the left wing of the hospital. Being the female sector, it would normally have been improper to venture to this side, Mr Broad told himself. He nodded agreement at his gentlemanly thoughts. This, though, was a mission of monumental gravity. Investigation on behalf of the crown overrode all other considerations. He nodded again. Electing to proceed with caution, Mr Broad crept towards an area of the hospital that he hadn't previously explored. Still perturbed by the lack of the reassuring presence of the daring Noyall or the irresistible Harriet Porter whose charms could disarm a crew of Barbary corsairs, he hesitated. At the same time, the thought of his heroics pleasing them both soon shovelled him onwards. Moments later his face contracted into a series of spasms: a response to the discomforting feeling that somebody was watching him. Mr Broad shuffled his body around, straining his head even further. He saw a tall gentleman, standing motionless on the soft lawn, and staring unequivocally in his direction. Mr Broad studied him cautiously. At least this wasn't the lunatic pugilist Big Jack Collins who Mr Broad wished to avoid at all costs. He evaded direct eye contact by shifting his head to either side of the stranger as if trying to discern something behind him. He noted that this tall and mighty man was smartly dressed, wearing a high hat, and that his hair, moustache and eyes were distinctly dark. Mr Broad shuddered. Only the lower limits of this man's cape fluttered in the breeze. Otherwise he was as still as a statue. Then it occurred to Mr Broad that this towering individual might be another detective. Of course! He certainly possessed the presence of authority. Mr Broad weighed up his options for a moment, then decided that he ought to perhaps go and introduce himself. After all, not only was this man probably an associate of Detective Inspector Noyall, but also it would be best to point out to this eminent-looking detective that he too was engaged in official police business for the security of Her Majesty's Empire. Mr Broad wanted to avoid any misunderstandings. He didn't want to be arrested as a peeping Tom. He set forth with a couple of paces but soon realised that the tall detective had ceased eyeing him, and was now watching something behind the corner of the wing. Mr Broad paused once more. After several squints of consideration, with his lips pursed and squirming like two worms on an angler's hook, Mr Broad boldly made yet another decision. He turned back to the rockface of the mighty hospital edifice, and trod even more slowly towards the corner of the wing. Just around its side, but inaudible to Mr Broad, an irate Dr Strange was berating Mr Garbett and wagging his finger with a violent flourish of his wrist.

"I told you not to meet me here for the time being, damn you man."

"I keep tellin' ya, Dr Maxwell, I think the pigs is onta me. It went 'orrible wrong."

"So you reckon they know it was you who committed the Nudd burglary? Well do you – or do you have an even worse misdemeanour to hide?"

"I ain't sure 'bout that. 'Bout being rumbled for the burglary. No, I ain't got nuffink worse to Jekyll, neither. Course I ain't. Nuffink. I'm scuppered, though. Was givin' that French bit a right grillin'. That chapel in France you told me to ask her 'bout. Was givin' her a right 'ard time of it, like. Then this big man appears, don't he? Outa nowhere. Out the fog. Well-dressed, well smart. Like he were some official big shot. He weren't no common bluebottle. If it gets much hotter fink I'll be orf. Try me luck in Argentina."

"Just how hard a time were you giving *la femme*? No. Don't waste my time telling me. I don't really care about that now. Although

I'm wondering if there is any other major reason why the police might be onto you," Strange asked through a flashing grimace. He put on his spectacles and stared into Garbett's face with his curling-lipped leer.

"I reckoned I oughta tell ya, anyhow," Garbett responded.

"Hang on," said Strange, who then peered to his left across the lawn. "I thought I saw somebody. No. Either I was mistaken or there wasn't anyone to concern us."

Garbett took a look.

"Gotta be on one's guard," he grunted.

"Indeed, Mr Garbett. I'll see you in Whitechapel. Get the hell out of here," ordered Strange, while Mr Broad, approaching from the blind angle at the pace of a sloth, was alerted by the voices. As he neared still closer, his nose perceived an unpleasant odour, and he crouched down amongst the fallen golden leaves at the corner's threshold. In position, he turned to look back. The tall man on the grass had gone. Crab-like, still squatting, and with damp leaves plastered over his boots, Mr Broad peered across the lawn but was unable to detect the tall man's presence anywhere. He had somehow totally erased himself from view. The conversation around the corner nudged Mr Broad to the good idea that he should be listening, and he awkwardly twisted himself into a better position – one that enabled him to recognise the voice of Dr Strange.

"Whitechapel at the Nag's Head. No, tomorrow night is impossible. Make it three days' time at around eight in the evening. Now go," Mr Broad heard the physician say. Just then, with his head tilted forward, a gust of damp wind swiped off his billycock and bounced it into the view of Strange. The young physician pointed to the hat.

"Some geezer's lost 'is tit fer tat," said Garbett, and the physician pushed the palm of his hand towards Garbett to silence him. Strange leaned forward as close as he dared to the stinking man.

"Just go along with this," he whispered, before raising his voice loudly, "Like I just told you, I'm absolutely sure Dr Norton is not able to see you here. Indeed it may well be the case that you need some therapy for your psychological affliction, Mister – I'm sorry but I don't think you mentioned your name. I don't need to know it. But Dr Norton is quite unable to see you here yet because you haven't been admitted through the normal procedure."

"Er. Whitechapel then?" asked Garbett.

"Yes, whoever you are. In three days' time. That's when Dr Norton usually visits Whitechapel. Though don't ask me why," said Strange, as he closely watched the unrecovered billycock wobbling in a shallow puddle. "Dr Norton will be able to meet you in Whitechapel in the Nag's Head at eight in the evening. I'll give him your description. And one other thing. None of your friends or acquaintances. The time before last when Dr Norton interviewed a patient in Whitechapel he was, so he related, distracted by the ugly presence of two of the man's associates. He described them to me graphically. A nasty sounding pair. So be on your own. Are they likely to be in the Nag's Head, any of your associates?"

"Dunno. Maybe, yeah. I ain't no clairvoyant."

"How about the Queen's Arms? Any of your associates likely to be there?"

"Erm, p'raps not. Don't fink so. But I don't go in there very regular."

"Good. So then Dr Norton will meet you in the Queen's Arms at eight in three days' time. I'll inform Dr Norton that it'll be the Queen's Arms," Strange reiterated loudly, and nodded as Mr Broad finally emerged from behind the corner to retrieve his hat. He instantly recognised the man from Noyall's photograph, although his sense of triumph was, during this moment, knocked back by some startling jabs of anxiety. But he hadn't been floored by discovering Mrs Porter in an intimate clinch with Dr Strange. Such was his relief that Mr Broad regained some confidence. He looked up, replacing his soggy hat, and saw Dr Strange nodding at him with a sour smile. The Fenian man from the photograph turned and scooted away across the lawn. Mr Broad nodded back.

"Dear me, Mr Broad," said Strange. "All alone and without Mrs Porter to hold your hand? As you've just witnessed, all sorts of people come pestering us here every day. As if we don't have enough work to keep us occupied without attending to every idiot, stray, tramp, vagabond, degenerate, maniac, or didikko who knocks on our door demanding therapy. Now don't tell me you also are seeking the professional advice of myself, of Dr Norton, or any of my other eminent colleagues, Mr Broad."

"Oh no. I'm feeling quite alright, thank you. Pardon me but I was just on my way to see the Reverend. I thought I would take a stroll first to see if the Reverend might be out here enjoying the fine weather. He does, you know, enjoy the fine weather."

"You are quite sure that you haven't come soliciting our assistance, Mr Broad?" asked Strange. "The weather isn't fine. It is windy, the skies are grey, and now it is raining. Good day to you, Mr Broad."

Dr Strange walked off towards the portico. The Fenian man from the photograph was, like the tall detective figure from the lawn, now out of sight. Deserted, Mr Broad stood blinking and twitching. He felt his heart thumping and his knees shaking. He decided to shuffle along the wing to the main entrance where he slowly ascended the steps. Heavier raindrops pummelled his billycock and rivulets dripped off the brim. Under cover of the portico, Mr Broad approached an elderly man sketching on the pages of a moleskin notebook. He reminded Mr Broad of his bank manager. This artist made Mr Broad a little wary because his bank manager was always, with that stern expression and cross voice, advising Mr Broad that he should be depositing more money in his account and removing less. But alone at Bedlam he was emboldened by his bravery in the face of all the ghastly risks he had been taking. And he now knew that Mrs Porter wasn't cavorting with Dr Strange in her mysterious absence. So, uninvited, Mr Broad stretched his neck to see what this man was drawing. The artist ignored Mr Broad's intrusion, halted his handiwork, and began giving directions to part of the wall.

"That's it. You. A little to the left. Not too close together! That's it. Hold it like that. Oh no. No. No. No. No! I told you to keep still. Now hold it there," he instructed. Mr Broad was able to discern that this man had begun sketching several sections of brickwork. All but one had been abandoned with diagonal lines dashed through them. "Excuse me," Mr Broad tried to get the man's attention. "I said pardon me for interrupting you."

"You can see the difficulty I'm having," replied the brick artist, finally crossing over into the world featuring Mr Broad. "They won't keep still or do as they are told. They have no idea how to pose or how to conduct themselves in a civilised manner."

"Oh dear. That's a pity. Only I was just wondering if you had seen a very tall man, smartly dressed, wearing a tall hat, and who is most probably a detective. He was over there on the grass a few minutes ago. Did you see where he went?" asked Mr Broad. He may as well not have bothered. The brick artist's consciousness no longer included Mr Broad's existence, and he continued to sketch and direct the bricks with escalating irritation.

14

Three days later Dr Norton stopped Dr Strange in the corridor not far from the physicians' room. Norton was wearing a new suit.

"I've just been to have a quick word with Mr Nudd. His wife has suffered such terrible traumas. After that awful business when her home was burgled, I now gather that a family friend was viciously assaulted by a street-trader shortly after visiting Mrs Nudd. Nevertheless, as you are aware, Mr Nudd has now discarded his bizarre attire – the robes, everything – for more modest and dignified clothing. But by Jove it gets better. Generally things are suddenly progressing at a rapid pace. Mr Nudd has now actually agreed to disband his little church and move out of London when he is fit and able to do so. Excellent news, isn't it? Er, not about the burglary or the assault, of course. And I apologise, especially because you are a man of such fastidious elegance, for my own new and uncharacteristic outfit. For many months Mrs Norton has been urging me to buy this grey Inverness cape with matching trousers. She said it would brighten me up – as much as grey can. Personally I think brown is a better colour to match my eyes. I won't however, be badgered into following your example and shaving off my hair. Our three young grandchildren are visiting us later today and I wouldn't be surprised if my Inverness cape provides them with a considerable source of mirth. I'm not at all sure if it's my sort of raiment, but it does keep me rather warmer as the winter approaches."

"Does that mean that you will be sending our Mr Nudd home imminently?" asked Strange through barely parted teeth.

"Well no. Not straight away. We need a period of adjustment for Mr Nudd. We need a period of appraisal to make sure that Mr Nudd is solid in his conviction, that he neither wavers nor undergoes another personal crisis. After all, it cannot be a simple transition to abandon what one had genuinely believed, possibly convinced oneself, was an important spiritual mission."

"Yes," hissed Strange. "I see your point entirely, Dr Norton. You are absolutely right that this must not be done with haste. Several further months. I can't agree more."

"Who knows? Maybe much less. I'm not sure how the extant members of his congregation will embrace the news. Mrs Porter in particular. In fact I've just seen her on her way to visit Mr Nudd. And, unusually, she was without her companion, Mr Broad," Norton added.

"Umm. Despite her protestations to the contrary, I fear she has been thoroughly revelling in her role as Nuddite Church incumbent prayer-leader. But there are plenty of similar religious organisations that would gladly take *her* ample bosom into *their* bosom, no doubt. And you say she was without her loyal companion, the splendid Mr Broad?"

"Yes. That's correct. They always seem to be together like a discordant pair of twins. It's an odd sort of chemistry between them."

"Perhaps he *is* here, but had to excuse himself for a visit to the gentleman's room. If not, I've no doubt that Mrs Porter will nevertheless be relating Mr Broad's latest bowel and bladder problems to her high priest. On the other hand, perhaps not. Now that Mr Nudd is no longer her or anybody's high priest, that thunderbolt could sufficiently distract her from discussing the excretions of Mr Broad."

"I expect you are right. Although she might be trying to persuade Mr Nudd to return to office on the grounds that this thunderbolt has wreaked havoc with his problematic bowel function," smiled Dr Norton. "I'll discuss the other patients with you later," he added, and walked off towards the main staircase. Strange hesitated as he was about to proceed to the room shared by Norton and the few other physicians. His face frowned. Taking a step forward he noticed the door to the physicians' room swing open. A tall, dark-haired stranger emerged and bolted with giant strides away along the central corridor.

"Hey! You! You carrying the high hat," shouted Strange. "I insist you stop. Who are you that thinks he has business in the physicians' room? What is the meaning of your intrusion? Stop, I tell you," Strange continued. And then the unknown visitor did as commanded. Just for a moment he braked and looked back at Dr Strange, who had never before seen such black and potent eyes staring directly at him. Strange called to a youthful male steward who had been alerted by the shouting and scampered out of the stewards' room as the intruder strode past.

"Stop that man, will you. Apprehend him immediately," Strange ordered. The steward hurried after the mysterious intruder, with Strange now following a safe distance behind, and after turning left as the corridor merged into a male gallery, the steward stopped and turned back to Strange.

"I said apprehend him, man," barked Strange.

"I can't, doctor, sir. He's gone. He's not there no more. Like a candle snuffed out by the breeze. Gone," the steward apologised.

"What are you talking about, man?" snapped Strange, pushing the steward aside to take a look. "Get out of my way. Dear God! He *has* vanished. Where could he have got to? Gather some of your colleagues together. Form a posse. I want a thorough search made of this hospital, the grounds, in fact the whole of Lambeth. If you don't find him you'll fast be doing some more searching – for a new employment. Move," Strange shouted, before inhaling some deep breaths to help contemplate the episode.

"Yoohoo," cried a female voice. "Yoohoo, Dr Strange."

"Dear God. Not now," muttered Strange, recognising the voice and turning around to face back past the physicians' room and towards the female wing. Having exited the visitors' room, clacking and clucking towards him like an excited duck on stilts, Mrs Porter waddled awkwardly as her ankles buckled above the pencil-length heels. Preceding her by some distance was the gusto of her perfume.

"Appalling tidings, doctor. The very worst. The Reverend is forsaking his flock. He is abandoning his Holy duties, you understand. No more prayer meetings, you see. It's truly hideous. No more *Reverend* Nudd; no more Holy World Nuddite Church; no more attentive congregations. What purpose can he now serve me having discarded his faithful followers in favour of his children and insipid wife? What will become of me, dear doctor? I'm so gravely sorry that you will not be able to attend a prayer meeting, what with your magnificent presence stood illuminating and fortifying my side. It is catastrophic – the horror to eclipse all horrors. Woe is me."

"Mrs Porter. What an exquisite pleasure as ever. But I really do have exceedingly pressing matters that require my full attention. You'll just have to deal with this yourself. Or locate your faithful friend, Mr Broad, for comfort. He'll be more than willing to oblige you," Strange replied.

"Oh! Oh! Woe is me. I'm feeling light-headed. I'm coming over all dizzy. Clutch me, hold me, doctor. Embrace me firmly in your strong, manly arms," Mrs Porter implored.

"I fear, Mrs Porter, that you are being overwhelmed by the quantity of your immoderate scent," Strange remarked. A second later the woman spiralled downwards like a histrionic actress, collapsing into a mess of doughy flesh, fabrics, and the crinoline and steel hoops of her petticoat on the floor. Dr Strange turned his face away and stomped past.

15

The stewards may not have found the intruder, but in the grounds of
Bethlem they would have passed Mr Broad in conversation with
another – an irate Irishman. Mr Broad was being severely castigated in
words that didn't need volume to stab like a blade. A few minutes
earlier Mr Broad had trodden inside a patch of tall shrubs to urinate on
the carpet of discarded leaves. The moment he had emptied his
bladder, with his trousers still around his ankles, a sudden voice from
right behind had sent him toppling over in fright like a dropped
custard pastry. Scrambling himself and his trousers back up, Mr Broad
beheld Noyall standing with his hands on his hips.

"What a soight for sore oiyes. Caught red-faced again wit yer
trousers down, eh, Mr Broad? Disappointed not to be after beholdin'
Mrs Lady Lash poised to discipline ya? Are ya? Still a-janglin' wit
froight are ya?" asked Noyall while Mr Broad picked up his spectacles
and his billycock.

"Oh! Oh dear. You startled me, Detective Inspector Noyall. You
must have got my note I left for you at Scotland Yard."

"You did *what*? Left a note for me at da Yard? Mary, mudder of
Jesus, don't tell me now dat ya *spoke* to anyone dere."

"Oh no. I just left a note for you saying I needed to meet you
urgently because the Fenian man will be meeting Dr Norton at eight in
three, actually, tonight, in the Queen's Arms in Whitechapel. That's
all. That's mostly all."

"Well, never moind Lady Lash, because maybe *I* oughta damn
well discipline ya, you reckless idiot. I should have you trown straight

146

inta Pentonville gaol wit da key trown away, you ossified baboon-brain. Dis is hoighly, hoighly dangerous undercover work, Mr Broad. And you're prepared to jeopardise da whole operation. Dat's tantamount to treason, Mr Broad, and dere was me tinkin' dat you were a foine, upstanding and hoighly intelligent defender of Her Majesty's empoire."

"Oh dear. I'm terribly sorry. Oh dear. It was so important, Detective Inspector Noyall, that I had no alternative but to leave a note for you at Scotland Yard. So important I even went all the way from here to Whitehall Place first. Then I remembered that Great Scotland Yard has been replaced by New Scotland Yard on the Embankment. It's much closer to Bedlam. It's just across Westminster Bridge, and if I'd remembered I wouldn't have had to walk anything like so far."

"I don't need to be told how ta foind Scotland Yard, you gabblin' bogbonce. And to tink dat ya first troid yer luck at da old premises. Yes, where da Fenian bombers blew a huge hole in da wall – even bigger dan da one between yer ears, Mr Broad – only fifteen years back. Dat just goes ta show da toiype o' people we're after dealin wit and just how important it is to obey me every word. I'm *undercover*, Mr Broad, loike da *whole* operation. Ya never know who's eavesdroppin' and a-watchin' da comin's and goin's at da Yard. Mary mudder of Jesus, have mercy on me soul and save me from da consequences of da reckless actions of a fockin' idiot."

"I'm so very sorry. It won't happen again," bleated a cowering Mr Broad who took a step backwards into a thorny branch. "Ouch. I just pricked my rear. Ooh. I'm sorry, Detective Inspector. I hadn't seen you around here and I needed to contact you urgently. I thought I was doing the right thing and using my initiation. Mrs Porter says I should use my initiation more often," he appealed. The alarm in Mr Broad's eyes was no longer visible to Noyall. The clouds had been ripped apart, and the tatters were being swept away by the wind. The sun drenched St George's Fields in a lively glow, a shaft plunging into the shrubs and reflecting fiercely off Mr Broad's spectacles lenses.

"Da roight ting, indeed! Initiative, indeed! Wit a bit a luck o' da Irish, dat desk sergeant will have tought you were a crazy simpleton and trown your note out wit da garbage – which is where I oughta be trowin' you, Mr Broad. *Initiation.* I'll be givin' you some initiation, to be sure. No! Of course I didn't get da note. The desk sergeant along wit most of dem at da Yard won't have heard of me, you idiot. Just loike dey won't have heard of me colleagues Boyle and Regan."

"What about Detective O'Hara?"

"Him neider. Nor detectives Foyle, Moyle, Doyle, O'Doyle, Hoyle, Coyle, Kilfoyle, and Murphy. All of dem undercover, and all wit aliases, you dunderhead."

"I saw one of them just before I saw that Fenian man you're after. He was watching on the lawn over there," Mr Broad pointed. "Maybe it was Detective Boyle or O'Hara. Or Regan."

"What are you talking' about? What man standing over dere?"

"A tall well-dressed man wearing a high hat. He was watching the smelly Fenian talking to Dr Strange."

"Was he now? And why do you suppose dat he was a detective?"

"I'm quite sure he was watching, surveillancing, as you detectives say, and he possessed this air of authority. Very calm and official-looking. Then he just disappeared. I don't know where."

"You're certain about dis, are you?" Noyall asked, and Mr Broad vigorously nodded, nearly losing his hat in the process. Noyall lit up a cigarette.

"To be sure, it was Detective Boyle, Mr Broad. And is dat da only toime you seen him?"

"Oh yes," confirmed Mr Broad who was busily scratching flakes of dry skin off his puggish cheeks.

"You don't never ever approach dis man," warned Noyall, puffing unravelling spheres of smoke into Mr Broad's face. "Not even if you tink ya need to pass me an urgent message. Do you understand? Ya moight blow his cover, do ya understand? Now heed my words, Mr Broad. You mess up one more toime and it's da gallows for you. But as it just so happens it moight well be a knoighthood if your information is accurate. And you say it was definitely da man in da picture dat you saw, and dat Detective Boyle was also observin'?"

"Quite definitely the Fenian man. Very rum-looking. Well I think so."

"And he stank to hoigh heaven?"

"It was terrible. The worst affliction of cat's dropping malodour ever to have violented my nose."

"And he will be in da Queen's Arms in Whoitechapel at eight tonoight?"

"That's what Dr Strange told him, in order that he can meet Dr Norton."

"And why would he be after wantin' to meet wit dis Dr Norton?"

"I'm not too sure. I think he wants some professional therapy."

"*Professional terrapy*? Does he now? I seem to recall dat you've spoke about dese two physicians before, Mr Broad. I smell a rat. Actually I smell several. I'm tinkin' dat dis is all toid up wit da reason why our stinkin' Fenian renegade was seen here previous by Mr Potts. Som koind a connection wit da two physicians. So what else do you know about dese two physicians, Mr Broad?"

"Just like I said. The burglary! The burglary at The World Palace of the Holy Nuddite Church. I knew Dr Norton had to be involved. And that Dr Strange. I don't care for him much neither. Not at all. Mrs Porter likes him but I don't know why. It make me come over all angry. I think he also needs to be arrested."

Noyall, without expression, contemplated Mr Broad's face. His own face pinched itself to reveal a trace of a rare inner feeling when he studied the light green slime that was oozing like an oil leak from Mr Broad's nose.

"You're a clever man indeed, Mr Broad. Quoite brilliant," said Noyall, still inspecting the nasal mucus. "What about your lady friend? You say dat she's better acquainted than you wit da other physician who was talkin' to da Fenian. Moight she be after bein' up to no good? She's always talking to your friend Nudd wit his crazy robes one moment, and yet she's well acquainted wit da physicians. Moight she be passing on some kinda information, now? Moight she be an accessory to burglary?"

"Oh dear. Heavens no. No, Detective Inspector. Mrs Porter is a very honourable lady. She is also one of God's chosen servants. She told me so herself. I would defend Mrs Porter's honour as if I were the last soldier standing at Rorke's Drift. I've told her that before many times and it makes me feel all lufflee," said Mr Broad excitedly.

"Indeed, Mr Broad. I can just picture dat. And I can just picture Her Majesty pinning da Victoria Cross to your foine example of a chest for defending Mrs Porter's honour to da very last."

"Yes, I can picture it too. I can also see myself escorting Mrs Porter to some of the great spectacles and exhibitions in London. Her late husband, Mr Porter, took her to see Buffalo Bill's Wild West show at Earls Court. He also took her to watch Barnum and Bailey's Greatest Show on Earth at Olympia. She often talks about them. I can picture myself, Sir Joshua Broad, with my Victoria Cross watching a spectacular circus at Olympia with Mrs Porter at my side."

"Circus, did ya say? Ya must be afoolin' wit me now. You, Mr Broad, will be after escorting Mrs Porter to da teatre, da opera, and da ballet, you will. And you'll be sitting dere in a proivate box for da aristocrats."

"Lufflee. Sir Joshua Broad and Mrs Porter together in a box."

"No, no, Mr Broad. Not any old proivate box. You'll be introduced to da audience and da cast before da performance begins as Queen Victoria's foinest son. Sir Joshua and Lady Broad – it'll be announced to all."

"Lufflee. Lady Broad. My mother always warned me that the ladies will all be wanting to ensnare me in front of the altar. She warned me that I must bide my time before diligiously choosing the right bride."

"I'll wager dat she knew ya problems wit all da ladies as only a mudder could. Foine and *diligious* specimen of a man dat you surely are, Mr Broad, wit plenty of *initiation*. No Bryant and May match girl fer you. No need for you ta kiss da Blarney Stone ta captivate all da ladies wit yer charm and yer epic stories. Ya have da pick o' da ladies and it's Mrs Porter who'll be havin' all da luck o' da Irish."

"Mrs Porter becoming Lady Broad. The perfect choice."

"Totally roight. Just tink about da picture we was paintin' at da teatre. At da point, loike, after bein' introduced to all and sundry. Tink about everybody roisin' to dere feet and cheerin'. Den, Sir Joshua and Lady Broad, you'll be sharing' da Queen's very own proivate box gilded wit gold after da entoire house has given' you dat standin' ovation. Tink about it. Savour yer foine prospects. Taste every last drop. But remember dis," Noyall resumed his grave tone. "Roight now it's da toss of a penny as to whetter your fate will be at the gallows of Pentonville for treason, or whetter you will be honoured as a hero of da Empoire. You wouldn't be aholding anyting back from me would you, now? You truly wouldn't want ta be after messin wit me. Or I'll clobba ya hard, and when yer not expectin' it. Comes wit bein' a sowtpaw."

"It's out-pour?"

"No, you idiot. A sowtpaw. S-O-U-T-H-P-A-W. From da baseball game in America. Boston Red Stockin's and New York Goiants and the loike. When da pitcher is left-handed. Now are ya aholdin' anyting back – before I give ya a demonstration of how ta hit from da sowt?"

"Oh no. Not about Mrs Porter. Not about anything. Honest," answered Mr Broad, ducking backwards as he wiped his nose with a sleeve cuff. "But don't forget that my suspicions are right about the doctors. Are you going to arrest them, Detective Inspector?"

"All in good toime. All in good toime. I tink fate is tippin' in favour of yer ennoblement for your brilliant detective work, Mr Broad. And dat's not forgettin' da handsome sum of cash dat will be fillin' your pockets. But, and dis is crucial, now – so you'd better pay attention and heed my words well Mr Broad – unless you want more dan a truly *violented* nose. If you're not after wantin' to swing from da gallows you don't utter a single word o' dis to anyone, do ya hear? You keep your mouth shut, now – or you'll be hearin, da wails of a banshee. And you never ever visit Scotland Yard on moy account. You never approach dat other man you seen – Detective Boyle – and you don't know nuttin' if he approaches you. Nuttin', Mr Broad. Not today, not tomorrow, not never," Noyall briefed, aiming his finger like a cocked pistol. "I'll foind you, Mr Broad. Is dat understood? Good. It better be. And one foinal ting for now. How do I know I can truly trust ya, Mr Broad? How do I know yer not an enemy of Her Majesty's empoire?" he asked. "Bein' such a brilliant man ya could've easily been a-foolin' me all along, loike."

"Please, Detective Inspector Noyall, you must believe that I would never, ever, be an enemy of the empire. Oh dear, no."

"Is dat so? So are ya ready, since you're such an exponent of initiation, to undergo da special initiation ceremony here and now to prove yer allegiance to a police officer of her Majesty's Empoire? Dis would officially make you a special undercover police assistant, don't ya know. But it's all hoighly top secret, Mr Broad. Are ya ready here and now to prove dat moyself along wit Her Majesty, who'd receive a special report about dis, dat we can both trust ya now?"

"Oh yes, Detective Inspector. Just tell me what I have to do or say," agreed Mr Broad before wiping away a new thread of nasal mucus hanging from his nose.

"Roight. Nuttin' to it, and nuttin' nasty. No cat's droppin's up ya nose or nuttin' to make you go a-frettin' now. Ya just have to get back down on your knees in front of me, state dat you, Mr Joshua Kenyon Broad, pledge yer allegiance to me, Detective Inspector Noyall, and also to Her Majesty da Queen Victoria. Den ya have to lick each of me boot caps tree toimes. But never, ever, Mr Broad, mention dis top secret ceremony to anyone. Her Majesty will be duly informed. She'll be so pleased wit ya. Truly deloighted. Is dat clear, now?"

"Oh yes," agreed Mr Broad who lowered himself to his knees.

"I, Mr Joshua Kenyon Broad, pledge my allegiance to Detective Inspector Noyall and to Queen Victoria."

Noyall then stuck his right, and followed by his left foot, under the nose of Mr Broad who was poised holding his hat to his head. He closely watched Mr Broad lick each boot in turn as a canopy of cloud, as grimy as an old floorcloth, drew towards the sun, gradually obscuring it and dimming the light.

"Did you appreciate da full symbolism and implications? How did moy boots taste, Mr Broad?"

"Ooh. Erm, lufflee," said Mr Broad, with a burgundy leaf flapping from the rim of his billycock. "Absolutely lufflee, Detective Inspector."

"Up on yer feet. It's all official now," declared Noyall. "Any bunglin' or failin' to obey me orders is a treason offence punishable by death. Dat's also official. I'll be off now. Away wit yourself."

16

Strange leant over as close to the dripping wet Garbett as he dared, bracing his nostrils to face inhaling the worst. Strange had arrived at the Queen's Arms at the appointed time. Slowly supping his ale with a view of the door, his eyes jumped when a rather nondescript man in jaded green had rushed into the pub shouting:

"Everybody put your drinks down and vacate the premises."

There was something of indistinct familiarity about this man. He could always be spotted in every large gathering of people. He was rarely noticed but always there if one searched hard. The man walked briskly across to Strange. Some straggling murmers petered out and the pianist pulled his hands away from the keyboard.

"Put down your drink and take yourself outside. NOW," he ordered.

Strange slowly looked up and calmly responded.

"There is nothing illegal about having a quiet drink in a public house, my dear fellow. I'm sheltering from the rain."

"And who, sir, might you be? Your name. Tell me your name."

"My name is Norton. I'm a physician," Strange answered. The bearded landlord wandered over.

"Show us yer warrant," he asked. "Let's take a butchers."

"He ain't no rozzer," screeched a young woman with a large graze across a corner of her forehead. "He's a lunatic."

"Never mind warrants. Everybody out," insisted the nondescript man.

"Nobody move," countered the landlord. "On whose authority, then? Where's yer badge or buttons?"

"On God's authority."

"Get out off of me property. Go on, hop it or I'll have you thrown out. And it won't be no horseplay for ya, neither." The landlord turned to Strange. "You wanna help?" he asked.

"Let's all calm down shall we," Strange suggested. "I'm a physician of the mind. Allow me to parley with this gentleman. See if I can placate him – or otherwise encourage him to be on his way without further ado."

"He ain't no rozzer," laughed the young woman. "I said he was a loony."

"Oh no, sir. Don't think I'm going to sit with you while you pour down your throat the poisons of Satan."

Dr Strange stretched out his smile, pushed aside his pint, and pulled back a chair for the nondescript man.

"A sinner I may be," he conceded, putting on his spectacles. "We all are to some extent. We're only human, as God created us. But I am a physician because I *do* care about my fellow man. I never drink myself even remotely into a state of drunkenness. Now please sit down. You are patently a theologian of stellar intellect and moral superiority. Your qualities are so visually ablaze like hill-top beacons that I instantly knew you couldn't possibly be a policeman. Sit yourself down and we can discuss the ills of the world like intelligent men touched by the righteousness of God."

"You are half an hour late, Mr Garbett. Forget about buying a jug of ale," said Strange. "We're going to take a walk outside."

"Nah. I'm soaked to the skin, and I'm 'aving me a pint. It's bleeding raining cats and dogs out there," said the pot-bellied Garbett. "Take a pew somewhere, Doc."

"No thank you. Not after what I've just had to contend with while I was waiting for you. What a waste of a quarter of an hour of effort. Furthermore it's still too quiet in here for my liking after that nonsense, and believe me you won't want anybody to overhear our conversation. Just follow me, will you," Strange insisted, as he pointlessly flicked at the dampest patches of his frock coat. Garbett reluctantly followed the physician outside. The streets of this part of Whitechapel, clustered around the Commercial Road, unusually, were almost deserted though no less noisy, the clattering of unrelenting rain replacing the more familiar din of assorted by-products of human excesses. Strange led Garbett along the road to a small archway that encased a wrought-iron gate. En route, Garbett developed a twitch. He pulled down the peak of his cap, flipped up his coat collar and bowed his head – but less to cloak himself from the downpour. His shifty eyes glanced back a few times to a position at the entrance of a fishmonger's shop, across the road and directly opposite the front entrance of the Queen's Arms. The archway offered just enough shelter from the driving rain for two men to hold a discreet conversation with a modicum of comfort – although being cooped-up too close to Garbett was never congenial. Dr Strange grimaced under the archway.

"What was it that you wanted to tell me the other day, Mr Garbett?" he asked. Instead of answering, Garbett poked his head out towards the spot opposite the tavern. His eyeballs widened and jerked from side to side. Strange was becoming irritated. His composure lapsed.

"God damn it, man. What is the matter with you?" he asked.

"Probly nuffink, guv. Just thought I saw a nasty lil face from me past. Most unwelcome, I can tell ya. Nah. Can't be. Nuffink to bovver about."

Dr Strange knew well that, in addition to all those who arrowed by without ever looking up or aside, plus the many who stumbled and fumbled their way around, there were always a few others: a handful of faceless figures lurking in the Whitechapel shadows, as still as tailors' dummies, and as busy as gravediggers' spades. Nevertheless he had many reasons to feel uneasy on this occasion.

"Not that giant brute with the big shaven head and marble-eyed stare?" he asked.

"Whah? Nah. Not 'im."

"Surely not that odd little runt with the paunch and the grey hair and the tatty hat?"

"Who?"

"That grubby little man with the baggy trousers who I once saw keeping your company along with that shaven-headed brute in the Nag's Head."

"Oh 'im. Nah. No chance. Old Sparky's long gawn orf, anyroad."

"Then what are you talking about? A face from where?" inquired Strange, taking a quick look towards the fishmonger's. "Nobody that I can see there at the moment. Maybe moved on or merely an illusion. You mentioned at the hospital the other day that the police might be onto you."

"A face from New York. Gawd. Blimey. Nah. Can't be. I was over there for a bit, see. In Hamerica."

"Yes," agreed Strange, protracting the syllable. "If there was anyone it was most likely a doppelganger. And visibility is poor in any case. So what about the police? What exactly happened with that French woman connected to the Nuddite Palace?" he asked, and while a horse-drawn cab slowly rattled along the cobbled road, Garbett muttered and Strange listened intently. He cupped his strained ear towards Garbett while the rattle of wheels and the rapping of iron-shod hooves against the cobbles were amplified by the presence of water. Once the cab had carried its passenger and noise well beyond the archway, Strange probed Garbett further.

"Tell me again, and with precision, what this *assumed* detective – for it is only conjecture on your part, Mr Garbett – looks like."

"Like I said, and he were no common blue-bottle for starters. More yer top-dog rozzer. The London particular was comin' down. Getting' thicker by the second. But from out the mist there he was stood. He were very tall. Dressed all natty and expensive-like. Wiv a high hat, wiv dark whiskers and 'air, a moustache. Wiv the blackest eyes you've ever seen. You ever seen two lumps of coal? Two stuck out the fresh snow? That's how dark they was, like. And what's more, Dr Maxwell, he had this queer look. A strength and calmness all abard 'im. One like I ain't seen much before, neither. Almost like he weren't real."

For a moment Dr Strange leered in silence towards Garbett's face without actually focusing. Following this lull, Strange rubbed both eyes and discharged a lengthy sigh before trying to delve further.

"And this definitely isn't the man you mistakenly thought you just saw over there?" Strange asked, nodding towards the fishmonger's.

"No. That son offa pox sore he's a different kettle o' fish altogevver. He don't look much. No. But he's more yer professional nobbler. Top drawer. Once he's picked up yer scent you've 'ad it."

"I concede," recommended Strange, "that all of this is causing a tingle of alarm. I'll return to that issue in a while. But lest it slips our minds, you said that before being interrupted in the act of *getting her to talk,* the French woman gave you a name of some primeval community in the Breton Marshes that included the word *chapel.*"

"Yeah. Sounds prime evil, like ya says. I wrote it down after. After I'd made a run for it. 'Ere. Stuffed in me pit," Garbett said, and he pulled out a scrap of paper from inside his jacket. "Yeah. It were *Chapel Sewer Lee Marry.* Not *Chapel Day Marry.* I written it down. Wiv me lead pencil."

"You are full of surprises, Mr Garbett. First I discover that all the police from *both* sides of the Atlantic are hunting you, and now I'm recoiling from the considerably greater shock that you are, at least, semi-literate. Give it to me," he instructed, snatching the piece of paper from Garbett's grasp. He inserted it inside the protection of his wallet that he shoved back deep into his own frock coat pocket. "Chapels, Whitechapels, *PE* chapels and French bloody *marais chapelles*. My world is suddenly cluttered up with a pestilence of chapels, Mr Garbett, just as surely as yours is with police officers. Now listen to me very carefully," Strange continued with a snarl. "I've got one more little job for you. You'd be well advised to execute it, and you'd be well advised to mark my words. Firstly, don't you ever venture near the Bethlem Hospital again. It's simply too risky. *I* can find you *here* in your more natural habitat. That man you saw – and let's assume he is a detective – the one with the dark eyes, could be a genuine problem. I've also seen him, snooping around the hospital. He must have followed you to the Bethlem – and after I had specifically instructed you not to call on me there. Which means, Mr Garbett, he probably saw you discoursing with me."

"Gorblimey."

"Hang on. I do remember thinking for a moment that somebody *was* watching us at Bethlem, but I can't be certain. Now if you recall, there was somebody else who might also have been prying – an imbecile called Mr Broad who just happens to be an associate, would you believe, of the man whose diary I have commissioned you to obtain for me. It may be the case, Mr Garbett, that I did indeed manage to convince the feeble-minded Mr Broad that the purpose of your visit to the Hospital was to seek a psychological consultation from my colleague Norton. But that detective, however, if he *was* about at that time, may well have been out of earshot of my little charade. As for the man you think you recognised just now, well we'll assume you were mistaken. Personally, I don't care a Colchester sprat if the police arrest you for your career of crime, but I don't want you dragging *me* into anything awkward. *I,* Mr Garbett, will not be easily defeated. I will not be defeated at all. And no dim-witted policeman is going to obstruct the ambition of superior intellect and breeding. *You,* Mr Garbett, will burgle that address in Pimlico one more time for me – and I don't wish to be kept waiting. You turn that house upside down and inside out if you have to. Dismantle the entire property brick by brick if needs be. Just find me that diary, year eighteen hundred and eighty-three, keep it safe and keep your head low. I will collect the diary from you here in Whitechapel at my convenience. I give you seven days. And one other matter. Don't expect any further remuneration. Coupled to the fact that you have attracted too much unwelcome attention, I have already paid you handsomely for this task which, to date, you have failed."

"Now 'old onto yer 'orses," Garbett protested with a shake of his head. "I already told ya. I ain't goin' back there in no 'urry. I told ya why previous."

"Oh yes you will, or," Strange said with the grinning leer returned to his face, and the lips beginning to curl upwards, "I'll help the police locate you. You see I happen to know why the police are looking for you, Mister whatever-your-real-name-happens-to-be."

"What ya talking 'bout?"

"Where do I begin?" asked Strange, pausing to put on his spectacles. "Well firstly, there's the little matter of a British soldier being absent for a very long time without official leave. Then we have some shenanigans in New York. You know, it's quite amazing what someone is prepared to brag about to a gutter whore when badly under the influence of strong liquor. And it's pointless to consider disappearing into the crevices. I know too much about you – and like a slug you will leave too many slimy trails."

"Hold on, will yer. You fink you got somefink over me? 'Cause of what some glocky lushington Judy says wiv a brain addled by liquor? You ain't got nuffink. Nuffink!"

"Mr *Garbett*, if that's what you insist on being called, you take plenty of risks in your daily business for a man with such a precarious status in society."

"Well, a man's gotta get by, like. Best he knows how, ain't he. Nuffink more than a lil caper here an' there. Ain't gonna end up some shivering jemmy."

"You'll end up worse than that if you don't do as I tell you. It would be the biggest risk and the worst mistake of your grubby little life."

"Well allow me to tell *you* somefink, doctor." Garbett responded. Strange waited for the revelation, and it came quickly, catching him off guard. A blow from Garbett's right fist smashed into the side of the physician's face, partially dislodging his spectacles. A second blow followed into Strange's stomach, and to limit the impact of further punches he pulled Mr Garbett tightly into his clutches. Strange's spectacles flew completely off his face as the two men grappled, and then toppled onto the wet pavement with a splash. As they rolled around, blood from Strange's face streamed onto the ground, forming red blotches that were rapidly diluted and dispersed by the surface water. Someone ran towards the two men now exchanging cumbersome blows on all fours. Garbett looked up at the interloper, wriggled free from Strange's clutches, leapt to his feet and fled.

"I'm a police officer," an Irish voice shouted through the rain at Strange, and the physician watched the wiry man haring after Garbett, water exploding from the cobbles and paving stones in his wake. Strange got up. After retrieving his undamaged spectacles he replaced them in a pocket. He picked up his hat, shook it, and gripping it tightly joined the chase.

"He's been pestering me for months," the physician shouted ahead. "Won't leave me alone... I don't know what he wants... Keeps pestering me. Decided to have a word. Find out... He attacked me," he further shouted between deep breaths, pounding on and crashing through the puddles. As the water detonated around his feet the physician's trousers and socks became so drenched that he might have been wading knee deep. His torso had become equally wet, sweat pumping through the pores of his skin and against saturated cloth. All too soon Strange's legs had become heavier than he could remember – as if he was battling through treacle while the police officer's legs sliced through the yards of street like a wire through ripe cheese. None of the men noticed the dance hall that they passed recently closed down by the police. Then the Jewish grocers, the Daily Bread bakery, signs in Yiddish, the Bricklayers Arms public house, Goldman & Goldman pawnbrokers, the Nag's Head public house – all were outstripped without so much as a glance. Bringing up the rear, and struggling to keep up with the pace, Strange could see that after his initial sprint, Garbett's strength was also wilting. It was now obvious that the Irishman could easily have already caught up with Garbett but seemed to be toying with him. Garbett ground to a halt. He gasped then coughed and gasped again. The detective stopped thirty paces behind. Garbett, stooping, stumbled forward until he cranked up his momentum into an awkward trot. The Irish detective, waiting, upright and still, then followed at the same pace. It occurred to Strange that the slighter and fitter Irishman was waiting until Garbett was completely exhausted before attempting to make the arrest. Damn you man, thought Strange, just get on with it if you're going to do it. The three men had now entered a torpid zone of the district. Factories and works yards slept oblivious to the unfolding drama. The Irish detective was suddenly catching up again. The desperate Garbett still had about fifteen yards over his pursuer. He staggered out of sight in the darkness as if merging into stone and mortar. The Irishman accelerated. He ran a little further and stopped. Strange could see him sniffing the air like a hungry dog, then walk a few more paces to inspect a recess. He didn't dally there, and as he turned away, Garbett re-emerged from his hidey-hole a few yards up and lumbered forward. The Irish detective sprang from his blocks. A few blurred strides later he grabbed the slumping Garbett and slammed him against a wall, pinning him upright against the bricks with his arms locked straight. Strange, staggering on, turned his head into the recess that the Irishman had investigated. Just inside, and exuding foul odours that were a match for Garbett's, the puffing face of an elderly simpleton – missing all his teeth, tongue flapping out, and the tip of his weeping nose eroded into a hollow – grinned back. He was mounting from behind an obese young whore who, bowed forehead grinding against the coarse brickwork, was clutching a bottle of gin. As her liver dissolved and she filled with disease, it wouldn't be long before firstly her flab and then the remainder of her flesh shrivelled away. Her soul had already decayed to almost nothing. Strange averted his eyes from the disgusting side-show. He coughed and spat out a dollop of phlegm. He switched his attention back to the predator and his quarry, and, now less than ten yards away, wondered whether it would be in his best interests to make himself scarce. He reminded himself that, under arrest, Garbett might talk – mentioning a Dr Maxwell from Bethlem – and decided to renew his complaints against him.

"He's been pestering me. I don't know who he is. He attacked me when I was trying to ask him why he wouldn't leave me alone," he explained, bent forward with his hands propping himself up from his knees. "Have you formally arrested him?" he gasped. The Irishman glanced dismissively across at Strange. He didn't respond to the question. Instead his eyes cast their net to the depths of the road before pulling back to Garbett.

"No bobbies in soight," he audibly concluded and thrust his head closer to Garbett's. "Dis will do noicely. A quoiet spot for a proivate reunion you've koindly led me to."

All three men seemed frozen in their respective positions for a moment. It may only have been for a handful of seconds, but during this lull Garbett saw himself back in profitable New York and getting up to all sorts. He recalled standing on the deck of the liner as it docked at Ellis Island. This was where he would reinvent himself as Paddy O'Halloran at the immigration centre. After establishing baiting rings in Manhattan he was soon stuffing dollar bills into his pockets, raking in the cash from spectators who gambled on fighting dogs pitted against half a dozen rats. At one of his baiting events he had been introduced to Micky Malley with whom he had soon set up a rip-off dive near The Bowery in the midst of the Tenderloin district. The Five Card Trick, on an occasion when enjoying a whisky in the tawdry office with Malley, was where he had first seen the rust-haired Irishman. Others had been present, and suddenly as if from nowhere they all reappeared to the snared Garbett as if he'd been there with them five minutes earlier. He visualised 'Cross-eyed' Jerry, Jack 'the Pig' Mitchell, Pat 'the Pincer' McManus, 'Fatso' O'Rourke, 'Turpentine' Jake, Valentino 'Shorty' Mancini, Al 'the Goon' O'Sullivan, 'Groping' Joe Hickey, 'Free and Easy' Rick Tompkins, and somebody called 'Flat face'. The Irishman who had finally caught up with Garbett had been known only as 'the Blade'. Present too was a ragbag of women: 'Blonde' Lizzie, 'Scar-bellied' Rose, 'Two-cents' Alice, and 'Russian' Anna helped run some of Malley's other enterprises. These were clip-joints entitled the Crazy Mare Dance Hall, the Ruins of Cairo Saloon, and Top Hats and Pussycats. The Five Card Trick dive had been easy pickings. The clients, typically foreign sailors, upstate farmers, or other naive visitors, had paid good money to drink remixed beer dregs. Garbett remembered how Malley had taught him to target a victim with something worth robbing, and then lace his beer dregs with drugs. Encouraged to keep drinking until unconscious by the promise of a dance in the sawdust dance-pit with a scantily clad woman, these clients were subsequently robbed. Dumped nearby, they had awoken with painful and scambled heads, lipstick kissing prints smattering their faces, and a crucial lack of memory of what had taken place. He remembered a British victim whose personal belongings had identified him as one Albert Pitts – or Potts, perhaps. He could picture that bloated face. The name didn't matter. This greedy buffoon, who had been bragging about all the gifts he had showered on young actresses and reeked of the wealth he carried about with him, he'd been child's play to suck in and then fleece. These were the halcyon days, despite Malley's dire warning about the fate of those who doublecrossed him. O'Halloran, as he then called himself, or 'Fragrant' Paddy, as he was known by associates, had plenty of cash and for once felt like a bigshot. But this particular dive, like most other illegal establishments in the vicinity, was under the protection of a crooked police officer. Before Garbett had had the chance to grow fat on his earnings, the crooked police officer was arrested. Garbett, in return for immunity from prosecution, had testified against both Malley and the police officer in court, and further admitted that his real name was Benjamin Barrow. However, like many of the city's corrupt hierarchy, the police officer had friends in high places. He was declared not guilty, handed back his badge, and returned to work for the department. Garbett had been nothing more than a small-time operator who'd mingled with the major league boys. At a stroke much of Garbett's immunity had been cancelled, and he was now a nark and potential felon who had fallen foul of both the police and the underworld. Malley had somehow managed to dodge even a gaol sentence, and Garbett remembered seeing the red-haired Irishman, who was right now pinning him against the wall, for the second time in the court house with several of Malley's other associates including Jack 'the Pig' Mitchell and Al 'the Goon'

O'Sullivan. 'The Blade' had been sitting without movement or murmur, just flitting his sharp eyes back and forth from witness Garbett to defendant Malley to witness Garbett. Recalling sheer panic and fear for his life, he was doing so again back at the present in Whitechapel. Garbett flipped back to the terrors of New York. With the Police Department, one officer in particular, plus Micky Malley and his cronies all hungry for emphatic retribution, O'Halloran, as he still called himself, had to hastily consider his shrinking options. There had scarcely been time to pause and take breath. Staking a claim in an exhausted, dusty town like Tombstone was a fleeting consideration. So too was pushing further south and across the Mexican border. Competing amongst the chills of Dawson and the Klondike river sediments suggested wealthier prospects if in luck – something Garbett conceded had deserted him for the time being. On the other hand melting back into urban England would be easier, he had realised – and urgent before the issue of deportation arose. After fleeing back across the Atlantic he had relocated in London under yet another name – Freddie Garbett – and now his luck had finally run its course somewhere along the Commercial Road.

The Irishman terminated the last throes of Garbett's flashback.

"I'll just be after, Mr O'Halloran, Barrow or whatever ya moight be callin' yourself dese days, be passing on da compliments of Mr Malley. Noice to see you've been after takin' a long shower in da rain. Noice to see you've rinsed yer filty clothin'. Noice dat you're still fragrant for da big occasion."

Then, in masterly motion of lightning speed, he whipped out a knife and plunged it repeatedly through Garbett's ribcage. Noyall watched with his head tilted as Garbett's legs collapsed and the pot-belly slid down the wall with the rest of him into a heap on the pavement.

"Mary, mudder of Jesus, don't ya have anytink ya want me to pass back to Mr Malley?" Noyall asked the corpse. "I were only after passin' on Mr Malley's compliments. Sorry you took it so bad," he casually added and, with a shrug of his shoulders, looked over to Strange who was hauling himself fully upright.

"What in God's name are you doing, man?" Strange asked. "You've just killed him."

"Indeed I have," agreed the assassin, rain dripping off his chin. "Hope I haven't inconvenienced you, so I do. Noice meetin' you anyway, Dr Norton. And be sure to pass on moy sincere gratitude to our mutual friend, Mr Broad. Tell him it's been a great pleasure workin' wit him. Don't forget to tank him, now, Dr Norton. I tink dat good manners are proiceless. Talkin' of proiceless tings, you can also tell Mr Broad dat I can't go arresting you or your colleague Dr Strange neider. I wouldn't be after expectin' physicians to be behoind burglin' houses, but den again dere aren't many secret doiaries wort more dan dere weight in gold. Rest easy for now, Dr Norton, as I won't be apprehending you. I tink I'm roight in believing' you need to be a police officer to be after doin' dat koinda ting. Must go," he declared, then sprinted away. He snapped left towards the Whitechapel road and then, at a guess, onwards to the Bethnal Green road.

Strange watched aghast for the few seconds the Irishman was visible. He unbuttoned his frock coat and groped in his pockets for his spectacles. He wiped them against his damp shirt and pushed them over his eyes. He then gazed down at the body. A knife handle was sticking out of Garbett's chest, and torrents of blood were still gushing from it as fast as they were being washed away with the flotsam of street litter. Strange opened his mouth to gulp at the air and, for a second, thought he recognised the distant but shrill sound of a police whistle squeezing through the pounding rain. Strange couldn't be sure. He couldn't discern anything much under the cascading black skies – not even a single specimen of all the slim, towering chimneys, some of which still belched smoking stench into the atmosphere. He inspected the corpse. The blackened red flow was slowing. Strange scanned the area. The sparse gaslights offered feeble assistance. He hadn't noticed any night watchmen during the pursuit. Nor had he seen any beat constables or activity around a couple of police stations they had passed. Fortunately, all the slack eyes of the law must be sheltering from the rain, Strange reckoned. There was no glow of moving light from a Bull's eye lantern, but either way, his sole option was to flee the scene without delay. Watching out for policemen or anyone at all, he lurched off in the opposite direction from where the Irishman was heading, hoping to avoid the docks and to find his bearings by reaching the Tower. With both hands Dr Strange wrenched his drowning hat back low over his head. With his mind disengaged from the leaking cut by his eye, he turned off the thoroughfare at the first opportunity.

17

"I almost failed to recognise you," Dr Norton told his colleague the following morning outside the physicians' room. "Goodness me! You look like you've been involved in a fight, and you've been looking so dapper in your frock coat. I think the word I'm looking for is *fashionable*. Dare I presume that you are following my lead in a change of raiment?"

"I took a long walk last night to consider my career. Some honest reflection. Alas, I got caught in that frightful downpour. I had a long walk home, and there wasn't a single cab or omibus in sight."

"Ah! Good ideas aren't always blessed with the luck they merit."

"Not even the lowliest of horse-drawn contraptions," Strange continued. "There never is when you need one. I took a severe drenching and I reckon it will take a week for my clothes to properly dry out. And of course one must never wring out high quality cloth like that," he lamented.

Dr Norton's face initially smiled gently before straightening.

"Such are the perils of a British autumn. But how did you acquire those nasty-looking bruises on your face? And that cut?"

"You can never ever find an available cab or omnibus seat in the evening when it rains. Even if there is a suitable underground train line nearby, they always seem closed for use whenever you most need the service. Anyway, I thought I spotted a Hackney carriage, made a dash for it, slipped, and collided with a tree. I came off worse."

"Oh dear. That is rotten luck. Still, I assume the damage is only superficial. Perhaps, considering the problems of transport, you should invest in a bicycle. When travelling unaccompanied, my bicycle is quick, doesn't require hay or water, and the exercise keeps mind and body in good health. Although I do admit to being grateful for the modern safety bicycle. I feel much safer now than a few years back when I tried the penny-farthing for a month or two, and suffered a spate of nasty grazes and bruises. Get yourself a bicycle, one of mankind's greatest inventions. And apply plenty of cold water to your face today. That's my advice."

"Actually, I'm biding my time until I can afford to buy what will prove to be a far greater invention. An ambition is to be the owner soon of a motorcar – especially since the law has now been amended allowing them to be driven faster than walking pace without the requirement of hiring a flagman. And I'm not referring to a cheaper little model like the Benz Velo, nor some steam-driven French piece of junk. I have in mind an elegant horse-carriage chassis with a petrol combustion engine. I'm picturing myself behind the wheel of the Daimler Cannstatt. The motorcar will soon make horses obsolete – and not before time. The ghastly creatures kick and bite. It's something I actually have in common with our friend Percival Nudd, awaiting equine replacement by the motorcar. And I am determined to have my very own transportation machine soon. In the meanwhile during foul weather, I, along with my finest garments, have too often to suffer on foot."

"Or procure a bicycle," the senior physician reminded Strange. Like an elder brother he then put his arm around Strange's shoulder to guide him into the physicians' room.

"Take a seat," suggested Norton as he sat himself down. "I must say that I'm encouraged by your desire to reflect on your career. I've become concerned that you were developing an unhealthy interest in the aetiology of Mr Nudd's problems. Dare I say that I feared it was becoming pathological? An obsession perhaps?"

"Lord, no." Strange laughed dismissively. "Merely a fleeting idea for a minor paper that might contribute, if published of course, to the understanding of religious mania and its many by-products such as messianic delusions. Just a notion, my dear fellow. Trust me."

"So am I to understand that you have now discarded this notion altogether?"

"Jettisoned weeks, no, months ago. Rest assured, my dear Dr Norton," Strange insisted. Norton's lack of response invited Strange to elaborate.

"And you were quite right to point out that Nudd's cult leadership is atypical. Thank you for digging out for me all those case histories on cult leaders and former cult members. You are quite right that Mr Nudd's church is probably based on guilt and the need to find purpose. This contrasts with the cults of the outright fraudster or the monster egotist who claims to sacrifice his life to his members when in truth they are sacrificing theirs for him. And no need to mention the usual sexual exploitation in the latter cases. You were absolutely correct that Nudd does not fit the mould of the conventional guru."

"That is excellent news," said Norton. "I'm delighted. After rummaging around for all those papers I'm also encouraged that you've evidently taken the time to read through them. Yes, I'm greatly heartened. Though it is only fair to inform you that I have been asked to watch you with more diligence. Let's call it closer supervision. I haven't in turn, however, imparted anything of your particular interest in Mr Nudd, or of your impatient professional ambition. Not so far, anyway. I hope you'll appreciate that I can't just turn a blind eye to recent excesses. Additionally I deem it apt to mention that I watched the great WG Grace batting during the height of the summer. He is a supreme technician equipped with both natural and honed talent, with experience, and with unshakeable application. His ambitions are so great at each visit to the crease that he even contests an umpire's decision when given out. Defeat is anathema to him – something very admirable up to a point. Yet notwithstanding his natural ability, he has learned how to compile huge innings from the profits of practice, experience, and even familiarising himself with the idiosyncrasies of the pitch during a match. As he becomes more accustomed to bowler and pace of the wicket, he gradually accelerates, playing increasingly flamboyant shots that he ascertains to be without great risk. Batting successfully, like practising medicine, is all about accumulating experience and knowledge at an eager yet appropriate pace. Conceding defeat, although WG might disagree, can sometimes be the best way of allowing oneself to move forward. I hope you'll think about that, Dr Strange. I also have a confession to make. You have mentioned visiting dog fights – illegal for many years, and rightly so. You've mentioned visits to Whitechapel, and the maid who cleans your lodgings informed me that on several occasions she has come across rotting human remains. She wasn't happy. She spoke of a skull, boiled clean in my opinion, and of some soft tissues in a pickling jar. I examined both and the latter was easily identifiable as cerebral tissue in formalin. It's been a source of such disquietude that I took the liberty of visiting Whitechapel myself in order to determine the nature and extent of your activities there. Of course your private life is your own, and certainly not any of my business. But I couldn't help thinking that I needed to know what was going on. I have not only a responsibility to our patients but also to you. I apologise for this intrusion, Dr Strange, but I feared greatly that some of your activities were intruding detrimentally on your prospects. It was very nearly a risk too far because I almost got myself killed in the process. I paid some utterly lost soul a shilling to answer a few questions and was, at her insistence, conveyed to dreadful room where I was almost the victim of a violent robbery."

"I know," Strange calmly interrupted. "I heard about that on the grapevine. I heard quite a bit about to whom you spoke and the questions you asked. My dear fellow, you are correct that there is much to learn, and gaining a better view inside the human mind is not without risks. You now know this only too well. And although I'm disappointed that you have had so little faith in me, I can forgive you. My late father would have described your unwarranted snooping as *poor show* or *bad form*. Actually, and since you are so keen on the game, he would probably have described it as *not cricket*. I, however, fully acknowledge that you had my best interests at heart. It has not gone unappreciated."

"We'll swiftly move on then, shall we? So did you perchance arrive at any conclusions or objectives – other than owning a weather-resistant motorcar – during your period of reflection? Anything that you would like to share with me?" Norton inquired.

"I'm glad you should ask that," Strange replied. "It's just that, and despite searching deep into my soul, I eventually arrived at but a solitary conclusion. Specifically that I require as a matter of urgency a short sabbatical to better determine if I am truly suited to a career of physician of the mentally afflicted. I'm being earnest, Dr Norton. I would fail in my duty to you and the patients if I were to be anything less."

"A brave admission and noble sentiments indeed. However I envisage a considerable obstacle in the way of your wishes. I could be wrong, of course. I anticipate, though, that you will have great difficulty in persuading our Physician Superintendent to grant you your request – unless he were to be made aware of several details that I've withheld. Of course, I can put in a word for you and try to provide a compelling case *without* revealing these details. But I fear it might be to no avail. Understand that we are all of us bedevilled from time to time with that potentially debilitating blighter known as self-doubt. It is only natural for a conscientious professional to be so. Such doubts have visited me on many occasions, sometimes extinguishing almost as fast as they arrived, and at other times lingering disconcertingly. Perhaps in a day or two your dilemmas will have all been resolved, and you will embrace your work with reawoken vigour. Although that recent episode, when you scattered our stewards far and wide in search of that intruder, did, I concede, make me question your judgement. As for that particular episode, is there anything you haven't told me?"

"About what for example? No, no, no. Of course not. I may have over-reacted a touch, but the security of all staff and patients is paramount."

"And you know nothing of the intruder's identity or purpose of his visit?"

"I'd actually been wondering if you've been keeping the very same information from me, my dear fellow. I don't know him from Adam – or anything about him."

"Good. Although the mystery, like my undeniable curiosity, endures, I rather hoped not. Perhaps, then, some leave is not inappropriate," agreed Norton.

"I think'" Strange decided, "I will broach this matter with our esteemed Physician Superintendent. But at the same time I am comforted, Dr Norton, and enormously reassured by your words of experience."

He stood up to offer his hand to Norton and a thumb-sized glass bottle fell from his trouser pocket onto the floor. Strange picked it up and dropped it back into his pocket where it clacked against more glass.

"Just a few empty phials for my mother. I clean them thoroughly first, of course, and she uses them to store some of her scents and oils. It's not a problem is it?"

"Of course not. Life must have been very difficult for your mother since your father's death. I commend you for doing these little things which undoubtedly mean a great deal to her. Thinking of visiting your mother soon?"

"It's a strong consideration," replied Strange whose thoughts for a moment drifted back to his father's funeral. He remembered a little further back to the day when his mother explained his father's frequent absence from home during leave from his duties as an army surgeon. He recalled his mother eventually explaining that his father had taken up partial residence with a mistress half his age. Strange recalled himself successfully preventing laughter spilling from his lips while his mother was strenuously trying to stop the tears dropping from her eyes. Strange's thoughts hopped forward to the funeral. He recalled all the absurd references made by the clergyman: his father being eulogised as the perfect, wholly virtuous, devoted, and much-loved husband and father. Strange recalled being surprised at how unemotional he felt, only aware instead of being irritated by the ridiculous tributes. Perhaps he might be roused by the entertainment of a fight between his mother and his late father's mistress. But the sham dignity of the occasion hadn't been reduced to an even worse fiasco since the latter hadn't bothered to attend. His mother, misreading Strange's demeanour, had thanked her son for being "my pillar of strength". As Strange reflected, his leer returned to his face. He removed it before responding to Norton.

"Like you, mater offers a wide ear."

The senior physician shook Strange's hand firmly, then watched as his junior departed. But Dr Strange had only been gone from the room for less than a minute when he returned accompanied by two police officers. Strange's composed manner was contradicted, if one looked closely, by a tint of facial perspiration as he introduced the two policemen to Norton.

"They were on the point of knocking when I left the room. This is Detective Constable Coates of the Metropolitan Police CID," Strange gestured to the youthful un-uniformed officer as Norton arose, "and this is Constable Smith," he continued with a nod towards the burly and much older bobby with a bushy grey moustache. "And this is my esteemed senior colleague and mentor, Dr Norton," he added, during the handshakes.

"So, gentlemen," asked Norton, "how can we help you? Do you have a new patient for assessment?"

Coates, with red cheeks and lacking a hat to cover his mop of brown hair, cleared his throat. During this fleeting moment his struggling moustache exposed the extent of its fight to establish itself.

"As a matter of fact, sirs, we don't – and please forgive us interrupting you. It's probably the work of a lunatic – possibly one of your patients here at Bedlam – but I'd just like to read you a note and see if you have any comment to make. It was handed in to the desk sergeant at the Yard a few days ago. It states thus: *My dear Detective Inspector Noyall,*" read Detective Constable Coates, "*I have urgent information to give you so pardon me for trying to contact you here. I have seen the Fenian man at the Bedlam lunatic asylum. He looks like a horrible ruffian. It was yesterday. I smelled him too. You were quite right about that. It was so bad it made me come across all queer. I felt awfully noseous. I am not in a position to say too much now for undercover security reasons that you will understand. Please come to Bedlam tomorrow and wait for me there. I will reveal everything I know about the stinking Fenian man's movements and more besides. I was correct in my suspicions about Dr Norton of Bedlam. It may be only a coincingdence that he will be meeting the Fenian man, but I am more certain than ever that he is the mastermind behind the burglary at the Holy Belgravia residence. You must only arrest him after you have first arrested the Fenian man. I will explain this later and be more pessific, but I must do it before tomorrow evening. If I am not mistaken I believe you must also arrest Dr Strange. He works with Dr Norton and is probably part of the villynous gang. I don't like him anyway even if Mrs Porter does. She is smitten with him. It makes me so angry. Even as I write this I am red with rage about Mrs Porter's feelings for Dr Strange. I have also seen these two physicians frequenting a transvestitite brothel in Ludgate Square. I saw the society wit Oscar Wilde at this den of soddyming inquiousness once, and also the Reverend Bream of St Peter's Church. Surely it was him but when I asked what he was doing there he told me he didn 't know what I was talking about and that his name was Mr I M Incognito. It isn't. Actually one of the transvestitites looks very similar to Mrs Porter but not close up. It isn't her and she doesn't pardon my French have a man's organ bits. I also saw somebody highly important of Royalty visit these premises but I shouldn't ellabyrate on this sollum situation as you know. I don't want to cause distress to Her Majesty the Queen. Not now she holds me in such high esteem because she might not believe me and change her opinion of me. I know all this about the transvestite brothel because I saw these people go in and out on some occasions a few years back when I just happened to be passing. I followed the physitions in once but departed quickly when I saw the degrydation. It is a filthy place and Doctor Norton and Doctor Strange are guilty of the foulest behaviour of which you and Mrs Porter ought to be informed. They must be sent to gaol. This is most urgent, but most especially regarding the Fenian Rennygrade. Sincerely yours, your most humble, obedient, and brilliant servant, J Kenyon Broad. Or, Sir Joshua Broad, if I may presume to call myself by this title in anticipation. PS I will win Mrs Porter in the end because I look after her and love her like no other. My advice to you, Detective Inspector, is that if you have a lady friend, fiancée or wife, then you should wrap her up in cotton wool. If you don't yet have a special lady, then I can always give you the benefit of my expert advice on how to woo and court a lady. Dr Strange and Dr Norton are crimmynals.* And that is it, gentlemen. Any comment either of you wish to make?"

"Goodness me. By Jove! How utterly extraordinary. And mention of visits to a brothel. A transvestite brothel. Extraordinary," commented a baffled Dr Norton with one eyebrow still higher than the other. "Does any of that make a jot of sense to you, Dr Strange?"

"Ha, ha, ha, ha, ha, ha! Ha, ha, ha, ha!" roared Strange, incapable of containing his initial mirth before eventually calming into his open-mouthed sneer. "I shouldn't laugh, I know, but that is surely one of the funniest things I've heard for a long time. And believe me, gentlemen, in addition to all the tragedy there are a fair few comic sights in here. As a matter of fact we *have* encountered Mr – or *Sir* – Joshua Broad, Detective Constable. To borrow his word, we can be quite *pecific*: the man is a half-witted fantasist. He's a feeble-minded inadequate who frequents this establishment to kowtow to one Percival Nudd, a self-styled religious guru who has, in recent years, become something of a regular fixture at lunatic asylums. It does rather sound as though poor Mr Broad is as deluded as his saviour Mr Nudd."

Norton felt that Dr Strange's response necessitated his intervention.

"I'm pleased that something has brightened your mood, Dr Strange. And whilst I essentially concur with your observations, these do sound like rather serious allegations, no matter how bizarre."

Detective Constable Coates again cleared his throat.

"So can I deduce from what you are saying," he asked, "is that you know nothing whatsoever about any of the allegations in this Joshua Broad's note, and that you further consider him to be a deluded fantasist?"

Norton nodded.

"That would, on the face of it, very much seem to be the case," he confirmed. "As my colleague Dr Strange here averred, we do, indeed, know Mr Broad. Some of the man's eccentricities *have* come to our attention. He always comes to visit Mr Nudd in the company of one Mrs Porter, also mentioned in the note. Mr Broad seems unable to detach himself from her – either physically or emotionally – and Mrs

Porter in turn seems unable to detach herself from our patient, Mr Nudd. I'm sorry we can't offer any further assistance," he added.

The young police officer shrugged by twisting open his hands.

"I can only apologise, sirs, again for the interruption. It has been our belief from the outset that this was nothing more than the scribblings of an idiot. After all, what I haven't already told you is that the note is addressed to some supposed police officer who doesn't actually exist. We are, however, obliged on several counts to follow it up. My gratitude for your time. Oh. Just one other little thing. We are, as a matter of fact, familiar with the premises in Ludgate Square to which this Broad character refers. And we need to be because as he quite rightly states, they are indeed frequented by a very senior member of the Monarchy who, God forbid, will one day become our King. It is a most delicate matter, but rest assured we have a very good idea of all those who patronise this particular establishment and your good selves do not feature on our list. I apologise, sirs, once more."

"Think nothing of it, gentlemen," said Dr Norton with smiles and parting handshakes while Dr Strange was muttering something that amused him about Mr Broad. "If you ever need any further assistance," added the senior physician, "about this or any other issue, don't hesitate to consult either myself or Dr Strange."

"Yes," agreed Strange with a straighter face. "Of course you have to do your work, and we have to do *ours*. And it does so happen that I have a pressing engagement with the Physician Superintendent," he added, pulling open the door, before ushering the two policemen towards it, and following them out.

Norton was a busy man. Even for one so dedicated, every morning presented him with a mountainous workload to climb. On this occasion the ascent had stalled with the physician unable to determine a clear path upwards. His thoughts had been distracted by Dr Strange's behaviour. Norton's drifting eyes stopped on an old copy of *Punch* magazine left on a table by another colleague. A publication never shy to lampoon Bedlam's therapies or grand balls – heaven forbid a caricature of an unstoppable Mrs Porter flouncing by in her most extravagant reception costume – he'd already browsed through this edition, memorable for the curate's egg cartoon. Dr Strange unequivocally had his good qualities, but, Norton wondered, just how rotten were the bad parts? Norton retraced his thoughts back to the point just before he became distracted by the magazine – and just after the departure of the policemen. In addition to having confessed his distasteful investigation to Strange, whose explanations still failed to fully convince, Dr Norton had been further reminded of his Whitechapel experience by the visit of the police. Even his preceding questions to Strange about the hospital's mysterious intruder had evoked the same smell of trouble. Just why had this intruder's presence at the hospital alarmed his junior colleage into emptying the establishment of its staff in an effort to catch him? And whoever he was, had Norton already come face to face with him? Norton cast his mind back to that Whitechapel rookery. There the withered prostitute had instructed him to wait inside a cramped and dingy room with peeling wallpaper, sooty swathes of damp infestation, a filth-encrusted floor, and an unmade bed. She needed to visit the bathroom, she explained, leaving the physician alone. Norton's eyes wandered around the room. So did his nose. The unpleasant smells provoked him to cough to clear his throat. He continued to wait, barely moving his feet. He took out a handkerchief and blew some of the dust and pungent fungal spores from his nasal lining. Eventually the door opened. Norton was perturbed to see not painted Nellie but a man enter the room. He looked substantially younger than the prostitute, and his grimy clothes and popping eyes prompted Norton to retreat a step. The man pulled out a knife. Norton raised his brolly and snapped it into a defensive position, ready to swipe or thrust, or whatever those fencing lessons all those years ago at school would recommend.

"Giss yer wallet, yer watch and any other valubals or else you get it bad and I cut yer heart and yer liver and yer kidneys out and throw 'em to the dogs. Now! If ya know what's best fer ya," shouted the knifeman. As Norton reached towards his pocket, still pointing the brolly forward, his attention was diverted by another man entering the room.

"I think you should look behind you." the physician advised. The knifeman looked over his shoulder and froze. He saw a huge, well-dressed man with black hair and eyes, an elegant moustache, and as steady as a column of basalt filling the doorframe. Such a moustache on such a big man, noted Norton, worn by one togged-up like the flying trapeze artist Jules Leotard, would be the embellishment of a circus strongman. On a man dressed as splendidly as this, however, such a moustache bore the grade of finesse – and this distinguished gentleman was aiming a gaping pistol barrel directly at the knifeman's head.

"My Gawd!" yelled the prostitute from the corridor. "It's Jack the Ripper. Or maybees me John inside is. You a rozzer come to arrest the ripper?"

Her question was unanswered. Nobody moved.

"Yeah, me friend thinks so," the woman continued, "which is why he come to protect me. Honest, he only come to look out after me. You a rozzer then?" she repeated, and the tall, swarthy stranger ignored her. He stood to one side and, still staring at the knifeman, still aiming the pistol at his head, pointed to the doorway. The knifeman began walking cautiously towards it, and then darted through.

"Come on Mabel. Let's get the hell outa here," he cried as they fled. The stranger nodded at Norton and dropped his pistol to his side. Norton lowered his brolly.

"I can't thank you enough for rescuing me," Norton uttered, still shaking a little but wearing a face of bewilderment. His words failed to elicit a reaction. The tall man, having said nothing at all, turned and departed. Norton waited for a few seconds to gather his senses. The discovery that the haggard, painted woman had been addressed as Mabel instead of Nellie was the least of the surprises. He inhaled on the musty air, coughed, and hurried after the imposing stranger. After first catching up with his rescuer the ensuing objective would be to locate a policeman. Norton retraced his path back through the brick maze: under the railway arch, past Blind Billy's yard, across a rubbish-jammed quadrangle, and along Wailing Waif passage. Norton struggled to penetrate the fog. Like muslin cloth, it draped his face and choked his throat. Norton's eyes strained against every viable direction. But like the dishonest whore and her accomplice, Norton's mysterious saviour was already nowhere to be seen.

18

The two senior citizens strolling down Fleet Street in their weekend best had known each other since boyhood. Some of their young friends had perished during the typhus outbreaks of the 1840s, others had succumbed to cholera in the 1850s, to smallpox, consumption, and also the military battlefields a long way from home. There, too many men were shunted into bloody oblivion by the command of a gentlemen's club of blundering officers. They were often picked off with ease in their bright and beautifully presented uniforms while marching in flawlessly drilled unison. If enemy weapons hadn't disposed of them, then malaria, dysentery or malnutrition prevented an abundance of them from ever setting foot on Albion again. These two, however, had survived unscathed despite sharing the grime and the germs cultivated by the heat, the water, and the congestion of the city. Their means had been modest, but throughout their working lives they had saved enough to find new pursuits in semi-retirement. After being persuaded to part with significant chunks of their savings for what they had believed to be an especially good cause, full retirement had bolted out of sight into the distant future. Both gentlemen had once been followers of the teachings of Nudd. The ivory-faced Mr Hughes and beetroot-faced Mr Rooney, sipping steaming refreshments from a coffee stall, hadn't finished arguing over the best venue for their Saturday afternoon perambulation.

"I would have preferred to visit Regents Park. It's been ten or so years since I last explored the gardens."

"It's dull. Dull, I tell you," Mr Rooney replied, thrusting back his cup to the stall owner. "The zoological gardens offer little but a collection of stupid beasts. I said this not half an hour ago. They smell, they make frightful noises, and they defecate with abandon. What's more, there is little shelter offered against the rainshowers of this time of year – though they grant plenty to the dumb animals."

"The Park's Botanical Gardens, Amos, might have made for an interesting stroll," said Mr Hughes.

"At this time of year, George? Balderdash! There's little to see amongst a tedious collection of plants that are shrinking out of bloom from the elements. Unless you want to amuse yourself squashing the stains out of the inkcaps and booting the soot out of the puffballs like a ten-year-old. I think not. Onwards towards the Embankment. Have you drunk all your coffee yet?"

Mr Hughes didn't hear the question flattened under the stomping yells of a pieman.

"Freshly baked pies. Getcha lavley 'ot fresh pies 'ere. Freshly baked pies. Finest meats selected first fing at Smiffield. Freshly baked pies."

"I hear a rumour," said Mr Hughes as he returned his cup.

"You've got a tumour?"

"No. I hear a *rumour*, Amos."

"A *rumour*. I wish that awful man would shut up about his blinking pies."

"Yes, a rumour that they intend to demolish these streets. They are planning to erect a new area to be called The Aldwych," Mr Hughes continued, as the two looked left down Holywell Street.

"Nonsense," Mr Rooney contested. "Just look. The place is thriving. Why knock it down? Look at 'em all, courtesy of the Saturday half-holiday. Too many people."

"Yes. It encourages the hooligan instincts. Oh! I say," exclaimed Mr Hughes with a nod of his head. "There. Halfway down Holywell

Street. Isn't that the billycock fellow from the Nuddite Church? The one who was always stuck to that Porter woman like a limpet? That dumpy little fellow with bad eyesight and an even worse complexion?"

"I know the one, George. The name is *Broad,* I believe. Always stuck to Mrs 'the Duchess' Porter like you say. Rather a tick than a limpet. A bloated, motionless tick. The billycock man. Where? Where did you see him?"

"Pies. Getcha lavley 'ot fresh-baked pies," boomed the pieman.

"Where did you see him, George? I asked where."

"Down there," waved Mr Hughes. "Down Holywell Street. He alighted from a hansom carriage. Look there he is."

"Can't see the useless blighter. Where?"

"Goodness me! I do believe, Amos, he's just had his pocket picked by an urchin who deliberately bumped into him. Look. There goes Broad with his billycock. He's entered a bookshop – and without his wallet if I'm not mistaken. And there goes the urchin in his baggy cap. See? Just look at him skeddadle down the road."

"Never mind him. Which bookshop? There are dozens down there. Dozens of people milling around too. I wouldn't mind finding him I can tell you. *Wrap 'em up in cotton wooool! Wrap 'em up in cotton wooool!* I'd like to wrap him up in string and throw him into the lion enclosure at the zoological gardens. I certainly wouldn't mind finding him."

"Me neither. Follow me and let's see if he can answer our questions about the Reverend's whereabouts. Let's see if he knows what has become of our hard-earned donations."

"But we know. Some converted into marble, and the rest into thin air just like the Reverend," remarked Mr Rooney as he followed his friend past a whelk and cockle counter, a potato cart, and then a scruffy parade of second-hand bookshops.

"This, if I'm not mistaken, is the one," decided Mr Hughes, and the two men stepped inside Otto's Page & Print Market – We Sell and Buy.

A minute and a half earlier Mr Broad had shuffled over to the bland and neatly dressed Otto, and inquired if he had any new stock of "particular interest to hearty and discerning gentlemen".

Otto, whose small size, balding head, and paint-brush beard reminded Mr Broad of his late father's accountant, leaned his mouth up to Mr Broad's ear.

"Indeed we do, sir," he whispered in a flat voice. "If you would care to deport yourself through the usual door marked *Private* you will find the newer publications, as always, on the table to the left. Usual conditions if you don't mind, sir: no more than five minutes to make your selections; the usual obligatory purchase of at least one item, sir," he added.

Mr Broad, with his billycock pulled so far down that the rim was almost dislodging his spectacles, bowed his head and walked straight into a display of *Historic Fiction.*

"Try half a dozen paces to your left, sir," Otto directed him. "No, that's quite alright, sir. I'll pick up the books you've knocked off the shelves," Otto said, as Mr Broad, crouching on one knee, dropped the two books he was clutching back onto the floor. He got back to his feet, shuffled to his left, and, his chin wedged into the gap between his shoulder blades, disappeared into a small room by pulling shut the door behind him. Mr Broad, so he thought, was about to spend the bulk of his weekly shopping budget, as calculated by Mrs Porter, on his favourite type of reading material. His tastes would have been better satisfied by the more emphatic stuff that Mr Garbett had once peddled, but the greater the explicitness, the more destructive its impact on his budget. Even more devastating to his withering funds were the occasional visits to discreet addresses. Furthermore, all these transactions necessitated masking from Mrs Porter's awareness. It wasn't that straightforward for a gentleman to balance his books: choosing between the longevity but lesser pleasures of a booklet, or the ephemeral but vastly more gratifying and direct experience afforded by a visit to a discreet address. Marriage to Mrs Porter would more than remedy the problem, he believed. In the meanwhile, as a connoisseur, his overdue payment for assisting Detective Inspector Noyall would boost the procurement of his requirements. Until then, and after careful assessment, purchasing his favourite reading material would always have to be but an infrequent treat for an epicure, as Mr Broad also defined himself. He had already spent a small fortune on his hansom carriage, and would do so to return home. He was wary of travelling on trams and omnibuses, unless accompanied by Mrs Porter. People were always giving him menacing stares. Even some of the children would point at him, pull faces, stick out their tongues, and make disrespectful comments. And that jacksprat brat in Holywell Street had been so impertinent as to aggressively yell, "Whatchit Mister," and "Watch where ya bleedin' goin', will yer," after running into *him*. Indeed, even with the security of Mrs Porter's company, Mr Broad was reluctant to travel on the open top of a tram or omnibus. He was convinced somebody would throw him over the edge. The underground trains were altogether too unnatural and terrifying – and the last time he had taken a single-storey omnibus he feared he wouldn't get home alive. This particular incident had occured after travelling to an address near the Walworth Road just beyond the Elephant and Castle. He had been intending to visit a certain Mistress Celia Stricte, but having journeyed nearly two miles fell a few yards short of her speciality correction rooms. Mid-point between the bus stop and Mistress Stricte's address a terrible commotion had spilled across from some neighbouring streets and directly into Mr Broad's path. Two gangs of young ruffians – Mr Broad later read in a newspaper that they were named the *Borough Boys* and the *Elephant and Castle Club* – had been viciously fighting each other with knives, belts, clubs and chains. It had been a fearful sight, with prostrate bodies being kicked and beaten, and others, with blood running from slashed and pierced faces, charging groups with similar injuries. When five youths chased a pod of three towards him, shouting, swearing and flailing their weapons, Mr Broad was nearly knocked over and trampled by the stampede. When not fighting each other these gangs would often amuse themselves by toff-bashing. As a distinguished man of leisure, Mr Broad was in no doubt that he might be targeted as an easy uppercrust quarry. After rescuing his billycock from the pavement, Mr Broad had retreated all the way home like a rabbit racing to the safety of its burrow. Inside, he locked all doors, internal and external, and bolted all the windows shut. When alone, Mr Broad now travelled only by hackney carriage. The two-wheel, one-horse hansoms were elegant and swift. They weren't, though, inexpensive.

"Can't see that Broad geezer anywhere in here," complained Mr Rooney as he looked around and around the cluttered little shop. "Are you sure it was this place, George?"

"It's very odd. A strange affair. A queer business without a doubt as I was sure it was this one."

"Seems you were mistaken, George. More's the pity. I'd like to get my hands on him. See if we could make him squeal about the whereabouts of Nudd and our money. Cursed luck."

"I don't understand how I could have been mistaken, Amos. But as you always say, if we went back to that Nuddite Palace, they'd all close ranks, hide behind the safety of each other, and tell us nothing. Like last time."

"I doubt they'd even let us in through the front door again after that disagreeable exchange of opinion," said Mr Rooney. "Shall we search in the other shops, or shall we browse the goods now that we're here, George? This section seems interesting. Enough to whet my appetite. Look here. *Religion, New Religion, Spiritualism, and the Occult.*

"Yes, I dare say I may well have somehow erred. The scoundrel would probably have been of little use had we cornered him in any case. Browse away then, Amos."

Messrs Hughes and Rooney spent several minutes picking up books of all sizes and thickness, flicking through random pages before trying another. Mr Hughes scrutinised the cover of a book entitled *Demons of the Dolmens* by Henry Spudge, and exchanged it for a fraying copy of *Lethal Plants and Shamanism* by Professor Frederick Beavis. If he had cast his eyes a fraction further right, he would have noticed a compilation volume entitled *The Royal Society for the Investigation of Strange Phenomena: 1882 Lectures and Papers on Atmospherical Enigmas*. Had he then investigated this, he would probably have discovered an article on ball lightning written by the very man he sought to confront about his lost savings. Mr Hughes instead pulled out another book and began reading some snippets.

"I say!" he exclaimed, "Listen to this. It's just our sort of thing and it's entitled *Monsters and Magic: an investigation into time, spirits, witchcraft and chimeras*. Read this bit here in the introduction," he added, handing the open book to Mr Rooney who read out the passage for his friend's benefit.

"*Many years ago, during Robert Peel's second occasion in office as Prime Minister, I met an astonishing Frenchman who opened my eyes but has left me bewildered to this very day. He was visiting England to observe, so he said, some members of a travelling circus who performed astonishing feats of trickery. In this man's opinion, it was possible to not only voluntarily change one's form beyond recognition, but also to alter one's presence in the course of time. He said that he was still to unlock the secrets of the latter, but was gradually perfecting the former art. He elaborated that shifting and distorting the body in both time and space were, in his opinion, feasible. I asked him for a demonstration for I understood not what he was saying. We were both passing the night at a coaching inn not far from Portsmouth, and this astonishing Gallic cousin suggested we retire to my room for a demonstration. Once inside, he performed a number of amazing tricks with some coins, making them disappear and then reappear in an assortment of unexpected locations. I was spellbound and suspected the Devil's work, but this Frenchman insisted that his trickery was nothing more than sleight of hand, clever illusion, and indefatigable practice. The next trick he performed was so extraordinary that I confess to being scared out of my wits. He retreated to the rear of the room near the bay-window. Then he asked me to stand by the door, and to drape my jacket over my face so as to thoroughly blind me to his activities. Though hesitant, I did as was told, and then waited for the three minutes that I counted aloud as instructed. On emancipating my eyesight, I saw another man unknown to me standing before the window. This French magician was tall, swarthy and finely dressed, but the man I now saw was shorter, with long grey hair, and clothed like a common beggar. I immediately asked him to reveal his identity and whence the Frenchman had been transported. He responded that he was that very man, and true to his word, his voice was the likeness of the Frenchman. I was fearful for my life, and considered taking flight without delay. The Frenchman smiled and walked past me and into the passage. On entering his room he requested that I wait outside. Not two minutes later he emerged from his room looking exactly the same as he had been before his transformation. I postulated that this trick surely, had been the work of the Devil, and he replied that neither the Devil nor God had conspired in the hoax."*

"It's fascinating stuff," interrupted Mr Hughes, "don't you agree, Amos?"

"Nonsense I say. Flimflam. Utter bunkum, George. I read Mr Wells' novel *The Time Machine* only this spring. Waste of my time. Now angels, however, Holy spirits, prophecies, witchcraft, wizardry, demons, and not forgetting of course spiritualism, dowsing, tarot…"

"Crystal ball reading."

"Precisely. And crystal ball reading – I naturally believe in all of that. Only blinkered numskulls wouldn't. Shifting in time and space? Does the author take us for fools?"

"It's probably a hoax, Amos."

"It's complete and utter nonsense – although if you weren't mistaken, that billycock man seems to have just vanished into thin air," said Mr Rooney as he placed the book back on the shelf. "Mind you, do you think the Reverend Nudd is a hoax?"

"You know, Amos, there was once a time when I genuinely believed that the Nuddites would watch the erasure of the Hittites and Canaanites and the Nonnuds and all the rest of them from the face of the Earth while the Nuddites established a new world order. You may be right about that. We may have been hoaxed. The Reverend Nudd fleeced us of the best proportion of our nest eggs before *he* vanished into thin air. I'd wager that he's also perpetrated numerous insurance swindles."

"Investment too, the rotter."

"I suspect, Amos, that Mrs Porter has some sinister involvement in all of this. At the very least she surely knows of Nudd's whereabouts. I heard a rumour that he is resident at Bedlam. I'm unconvinced, Amos. I smell a rat."

"It's nonsense, George. Why would he be there? You don't think he's hiding out in the Tower of London do you?" asked Mr Rooney. "Or might he have been murdered, poisoned to death. Just look around. Outside, I mean. Along with all the bookshops here in booksellers row and next door, of course, in Wych Street, you'll find a number of chemists of shady repute," he continued, and led Mr Hughes back outside the shop where they nodded their heads as Mr Rooney expounded his notion.

"Administering poison is the favoured way of disposing of somebody these days. It is all too easy to obtain the potions from these chemists, to administer them undetected, and for the cause of death to remain forever a mystery. I wouldn't mind disposing of the Reverend Nudd myself if he is still alive – if I could only find the swine. And *only* after we'd got our money back."

"I share your feelings, Amos. I say, another thought has struck me. Maybe, God forgive me my presumptiousness, he's a secret bastard son of Her Majesty the Queen?" suggested Mr Hughes.

"Nonsense. You're allowing your head to fly off with the fairies, George. Although Nudd could be a Russian anarchist."

"Or maybe one of President Kruger's spies sent over from the Transvaal."

"A sodomite and associate of Oscar Wilde? Mr Broad likewise?" wondered Mr Rooney, peering back through the shop's open doorway. Inside he saw Otto look up at the clock mounted on the wall, and then glance across at the door marked *Private.*

"Good thinking, Amos. I say, you don't think he might be Jack the Ripper, do you?" asked Mr Hughes. "That beast never has been identified."

Jack the Ripper remained firmly implanted in the consciousness of the nation. During the night he returned to stalk the subconscious of many heads that had nestled into their pillows hoping for sweet dreams. In Whitechapel, where the unmasked fiend had left his trail of carnage in the previous decade, the perils of seeking out subsistence on the fringes of society had not diminished. They had been present both well before and since the notorious slayings. Danger was often a footstep away, and as likely posed by a familiar face as by a visiting stranger. The slain body of Benjamin Barrow, alias Freddie Garbett or Paddy O'Halloran, was another recent case for the police to solve. Though they knew that witnesses had seen this lowlife leaving a public house in another man's company, few people offered the police more than the odd crumb of information, and few of the police investigating the murder felt particularly motivated to catch Barrow's killer. For many, however, the biggest threat was the harshness of existence that slowly demolished victims with the contents of bottles when not mugging them with disease. At the very moment the two senior gentlemen were speculating on both the identity and whereabouts of Mr Nudd, a body lay cooling in a garret room above a pawnbroker's shop in Whitechapel. Wexford Cathy had finally yielded to the inevitable a few hours earlier. Nobody else knew yet, and nor would they care. She had been murdered long before, whilst still a girl in Ireland, but it had taken all this time for her to finally expire.

19

Norton was sitting at his desk. He was leaning forward like a botanist studying a leaf. Through the monocle in his right eye he was reading a note he had just pulled out of an envelope addressed to *Dr Norton, Senior Physician, St Mary of Bethlem Hospital.* The note accompanied a round fruitcake just handed to him by a delivery boy. Norton admired the magnificent cake. It was a pity, he thought, that Dr Strange would not be able to enjoy even a solitary slice – irrespective of his recent conduct. Strange, who had been denied formal leave by the Physician Superintendent, had not been seen at the asylum for three days now. His lodgings, missing a bag, some clothes and personal grooming items, appeared deserted. Norton adjusted his monocle to read the note once more:

"*Dear Dr Norton,*

A peculiarly grateful and thoroughly cured lady wishes to express her sincere appreciation for all your indisputable assistance. It has been a while since I was discharged from your God blessed care, but the compulsion to thank you in a fitting manner has ultimately proved impossible to resist. I wish to remain anonymous, you understand, but would nevertheless like you to know that you are a wonderful man and first-rate physician with the patience of a saint.

Please accept this modest token of my appreciation. Please also share this cake with your brilliant young colleague, Dr Strange, who has also provided invaluable assistance in my complete recovery. My family and I cannot thank you enough.

Our sentiments may be a little premature but we wish you a merry Christmas and a happy new year. Thank you humbly."

Alas, it was too late to question the delivery boy. The whippersnapper had skipped off the second after Norton had tipped a halfpenny into his outstretched hand. In any case, the physician thought respectfully, the former patient desires anonymity. Something occurred to Norton and he raised an eyebrow. He reached across to inspect another item that had arrived the previous day. It was a furious letter of complaint written by Mrs Porter, and was the fifth and latest of a string of letters Mrs Porter had written to Norton in recent months. In two of these Mrs Porter had offered her *"not wishing to sound immodest, you understand, pre-eminently lauded singing and acting talents"* to the hospital's annual pantomime production, performed by members of staff and supplemented by members of their families. The third reminded Norton that she hadn't yet been invited to *"adorn"* the pantomime, and the fourth complained that she still hadn't been invited to a Bethlem ball. The latest letter was very different. The tirade accused Dr Norton of ruining her life by forcing the Reverend Nudd to forsake his sacred mission and instigating the collapse of the Nuddite Church.

"You have fraudulently manufactured a change in the Reverend's personality," she had written. *"Never in my wildest imagination would I have envisaged the ignorance of a NONNUD allow someone to stoop as monstrously low as you have. I wouldn't be in the least surprised if I discovered you to be a MENNECK. Yes, a MENNECK! Your claim to only have The Reverend's best interests at heart is nothing more than humbug! No doubt Mrs Emily Nudd has colluded with you in this. The Reverend once promised to employ a scullery maid to assist her. He need only take a closer look at his wife who, in addition to lying on her back for the purpose of bearing children, has little more herself to offer either man or household than the labours of a scullery maid. Any woman, you understand, can lie on her back to*

take a man's seed. Though this is a grotesque affront to all those unable to spawn that the likes of Mrs Emily Nudd are blessed with unbridled fertility. I don't know who is the greater villain. I don't know if it is that wretched woman or you. It takes, Dr Norton, all my sapping powers of restraint to phrase this so politely. For you have disrespected The Reverend's sacred mission, and reduced his dignity to ruins. In so doing, my divine purpose also has come crashing down like the walls of Jericho, whilst you, Dr Norton, blow loudest on the trumpets. You are no Joshua. You are the beast of sixes documented in the Book of Revelation."

These words cued Norton's memory yet again to a day earlier and his second Whitechapel visit. After searching fruitlessly for a glimpse of Dr Strange, he had been harassed by a soap-box preacher. Norton had been sifting his sore eyes through the East End's gassy intestines, stuffed with people and litter and hungry dogs and dumped boxes of rotting fish. Thank goodness for the aroma, if not the extra smoke, of roasting chestnuts, he had once told himself after a squint and another coughing fit. From the side of his eye he noticed a finger, and then a pair of eyes, pointing at him. Yes, at him, and not at the nearby shopkeeper wearing a long striped apron and leaning on a broom as Norton had initially assumed.

"Yes, you sir," shouted the little man wearing a jaded green suit and fawn high hat collapsing like a soufflé. "You have come to feast your filthy lust on the harlots of Sodom and Gomorrah. Think not that God hasn't been watching your every step. Think not that He hasn't been listening to your every disgusting thought. As surely as you strut around this cesspit of vice in your fine garments, with your superior airs and graces, and with your stiff phallus bursting the seams of your pants, I swear by God almighty that if I unclothed you I would find the sign of the beast upon your condemned flesh."

Norton had looked away, hoisted high an eyebrow, and walked on. The preacher jumped off his soap-box and pushed his way over to him.

"I'm talking to you. Don't think I don't know who you are, sir."

"I think you must be mistaken," responded Norton.

"I know that I am not. For it is writ in the Book of Revelation. You, sir, sit astride the whore of Babylon, and you fornicate with her. You fornicate, FORNICATE."

"I understand," said Norton, "that you have concerns. Believe me, I share some of them. But please allow me to continue unimpeded on my way."

"I am *not* one of the ten Kings sharing one hour's worth of dark Kingdom with you, sir. They are all politicians who sit in our Houses of Parliament. Just like you. Don't think I don't know. Don't think I don't know who you really are," shouted the preacher into Norton's ear.

"Actually I'm a physician."

"Aha! From the London Hospital up the road? Mr Ripper, surgeon of Satanology? Carrying a hidden collection of surgical knives to mutilate the vulnerable?"

"Certainly not. I'm a physician at the hospital of St Mary of Bethlem. I'm a busy man and I really must take leave of you."

"Aha! Bedlam! Then you will know of the great and good Dr Strange."

"As a matter of fact I do. Good grief! Have you seen him recently?" asked Norton.

"No, no no, no, no. You won't trick me. I've never had the pleasure of meeting him in any case. You won't trick me, dastardly sir."

"I'm not trying to trick anybody. My name is Norton and I am merely concerned about my colleague, Dr Strange, a bit of a habitué of these parts, who has gone missing."

"Aha! You don't fool me for one second, sir. You are only interested in getting your clawed hands on the diary of the false prophet Nutt for purposes diabolical. I know nothing of Nutt or his Nutty Church. You won't trick me. The real Dr Norton has an interest in this diary and, sinner though he may be, he has not lost sight of God. But you? I know who you are. Oh yes indeed. You are an imposter, you are *not* Dr Norton, and you *are* the beast."

With that accusation the preacher returned to his soap-box with a hop and Norton continued on his way. Above the general din he heard the preacher resume his self-appointed duties.

"False prophets, watch your steps, because the end is nigh. Cult leaders abandon your flocks for they worship you and your vanity, and not God and His son Jesus Christ. Eat not meat, drink not alcohol, and smoke not opium – for they all fill man and woman alike with lust and violence. For these are the paths to ruin. RUIN, I say. Look about you, you excrement of the world. You are the sisterhood of Satan and the brotherhood of Beelzebub. You are undone by your vices and you will be left behind to burn in hell of your own making when Christ returns. The beast is here, for I have just seen him. The final battle is nigh. Pour away your liquor and banish your lust, you filthy excrement on the face of God's Earth. Repent, nay drop to your knees and beg God's forgiveness – and you might be saved yet. The antichrist walks among you and tosses the whores shillings to satisfy his vile lust so they may purchase more liquor to poison their bodies and drown their souls. Beware the false prophet Nutt and his Nutty followers, and beware most of all the man who sometimes calls himself Dr Norton of Bedlam."

The man who *was* Dr Norton cursed Nudd for the first – and last – occasion.

"Blast stupid Percival Nudd and his good-for-nothing diary."

He visited a few pubs, rebuffed numerous solicitations from both hawkers and women, and made some inquiries. Norton felt relieved not to have caught sight of Nellie, or Mabel, or whatever other name she called herself. He was disappointed not have spotted his mysterious tall rescuer. Norton returned to St George's Fields none the wiser about Strange's whereabouts. He arrived back shocked and unable to make convincing sense of his encounter with the preacher.

In the physicians' room Norton had been telling himself that Strange must have at some time engaged in conversation with the preacher. He had used his charm to endear him to the man, and probably moaned about his senior colleague's reluctance to allow him a free rein to do as he wished. The preacher's recollections must have subsequently, and quite plausibly, become completely muddled. As muddled as The Book of Revelation itself. Norton blinked extravagantly. Yes, poor Mrs Porter had also become muddled and very irate with her frustrations. In view of the anonymous cake delivery, perhaps it would be prudent to review her correspondence and handwriting style, he told himself. Norton regained his focus on the letter and read on:

You have corrupted The Reverend's mind and at a stroke destroyed my social position. You have even persuaded The Reverend to deign to undertake some common household chores at your ghastly and most inhumane of establishments. It's an outrage. You are intent on destroying my status. Nor have you stopped there. You are even intent on crushing the beautiful, awe-inspiring and God-blessed blooming of my heart by driving away your magnificent, manifestly superior, and thoroughly brilliant colleague. It is abundantly clear that you have forbidden my darling Dr Strange to pursue his romantic attachment with me. Oh yes, Dr Norton, my late uncle Major Bertie Birchall would have known what to do with a man of your despicable ilk. A courageous, intrepid and thoroughly heroic man, uncle Bertie probably shot dead more exotic beasts around the globe than any other Englishman in the whole of this century. Likewise he probably slaughtered more savages during military campaigns and expeditions than any other good Christian either living or deceased. He would have thrown you into the jaws of a maned lion, most decently allowing it a final meal of your scrag-end flesh before shooting it. That, or he would have thrown you to the merciless savages like the horrible ones who frequent the shores of Lake Chad. He could, of course, have sent you running for your life through the forests where he would have hunted you down and felled you like a stupid gorilla with a single shot between the eyes from a hundred paces. But God Almighty, you understand, will be more than simply your judge." God, she assured Norton, in an act of retribution so grave that she dare not contemplate it, would apparently soon smite him down. And due to the actions of Dr Norton she would never now be privy to the *"Final Solution"*. Instead she would be *"eternally trapped in a Nonnud wasteland"*. Nor would she quite properly ever find it within her to forgive the hospital for not inviting her to one of the balls. Not even to a fancy dress ball. Mrs Porter had also mentioned that for now she would have to find some comfort at home by baking her *"country-wide famous cakes"*. Norton compared the writing of Mrs Porter's rambling letter with that of the anonymous note. After examining both he walked over to his spare cricket bat and, with his monocle still attached to his eye, played a couple of defensive pushes. Dr Norton replaced the bat against the wall and returned to his desk. He slipped the monocle into his waistcoat pocket and shook his head. What a stupid notion, he admonished himself. The physician leant forward to sniff the cake. As much as Dr Norton was as intrigued he was equally delighted. The sponge was stuffed full with a glut of nuts, peels, and glazed or dried fruits. The cake exuded fumes of spiced brandy blended with marmalade and rich molasses. Norton was feeling a little better now. If only Dr Strange, he thought, were here to see that he also was appreciated. This might have reassured him, perhaps smoothed away those bumps of doubt. For a while Dr Norton's thoughts remained with his headstrong young colleague. If and when he returned, Dr

Strange would at the very least be subjected to the inquisition of a disciplinary panel. Norton would discreetly, and without urgency, seek answers about the preacher's diatribe. Probably Strange had settled on visiting his mother in Leatherhead with her collection of perfumes, aromatic oils, and toilet waters. She wasn't connected to the telephone system but Norton could write to her. Alternatively Strange had perhaps headed to a seaside resort. There he could solicit the fortification of therapeutic sea air whilst pondering his future along a windswept beach. But Norton knew he couldn't dally on this speculation for long. With Strange absent his workload had doubled. He found a table-knife in a drawer and began cutting away a small slice of cake. He had decided to enjoy a quick nibble before returning to the professional matters of mid-morning. While still carefully prising away his slice, Norton was abruptly interrupted. Someone was knocking with urgent vigour on the door. Slightly startled, and before Norton had fully articulated his invitation for whomever to enter, the door flew open. The tall and suave gentleman with the darkest of eyes and hair, the waxed moustache, and tall hat clutched into the angle of his arm, burst into the room. This was the very same man, Norton instantly recognised, who had rescued him in Whitechapel. Without saying a word, the stranger merely nodded courteously to the physician and snatched the entire cake from the desktop.

"Excuse me," uttered an astonished Norton. "I was about to express my considerable gratitude and also my surprise at seeing you here. For unmistakably you are the man with the pistol who probably saved my life not long past."

The tall stranger totally disregarded Norton, and carried away the cake as quickly as he had arrived. Norton leapt up to follow, sending his chair flying backwards onto the floor.

"But what in the blazes do you think you you are doing? Excuse me!" he called out. He watched the stranger stride along the corridor towards the male wing and turn left. Norton managed to tail the intruder sufficiently well to rediscover him standing outside at the back of the building near the airing ground for convalescing patients. Positioned a few paces back from some rubbish bins, the cake-snatching intruder rose like a stone effigy of ancient might from the ground. Then he moved, turning towards Norton. Still mute, he beckoned Norton over. He pointed to the crumpled cake that lay in a deformed mess at the foot of a bin, and raised his hand to persuade Norton to wait. The physician, by now fascinated by events, chose to do as indicated. Norton had long strived to avoid judging people too quickly – and somewhere down the line he had learnt to avoid the rush for conclusions when initially confounded by an experience. In any case, Norton felt calmed rather than alarmed, both by the hypnotic qualities of the dark eyes, and also by the stranger's general demeanour of sophistication and authority that others had already noted. And in still silence the two men waited together for a minute or so until some noisy starlings disturbed the surreal calm by flying down to peck at the cake. Norton continued to watch the hungry birds gobbling at their unexpected bonanza. Some sparrows gathered nearby and a plucky flew dived in amongst the starlings to snatch a crumb or two. Then an odd thing happened. One by one some of the birds keeled over, and another dropped dead from the sky as it attempted to fly away. Norton knelt down and gently picked a waning sparrow. As he stood up the bird's little claws clung on to Norton's fingers, and its open beak seemed to be either gasping for breath or attempting to emit a peep of warning. Cradled in the doctor's hand, it was now motionless and he replaced it on the patch of accumulating massacre. This was halted by the intruder who strode in amongst the birds to wave them away. Norton raised an eyebrow, looked up at the intruder and connected with his eyes. The intruder stared back before his face adjusted into a modest, though warm, smile. Norton responded likewise, but was unable to restrain his curiosity any longer.

"I am enormously indebted to you, sir. Not for the first time. But would you do me at least the honour of revealing your identity?" he asked. The question was unanswered. "You are, isn't it the case, the gentleman who was also recently spotted leaving the physicians' room and then chased along the corridor by my younger colleague?" tried Norton, again without a verbal response.

The tall stranger nodded courteously, waved away a few curious birds, then briskly walked off. Dr Norton was left gripping his scalp whilst trying to identify something intelligible within the macabre little scene. In any case, Dr Norton knew, it was pointless pursuing a man who shackled his lips from releasing the slightest murmur.

20

Nine weeks after the mysterious cake incident, Dr Norton was cycling along the path towards the Bethlem portico. His trouser bottoms were clipped tight by the ankles under a rainproof cape. From afar this resembled a slackened wigwam on wheels, through which a neck, thrust above the apex, held a steady and illusory rounded head. The physician preferred to wear a bowler hat when cycling, and he usually exercised on his bicycle for a mile or two before the start of each working day. It was what he described as his "constitutional". Dr Norton hadn't noticed the man closely observing him, loitering behind a dense tangle of leafless shrubs some thirty yards away near the entrance to the hospital grounds. Had he done so, he would not have recognised the vagrant figure in tatty clothing bent uncomfortably onto a walking-stick. This disfigured wreck of a man, who Norton might have guessed to be an invalid war veteran reduced to a miserable existence on the road, soon hobbled away. A few hours later Dr Norton returned grim-faced to the physicians' room after visiting some patients in their rooms. His professional duties were still onerous, bereft of either Dr Strange or a replacement. A smile loosened his face when Norton found an attractive beige-haired woman of uncertain youthfulness waiting outside the door.

"Good day, madam. May I be of assistance?"

"Good day, monsieur. I am looking for a Docteur Norton," she replied with French in her accent and tremors in her eyes.

"Well, you have found him," Norton announced, and encouraged the woman into the room. After accepting the invitation to take a seat she preceded to narrate an extraordinary tale during which Norton, from a combined product of good manners and astonishment, listened without interrupting.

"Monsieur, I come to speak with you about a terrible *histoire*. I think a Docteur Maxwell was working here, non?"

"Maxwell?" queried the physician.

"He was I believe here until about two and a half month ago," the woman explained, and began describing the features of Dr Maxwell.

"That would be Dr Strange. Dr Kenelm Maxwell Strange," recognised Norton.

"Yes, he become very strange. First cut his hair very short, then..."

"Actually, his *name* is Strange. His surname. I have, as a matter of fact, learnt that he sometimes uses the name Dr Maxwell when elsewhere. Whitechapel, for example."

"Ah! *Ca c'est son nom de famille.* Maxwell-Strange. Alors, I think is terrible for him. This Docteur Maxwell-Strange, maybe he is dead, monsieur. I do not know for certain. I know him from his visits to Whitechapel, monsieur. He see me there sometime in the evenings. But this one time, ten weeks ago or maybe a little more, he come to me in a tavern and tell me he has a special job for me. Monsieur, normally I find some work in these taverns with the... with, with mens who needing some feminine company. *Vous comprenez ce que je veux dire?* You understanding? He tell me he want me accompanying him to France. He tell me he pay me good money for this, and he tell me he need someone with him who speak French like me, a French woman. He say he need me to interpret for him because he don't speak French so well. *Alors, bien sûr je peux traduire.* I say okay if he pay me some of this money in advance so I can pay for the care of my childrens while I in France. The oldest he is only fourteen. The docteur, he agree. So a few days after we travel to a place in France I do not know. This is really a *terrain sauvage*, south of la

Loire, and *littoral*. Flat and dangerous, this lonely terrain. Many tempests here, monsieur, and crude habitants with the ways and belief of the ancients. This is in the Marais Breton – Breton Marshes of the northern *Vendée*, monsieur – at a village I think condam-ned by God called la Chapelle-sur-le-Marais. We stay in the *auberge* of the village, separate rooms, Monsieur docteur, and the first breakfast at the *auberge* Docteur Max, Docteur Maxwell-Strange, he telled me what he want to know about this place. He say he want to find out about the visit of a man called Percival Nudd who was there fifteen year ago. He didn't tell me why. Ah. You know this man Nudd?" asked the woman, after Norton grimaced and wiped the side of his forehead.

"Yes, I do. But please continue."

"Next, Monsieur le *médecin* Maxwell-Strange he say he first want spend two days exploring the marshes alone. He hire a horse and depart in the morning and return the afternoon like this for two days. He always, always, always complaining about horses. He don't like them. Me? I stay in the *auberge*. And I like horses. For me it is much *ennui*. But when I take some little promenades in the village, I see that the people they are not so friendly. They either prefer to say nothing and look the other way, or they ask me why we passing the times in their village. I say I am not sure. I know they are not content. Madame *la patronne* of the *auberge*, she is old and very polite, but I see she always looking at us with big anxiety from the side of her eye. I can tell you, monsieur, before my residence in England I was born in France and I living there nineteen years. Mostly I was in Paris but I visited some other places also. But, monsieur, never, absolutely never did I feel this *inconfortable* anywheres or any places in France like this time. It was like very bad dream. On the fourth morning Docteur Maxwell-Strange he ask me to ask the peoples if they remember this man Percival Nudd from before. First I ask madame *la patronne*. She is not happy with this question. She don't answer this question and she counsel me not to ask other peoples this question. She say me that people who speak too much and ask too many questions, they sometimes lose their tongues. Sometimes, she say, they lose more than their tongues. They lose everything. I tell all this to the docteur, and he say he pay me so I must to ask other people. I ask five older habitants of the village, and they tell me nothing. Docteur Maxwell-Strange, he ask me to ask the *prêtre*. I find one in the church, is the chapel, and after I ask him he say nothing but he shake his head and make the sign of the cross. In the afternoon the docteur he ask me to ask the habitants if they know a man of the marais – a marsh man. I don't know what is this marsh man. I am very afeared because I know the peoples really don't like this question. When I ask madame *la patronne* she only counsel me that we must leave very *rapidement* and not to ask more questions. I tell monsieur the docteur this, and he laugh very much. Very much. This is like a very bad *cauchemar*. Bad dream. Then a man – he was coarse, younger man and I didn't like him – he tell me to tell Docteur Maxwell-Strange he must meet late afternoon in the dark in the marshes nearby if he want to know more about this marsh man. He say six o'clock. I tell all this to the docteur and I tell him I think he must not go there for this rendezvous. But he laugh again and then he go there. I wait and I wait but the *médecin* docteur he didn't return. I waited all night and he didn't come back. The next day I ask the habitants if they saw him and they always say nothing – except madame *la patronne* and one other habitant who say I must leave. But I think I must wait for the Docteur Maxwell-Strange. Then, after I waiting all day, an older man knock on the door of my *chambre* and tell me that the docteur he has returned to England and I must go also. I thank him but I do not believe this. I decide to wait more. Then later, in the middle of the night, someone else knock on my door. He is a very big man with dark hair and eyes, and a *magnifique* moustache I can see with the light of the candle. He is *sophistique* and surely not from this village, but I think he is also

French because although he is not speaking at all, I know he understand my words. He show me to speak very, very quietly, and he lead me out of the *auberge* with my bag and take me to a big horse. It is black outside, like this man's hair and eyes, and like his fine cloth, and then he put me on the back of his horse and we ride for many hours to a small town, I think it is called Machecoul. This tall man he never ever say one word but all the time I trust him. I didn't know why. At Machecoul there is waiting a horse carriage and the tall man put me inside. Then the tall man he bow his head to me, and the carriage driver transport me away to Nantes. The carriage driver he does speak to me *un peu* – only a little – and tell me he will get me back to England on a ship. He buy me a train *billet* for Dunkirk, and he give me a billet for the ship to Dover. I ask him who is this tall man but he only say it is *son maître*. His master. I ask him if he know about Docteur Maxwell-Strange but he say *non*. This is all can tell you, monsieur."

"Madame, I certainly appreciate you coming here to divulge all of this," Norton responded, trying to ignore, just for the time being, the description of the man who had rescued his intriguing, and admittedly beguiling, visitor. "You have surely done the admirable thing. And I am distressed to learn of your terrible experience in addition to the disappearance of Dr Strange. But, permit me to ask, why have you waited so long to inform me if you arrived back in England weeks ago?"

"Yes. At first I was afeared for about a week. Then I try to find where Docteur Maxwell-Strange he works. He didn't tell me it was here. He didn't tell me it was this type of hospital. I ask at many hospitals for Docteur Maxwell, but nobody they don't know him. I remember he once mentioned your name but I cannot find it in my head. Then, last Tuesday I remember your name because a crazy *pasteur* in Whitechapel he was crying out many things about the Devil. And he was crying out the name Docteur Norton just the moment I passed him by. He was warning peoples about a man who say he is Docteur Norton but who is the beast. But it was like he was talking about Norton just for me. He was *un fou* – madman – and next he was trying to tell the whole world not to read the diary of Nutt. Yes, like *noix* – perhaps a walnut. But perhaps this is not Nutt but is Nudd who interested Docteur Maxwell-Strange. I don't know. *Jai pas compris.* He say this Nutt diary is not Holy Grail. He say it is only a trick of Satan, and that to search for this is the road to ruin. I don't know what this means, but this madman he say your name, Norton. *Alors*, I ask again at some hospitals and suddenly a *médecin* from St Bartholomew Hospital tell me this morning he know a docteur Norton here at Bedlam. *Voilà.* I come quickly, monsieur. *Tout de suite.*"

"And you have neither heard nor seen nothing of Dr Strange since?" asked Norton.

"Not at all, monsieur. I am sorry."

"No. It's not for you to be sorry, madame. It is I who should be sorry. I realised that there had been a problem with Dr Strange: call it an obsession, if you like. I think I know why Dr Strange wanted to visit this place in the Breton Marshes. As a matter of fact I'm quite sure on this. I should have listened closer to my better judgement and intervened at an earlier stage. Had I done so then this doomed trip, for one, would never have happened. I put his behaviour, regrettably, down to the ambitions and impetuosity of youth. A certain arrogance. When Dr Strange went missing I assumed he was visiting his mother so I wrote to her. She replied that she hadn't seen or heard from him, and I couldn't shake off that feeling that he was recklessly up to no good. Unfortunately the attitude I had adopted was...."

"*Laissez-faire?*"

"Precisely. Forgive my manners. I have been most discourteous. I don't yet know your name, madame."

"Just call me Frenchie, monsieur."

"Forgive me for ask..."

"This, monsieur, is *veritablement* a difficult experience for me to come in this type of hospital. I don't feel so good about it."

"Please, Madame, rest assured that you have no reason to feel uncomfortable as a visitor to this hospital. It is quite safe, and the patients here – most of whom will recover fully – are to be understood or even pitied. They are not to be feared."

"No, monsieur. I do not fear them. Yes, I pity them like I had the pity for my mother when I cry for her when I visit her in the Paris hospital *Salpêtrière*. I had thirteen years old and this was the first I see her since I am a little girl."

"I'm so sorry," expressed Norton. "I obviously had no idea. Forgive me for being presumptious."

"*L'Hopital Salpêtrière* is also a hospital for the lunatics, monsieur. Mainly for *les folles*. The womens," said Frenchie. She stood up. "I think is time I go now, monsieur."

"Please wait, madame, unless you really must go. Please sit down again for a moment," Norton requested. His eyes communicated both kindness and concern, and he waited for the woman to lower herself back onto the chair with her knees and ankles together.

"Yes, I am indeed familiar with this hospital's reputation," the physician resumed. "A brilliant physician there a few years ago, a Monsieur Gilles de la Tourette, identified a nervous disorder causing baffling and debilitating social behavioural problems. An altogether brilliant man. The old gunpowder works – these days a most noble institution. So, your mother. Did she make a good recovery, madame?"

"Non. Unfortunately she had a terrible problem with an infection of *l'arsenic*." She was working in a factory many years with the manufacture of wallpapers and there was much *arsenic* put in this like with many wallpapers and it infect her badly. I didn't see her for eight, I think, years, and my older sister is like a mother to me in this time. Then my sister, and *aussi* my father, he had a big problem with the consumption, they finally tell me the truth and take me to see her just before she die. I tell her that I always loved her. But I think she didn't know I am her daughter."

"That's very sad. I'm so sorry. Maybe she *did* know who you were. I expect she died a lot happier having seen you. Having felt deeply comforted by your words. Perhaps she was simply unable to express this lucidly. But it's very sad. I've seen a wallpaper manufacturer in this country destroyed by arsenic. I've also witnessed several hat makers rendered insane by mercury poisoning from, er, the lead stiffening process, and before their internal organs and their nervous systems completely failed. The use of some of these metals and other toxic elements in industry is a treacherous business. It's about time, actually long overdue, that both wealthy factory owners and society as a whole took more care with these dangerous elements, and looked after the welfare of the workers who earn them their riches and take all the health risks. You have my deepest sympathy, madame. I strongly suspect, though you may have been unaware of this, that your visit provided immense comfort to your suffering mother. More than you could ever know."

"Thank you. Monsieur Norton. I hope so. You are a gentle man," responded Frenchie, and a tear spilling out of a moistened eye gathered pace and ran down her cheek."

"Forgive me for asking, Madame Frenchie, but just before you revealed the tragic circumstances of your mother, I was about to ask if you are still struggling to, er, earn a living at Whitechapel?"

"Yes, monsieur. Even the good days, if you *comprend* me, are bad."

"I empathise fully. And forgive my impertinence, for I am aware of the culinary expertise of the the French, but can you cook?"

"Yes, monsieur. Of course."

21

Only the solitary candle in the middle of the circular table now provided erratic glints of light in the room. Eight people sat around the table holding hands. A ninth, the medium, sat slightly back like the detached segment of an orange. With closed eyes she motioned with her hands as if trying to unwind invisible string out of her forehead. Amongst the shadowy circle, Mrs Porter, gripping hands with immediate neighbours, was breathing heavily. She desperately wanted to shatter the tense silence of the eerie room with a scream. Finally, to Mrs Porter's gasping relief, the medium's voice dramatically boomed into action.

"Meessiss Porter," she shouted with an indiscernible accent. "I haff one departed from our vorld who eess attemptink communication. I am tryink to get a name. I haff a letter *F*. Frederick, perhaps? Duss theess name mean anythink to you, Meessiss Porter, or to anybordy here? No? Vait. Maybe Francis, or Frances. Maybe Francesca. Duss anybordy know theess name of a dear departed one? Vait. Pleasse vait. Eet eess clear now. Eet eess a letter *E*. Does anybordy know Edith? No? Vait. Vot about Elsie, Emma, Edna, Eliza, Eleezabeth, Esther, Eve, Ella."

"Yes!" cried a man with a luminous beard. "My late mother once had a friend called Beth – although I don't think she had seen her for over a decade by the time my mother passed on to the other side. She went to live with her son's family in Suffolk."

"Vait a moment. I can hear more clearly now," continued the medium. "A voman called Beth eess speakink to me. She eess vith herr frient now, and she eess so happee to be vith herrr in the speerit vorld because she hadn't seen her for more than ten years in the material vorld ven her frient passed on. The frient of Beth is called, is called..."

"My mother's name was Agnes," stated the bearded man.

"Shusssh! Vait. Her name eess, eess, it eess comink, eet eess Agnes. Ah yes. Beth eess sayink that Agnes horself eess not ready to communicate now, but she vonts her son to know that, that... no! Vot a peetee. Beth hass now gone. But Beth said that Agnes vill be ready to communicate soon. She has messages for herrr son. Maybe next veek. Maybe the veek after – or the veek after that."

"How wonderful!" exclaimed the bearded man. "Verily this is superb news. Mother, if you can hear me, I shall be right here. Mother, I shall be awaiting you. Mother."

"Shusssh! Vait. I *must* haff silence. I must return to my trance. I ham now receivink visions of the futurrrr. No vait. Vait, vait. Theess are fadink. Zay haff gone! Ough! My head eess speenink. Please excusee. Excusee. I must take somm varterrr. Pleasse stay in your seats. No vun moof," she ordered. The medium stood up, snatched the candle and staggered out of the room into a well-lit corridor. She slammed shut the door behind her on which a poster-sized notice was affixed. It read:

NOTICE

Please read before entering.

Madame SOPHIE VLATINSKY does NOT CHARGE A FEE for her exceptional and unique services.

These services render her EXHAUSTED and EMOTIONALLY DISTRESSED.

The RENTAL of her exclusive SALON is NOT INEXPENSIVE.

A DONATION of NOT LESS THAN HALF A CROWN is respectfully anticipated from each sitter at each sitting. Please make your donation BEFORE the sitting COMMENCES. Donations are not refundable at the conclusion of a sitting.

THANK YOU

Madame Vlatinsky hurried along the corridor wrapped in a thick black coat. Generously, one might describe her as middle-aged. She was dumpy with grey hair tied behind in a bun. Contrasted against her chalk-dusted face, her puffy eyes, plummeting beneath pencil-drawn eyebrows, were plastered with so much makeup that she wore the quizzical expression of a mannequin with features painted on by a child. She opened a door and entered a kitchen. Mr Broad was sitting there. He was wearing his billycock as ever but was without the Nuddite locket and chain that were now the property of bookseller Otto. He had been picking his nose and thumbing through his copy of *GLUTTON FOR PUNISHMENT AGAIN – MR HORACE DIMPLE BEGS FOR MERCY,* when, upon hearing footsteps approaching along the creaking floor, had inserted his booklet inside his waistcoat.

"So, Mr Broad, tell me again," instructed the medium, "What was Mrs Porter's late husband's Christian name?"

"It was *Gordon* Porter."

"Gordon. Right you are. Will you wipe your nose for Gawd's sake. That 'orrible mess ain't greengage jam. And remind me about that Nudd fellow's chapel. Whotsit for?"

"It transmits protective energy from God to a chosen individual after we have put the energy into it with our prayers. Pardon me about my nose."

"Right you are, cock. Protective energy, you say. Gibberish, innit? And it's Gordon. That Porter woman will be as good as all yours by the time this seance is done."

"Lufflee. Lufflee."

"Oh! Nearly forgot summit. The dog. And the breed she's wanting is a Pug or Peckingese, yes?" checked the medium, and Mr Broad nodded, grabbing his billycock before it slipped off his head.

"Best get back in there now and get on with the show – and you don't forget to stay put exactly where you are until I says you can leave. Or there'll be hell to pay. I *do* have powers, you know, and I'll set some abominable spirits onto you unless you know what's good for you."

Back inside the rented drawing room, the candle replaced on the table, Madame Vlatinsky resumed the seance.

"Meessiss Porter. I am seeink the futurrrr. The speerits are communicatink vith me. Eet eess gettink *very* cold. I said eet eess gettink cold in theess room. COLD IN THEESS ROOM," Madame Vlatinsky repeated loudly, and a little man – all the while hidden behind fractionally parted velvet curtains – quietly opened a window. The chilly air surged into the room, and the candle-flame danced maniacally from its wick. Mrs Porter juddered, and clasped her neighbours' hands even tighter.

"Isn't it marvellous?" she whispered.

Unbeknown to Madame Vlatinsky the landlord of the property had just opened the front door to three men. But she did hear some faint voices towards the kitchen area and, irritated by the disturbance, emitted a sigh before drawing a deep breath and thundering back into action.

"Meessiss Porter, I can see you vith a vunderful man. He eess not the likeness of Adoneess – but hee eess a vunderful and remarkable man. He vares a beellycock hat and, vait a moment, hee eess called Jonah, Jonah, vait, Jonah Brode. No *vait*," she screamed. "Hees name eess comink to me now. It eess Joshua Brode. *No.* Eet eess Joshua *Broad*. I can see eet all now. Only vith theess magneeficent man can you find true happeeness. Yes, vith Sir Joshua Broad. I can see heem being kernighted by the Queen Victoria. I can see you so haappy vith theess magneeficent man, Meessiss Porter. I haff seen theess man in a vision vith you. Do you know a man of theess name?"

"Oh! I, er, do," replied Mrs Porter hesitantly. "Oh! I really don't know what to say. Words elude me. This would not amount to the bliss I had been anticipating, you understand. Isn't there a Holy man re-established on his sacred mission, or perhaps better still a young physician called Dr Strange anywhere? You see..."

"*Shussh*! Meessiss Porter. I am connectink again vith the other side," said Madame Vlatinsky. She dipped her face, covered by her left hand from just beneath her closed eyes, so that her forehead touched the table rim. With her right hand she slid open a little drawer under the table and careful removed a ten inch stretch of cotton wool, inserting one end up her hidden nose. She began breathing with audible speed before raising her head back up to reveal, in the eerie light, an apparently unspecified blur of white issuing out of a nasal cavity. There were gasps of astonishment from around the table. A young woman shouted,

"Ectoplasm. Just look. It's ectoplasm."

"Isn't it marvelous?" remarked Mrs Porter.

"Yes, yes," cried Madame Vlatinsky. "You are overpowerink me. You vill haf your say. Retreat," she added, and then dropped her head to the table again, obscuring her nose and free hand that expertly whisked the cotton wool away and back inside the drawer. She sat up still breathing heavily.

"Meessiss Porter, I am receivink a message from the speerit vorld. He arrifed in the ectoplasm. He must haff somzink very important to say. Vait a moment. Vait. Meessiss Porter. He is tellink me heess name. Do you know somebordy vith the name, vait... Eet eess comink to me. Heess name eess Gordon. I can peecture heem now. He eess much older than you. He hass sadness in heess eyes. Eess theess Gordon your deceased father?"

"Oh! Glory be! Actually Gordon was my dear, dear, dear departed husband."

"Meessiss Porter. He eess sayink he forgeeves you. He eess saying he alvays lurves you. Do you understand theess? What theess meanss?"

"My poor Gordon. Yes. Yes, I understand this. Thank you so much, Gordon. Thank you so very much with all my heart."

"Meessiss Porter, Gordon eess sayink to me that all the protectiff energy from the, from the chapel – I don't know vot theess chapel energy eess all about – he eess sayink eet eess vith you and Meester Sir Joshua Broad. He eess sayink that a man called Nutt, maybe Nod, eess feeneeshed, and he is tellink me that he vill be haappy een the eternal speerit vorld if you becump Meessiss Lady Broad. He knows you are vontink a little doggee – he eess tellink me theess eess a Pug or a Peckingnese – for zee company arount the housse. Gordon eesss sayink you need company from the man vith the beellycock, not a little doggee. He gives you heess blessink."

"Oh! Gordon! I am overcome with emotion – and confusion. I'm feeling awfully flustered, you understand. Appallingly. But marry Mr Broad? Are you absolutely sure about that?"

"Vait. Vait a moment pleasse. Gordon eess sayink he eess sure about theess, but he eess fadink. I am loosink heem. He eess fadink," wailed Madame Vlatinsky, and before she could continue the door opened and two policemen marched in. The first, a constable wrapped in his long coat, replaced his helmet to light his Bull's Eye lantern.

"Let's have some illumination, and nobody move," instructed the second officer dressed out of uniform and with a scarf around his neck. "My name is Detective Constable Coates and we are looking for a Mrs Harriet Porter whom we have reason to believe is attending this choice little soirée."

Madame Vlatinsky switched on an electric light and Mrs Porter stood up in the dreary room. She was sheathed to her ankles in a tight garment of pink cotton, and had discarded the bustle during late autumn. Her upper body was better insulated by a brown fur coat, and she needed this because snow was falling outside in the borough of Islington.

"I am Mrs Porter. Mrs Harriet Lavinia Porter," she announced.

The other sitters of the serrated circle, having now released their hands, were represented by five women of diverse maturity, plus another elderly gentleman in addition to the son of Agnes who sported a long white straggly beard. All of their eyes were staring at Mrs Porter who hoisted her bust and asked,

"What, gentlemen, do you want with me?"

"We'd like you to accompany us to the police station," replied Detective Constable Coates, "to answer some questions in respect of a fruit cake recently sent to a physician, by the name of Norton, at the Bethlem Hospital in Lambeth."

"But what exactly has this got do with me?"

"For your sake, Mrs Porter, let's hope it will be nothing at all."

"Oh dear. But how did you know you would find me *here*?"

"We too have connections with the spirit world," said Coates. "No. In all seriousness, it's called straightforward detective work, madam. It's what we do. We first went to an address you are known to frequent in Pimlico. The lady of the house gave us your home address at Fulham. Your next-door neighbour said you had mentioned something about visiting Madame Vlatinsky. We are familiar with these premises."

"I must protest that I have done absolutely nothing wrong. This is an outrage. Why can't you people do something useful like arrest Thomas Huxley for blasphemy? Why don't you arrest Dr Norton of Bethlem for skulduggery? For the false confinement and brainwashing of a divine leader? Why haven't you apprehended Dr Norton yet for burglary? Oh! A thought has occurred. Has Dr Strange returned to his duties at the hospital? If some female imposter is trying to impress Dr Strange with the gift of a cake she claims has been baked by..."

"Please come along, madam. We have already found your companion, Mr Broad, skulking in the kitchen of this property."

"What? Mr Joshua Broad? J Kenyon Broad? *Here*?"

"That is correct, madam. As I was about to say, your particularly splendid beau was apprehended attempting unsuccessfully to climb out of a window. Not a difficult task since Mr Broad got himself stuck in the window-frame. A third officer is holding him in the kitchen – along with an obscene publication he was lawfully obliged to confiscate – right now as we speak. Mr Broad *is* known to us for a variety of reasons. His eccentricity has previously been noted, and we are aware, Mrs Porter, of your association with each other. We shall be bringing him in to question him separately about the cake – and, quite probably, other matters too. Please come with us, Mrs Porter, and it would be advisable to do so with the minimum of fuss."

22

"Thomas! Thomas!" shouted a trim lady of demure elegance and with softly greying hair. "Thomas!" Mrs Norton shouted, as she approached her husband who was playing the piano on this Sunday evening at his Clapham house. Norton stopped and looked towards his petite wife.

"Thomas, there's a gentleman at the door. I'm afraid I haven't invited him in yet, though I'm reluctant to leave him standing there with it being so miserable outside. I don't know who he is, but he's asking for you and he claims he's Dr *Strange*. Young Kenelm."

"Goodness me!" said Norton, leaping to his feet. "We'd better invite him in. He *says* he's Dr Strange! Doesn't he resemble Dr Strange?"

"I can't really decide. It's possible – but this man better resembles a disfigured vagrant. The unfortunate is in a truly wretched condition."

"Good Lord!" exclaimed Norton as he rushed past his wife. In the doorway stood a gaunt man leaning on a crude walking-stick. Oversized filthy and tattered garments were hanging from him. His face looked as though it had recently been battered out of shape with an arsenal of clubs. The nose, flattened excepting odd bumps, had evidently been smashed. An eyebrow ridge was dented, the eyes bloodshot, and where the face wasn't overgrown with ungroomed whiskers, cracking skin was crisscrossed with scars. He presented himself without a hat that would have partially tamed the matted hair curling in all manner of directions. The sprouting unwashed locks, clogged with grease and filth, relinquished the occasional fair-hued strands to flicker in the breeze.

"It's me. Kenelm. Dr Strange," mumbled a vaguely familiar mouth that was now missing several teeth. "I am unable to speak easily since my jaw was fractured. Can't you recognise me?"

After a pause the man continued.

"Dr Norton. I seek sanctuary. I seek assistance. Help me, my dear fellow, I beseech you."

Norton pushed his monocle to his eye and and scrutinised his visitor. He recognised some features of the face and the voice, and he recognised what remained of a once splendid frock coat.

"Good grief," muttered Norton, his wife looking on behind him. "You'd better come in, man. Come in. We'll see what we can do for you. For a start I'm sure my wife can heat up some nourishing broth. We are fortunate to have a bathroom with piped water here. So perhaps first we can heat up some water so you can wash and relax in the bath-tub," said Norton. Even the sickly aromas of early blossoms decorating the Common were unable to placate the vile odours that now emanated from Strange – odours indistinguishable from those that had previously so repulsed him in the company of the man he had called Mr Garbett.

"I'll find you a change of clothing. Come on inside," said Norton without a second thought.

After Strange had bathed, he dined on mutton broth mopped up with buttered bread. Offered a comfortable chair in the drawing room near the hot hearth, he hobbled across with his stick – a splintering wooden shaft once neatly cut at a timber yard. Wearing some of his taller host's clothing, the trousers turned up at the bottom, he settled himself down more confortably. Norton poured him a glass of whiskey.

"You can tell me all in good time," said Norton, shoving a fresh log into the dancing, spitting flames. "When you feel ready, then you can tell me what's happened to you in these past three and a half months. I do, however, know that you went to la Chapelle-sur-le-Marais in France. It's a huge relief to discover that you are not dead, as I had most gravely feared."

"And no doubt it will have a come as a big surprise to my assailants." mumbled Strange, struggling with pain to sustain a flow of words. "Being bludgeoned to pulp... and left for dead at the bottom of a canal... in the middle of a cold night... in the middle of nowhere, it doesn't do a lot for one's appearance – or for one's tailoring."

"As I bear witness. But all in good time. First, Dr Strange, we need to see that you recover some strength and weight. I also suggest that you have a thorough medical examination. You don't need to have any immediate concerns over lodgings. If it is agreable to you, Mrs Norton can prepare a spare room for your requirements. Actually, she's doing so at this very moment. Have no concerns about that whatsoever, Dr Strange. Have you contacted your mother?"

"I'll write to her shortly. Dr Norton, tell me – and may I at this juncture... express my sincere gratitude to yourself... and Mrs Norton for your immense hospitality – but just exactly, how on earth... did you know that I had gone to that infernal place in the Breton Marshes?" asked Strange with words so muffled that they sounded as though they had been assembled in his throat rather than in his mouth. "And what a place. Thought I'd ventured into a lonely huddle of dumb sheep. More like an angry hornets' nest. Place needs to be torched." he added, staring into the fire. "How did you know?"

Norton dragged his chair closer.

"Your translator companion, the lady who calls herself Frenchie, she managed to find me in order to explain your absence."

"That, I can assure you, is no lady. The blabbing ha'penny whore."

"I think you are far too hard on her. She sought me, and not without difficulty nor considerable expenditure of her time, to relate what had happened. With genuine concern. It seems to me that your perceptions of this woman are quite inadequate. There is evidently more to her than you are aware."

"With all respect I think I know this common woman... from the slums of Bethnal Green, better than you do, I am embarrassed to admit... my dear fellow," Strange articulated. "I expect that as we speak she is earning a crust in some dingy back-alley with... with her dress hitched up and her legs apart. Excellent whiskey."

"You presume incorrectly, Dr Strange. Right now, if my timepiece is accurate, she will be returning home not too far from Bethlem Hospital having spent the best part of the day preparing meals for the patients there. Yes, we employ Madame Frenchie in the Bethlem kitchens."

"I surmise with horror that you are not joking."

"Indeed not. By Jove! Madame Frenchie is a most diligent, competent and appreciated member of our housekeeping staff."

"Well prepare yourselves for a plague of headlice. And since you know... you know something about my... little expedition to France, what of the great and holy Reverend Nudd?"

"Now here's a quandary. During your lengthy absence, I regret to inform you that you ceased being a student of the hospital. As a matter of fact you were only replaced by another student less than a month ago at the end of February. And by the way, I've so far decided to disclose nothing of your trip abroad to the Physician Superintendant. Frenchie is also unwaveringly discreet. Anyway, as a consequence, I am not therefore, as you will be aware, at liberty to breach patient confidentiality. On reflection, however, and considering your previous professional interest, I am prepared to bend the rules. Mr Nudd is still with us. He is rallying, but has found it difficult coping with the transformation from *reverend* to plain *mister*. We do, with well-founded optimism, anticipate his transfer in coming weeks to our convalescent residence at Witley. His wife has finally now visited him a few times, and we have all been greatly heartened recently by his steady progress. And it's not before time – not least since he has yielded to his wife's desires and agreed to authorise Mrs Nudd to put their house up for sale. I believe they will be looking to move out of London to a quieter location."

"Fascinating. That unremarkable lunatic has, one way or another, been responsible for drastically altering the destiny of a number of lives," remarked Strange. He winced and caressed his mandible before continuing. "Does that ridiculous Mrs Porter, and that grubby imbecile... I forget his name..."

"Mr Broad."

"The very man. Do they still frequent the hospital to support their Messiah?"

"Goodness me. Well things have moved on apace since I last saw you. Mr Broad, I can reveal to you, now frequents the hospital more than ever. Although Mr Nudd does his best to avoid him. Yes. The unfortunate Mr Broad is now one of our patients, occupying a bed on the ward upstairs from Mr Nudd on Gallery III."

"So he's now *officially* a lunatic. The feebleminded Mr Broad has at long last been certified. Ha, ha, ha, ha, ha, ha, ha! This is the first time, my dear fellow, I have laughed for a very long time. Ha, ha, ha, ha, ha! I shouldn't laugh. It hurts."

"No. Perhaps you shouldn't laugh."

"I always thought," mumbled Strange, "that Mr Broad was one of those types... with the fortunate – and utterly undeserving – knack of surviving without... without ever doing a stroke of anything useful to earn it."

After slowly excercising his jaw Strange continued. "I pictured him as a static parasite that had once... been fortunate to attach itself to a host animal of good health and lifespan. A slug, alternatively, that had stuck against the side of an animal's paw... and been brushed off into a vast cabbage patch. And it would not be unjust to add that this is a slug... coated with an infestation of mites teeming all over it. Anything interesting?" asked Strange, emitting a groan as he pointed with his stick towards a thin publication spilling just over the edge of the mantelpiece.

"The *Quarterly Journal of Inebriety*. Lastest edition."

"I'll have another whiskey if I may," Strange requested, following a pause, and with a restricted nod at the bottle. "A large one. It eases the pain, dear fellow."

"Umm. To continue, a little less than respectfully, with your metaphor," said Norton, pouring an extra measure into Strange's glass, "picture instead a slug that has worked its way onto the floating weeds of a pond. Slowly and haphazardly it eats its way towards the centre. There it becomes isolated, and starts eating its way through its leafy raft, until there is little left and the slug plummets to the bottom of the pond. This, I fear, is a better representation of the truth," Norton suggested.

"Thomas!" intervened Mrs Norton who was returning to the room. "What a grotesque picture you've just painted. As you admitted, quite disrespectful."

"Perhaps overly," nodded Norton.

"My dear lady," Strange addressed Mrs Norton, "your human decency and compassion are admirable – but you have not met this slug-man chimera. I have always detested slugs. At school I once found a slug in my lettuce during supper. When another boy wasn't looking I wiped... the vile creature off my knife onto his plate. Alas... the housemaster happened to be watching. I received six strokes of the cane. I ensured I was never caned again. I've detested slugs all the more ever since."

Norton smiled awkwardly at his wife and returned to Strange.

"And I was about to say that Mrs Porter has not, to my knowledge, visited the hospital for some time. It would appear that both Mr Nudd and Mr Broad have been expunged from her social circle despite being, until recently, the two principle components. Mrs Porter's relationship with both of them now seems, for different reasons, to be irreparably consigned to history. In any case the poor woman has not been without her own acute problems."

"No? Pray tell me more."

"She's been involved in a spot of bother. Something of a scandal. A trifle, actually," said Norton.

"The room for Kenelm is ready," Mrs Norton said to her husband, and smiled at Strange.

"Thank you so much, dear lady," Strange responded before turning his attention back to Norton.

"So tell me about this scandal involving Mrs Porter. I cannot contain my curiosity any longer."

"There wasn't much to it really. You know how these things are given the hyperbolic treatment to turn a mundane affair into a sensation. She was merely a prosecution witness at The Old Bailey."

"Come now, Thomas," said Mrs Norton. "It's been in all the newspapers. Kenelm is bound to hear about it sooner or later. He might as well learn about it now if he so wishes."

The physician's wife walked over to a cabinet and searched through some drawers before pulling out a publication.

"It's all here," she said. "I bought this penny pamphlet because Mrs Porter's name had already cropped up in our household over another issue. She had written my husband a rather angry letter, but that's not important now. Have a read of this," she offered, and handed a copy of *The Illustrated Police Budget* to Dr Strange. The headline amused him:

THE TWIST IN THE CAPTAIN DIXIE TRIAL – SENSATION AS SCANDALOUS KEY WITNESS MRS HARRIET PORTER IS EXPOSED.

Captain Dixie Walks Free whilst Mrs Porter's Reputation is Destroyed.

"Ha, ha, ha, ha, ha, ha, ha!" Strange erupted through his aching jaws. "While I was battered... to the precipice of oblivion, guess what survived... without a scratch inside my jacket?" asked Strange, grimacing as he pulled out his spectacles like a lead weight from a pocket, and heaved them in staccato jerks up to his nose-perch and over the ears. He gingerly massaged his cheeks, pulled the tract closer to his wide stinging eyes, and read on:

The rape trial of Captain Lambert Dixie took a dramatic twist on Wednesday, allowing the accused to walk free, and turning much of the attention onto prosecution witness Mrs Harriet Porter. Captain Dixie had originally been arraigned on a charge of raping Miss Caroline Rudge, a chambermaid aged seventeen years, during a train journey from Brighton to London on the fourth of October last year. The charge was amended to one of sexual assault on the orders of the Judge who stated that it was impossible to rape a woman who resisted. Captain Dixie had already denied the amended charge, claiming that he had only foolishly kissed Miss Rudge in an intimate clinch after she had vigorously encouraged him to do so.

Shameful Accusations

The dramatic twist unfolded with Mrs Porter on the stand, although initially Captain Dixie's prospects seemed bleak as Mrs Porter presented herself as a plausible and damning witness. As a key prosecution witness she had testified on oath that Captain Dixie had earlier tried to "impose himself upon (her) in a lewd and aggressive manner" during the journey. After resisting his "coarse advances", she claimed that Captain Dixie had stormed out of the carriage, returning some half an hour later with the claim that he had found "a younger and more wholesome piece of flesh upon which to satisfy (his) lust". When asked by the prosecution counsel, Mr Simon Craggs, whether she had responded to this comment, Mrs Porter said that she had asked Captain Dixie if the young woman had acquiesced. According to Mrs Porter, Captain Dixie replied that "she was a common harlot who kicked and spat at (him) while he forced (himself) upon her. But she'd had it coming to her, and should have been grateful that she had lost her virginity to such a handsome man of good breeding". Mrs Porter added that Captain Dixie, "spurned yet consumed with lust after spending time alone with (her)", was in her opinion unable to restrain his passion any longer. She commented that she had witnessed Miss Rudge alighting from the train in London whereupon the chambermaid sought a policeman to arrest her alleged assailant. Mrs Porter described Miss Rudge as "possessing the limited though possibly challenging feminity of youthfulness without wrinkles, rust or anything very much – but otherwise, as the discerning eye can see, quite unremarkable in appearance".

The Trial, and Mrs Porter, Collapse

However the course of the trial was turned on its head when the defence counsel, Lord Crockingford, questioned Mrs Porter. In doing so the real Mrs Porter was to unravel before the shocked assembly. The verbatim transcript of this sensational sequence is as follows:

Lord C: Mrs Porter, you have averred that when Captain Dixie returned to your carriage, he was now frequently rubbing his shins as well as suffering from a swollen lip with blood trickling from it.

Mrs P: That is totally correct, your Lordship. He was manifestly in pain after the victim of his filthy advances had tried to kick him off her person. She had kicked him in the shins, you see.

Lord C: So as, to use your words, the prosecution's star witness, did you actually see this alleged assault?

Mrs P: Oh no, your Lordship. You see I was alone in my train compartment the entire time but it is obvious what had taken place, you understand.

Lord C: As a matter of fact, Mrs Porter, what you are claiming isn't obvious to me at all. As you know, Captain Dixie states that his thick lip was incurred after you had hit him with your bag for spurning your advances. He states that he fled from the train back in London to escape from you, that his shins only became bruised in the regrettable scuffle that led to him being restrained by a police officer, and that he knew nothing until that moment of the allegations made by Miss Rudge who, some believe, is nothing more than an opportunist seeking easy pecuniary gain from Captain Dixie. Are you stating, Mrs Porter, that you did not hit Captain Dixie in the train compartment?

Mrs P: I should jolly well have liked to hit him when he tried to force himself lewdly upon me. But I certainly did not. Like many men, you understand, he was overwhelmingly attracted to me and no doubt preoccupied with my luxurious bosoms. I could offer you a list as long as the road to York of men who have instantly fallen under my spell – including a breathtakingly brilliant young physician who tests electric quacking devices. But the fatal allure of a respectable lady such as myself neither represents a reciprocal feeling towards every admirer, and nor does it excuse that ghastly man's behaviour. I shall prove to the court, your Lordship, that Captain Dixie is but a filthy and brutal rogue who has done nothing other than lie about this whole sordid affair. As The Reverend Nudd once taught us, beware the toad dressed as a man – for beneath its finest military garments shall be found warty and poisonous skin. I wouldn't be surprised either if Captain Dixie's a Meneck like Thomas Henry Huxley who should be hanging from the gallows. I shall show you all. Just you wait and see. After devoting my life of late to God's special Nuddite mission, He has empowered me, you understand. And don't forget that I am the prosection's star witness. I shall show you all.

Lord C: No doubt the court will look forward to that with great anticipation – though not to the exposure of any warty and poisonous skin. Mrs Porter, as we all know, the worth of a witness in a court of

*law is dependent on that person's sanity. Would you consider yourself
sound of mind?*

*(At this point Mrs Porter insisted that she visit the ladies' WC to
powder her nose. At length this was granted and a brief adjournment
ensued. A court usher, who escorted her, later revealed to our
reporter that Mrs Porter must have needed to find urgent relief from
flatulence caused by the excitement of the proceedings. So loud were
tell-tale vulgar noises from the other side of the door that he was not
without sympathy.)*

*Lord C: Now that you have powdered your nose, I'll ask you
again, Mrs Porter: do you consider yourself to be of sound mind?*

*Mrs P: Without question, your Lordship. My intellect and
reasoning are much sought by those needing wisdom and counsel.*

*Lord C: Really? Yet you wish to see Thomas Huxley swing from a
noose. I fail to see the point, never mind the unprecedented practical
difficulties, of hanging somebody at the gallows who has already
departed this world nearly five years since (the courtroom erupts into
fits of laughter before Lord Crockingford continues).*

*Lord C: On that particular subject, the words "give enough
rope" and "hang oneself" readily keep returning to mind (there is
more laughter in the courtroom). Mrs Porter, as one of the privileged
few empowered by God, and who insists on being feted as the star
witness, you have made clear to the court your assertion that Captain
Dixie is a liar. However, would you say, Mrs Porter, that you are a
woman of utter integrity – this also being important to the worth of
your testimony?*

*Mrs P: Oh yes. My reputation of integrity spreads far and wide,
your Lordship. It is simply not a matter open to the merest hint of
dispute.*

*Lord C: So you are saying that your account of what took place,
Captain Dixie's alleged attempted assault on you, and additionally the*

discourse that took place between the two of you after he returned to your carriage, is completely honest?

Mrs P: Completely, your Lordship. Have no doubts at all.

Lord C: And did you not earlier state that you had travelled down to Brighton to walk along the promenade and enjoy the sea air?

Mrs P: That is correct, your Lordship. The sea air does wonders for the complexion of a lady like myself, you understand, who needs to remain at the very zenith of her prime to please a host of admirers. I am referring to proper gentlemen, of course. It will come as no surprise to you, though I naturally hesitate at admitting it myself, that I received a hundred and one covetous glances as I paraded along the seafront. Most particularly when I inhaled deep breaths of the sea air causing the enhanced prominence of my bosoms.

Lord C: And was this the sole purpose of your trip to Brighton? To take a stroll along the seafront – irrespective of displaying yourself to court covetous glances, Mrs Porter? Although wearing boots with five- to six-inch heels, as testified by several other witnesses on the trains and at the stations, and not usually a sound choice of footwear for lengthy perambulation, might explain a desire to attract all those covetous glances. So let me ask you again. Was a walk along the seafront on your six-inch heels the sole purpose of your trip to Brighton, Mrs Porter?

Mrs P: Absolutely and exclusively, your Lordship. After strolling near the beach for an hour or so I used my return ticket to travel home.

Lord C: If you used your return ticket as you claim, why did you travel outbound third class, and inbound first class? I might be wrong but I wasn't aware it was possible to purchase such a ticket. Did you defraud the railway company on your return journey?

Mrs P: Oh! Of course! Silly me! I discarded my return ticket and purchased a new first class ticket.

Lord C: This sounds to me like a rather extravagant whim. Or could it mean that you were, just prior to embarking upon your return journey, suddenly feeling wealthier than prior to your outward journey?

Mrs P: Oh! I suppose it does rather. I am not without means, your Lordship, and it is a woman's prerogative to change her mind, you understand, even about matters such as the class of one's train carriage. Perhaps, your Lordship, you are in need of getting to know the fairer sex rather better in order that you better understand us.

Lord C: I thank you for your advice, Mrs Porter, but as I intend to reveal, I believe I understand you well enough. I'd like to ask you about the events that you claim occurred before Captain Dixie's temporary absence from your first class carriage. You have stated that Captain Dixie attempted to impose himself upon you in a lewd and aggressive manner. Is it not the case that you spent most of this period outrageously flirting with Captain Dixie, and that having done his best to rebuff your advances politely, he felt the need to take a walk to escape your unrelenting advances?

Mrs P: Certainly not. This is an outrageous, a totally scurrilous suggestion. It is an heinous slur on my shining reputation. Just who is on trial here? Poor put-upon and totally honest me – Mrs Harriet Lavinia Porter – or that nasty man Captain Dixie? I'll remind you that I am the star witness for the prosecution.

(The Judge) Lord Chief Justice Waverley: Mrs Porter, would you please answer the questions and refrain from any further outbursts. This is a grave matter, and I am distressed enough to see a fine member of my old regiment in the dock without having a prosecution witness reduce proceedings to an undignified shambles.

Lord C: Mrs Porter, you have insisted that you have told nothing but the truth, and that furthermore the sole purpose and activity of your visit to Brighton involved walking by the seafront somewhat implausibly on your six-inch heels. I am, however, in the possession of a letter (Lord C holds up the letter and waves it) from a Major Garfield Hardy-Fisk who is a resident of Brighton. He is a widower of impeccable character, and a retired and very distinguished veteran of Her Majesty's army. By good fortune for the benefit of justice he is also a friend and former colleague of the accused's father. Not only has he written a glowing testimonial on behalf of Captain Dixie, but he has also and very courageously stated that, as far as the Major is aware, you travelled to Brighton for the sole purpose of visiting him. He further states that he paid you the exceptionally handsome fee of ten guineas to satisfy some of his sexual proclivities. He states that he contacted you by letter to suggest this arrangement, having previously known you by the name of Lady Lavinia Lash. Apparently Major Hardy-Fisk had visited you on several occasions a year earlier in 1897 at a London address for similar services. This is an address in Putney owned by a Mr Joshua Kenyon Broad who has signed an affidavit confirming that you provided such activities at his address. (Lord C hands both the letter and the affidavit to the judge after brandishing them at Mrs P.) I put it to you, Mrs Porter, that you travelled down to Brighton for the sole purpose of visiting Major Hardy-Fisk for an appointment of carnal titillation, that flush with his payment you purchased a first class ticket back to London, and that you were angry with Captain Dixie, feeling humiliated after he spurned your advances, and that far from being a woman of utmost integrity you have despicably fabricated lie after lie as an act of revenge in order to destroy Captain Dixie's good name. Mrs Porter, are you aware of the charge of perjury, and are you still intending to persist with your grotesque lies?

At this point Mrs Porter collapsed and had to be carried out to receive medical treatment while the trial was adjourned. The courtroom was in uproar. On the resumption of the session, a revived but bowed Mrs Porter admitted that she had, after all, travelled to Brighton for the sole purpose of providing sexual services to Major

Hardy-Fisk, whereupon the judge ordered that the case against Captain Dixie be dismissed. Further uproar ensued when Miss Rudge and her mother, Mrs Gladys Rudge, shouted a torrent of abuse at both the Judge and the acquitted defendant. Miss Rudge insisted that, despite the collapse of Mrs Porter's testimony, she had nonetheless been viciously raped by Captain Dixie. After the Judge threatened to have Miss Rudge and her mother indicted for contempt of court, the outbursts eventually subsided and the two distressed women were escorted from the building.

Mrs Porter Exchanges her Lash for a Tambourine

With her reputation destroyed and her immoral activities exposed, Mrs Porter found refuge upon leaving the Old Bailey amongst a band of Salvationists who had been singing hymns and banging on their tambourines outside throughout the proceedings. It is believed that their presence there was for offering Christian support, moral tutelage, and salvation to Miss Caroline Rudge. Miss Rudge showed no inclination to be received into their fold. But in the wanton and dishonest Mrs Porter they have found a new member who, it has been reported, has enthusiastically sought salvation among their membership. Perhaps the Salvationists will also be able to lead Mrs Porter away from the sin of gluttony. Before the trial commenced she had been witnessed outside the Old Bailey scoffing copious quantities of cake that, she claimed to astonished onlookers, would "therapise (sic) and fortify (her) delivery of star witness statements". Mrs Porter had also been heard making the extraordinary boast that her "prune and walnut cake was being developed to cure patients of all lunatic asylums, except the ghastly Bethlem Hospital that ought to be demolished, you understand, of their lunacy".

As for the dashing Captain Dixie, he received loud cheers from a substantial gathering of women who had, along with the Salvationists, been waiting outside the Court House. A number of these women flung themselves at the triumphant Captain to lavish kisses on his beaming face. At length the Captain was able to thank his worship the Judge, Lord Crockingford, and all his well-wishers. He pleaded to the crowd that "although many good people have advocated that Miss Rudge and Mrs Porter deserve to be horse-whipped all the way down the road to Newgate jail, I say that we must confer pity on these two wretched souls. They are sorely in need of God's forgiveness, and it is our duty to pray for them." He then announced that now it was "proven that (I) was victim of heinous falsehoods" his plans to become a member of parliament, at the completion of his officer's commission, were back on the agenda. This detail was greeted by further loud cheers and cries of "Captain Dixie for Prime Minister".

Read more about Mrs Porter's Debauched Life on pages 3 & 4. See more Realistic Illustrations inside including Mrs Porter Lashing a Client, Mrs Porter Pestering Captain Dixie with her Unwanted Advances on the Train, Mrs Porter Scoffing her Cake, and Mrs Porter Collapsing while at the Stand. But just who, we wonder, is the Reverend Nudd? Please contact the editor of this publication if you know.

23

Strange had presented Norton with another dilemma.

"Once I've recovered sufficient strength, I'll be able to return to my work at Bethlem," he had said. When Norton had queried this, Strange had answered that if Norton were prepared to go along with his plan, he would explain to the Physician Superindendant that he had been abducted by a ruthless gang of ruffians who had mistaken him for a senior railway employee. They had held him hostage for weeks, dispensing regular beatings, to coerce him into giving them precise details of train gold bullion movements. Eventually realising their mistake they had dumped him on the Hackney marshes.

"Let's see," Strange had said. "The gang leader is a huge brute with a shaven lump of a head. No, that's the principal henchman. The leader is a little man with spikey grey hair under a tatty old hat. His legs seem too small for his body and he wears baggy trousers. Also he's wearing a hooped shirt under his filthy jacket."

"How extraordinary," Norton had remarked. "A rather bad apple, if I'm not being unkind, just like the last one you described, turned up here not an hour before your unexpected but most welcome reappearance. I'd completely forgotten. A northerner with an exceptionally gravelled voice, he was after building or maintenance work and claiming falsely, we think, to be doing other jobs nearby."

Strange organised even the smallest details in his head, yet Norton was not convinced.

"But my dear fellow," Strange had insisted, "I am a chastened man. I also have much to offer as a physician of the psychologically afflicted. Why allow an inconvenience to destroy my career? I have never before permitted the slightest inconvenience to stymie my progress. That is the downfall of weak men. I remember at school when I was caught cheating during an exam by a boy I suspected of being the very sneakiest of school snitches. I uttered a few quiet but very well-chosen words into his ear, and his face turned grey. Ha, Ha! It did the trick. After all, there were surely plenty of others who cheated and I was merely keeping up with them," he had elaborated. "Certainly, it has always been a motto of mine that any hindrance to progress must be eliminated."

Norton, though, had let Strange know that he was an astronomical distance from being convinced. These comments troubled Norton, and for the time being both he and his wife felt the inconvenient need to reside indefinitely at the Clapham address until the moment of Strange's departure.

"The day before your disappearance you spoke to the Physician Superintendant. You requested leave that was denied. You additionally told him that you considered yourself already worthy of promotion from Clinical Assistant to Assistant Physician," Norton had mentioned.

"He must have misunderstood what I was saying," Strange had muttered back dismissively in the general direction of Norton's troubled brow. During the evenings Norton's conversation with his wife and his guest had been reticent. For long periods he preoccupied himself with practising on the piano or disappearing into the dining room with a cricket bat to practise his shots for the still distant summer season. At least, Norton reflected after eight days of convalescence at his home, Dr Strange had now put on five pounds in weight and he was gradually finding it easier both to speak and to move around.

Norton was sitting at his desk in the physicians' room chewing on Strange's gristly intentions to return to work at Bethlem. So far his guest had been urged to remain in the Clapham house and to refrain from taking exercise anywhere near the hospital. On this particular day Mrs Norton had sent a messenger to alert her husband that "their new lodger" had gone missing. The moment he received it Norton raised an eyebrow and began fearing the worst. He checked with the gallery ward staff. Only fifteen minutes earlier Mr Nudd's request to stroll in the large open gardens had again been sanctioned. Instinctively Norton enlisted the services of an available steward who followed the physician outside.

"Come with me, please. Don't question why. I'm following a hunch and might need assistance," he requested.

Nudd, now a regular sight in his conventional clothes, was finding some enjoyment from the fresh yet chilled air. He no longer pranced, but now walked with an unexceptional gait. He was, right here, distinctive only in that the Bethlem hospital grounds were otherwise almost deserted. Almost. Percival was undergoing metamorphosis into a new man, even if the younger version with great aspirations had been lost forever when first alighting on the soggy soil of the Breton marshes. Back here in St George's Fields thin crusts of overnight frost still covered patches of lawn, firming them like the new resolve that Nudd felt in every muscle-fibre of his body. As he strolled he was appreciative of the sunlight that blazed down from the clear sky. Discovering the pleasing bird chorus, Nudd had no idea that he was being tailed, nor that his physician was urgently seeking him. Norton might have been too late.

"You useless lump of diary-scribbling excrement," muttered Strange, stealthily limping closer. Nudd, meanwhile, had paused to admire a squirrel bounding along the grass. Strange, using the trees and shrubs bordering the path's blindside for cover, squeezed between two trees close enough to hug each other with their intermeshing branches. He was within an arm's length of the patient. Nudd remained oblivious, with his eyes tracking the squirrel that was racing up and down a tree trunk. Even a tittle-tattling magpie that fluttered down from the sky to grab onto an overhanging branch failed to distract him.

"You bastard son of a whore," bawled Strange as he flung himself from behind upon Nudd's back. Kneeling on the flattened Nudd, whose face was squashed into the turf, Strange flailed wildly at the back of Nudd's head with his walking stick. Then he tossed it aside and pincered Nudd's neck with his shaking hands in an attempt to throttle him. This lasted barely five seconds because Strange in turn had also been shadowed. The tall, dark-eyed and expensively-tailored man was poised to intervene yet again. On this occasion he was coming directly to Nudd's assistance.

"Over there," pointed the steward. "A fight yonder."

Across the lawns Norton and the steward hurried over and witnessed the tall dark-eyed man emerge from the background to rescue the Bethlem patient. They saw him rip Strange off Nudd's back like a loose top-blanket from a bed. By the time they arrived at the scene the huge man was holding the panting and unsteady Strange firmly in his arms.

The unforgettable jet-black eyes reconnected with Norton's, and without glancing away he hurled Dr Strange into the grasp of the steward.

"Don't you recognise me?" Strange gruffly asked the steward. "Don't you know who I am, you impertinent knave?"

"Just hold him tight, please," instructed Norton, who knelt down to tend to Nudd. His patient was still breathing. He would be fine, but for now lay inert in a state of shock.

Norton looked back up, and the mysterious tall man was still staring back without the slightest amendment to his face. It was devoid of expression.

"By Jove! I should have known that you would make an appearance. I am conscious of the fact that you won't speak, sir,"

Norton said to him. "I presume, forgive me if I'm mistaken, that it's just possible that you are *unable* to do so. I presume further that you are possibly missing a component of your oral anatomy. If, however, your auditory ability is unimpaired, I confess to being at a complete loss as to what to say to you except to thank you profusely. Since you will not – or rather cannot – speak, then I know you cannot vocalise any answers to the all the questions I have."

Norton received one last shock. The tall dark-eyed man's moustache flickered. He parted his lips and spoke.

"*Au contraire*, monsieur. I beleef and I 'ope zat beezness eez finally feenished."

Norton's jaw dropped, and the tall Frenchman smiled.

"Heavens above! Is there anything at all I can do to thank you?" Norton asked after widening his eyes and blinking. "Goodness knows I expect there are others. But as for myself, Mr Nudd, and, if I am not mistaken, a lady who goes by the soubriquet Frenchie, we are all heavily indebted to you, sir. Is there anything at all I can do for you to express my gratitude?"

"*Oui*, Monsieur. Take good care of Monsieur Nudd. Zees I trust wiz you."

"Of course. Of course. We are doing our best and shall continue to do so," said Norton.

He regathered his thoughts and turned to the steward who was holding Strange.

"Take him inside and continue to hold him, please. Get any assistance you may need. I'll see to Mr Nudd here," he said. He watched the steward dragging Dr Strange towards the portico before tending to Nudd. After a basic examination, followed by carefully hauling up his dazed patient into a sitting position, Norton glanced back to where the tall Frenchman had been standing. He was nowhere to be seen.

24

Percival Nudd, blemished by only a few temporary scratches and bruises, had wandered away from the rest of the the Bethlem hospital patients' outing party. Physically unscathed after being attacked near the hospital the previous day, he had agreed with Dr Norton that, to avoid the risk of losing his confidence when out and about, hiding away in the hospital was the last thing he should do. He needed to think and was seeking the solitude of an alternative setting, a complete change of scene, for some uninterrupted contemplation. Shortly before arriving at the Crystal Palace by omnibus, the group had passed a football stadium. Glancing across at this vast venue of international football matches, Mr Nudd half caught sight of the giant sign-board by the entrance:

WELCOME TO THE SYDENHAM STADIUM
Today's Fixture: NUDD versus HIS CONSCIENCE

Percival Nudd took a second look. The board was left blank after the words *Today's Fixture*. He turned to the two nearest passengers to ascertain if they had noticed anything unusual. Busy in discussion about investing money, they evidently hadn't. Nudd didn't know anything about these two gentlemen who would have more than passed muster. Nudd didn't even know the names of these fellow patients who presented themselves as the epitome of normality. Making the effort of getting to know them, however, might have raised a few doubts. So Nudd was unaware that Theobald R Theobald was a former town councillor and lay-preacher of temperance. Nudd was unaware that, after losing all his money earlier in the decade to the building society swindler J Spencer Balfour, JP, MP, Theobald had inclined since to erratic behaviour and heavy drinking. Nudd knew nothing of Z Quentin Ashcroft's troubles. This well-off and retired engineer was twinkling stars away from financial ruin. Yet he was adamant that a conspiracy to fleece him would force both himself and his wife into the workhouse. The conspirators, Z insisted, included his former butler; the Archbishop of Canterbury; an advisor to the German Kaiser called Johann Schmidt; and an Egyptian bellydancer called Fanny whom he had met once at the 1893 Chicago World Fair and who, Z suspected, transmitted sinister ciphers by the scandalous jiggle-wiggling of her hips. Nudd knew next to nothing about the young woman sitting behind who kept tapping Theobald on the shoulder and bursting into tittering fits. He had seen her around the hospital, noticing that she had the ridiculous habit of exploding into mirth for no obvious reason. Rather like spontaneous combustion, but at least, thought Nudd, she wasn't hazardous. Nudd frowned. He stroked his sidewhiskers. After some consideration he decided to introduce himself to the two sober-looking gentlemen.

Twenty minutes later, a little nervously, and he was exploring the grounds of the spectacular glass house that had been dismantled at Hyde Park almost fifty years earlier, and re-assembled here on an even larger scale in the green suburbia of Sydenham Park. Nudd had quickly managed to disengage himself from the Bethlem patient group on the terraces that elevated the visitors to the exhibition building, or lowered them back down into the park. Despite sharing a hospital ward for long months with many of these characters, he hardly knew a single individual. Of the few recognised by Nudd were the aptly named Jeremy Giggles; the hopelessly confused septuagenarian brothers Bounce; the violinist Gilbert Gilbertson; the tortured, sighing Mancunian sage "Pop" Eccles; the sluggish Miss Rosemary May; the squinting beanpole Edward Daniels – or possibly Daniel Edwards; the irritating little Bert Wigley; the excitable Italian grandmother with a difficult name; the pompous and smug somebody-or-other cobbler who incredibly believes himself to be the reincarnation of Julius Caesar; and a middle-aged man called Tin MacLeish. Yes, thought Nudd, it is quite definitely *Tin* and not Tim – though he had no idea why. For a few seconds he wondered. Perhaps he should ask. Perhaps now was the opportunity to belatedly become better acquainted with a number of them, to take an interest, and ask a few questions. This, however, would have to wait. Today, he decided, he had much bigger questions to ask. And Mr Nudd was dressed for a serious exercise in a sombre dark jacket, waistcoat and trousers, and completed by a short cylindrical gentleman's hat. Detached from company, and of inconspicuous appearance, Sydenham Park offered a cordial and fresh setting to help a storm-ravaged mind reorganise itself back into serenity. Dr Norton was probably correct. Nobody had any business to attack him here. Nobody or nothing at all.

Maybe Dr Norton *was* right after all about certain other matters, thought Nudd. He said I should confront my demons, and he wasn't referring to Satan, or to wild and lonely places. He said that they would inevitably remain in my head, in all likeliness multiplying, if I kept running away from the troubles of my past. It would only be possible to progress beyond this discord if the past was dealt with honestly and without fear. Norton had told me, Nudd further recounted with eyes pointing at nothing in particular, that it had been a Frenchman who had possibly saved my life from the assailant at Bethlem. Not any unremarkable Frenchman who just happened to be passing by, either. This one stood tall and calm, this one dressed with aristocratic distinction – and his hair and eyes were yet darker than a moonless night. It had to be him. Surely. God I beseech You, favour me with the truth. But whether he walks as a living man or a dead man, perhaps that doesn't truly matter one jot. This need not be an issue for lingering contemplation – even if it is difficult to totally ignore. The implications, that firstly he is watching out for me, and that secondly, he thus surely perceives me as blameless, Nudd reasoned, absolves my feeling of guilt. It should do. And by the same token transfers the burden onto the Frenchman. Or does it? My Lord God, could I have been so wrong? Could it be that this man, whether deceased or alive, or alternatively his family – as I have long suspected – is the source of our mysterious monthly funding? Nudd didn't hear the voice he had hoped for to answer his questions. The voice that spoke inside his head, as it had done one miserable night on the Breton Marshes, warned,

"Religious zealotry of a clos-sed mind, Monsieur Nudd. And burneeng ambition, and personal frustrations of zee man who always want too much, zees are ze causes of strife for heem and other peoples."

A few miles north of Sydenham Mr Broad was seated at a table on Gallery III writing yet another letter to Queen Victoria. Again he was requesting his payment and knighthood owing for special undercover services on behalf of the Empire. Outside, Mr Hughes and Mr Rooney were exchanging a variety of facial expressions at the bottom of Bethlem's portico steps, their backs towards the grand entrance.

"It's a fact! So the Reverend Nudd really *is* resident here. And he's gone on an outing to the Crystal Palace," remarked Mr Hughes.

"And they say we've only just missed him, the slippery scoundrel," Mr Rooney added, his lower lip jutting forward beneath a red face and fierce eyes.

"Do you suppose, Amos, that he's a *genuine* lunatic, or might he be a fake who has artfully gone to ground here?"

"A lunatic? Balderdash! He's a fake, a fake. He's a fake I tell you, George. He's faking lunacy because he fears that you and I want our money returned. He fears that others too will be preparing lawsuits against him. If we ever catch up with him he intends to plead lunacy. Mark my words."

"But Amos, we've already investigated the possibility of reclaiming our donations, and we've been advised that our chances are as slim as a thread of sewing yarn," Mr Hughes pointed out. "Not forgetting either, if I'm not mistaken, that the PE chapel was built with our blessing, courtesy of Nuddite donations."

"Bah! That's not what he thinks. In any case, what kind of chapel do you call *that*! It's nothing more than a marble garden ornament for Mrs Nudd to admire. It's a mere bagatelle. It's as hollow as the foundations of the Nuddite church are shallow."

"Or as Nudd is humbug," added Mr Hughes.

"Do you know I wouldn't be surprised if that kowtowing sackful of wet suet – Mr billycock Broad – if he's been fooling us all as well. It'll probably turn out that he's been on the trail of Nudd all this time while leading us to believe that he's an outright idiot. Probably turn out that he's one of Her Majesty's finest undercover agents."

"What a fascinating idea, Amos. The more I consider it, the greater the appeal. Of course! Nobody could *truly* be as thoroughly feeble as that man. It's all been an act. Dare I say, I think you're onto something, Amos?"

"Onto the Reverend Nudd. We've got him on the run. He's nothing more than a charlatan, George. He may be running, but little does he know that we're in hot pursuit," asserted Mr Rooney.

"Might he be hiding here, masquerading as an imbecile, to avoid reasonable suspicion while he plots some dastardly crime against the nation? Consider the consequences if he were preparing to assassinate Her Majesty the Queen."

"I wouldn't put it past him, George. The man is probably capable of anything – and I'm certainly not referring to his outlandish claims. Able to run to Oxford and back in a night indeed as that preposterous Porter woman insists! Utter nonsense! He'd truly require the ability to shift faster than quicksilver if he is to elude us now."

"Able to accomplish that particular feat you mentioned in under an hour, I was informed," Mr Hughes mentioned.

"We'll soon put his running abilities to the test, George. Time to send a telegram post haste to Newgate Prison's hangman to ready the noose for Nudd's neck. Pentonville, Wormwood Scrubs alike, the full length of the rope. We are fast catching up with the scaly knave like hounds after a fox."

In Sydenham Park, Percival Nudd hadn't conceded defeat with his efforts to reorganise his thoughts. The Nuddite Church was not solely based on the misperceptions that I told myself were factual, he thought. It was possibly also formed by a heart fearful of the truth, he suggested with horror. But perhaps not. Nothing is certain, despite the coincidence of my rescuer's appearance. And I unequivocally saw what I saw all those years ago with my own eyes. God, You spoke to me, surely? You have been directing me, surely? The Holy World Nuddite Church is *not* built on the foundations of a false prophet, surely? God almighty, where *are* You? I *need* answers, Nudd begged. Then, perhaps, he received one. The crashing boom of an explosion turned his eyes towards the Crystal Palace. Metal, timber and unrelenting glass shrapnel scattered high and wide: a storm-cloud of predominantly transparent, smashed components darkening the heavens. On the elevated ground below was a massive void, like a plinth bereft of its statue, where the structure had in an eye's blink earlier stood. Only Brunel's soaring water towers remained, minarets stranded without their mother of mosques. Small glass splinters rained down close by, and a plaque of gigantic proportions flew the one hundred yards or so towards Nudd, crashing only feet away onto the grass before he could take cover. It had landed with the inscription facing up, and Nudd, frozen like a stump of petrified wood, read the words *The Crystal Holy World Nuddite Palace*. As Nudd saw a second wave of debris hurled through the sky, including vast sheets of jagged glass catapulting straight towards him, he flung himself face down to the ground and covered the back of his head with his hands. Then, after a lengthy lull, he raised his chin to look around. He tentatively stood up. The Crystal Palace was intact. The most extravagant orangery ever constructed – conceived for Gargantua's nectar trees – was a whole that could, as the sun reflected off the glass walls and tubular roofs, have been chiselled out of a glacier by an army of fur-uniformed artisans. No explosion of any kind had occurred. No fireworks had been detonated. Nudd remained there for a long moment, brushing away grass blades from his soil-stained trousers and jacket, and gazing at the great glass folly that survived unbroken – in contrast with the Nuddite Church. Wiping off the remaining detritus from his clothes and shaking the last drips of madness out of his head, the erstwhile Reverend wandered away towards a lake. As he drew closer, his steps in the increasingly squelchier turf faltered a little. But he clenched his fist and pushed on as he repeated Norton's advice to himself. Any natural body of water – whether a pond, lake, stream or river, whether a trickle or an ocean – had been avoided by the Nudd for quite some time. Canals, though, conjured up the greatest terror. But now, if he could face up to an ornamental lake, then who knows what next? Perhaps even jellied eels, once a favourite, could return to his menu at the first opportunity.

Around the banks, with his pulse still racing and a queasy feeling infesting his stomach like tangled worms, Nudd encountered life-sized concrete sculptures of the enormous vanished lizards that had been named dinosaurs. He approached a pair of the fearsome-looking, snout-horned beasts that were labelled as *Iguanadons*. He read the additional details, and stroked one of his always fastidiously trimmed and slender sidewhiskers that were permanent fixtures striping each flank of his face. How, he asked himself, could the men responsible for these guessed reconstructions not accept that they were merely monsters that had perished during the Great Flood? Hadn't these blasphemous so-called scientists read the book of Genesis? You, Nudd said to the sculptures, are nothing more than forsaken beasts, monstrous both in size and stupidity, that God dispatched to the wilderness of non-existence. *You* were not deemed worthy of being summoned aboard Noah's Ark for salvation, Nudd continued. He turned away trying to ignore the contradictory arguments diametrically circulating his head. These pointed a giant signpost to the notion of evolution, as well as posing the question as to why a flawless God should in the first place create such beasts if He was then to discard them as surplus to requirements. Something caused a blood-surge into his limbs. Nudd looked back at the closest Iguanadon with a sharp twist of his neck. Something had stirred. He had heard the crackle of movement first. A ferocious roar of hostility ensued. The beast, from all fours, reared up at Nudd with its jaws open. It hammered the quaking earth as it crashed back down, and planted an enormous clawed foot towards him. Nudd didn't wait for the next movement. He turned and ran through the sodden ground. After beating a hasty retreat he looked behind to see if the beast was following. It wasn't, and furthermore the sculpture was in the precise and original fixed position when Nudd had first encountered it. Nudd felt his veins throb. Confront Satan alone. Confront the diabolical beast, he heard himself preach. Confront your problems, Nudd heard Norton preach. He had done neither. He had fled. Mr Nudd proceeded further away with a resumption of head-shaking, recalling again what he had seen on the Breton Marshes. He felt the sheer dread as if he were still there that awful night. Then he recalled, about a year after returning home to England, how he had begun experiencing those exhilarating sensations. These were the mighty moments when God and the spirit of Jesus seemed to fill him with joy, with special powers, and with the greatest of purpose. Everything and every sensation without exception had felt real. Nudd asked himself a question. Just what was or *is* real? And never mind the puzzle of gravity for now. Mr Crabtree, him from the adjacent room on the ward, calls me the Right Reverend Fool's Gold, Bishop of Bedlam. He refers to Mrs Porter as the Widow Flibbertygibbet. Can it possibly be that the discourteous reasoning of a Bedlam lunatic is sounder than that of the presumed sane? For Nudd, as he had experienced periodically over the years, a session of trying to find answers, as usual, resulted only in the propagation of more questions to be asked. He reconsidered the words of Dr Norton. The solutions must lie in confronting my fears, Nudd conceded. He recalled the day when Emily's parents had a rocking-horse delivered from a local toy shop as a gift to amuse the children. He had refused to accept the delivery, and negotiated with the toyshop to buy it back at half the price. The time had arrived. It was long overdue. Now he would deal with horses.

Percival Nudd navigated his way through the park until he reconnected with the central avenue. This led him to the exit at the opposite end from 'the Palace'. He ventured out onto the semi-rural road and waited. Watching some cyclists pedal by in dribs and drabs, Nudd didn't have to wait long until a rider approached on a large horse.

"Hello, there. Excuse me," Nudd called out with a raised hand to the man. "I say, forgive my intrusion."

The bowler hat-wearing rider halted his horse and looked down at Nudd through kind eyes. He was wearing smart clothes, immaculately tailored, slightly casual, and unpretentious. The more Nudd assessed the rider, the more approachable he seemed.

The man was roughly Nudd's age, and below his greying moustache that matched the hue of his horse, he smiled with extra impetus before responding.

"How may I help you, sir?"

"I apologise sincerely for interrupting your passage, but I have a request that you may consider to be a little peculiar," said Nudd.

"You have my attention, sir. Tarry not. Go ahead and make your request."

"Might I discuss the force of gravity with you?"

"Gravity? I have no expertise on the matter. I am able to concur, though, that your request is most unusual. Are you quite sure you have stopped a complete stranger to discuss the force of gravity, or did you really stop me for another reason."

"No. You are quite right. I didn't stop you to discuss gravity. Thank you. You are most patient. You are most considerate – and cordial. I'll try again. I have an affliction, you see. One that has gripped me for a decade and a half. It has nothing to do with gravity. It is a fear of horses. This has resulted in my preference to avoid these magnificent beasts during all this time. It may sound absurd, I grant you, but whenever I see or imagine a horse I am rendered a victim of overwhelming anxiety."

"It is certainly highly unfortunate, my poor man. Not so much absurd as incapacitating when one considers the proliferation of horses in the open spaces of our nation. Allow me to observe, sir, that I perceive no overt indications of your anxiety at this very moment."

"No. Perhaps not. Inside my heart is beating fast, but I am determined to contain it. I have resolved to confront my fear as a solution, a means, to conquering it. I was wondering if you would permit me to gently touch your horse, pat it lightly, and possibly even scratch its forehead?" Nudd asked. The rider smiled again, and dismounted.

"I see no reason why not. I may not be capable of assisting your understanding of gravity, but I might be of assistance in *this* matter. I'm in no hurry, my gelding is as docile as he is powerful, and I am loathed, sir, to ignore your brave attempt to bring your affliction to a conclusion. Go ahead."

"Thank you again," said Nudd, and he reached out to pat the horse at a rigid arm's length.

"How are you feeling, sir?" asked the rider. "To my ingenuous eye you are managing commendably. My name is James Thompson."

"And I am the Reverend, I mean Mr Percival Nudd," Nudd reciprocated, and the two men firmly shook hands.

"Would you care to mount my gelding?" asked Mr Thompson. "I do believe you could achieve this, Mr Percival Nudd."

"I am growing in confidence," Nudd agreed. "Yes. I would like to accept your invitation. It has been far too long since I sat astride a horse."

Nudd was helped up. He took hold of the reins as he sat stiffly upon the horse that was shuffling and twitching its long legs.

"Well done. Bravo!" encouraged the rider. "How are you feeling, sir?"

"A touch nervous but growing stronger, thank you, Mr Thompson. With the passing of each second my fears shrink and my confidence gains. This is a momentous occasion for me. It is an achievement that will hearten my wife."

"I'm delighted to have assisted – along with Silver, of course," said Mr Thompson, a second before becoming distracted by two men approaching at Nudd's rear. He turned back to Nudd.

"Evidence is fast approaching that there are others eager to congratulate you, Mr Nudd."

"I beg your pardon?"

"Two elderly gentlemen are fast approaching at your rear. Listen. They are calling out to you."

"Percival Nudd!" shouted Mr Rooney. "Percival Nudd!"

"I do believe we've found you at last, Percival Nudd." shouted Mr Hughes.

"You thought you'd seen the last of us, you rogue," shouted Mr Rooney. "We've come to get some answers."

"Most importantly we want our money back that you swindled us into giving you," spluttered a breathless Mr Hughes.

Nudd partially rotated the horse and watched aghast as the two puffing men trotted closer, Mr Rooney brandishing his walking stick and Mr Hughes shaking his fist. Nudd's first thought was to attempt the trick that restored the Crystal Palace of turning his head away and closing his eyes. This failed to extinguish the cries of Hughes and Rooney. It hadn't worked. On opening his eyes the two elderly men loomed within imminent impact. Nudd sat on the restless horse watching his two former followers approach – incapable of knowing how to deal with the situation. Mr Rooney, his face glowing like red hot embers, lunged up at Nudd with his walking stick like a bayonet, in the process breaking Nudd's locket chain. The horse fidgeted uneasily, Mr Thompson looked bemused, and Percival Nudd took decisive action. He roused the horse and galloped off.

Nudd urged his borrowed steed along the road that orbited the park. An automobile approached, being driven through the middle of the thoroughfare like the erratically swerving course of an injured snake. The vehicle's driver impatiently sounded his klaxon at the approaching horse. Startled, it careered off the road, vaulted a low wall, and galloped through the park.

"Oi!" yelled a young man escorting his ladyfriend as the horse galloped past across the turf. "Horses aren't allowed to be ridden in here."

"No horses, you idiot!" Nudd thought he heard somebody else shout as his hat flew off and he clung onto the charging animal. He galloped past a trio of familiar faces. Ashcroft was pointing at him and Theobald was yelling something and wheeling his arms like windmill sails in opposite directions. Pop Eccles just stood dumbfounded with his eyes as wide as saucers. He heard other shouts too, as he tried to direct the horse back towards a gap that would return him to the road. But the shouts became increasingly muffled by the sound of thundering hooves, and the thumping of his heart, and the terrifying rumbling of a second set of hooves – until he heard a distinctive French voice shouting through the chaos and drawing louder.

"Monsieur Nudd, Monsieur Nudd. Wait. *Attendez-vous*, please. You must stop runneeng away."

Nudd slapped the horse onwards. He glanced back to see a familiar figure on horseback. There was that ursine frame leaning forward clutching his hat under his arm, with the black locks and moustache, and even darker eyes that stared at him like the twin barrels of a shotgun. Each and every feature filled Nudd with utter dread. Just one glance was more than enough, and Nudd continued to flee in sweeping circles. Groups of onlookers were gathering in the park, and as Nudd thundered on and on they streaked past like grey smears. He was aware of other voices but suddenly all he could hear were two. Norton was calmly advising him to stop running away, and another was shouting at him to "stop *runeeng* away." He had not only again looked back for the wrong reasons, but it also suddenly dawned on Nudd that he couldn't run away anymore – not in circles like the turmoil of his mind. He brought the horse to a halt. He was breathing harder than the horse. He turned it around. There was nobody pursuing him. A group of ladies were the only people nearby. One approached him and told him angrily something he already knew about it being forbidden to ride horses in the park. Nobody else approached him, and nobody else was shouting at him. Only the lady's scolding voice now endured, disturbing the peace fleetingly, before fading from his consciousness. Nudd steered the horse at an easy canter back out of the park and onto the road. He recognised Mr Thompson in the distance and headed over to return the horse. Mr Thompson had been searching for Nudd alone. The two former Nuddites, still on Nudd's trail, were scouring Sydenham Park. But, with the diminishing pace of clockwork toys in need of a re-wind, their ageing legs were slowing and their energy reserves depleting.

"I cannot apologise enough. I panicked, but I have returned your horse safely," Nudd blurted as he dismounted, looking around for signs of the two elderly men.

"That's quite alright," responded Mr Thompson, taking his horse's reins. "It seems that you have a host of difficult issues to confront, sir, and I applaud you for facing up to your challenges. A reluctance to deal with more than one simultaneously is understandable. Anyway, Mr Nudd, I have something for you," continued Mr Thompson, smiling again and holding out Nudd's locket and chain. "In addition to losing your hat, you almost lost this. It's a fair exchange. Your golden locket for my Silver."

"Thank you again, Mr Thompson. You are a thoroughly decent man. I hadn't realised I'd lost it."

"Nor had I," said Mr Thompson. "I saw you clutching it above your chest when you were patting Silver, but like you I hadn't realised you'd lost it. Not until several minutes after you'd galloped out of sight. A big man with the strikingly dark eyes and hair, and of a decidedly aristocratic appearance, passed by on his horse, leant down and handed it to me. He simply nodded and instantly trotted away."

25

Down in the Bedlam basement Norton ventured into a sideroom to visit a newly certified lunatic. A day earlier the latest arrival had been bundled inside the hospital and inserted into a type of strait-jacket that secured his arms to his flanks. Now he was also clasped by forearm canvas wraps onto a restraining chair. Elsewhere in this constructed grotto was a bed equipped with straps and fastened by bolts to the floor; a small window beyond reach near the ceiling; two paintings depicting pastoral serenity hung high up; and an electric lamp that saturated the sparse contents with light. A pair of tough-looking male nursing attendants postured at each side of Strange. One of them asked Norton,

"Shall us gag 'im, sir? In the hevent of 'im tryin' ta bite – or maybe spit?"

"Goodness, no. There's no need for that. He would hardly be capable of inflicting a bite with such limited dentition. In any case, I am hoping for some discourse with Dr Strange."

Through his mutilated face the new patient's mouth widened to the limits and fully revealed the trademark leer to Norton for the first time in months.

"Dr Strange," Norton addressed him, "you are to remain here until the police have questioned you. I expect this'll be after the weekend – tomorrow or Tuesday. I anticipate that you will be later transferred to Broadmoor. I hardly need to remind you that this hospital does not provide therapeutic care for those deemed incurable or dangerous. Naturally I shall tender my opinion about the vicious beating to which you were subjected in the Breton Marshes, and not least those to your head. They may have caused damage – both organic and psychological – that significantly impairs your mood and as well as your ability to reason."

"Thank you, my dear fellow," responded Strange through his few remaining teeth. Though swathed rigid like a mummified has-been on his throne, the erstwhile doctor's head bobbed, and his mouth discharged. "I wish to again apologise sincerely to Mr Nudd, to yourself, and to all concerned for my behaviour. I fear that the injuries I have sustained, along with the recognised folly of my excursion, combined for an instant like spark and fuse to ignite all the frustration, and the hurt and misjudgement that will now blight my future existence. I cannot apologise enough. And after pleading *temporary* insanity as a consequence of my beating, I shall demonstrate that I have made a full recovery and, Lord willing, be released back into society to honour my Maker and serve a useful purpose. I had been left, as intended, for dead. However, the good Lord, evidently, has use for me yet on this earth."

"Quite possibly. And may I take this opportunity to inform you that Mr Nudd is fine. One can hope that you are as relieved about that as I am. Actually you may rather ironically have knocked some sense into him. He was suffering from shock but has recovered so quickly that I have consented to him embarking on his first patients' outing today. As a matter of fact, I vigorously encouraged him. You undoubtedly do owe him a huge apology. But tell me one thing: it is the least you owe me. Why did you attempt to fatally poison me with that fruitcake?"

"Oh come now, my dear fellow. I am completely ignorant of what you are talking about. I may well, in a fit of pique, have attacked Mr Nudd – but I'll be damned if I allow you to besmirch me with other fanciful accusations. Fruitcake? What fruitcake, and when?"

"You know the answers to your questions, and you know that I know it was your doing. Some of the poisons, having been identified, could have been procured from the less scrupulous backstreet chemists. Arsenic, mercury, laudanum, belladonna certainly. But sulphanol? And hyoscamine? Medicines we administer here? It is true that preparations of the latter can be extracted from henbane. As a matter of fact it was a good thing for me that you mixed in considerably more than just large doses of hyoscamine and belladonna alone – because those two poisons would not have proved fatal to the poor hungry birds that alerted me to the danger. Ah yes! And I nearly forgot the nux vomica. It was brought to my attention that an amount of strychnine had gone missing, noticeable since we only keep a minuscule supply. So I presume that the missing powder also ended up in that cake. Sadly I am left to conclude that in your twisted mind I became a potential inconvenience – one that might have thwarted your ambitions. I assume that you saw no alternative than to dispose of me as if I were a gnat to be swatted out of existence."

"Or a slug to be squashed underfoot. Ha, ha, ha, ha, ha, ha, ha!" laughed Strange, interrupted by one of the nursing attendants.

"Shall us gag 'im now, sir?" he asked Norton.

"Lord, no," replied Norton with a quick shake of his head like a baby's rattle. "But thank you, anyway."

"An interesting theory, Dr Norton," continued Strange camly. "But a ludicrous one."

"Maybe," Norton responded. "And it is one that I shall also tender to the police. It may well interest them, especially having occurred prior to the injuries inflicted on the marshes. Then there's also the issue of a certain Mr Garbett. I hadn't mentioned that on my almost ill-fated investigation at Whitechapel I learnt of his name in connection with you. This link has since been corroborated by Frenchie who has furnished me with extra details, including the man's bloody and unsolved demise," added Norton with a raised eyebrow.

After allowing sufficient opportunity for Strange to offer a response, Norton continued,

"Anyway, moving on, it's been a rather good weekend so far. Only one patient admitted – you, sadly – but three departing home. Amongst those formally deemed cured is Mr Albert Potts. He's the man you helped to look after here following his bad experience in New York if you recall. About a month ago he finally managed to overcome his fear of proceeding outside – the problem he mysteriously acquired last Derby race day. He has made rapid progress since. Yes! So far it hasn't been an altogether bad weekend for us at Bethlem."

"I share your joy," said Strange through his grin. "All the way until Monday. Although in the meanwhile I won't relish knowing at mealtimes that some of my food will have been prepared by a French whore."

"Not today, however. Frenchie, Marie-Christine, has a day off. Later, early evening, she and her sons will be dining with Mrs Norton and myself."

"How delightfully cosy. Just remember it's dog eat dog."

"I beg your pardon?"

"Dog eat dog, my dear fellow. I once warned you that you lack ruthlessness," grinned Strange.

"Is this, Dr Strange, the first move of some sort of game you are trying to play with me?"

"I just think it would be pertinent to remind you of a few crucial details at this point, while you snuggle up to Frenchie in your unwaveringly decent way. There's the fact, for example, that some believe *you* responsible for the Nudd burglary. Another fact that, whilst I did not have anything to do with Mr Garbett's demise, a witness – perhaps the assassin – places *you* firmly at the scene of the crime."

"That's all completely ridiculous as you well know. It also smacks of desperation. You may be unaware, however, that I made a second visit to Whitechapel. If it rendered me hopelessly confused at first, a peculiar encounter with a preacher is now making some sense. Dare I suggest that you gave yourself an alibi by using my name?"

"A preacher? Another lunatic like Nudd? Ha, ha, ha, ha, ha! Suggest what you like. Ha, ha, ha, ha! Now *that* is completely ridiculous. I am confident, however, that in good time some cogently interesting developments will render you more malleable to, let's just say, significantly helping my cause. Being ruthless, unlike you, I always make sure that I've first prepared a safety net lest I slip up and fall from the high-wire."

"This disrespectful game is boring me, Dr Strange. You are bluffing."

"Am I? I apologise if you are bored for now. Trust me, dear fellow, that before long the game will become positively enthralling."

"Its a great shame, Dr Strange, after all I, and, indeed, recently my wife, have tried to do on your behalf, both professionally and at our home, that you resort to this sinister nonsense. Though I really shouldn't be surprised since you've already made an attempt to dispose of me."

"You have no hard evidence that I sent you a toxic cake – because there isn't any. It's just conjecture on your part. And the Garbett murder? The same. My only crime, for which I have already expressed remorse one hundred times over, for God's sake, was my attack on Nudd. It was not pre-meditated but an accident of circumstances. It was a fit of rage. Certainly I was caught in flagrante delicto, and whilst I wanted to give the idiot a good hiding there was no intention of causing him any serious harm. I had, understandably, been pining for a sentimental look at the hospital, and came across Nudd by chance. Let's face it, if he hadn't withheld his infernal diary from my scrutiny I wouldn't be in the mess I'm in now: career perhaps terminated, body battered and disfigured. Of course I lost my temper when I saw Nudd ambling around without a care in the world. So just take a good look at me right now and use your blasted monocle if it'll help you see properly. Look at me, indistinguishable from a ventriloquist's dummy. Caged down here like a dangerous animal. It is *you* who is playing a sinister game with *me*."

Norton quelled his reaction by counting to ten.

"You used the word *sentimental*," he observed. "Sentiment is not an emotion, in my opinion, familiar to you. Any evidence I give to help convict you will include a personality assessment, believe me. Sinking in the quicksand of all the damning evidence, it'll be left to you to try pulling the wool over the jurors' eyes."

"Or, *if* any of your absurd accusations proceed to trial, to simply win the day. Dog eat dog. It's nothing personal, dear fellow," Strange said, re-forming his leer-smile hybrid. "Learn how to play games or join the army," he added. "The alternative was to get nowhere in life. At school I was force-fed Greek, Latin, and Christianity. Everything else was about team sports, military drill, and avoiding the rod. Imagination was forbidden. Individuality was forbidden. Stupid and unquestioning conformity, on the other hand, was richly rewarded. I learned to dodge the rod most of the time. I learned to covertly avoid conforming. Those free-spirited individuals of stubborn principles ended up being expelled, having wrongly taken the blame for a catalogue of others' misdemeanours. Not me. Not Her Majesty's army for me, either. I bid you welcome, my dear fellow, to my world of games without prejudice. You accuse me of all sorts and hold me in here. Here, where I have slaved hard to bring relief to the psychologically afflicted with dedication and acknowledged prowess. En garde, my estimable mentor. Whether you judge me or not, and whether willing or not, you are now a participant in one of my games."

Norton cleared his throat and hardened his voice.

"I think this interview is fast drawing to a conclusion."

"Off to practice with one of your cricket bats? It won't help, Dr Norton, because *this* isn't cricket."

Norton half-smiled, then chose to ignore Strange's advice.

"Being a free-thinking individual doesn't necessarily equate with committing deeds of evil. Dr Strange, your salutary experience is not the only one to have, in one way or another, resulted from our friend Percival Nudd's secret diary entries. They have, as you yourself not long ago remarked, served as the catalyst for changing the lives of many. Probably a lot more than we'll ever know."

"No truer words were ever uttered," interrupted Strange, maintaining his broad, leering smile.

"Whatever it was," continued Norton, "that Mr Nudd experienced in the Breton Marshes, clearly not the precise fate that befell you, is probably best forgotten. But, leaving your games to one side, perhaps you may be so kind as to tell me one last thing. Can you enlighten me – anything at all – about the identity of that tall Frenchman who pulled you off Mr Nudd?"

Strange's face stiffened.

"I was rather hoping, dear fellow, that *you* could enlighten me," he answered with a hint of annoyance. "Just who the hell is he?"

The door hinges creaked with a painful wail bisected by a sharp double knock.

"Who the hell," intervened another voice, "is who?"

Strange tilted his head to stare beyond Norton who swivelled to look behind him. Detective Constable Coates, carrying a briefcase and with a reluctant uniformed policeman lagging behind, crossed the floor slabs to greet Norton. He still lacked a hat, and hadn't abandoned his efforts to grow a moustache visible to the keen-sighted at more than five paces. Coates nodded with uncertain courtesy at the bundle of Dr Strange and chair, then he addressed Norton.

"My sincere apologies for interrupting your work, doctor, but I too must conduct mine."

"By Jove! Hello again, Detective Constable. Have you come to take Dr Strange away already?" Norton asked.

"Take him away? What for? I didn't even know he still existed until about an hour ago. I am not aware that we need to take him anywhere yet for the assault on your patient."

"So why are you here, if you don't mind my asking?"

"Do you know, doctor, that's a rather good question. I'm not even sure myself," Coates replied. "There have been some odd things afoot. That's undeniable. The poisonous cake – though despite our suspicions we can't pin that on Dr Strange here. Not yet, at any rate. Preceding that unpleasant incidence of heinous baking there's been the burglary at the home of your patient, Reverend Nudd. There's been an assault on a French lady who visits the Nudd home from time to time. On a regular basis, to be accurate. There's been a spate of unusual accusations about yourself and Dr Strange here. That's an understatement. There's been talk of a secret diary, mention of a Fenian agent – no less – and there's further been the murder of a distinctly objectionable character using the alias Garbett. To top it all, Dr Strange then absconds overnight," itemised Coates, who had spent much time over recent months moving pieces of paper around his desk top. On each square was written the basic details of each of these separate incidents in block capitals. Supplementary notes were scribbled beneath, and Coates had been swapping them around as if trying to solve an anagram. Usually, at the centre, was a piece of paper labelled with the name Reverend Nudd.

"Goodness!" remarked Norton raising an eyebrow, "the plot thickens."

"It certainly does, doctor. What's more, we know as a matter of fact that you've made at least one visit to Whitechapel. You were asking questions about Dr Strange here. Could I ask why you knew he might have business in the East district?"

"Because Dr Strange had informed me on more than one occasion that he visited the locality. At the time his behaviour was a cause for concern," explained Norton. "How did you know?"

"We were watching your movements with undercover officers, Dr Norton. One in particular. Men whose faces are not known on the beat of the Whitechapel – er, formerly *H* – Division. Keeping an eye on you."

"Ah! So, so the tall Frenchman – he's actually one of *your* men?"

"A *tall Frenchman?*"

"Yes, suave, sophisticated, tall hat, dark hair and eyes. The man who rescued me when I was about to be robbed at knife-point. The man who saved me from the cake. The man who pulled Dr Strange off Mr Nudd."

"I really don't know who you are talking about, doctor. Make a note of that, will you, constable," Coates instructed the bobby who was watching from the rear. "A tall, suave Frenchman rescued the physician at knife-point. No – it is not beyond my duty to inform you that our man on the job can transform himself into many convincing undercover characters. But he can't become tall – without, er, climbing up a ladder."

"Excuse me sir," the nervous constable nudged his superior, "We were informed that it was a Frenchman, if you recall, sir, who came to the rescue of the patient Nudd, sir."

"I think," said Norton slowly, "that I'm becoming as puzzled as you, Detective Constable. Probably considerably more so."

"I am at liberty to reveal that our man on the job is quite zealous in his characterisations. He sometimes likes to ruffle a few feathers. Put the cat amongst the pigeons and see in which direction they fly. The theatre's loss is our gain."

"How extraordinary," remarked Norton.

"Ha, ha, ha, ha, ha, ha, ha!" roared Strange.

"Good Lord! My second visit after Dr Strange's sudden disappearance. Good Lord! The preacher?" wondered Norton.

"Preacher, eh?" replied Coates. "I'm not really at liberty to specify our man's mode of disguise, doctor. Whitechapel is known to attract many a preacher. That I can confirm. Let's just say our man specialises in rat-catching, but not the variety with whiskers and long tails."

"Ha, ha, ha, ha, ha!" continued Strange. "What about groomed side-whiskers and long coat tails?" he asked. Detective Constable Coates casually swung his eyes at him.

"He had also been watching some of *your* movements, Dr Strange. He saw you at the Queen's Arms public house. It was the night the man calling himself Garbett was murdered along the Commercial Road. Our man reported that the victim entered the establishment to possibly keep an appointment with you, Dr Strange," Coates pointed out.

"So does that mean that your man saw or knows the identity of the murderer of this Mr Garbett?"asked Norton.

"Sadly, alack, not. He should have relieved himself in the Queen's Arms water closet before he exited the premises. As a consequence of neglecting to do so, he momentarily took himself inside another public house to empty his bladder. By a stroke of misfortune it would seem that it was during this brief ten minutes' absence from duty that both Dr Strange and this Mr Garbett departed from the Queen's Arms unseen. We have nothing to firmly place Dr Strange at the subsequent scene of the crime. Nor do we know of a motive. Anything to arouse suspicion is only circumstantial: putting him in the same public house as the victim around the critical time. Then his unexplained absconding a day later – perhaps within the hour of meeting him with your good self at this hospital for the first time. In fact we still thought Dr Strange was missing – until now."

"Ha, ha, ha, ha, ha, ha, ha!" laughed Strange.

"Dr Norton," asked the detective, "would you arrange for Dr Strange to have his shackles temporarily removed in order that he can sign a statement?"

"Yes, of course," agreed Norton. He nodded to the nursing assistants who released Strange's arms. Coates opened his briefcase and removed a pen, a glass inkpot, and a document.

"As you will see, Dr Strange, this is a simple statement that confirms you played no part whatsoever in the murder of the blackguard calling himself Garbett, and that further, you know nothing about how he came to be murdered," said Coates. He handed Strange the sheet of paper and the pen that he first dipped into the ink. "If this is correct you merely need to sign and date the document. You are under no obligation," he explained.

"Do you have his spectacles, gentlemen?" Norton asked the nursing assistants. The spectacles were passed to Strange who fitted them into position. He read the statement, and read it again. Norton watched with bewilderment. Strange signed the document, and passed it back with the pen to the police officer. His spectacles were plucked from his face and his arms were re-secured within his garment.

"Just as I suspected." declared Coates, nodding. "Dr Strange here is right-handed. According to the physician who examined the corpse and testified to the coroner, the, er, angles of entry of the stab wounds indicate with little doubt that Garbett's assassin was left-handed."

Though physically restrained, Strange's mirth once again was not.

"Ha, ha, ha, ha, ha, ha, ha!"

"So, Dr Norton," asked Coates after glancing at Strange, "why is there so much interest in Reverend Nudd's diary?"

"Ha, ha, ha, ha, ha, ha, ha, ha, ha, ha, ha, ha!"

"And tell me all you know, sir, about this tall Frenchman."

26

One hundred and fifteen years after it had been written, a diary came into the possession of a postgraduate student researching minor cults of the late nineteenth century. The diary's author, one Percival Nudd, had lived out the last phase of his life in rural Sussex at a small cottage he shared with his family. Life there had been frugal, Mr Nudd usually finding bouts of employment during the summer fruit-picking season. Otherwise he was largely unemployed. With such scant income, the Nudds were vastly indebted to a mysterious French benefactor who continued to send over sums of money on a regular basis. The cross-channel funds only ceased when Emily, a widow for eighteen years, was buried.

Percival Nudd passed away in 1919. A victim of the devastating influenza epidemic, his wife had risked infection to hold his hand as he took his final breath. Only months earlier Nudd had been notified that his only son, Percival junior, had died in battle. His arm and leg shredded by shrapnel in a muddy trench, amputation had failed to save him as gangrene had advanced faster than his battalion's push towards Amiens. The erstwhile Reverend had not seen his secret diary since living in London. Neither had anybody else for over half a century until, during the early terrors of the Blitz, a German bomb in 1940 destroyed the rear half of the Pimlico house along with its small, attached area of land. The missing diary was recovered undamaged from the rubble of a bizarre marble monument, reported to have been an obelisk, in the garden. In all probability, it was deduced, the diary had been hidden inside a small chamber designed for that very purpose. The owner of the property, fortunate to survive the explosion, traced Percival Nudd's only surviving child, his daughter Amelia, who in turn handed the diary on. It eventually came into the hands of Amelia's great granddaughter, Sarah Coggins, who had neglected it in her attic until approached by the student. She gladly lent him the diary to assist with his research. Although being a worthy source of material for the thesis, the tale that unfolded in the diary's entries provoked, for the student, far greater fascination than the short-lived history of the cult of The Nuddites.

PART II

The Diary of Percival Conrad Ignatius Nudd

18th September 1883

This morning I received a letter from a Monsieur Louis de Menec of The French Institute for Scientific Advancement. He had read a publication of my lecture earlier this year at The Royal Society for the Investigation of Strange Phenomena entitled "Ball Lightning: The Internally Powered Model Hypothesis". He was apparently sufficiently impressed to now invite me over to France to conduct some scientific observations in an area known as the Breton Marshes. These are to be in two phases. Firstly he wishes to discredit once and for all some of the local peasant notions that the prehistoric stones of the vicinity have magical powers, and also that they are frequented by goblins or some other fanciful "little people". Secondly, having completed the megalith study, he wishes to observe any occurrences of ball lightning and will o' the wisps to verify not only their existence, but also to endeavour to determine their cause. All the studies are to take place during the hours of twilight and darkness: the approach of sundown until sunrise. It seems that Monsieur de Menec is something of a maverick with aristocratic connections. I am uncertain who will be providing the funding.

I have just posted a reply to this Monsieur de Menec. Though unfruitful so far in discovering any references either to this gentleman or to The French Institute for Scientific Advancement, I shall be delighted to enrich his work by provision of my expertise and scientific understanding. I will be crossing the channel by steamer two weeks today. The prospects of a desolate nocturnal existence, for the duration, and with this gentleman Emily already refers to as deMonic, both fascinate and daunt me.

2nd October 1883

I arrived in Nantes just after noon and have found myself a suitable hotel where I can take a much needed bath, trim my moustache and side-whiskers, consume generous portions of excellent French cuisine, and procure a good night's slumber. It will be a fine thing indeed to sleep horizontally on a static bed that is neither rocking nor trundling forwards. A few glasses of Nantaise wine followed by a thimble of absinthe will provide an ideal nightcap for a weary traveller. I don't wish the green fairy to become a monster trampling my head in the morning. My timepiece will be on the bedside table, along with a photographic miniature of my dear wife and a gold locket containing a snipped tress of her hair. They reliably furnish me with some comfort and good luck whenever I have to travel in pursuit of scientific research. On such expeditions I trust both in God's grace and in the desire to return safely to my fair and dutiful wife, Emily. Tomorrow, a Monsieur Michel is to meet me opposite the Cathedral of Saint Pierre and Saint Paul. From there he is to drive me in a horse-drawn carriage along some, presumably, boggy and treacherous tracks (more suited to wild beasts with long claws), and into the depths of the Breton marshes. At length we are to finally rendezvous with Monsieur de Menec at the remote village of La Chapelle-sur-le-Marais.

3rd October 1883

My Monsieur Michel was awaiting me at the appointed time. Standing motionless by his two-horse carriage he was recognisable, as arranged, both by his black cap with a white feather and also by an autumn sunflower held in his hand. His countenance tended to be rather surly. A man of few words, he politely doffed his cap to me, nodded and grunted. He placed my baggage securely on top of the carriage and gestured for me to enter and take my seat. With the agility of an organ-grinder's ape he then clambered onto his driving perch, and we were soon rumbling out of Nantes and progressively further away from civilisation. Tally Ho! The spirit of adventure has entered my tingling veins.

Fortunately the journey to our destination passed without incident. The roads, although becoming increasingly like muddy tracks, neither ensnared nor toppled our carriage. It was often bumpy due to the coarse lumps of stone used in places to harden the track surface, and I was at times almost cast out of the seat. Perhaps it was fortunate that the land here was as flat as a vast French crepe, cut into irregular slices to feed the issue of Titan by the natural rivulets and the engineered ditches. My knowledge of engineering does not sit on a lofty stratum of my scientific portfolio, but I shall neverless take an interest in the reclaiming of this land from the sea. No doubt the Dutch were involved in this. As the carriage approached, herons and egrets launched into flight, deer stood staring before bounding away and, further upwards, swathes of waterfowl mottled the bleak sky whilst buzzards and harriers looked to harness a ride on the billowing winds. As my eyes dropped back down I watched sheep and bizarre donkeys with long shaggy coats munch on the lush marshy grasses, through which small furry creatures, too obscured for me to identify, scampered and scurried. Like a gorging reptile the wilderness swallowed us inside its gaping jaws. Our progress thus became slower and I was somewhat relieved when we finally arrived at la Chapelle-sur-le-Marais mid afternoon without having become marooned by a broken or submerged wheel. There, I was ushered into a tiny hostelry of sorts – the only one most probably for miles around. Monsieur Michel carried my baggage inside and deposited it next to my table. He then instructed me, in barely comprehensible English, that I was to wait there until Monsieur de Menec arrived. And this proved to be tedious. A rather burly woman presented me with a meal of shredded cabbage studded with mussels and shrimps, and some, I surprisingly point out, under-boiled potatoes. In fairness I should add that this was to taste astoundingly better than its appearance had suggested. A flask of watery wine was also placed on the table along with a rather haggard-looking goblet. I was hoping to start eating after the arrival of Monsieur de Menec. Though having waited for a few minutes I was vigorously encouraged to commence by the burly hostess, a Madame Rontard. Long after eating my tardy lunch there was still no sign of my new colleague. To occupy the time I turned, God forgive my vanity, to fantasy: I imagined delivering a lecture at the Royal Academy, being presented to Queen Victoria, becoming a leading scientific pioneer in the Empire and beyond, and making those haughty universities – for the repudiation of an able grammar school alumnus – look so thoroughly foolish. I had to pass the time and also comfort the soul in this elementary outpost of society where I was kept waiting. And I just continued waiting, hour grimly stacked upon hour, all the time ogled by various local folk who came and went. Some of them were courteous enough to afford me a nod. Others merely gazed at me as if I were an oddity abandoned by a travelling freak show. On occasions I stepped outside to inspect the surroundings. The chapel of the village name stood across a little square from the hostelry. There were two shops, as far as I could discern, one of which sold only the bread baked on its premises. Other than these there were about another score or so houses, and a couple of handfuls of stables and barns. Stretching past the village to the horizon, the terrain persisted stubbornly with its flatness. It is surely more level than the summer waves of the ocean that abridges this land fifteen kilometres due west. Loneliness prevails, and even here it seemed anomalous to behold the gatherings in the auberge during the course of my wait because there was scarcely a soul to be witnessed out and about in the village itself. The majority of activity was represented by the roaming of scrawny dogs, and the pecking of scruffy hens when not being sporadically chased by a ragamuffin boy.

Eventually at just past seven in the evening my long wait was over. A huge man, much taller than any Frenchman I had so far seen, and attired splendidly in a finely tailored costume and cape better suited for dining at the Savoy Hotel, appeared in the doorway. Monsieur Louis de Menec arrived with such suddenness, an apparition of such incongruity, that he might have been spirited here from another world – had I believed in that sort of skulduggery! His raiment cut from finest cloth, his hat of velvety felt rising like a pillar atop a human mountain, were all inky-black like his eyes and his abundant locks. He more than caught my eye. He gripped it with the authority of Mesmer, smiled, strode across to my table with an outstretched hand and almost snapped the bones in mine as he vigorously clasped it.

We both have a room here at the auberge – basic yet adequate – and I am scribbling this entry as I sit on my bed. Dinner was another interesting and splendidly nourishing affair. We started with half a dozen fresh oysters, and this was followed by stewed eels, potato slices set in cheese and cream, and a variety of delicious fried fungi which, I shamefully confess, I struggled to identify. Finally another cheese, one of firm texture, saline tang, and subtle fruity flavour, was produced that we devoured with some bread. With so much cheese I shall dream vividly tonight, no doubt, entering into this surreal world in haste. As I am now suffering from the effects of copious conversation, assisted by a plentiful supply of wine to moisten the tongue, I am more than ready to take what shall probably be my last night of sleep for some time. Exhaustion has pounced upon me with the grip of monstrous fangs that are pulling me down into prostrate submission. Resistance is both futile and inexpedient, and so I shall reveal more about my new colleague along with forthcoming activities in the next entry. Suffice to note that Monsieur de Menec speaks excellent English, and for that I am grateful, because trying to express myself in French would surely have exhausted me hours ago. I have imbibed to excess, and I fear that Emily would be none too impressed. Most certainly time for bed!

4th October 1883

Our scientific research commences this evening. After the comforts subsequent to my arduous journey – the overindulgence in the yields of this coastal land, and the undisciplined enjoyment of the fermented fruits of its neighbouring vineyards – settling down to the assignment will be welcome.

My colleague tells me that we are to spend at least a week observing the megaliths. These are located about seven kilometres southeast of here where the marshes have never penetrated and the terrain, consequently, is considerably firmer and drier. We are to investigate a pair of menhirs that stand like a devoted couple, Monsieur explains, and a dolmen situated about four hundred metres away. De Menec is to observe the twin upright slabs of stone which both reach a height of nearly five metres and which are separated by a distance of approximately seventeen. I have been designated observation duties on the dolmen. We are to carry lanterns but vision should be greatly enhanced by our celestial neighbour the moon, which is approaching fullness at this time. According to prevailing local belief, and very queer and superstitious their notions seem to be, both menhirs are believed to completely spin about their axes over several minutes commencing at the stroke of midnight. Furthermore, when the moon is full, they are believed, at irregular intervals, to dance about the pastures accompanied by little people before returning to their original positions after every occasion. The dolmen does not offer the animation of stone, apparently, but has some significance for goblins who are believed to congregate there during the night. This dolmen has partly collapsed over the multitude of centuries, but I am informed that it is still discernible as a circular pile of stones just managing to support several vast lintel type stones on top, and under which a restricted chamber might afford some shelter. Naturally both de Menec and myself consider these fanciful notions of the local peasants to be absurd. They are, however, all the same firmly anchored in the minds of the people of this area. Indeed similar notions are prevalent further north into Brittany, further south into the lower Vendée, and beyond: endemic across hundreds of French kilometres into the Alps and the Pyrenees. De Menec and myself should, as true scientists, keep open minds but we also anticipate disproving such notions through straightforward observational research. I presume that we are adopting an hypothesis that precludes spontaneous stone animation whilst including the imagination and other collective mental aberrations for the explanation of such beliefs. Alas, de Menec persists in being unsatisfactorily vague. I still await his clarification on this hypothesis, and my scientific expertise may be needed to lead the way. But I am becoming of the opinion that, for whatever reason, de Menec simply wants to challenge the people of this area and demonstrate that they are both wrong and asinine. In the unlikely, but most interesting occasion of any evidence being spotted to the contrary, the observer is to attract the attention of his colleague in the following manner: he is to low loudly like a cow and then raise his lantern thrice. At this improbable signal the other is to then make his way as swiftly as he is able towards that lantern and his colleague.

Monsieur de Menec is a most convivial gentleman. He is a great bear of a man but any bestial resemblance stops there – except for the matter of the soul on which I shall elaborate presently. His elegant and expensive dress-sense helps to cut a figure of fine breeding and dash that will be quite out of place for the fieldwork we are to undertake. Thick, black curly hair clings around the brim of his towering hat. His eyes are a darker brown than the natives' from deepest Africa, and have the potency and the mystery of a witch's brew. Arguably they are black. Beneath a bony nose his waxed, black moustache is sculptured with pride. This moustache, I believed termed "natural", is grandly dinctinctive without the ostentation of over-exaggerated length, flopping droop or upturned curls. Like a low-lying triangle with an expansively oblique apex, it slopes down gently to form sharp corners with the level base. It is difficult to know much about his family background as he is reluctant to discuss anything at all to do with his personal details, although he has once declared that this project has something to do with unfinished family business. He is possibly five years or so older than me, and climbing towards the half-century a decade hence. Beyond that, all I can ascertain is that this fine gentleman is an energetic and educated conversationalist, and something of what the French would call a "bon viveur". I should record that, approaching its conclusion, some of the conversation did disturb me a little, though, and I have attempted to record the dialogue as accurately as my memory serves me. When alarmed by something I deem it best to reconsider, with as much accuracy as possible, at a later time when feeling fresh and becalmed of mental tempests. So, to the best of my ability, our discourse was as follows. Being protestant I asked de Menec about the fate of my French brethren, the Huguenots. Monsieur responded by asking if possessing any ecclesial faith was relevant to the pursuit of scientific knowledge. I was astonished and dared to presume that my colleague was a Catholic. He looked me in the eye and asked me what I should care of a denomination who had massacred the Huguenots three centuries ago on the day of Saint Bartholomew. I responded that three centuries was a long time past and that we were, notwithstanding, all Christians who now got along and respected each other. De Menec then asserted that whether Christian or otherwise, theists all have varying beliefs and that they cannot accordingly all be right. I concurred to a point, but stopped short like a stubborn mule refusing to advance when he added that, by supposedly the same logic, theists could all therefore be wrong.

"As a man eenterested in scientific understandings, 'ow can you beleef in zees zings?" he asked me. "The great Breetish man Monsieur Darwin as shown all zee stupid peoples zat evolution eez responsable for all ze living theengs of now and before. Zis is not God making theengs in six days. Maybe you should read ze works of Cuvier."

"No. You are correct about that." I answered uncomfortably. "But the creation of everything, here and in the heavens, demonstrates a power and precision beyond anything that could be conceived by chance and without the great love of a nurturer. Have you not heard of the Reverend William Paley's analogy of the Almighty Watchmaker? We reasonable people can all accept that the earth is thousands of years old and was not created in the year 4003 before Christ's birth, as calculated by Archbishop James Ussher. "

"Millions, Monsieur, enormous millions of years old. Anuzer Breetishman, a Scottishman called 'Utton 'as shown zees. And never forget zat one time you would 'ave bin burned at zee stake not so long ago for explicating zat zee sun and ze stars are not going round ze earth."

"Yes, of course I am familiar with the work of Hutton – and Cuvier as well," I replied with a hint of irritation. "And regarding Monsieur Cuvier, of course I accept that fossils are the remains of beasts long vanished from this Earth, and further that many are probably not the remains of creatures that perished in the great flood. But however one interprets the book of Genesis, we are only here due to the miracles and benevolence of God. In Him I trust. In Jesus I trust, and in the Holy Spirit. God does indeed move in mysterious ways, Monsieur, and it is not for us to think we can understand His power, His wisdom and His methods. We can thank Him for His grace and for creating us and all else in His Kingdom. We can thank Him for revealing some of the secrets of His Kingdom to scientists like you and me. We can thank Him for blessing us with a soul. Do you not think so, Monsieur?"

"I think you have zis faith because it is ze faith of your farzer and 'iz farzer and 'iz farzer. I don't like zis concept of soul. But, Monsieur Nudd, I do beleef in ze spirit. For example, I beleef in ze spirit of discovery, and I 'ave faith in ze spirit and ze wisdom of my grandfarzer," De Menec announced sombrely, and stared into my face with eyes so dark and fathomless that they seemed to be twin portals through which one could plunge into hell itself. I shuddered momentarily then said something too hastily.

"Monsieur. Please take no offence but are you a follower of Satan?"

At once I regretted this foolish question but after a pause during which he scrutinised me, De Menec roared heartily with mirth before responding with composure, "Monsieur Nudd, to worship ze Devil one must beleef in ze Devil. To beleef in ze Devil one must beleef in God."

"Don't you have any religious faith at all. Monsieur?" I inquired. "I should point out that I have my faith and can trust in God at all times. I have put my trust in God for the safe undertaking of our work in such a desolate place as this with its many dangers, and then to deliver me back into the arms of my dear wife."

"And so eef you was afflicted wiz, per' aps, consumption would you place your trust in God or in a physician of *bon reputation*? Or per'aps, Monsieur Nudd, you would place your trust wiz ze skilled physician and *explique* after recovery zat it eez ze will of God zat you get better because you 'ave put your trust in 'im. *Simplement*, for zis work we make 'ere, I trust in me, I trust in my granfarzer, and I trust in you. I think it to be foolish to trust in anysing else. Just look at zees peoples of zis region. Zay 'ave strong beleef in little peoples, in moving stones, in superstitions, in a virgin 'aving a baby, in God. Zay search for ze Devil heverywhere but zee Devil is only in zem. Zees peoples know nussing. I 'ave faith in us. To us, Monsieur. *Santé!*" he toasted zestfully, raising his glass above his head. "And to my grandfarzer," he concluded, and I raised my glass respectfully.

It is now late afternoon. We have reposed for a few hours in an attempt to facilitate the sustaining of not merely conscious but lucid minds tonight. After all, unless something most unanticipated occurs, tonight – and the ensuing six – will be periods of great tedium with ever lengthening hours in the dead of night. Monsieur de Menec has procured two horses to transport us to our remote laboratory and after dining early we shall set off at six o'clock. Subsequent entries of this journal will be written on awakening early afternoon following work, rest and nourishment.

7th October 1883

Father Time seemed to have placed his scythe and hourglass on the ground so he could lie down to rest beside them. Naturally I have been contemplating Monsieur de Menec at length. Despite his apparent rejection of our Lord – and I pray that his soul might be saved yet – I must confess that this man is otherwise a most agreeable example of God's creations. He is cheerful, continues to be an able and fascinating conversationalist, and his very presence imbues one with confidence. In de Menec I certainly trust. My mind has since been wandering to other matters such as my Emily, and I have been attempting to invigorate my motivation for this expedition with thoughts of great discoveries and of being invited to speak at grand scientific conventions. And as this has continued I have begun to exhaust my cache of fantasies to fend off the solitude and slumber that threaten to interfere with the task at hand. Yet just when the nights were becoming so indeterminately stretched, at last there is something interesting to report. I had, as usual, been gazing towards the dolmen with my imagination playing tricks on my efforts to concentrate. I had been picturing myself comfortably in bed at home in Pimlico with Emily purring softly as she slept by my side. Suddenly I was roused from this narcotic vision when I began to think that I could hear someone, or some thing, moving around near the monument.

"Is that you, Monsieur?" I asked, in the unlikely event it was my colleague. There was no response and so I manoeuvred stealthily towards the dolmen. Since the clouds were overcast and sprinkling the occasional balm of drizzle, the moonlight was unhelpfully absent. Thrusting my lantern towards the low dark entrance I then perceived some movement. At this point I stood back and lowed as loudly as I was able before thrice hoisting the lantern above my head. After a few seconds de Menec's lantern could be seen to be approaching, and before long my colleague had arrived with bounding strides and tempestuous puffs of breath that blasted the air more forcefully than the Atlantic gales.

"Is everysink all right wiz you, sir?" de Menec inquired anxiously. "'Ave you seen somesink *remarquable?*"

And so I described the occurence and we strode across to the mouth of the dolmen. Crouching, we lowered ourselves, lanterns first, to peer inside the darkness. Then we made a discovery. No it was not a goblin, nor wildcat, nor phantom. Lying down and recoiling from our presence, however, was as tatty and sorry a looking wretch as I have witnessed. He was clutching a bottle of liquor and clearly in a state of inebriety. De Menec questioned him and the wretch explained that he was an itinerant fisherman whose existence depended on catching eels in the marshes at night. I confess that, with my lack of complete fluency in this man's language distorted by his drunken slurring, I had difficulty in grasping the full picture. I had to keep asking my colleague for assistance. De Menec explained to him that we were conducting scientific research that would be seriously jeopardised by his presence and offered him some money to leave. The poor wretch at once declined and began jabbering something about being too terrified to return to the marshes because of somebody he referred to as "l'Homme du Marais". Heavens above! This was as perplexing as it was inconvenient. He persisted, his face contorting, in mentioning this man of the marshes, and I requested confirmation from de Menec that my interpretations were accurate. De Menec dismissively splayed his hands away and told me that this man was merely a drunken lunatic whose own deranged mind was conspiring to frighten him. At length he offered the man yet more money, which was accepted, and ushered him on his way.

Nothing else of note occurred after this. How far away the wretch actually deported himself I cannot say but I was not aware of him subsequently. My colleague too had shrugged his shoulders, muttered something about the ravages of alcohol, and returned to his post. Little was said riding back but then we were both typically weary. My fading mind couldn't totally dismiss that poor man's expression as he ejaculated his fear of his imaginary marsh man.

"Alco'ol, sir, eez 'iz only beast," de Menec had determined.

11th October 1883

The Megalith project has been concluded. It ended at daybreak this morning and for that I am a relieved soul indeed. An ovation has been earned as has the opportunity to respond with a bow. In the circumstances the effort required to remain awake when endeavouring to focus the attention on barely visible stones was of Trojan proportions. Of course, not all scientific work is entertaining, contrary to widespread, uninformed opinion. We don't all conceive the fixed images of photography like one ingenious Monsieur Niepce. We don't all engineer steam engines like Mr Watt, isolate bacteria for the creation of vaccines like Monsieur Pasteur, change our understanding of the origins of species like Mr Darwin, or develop electric lamps like Messrs Swan and Edison that can illuminate an entire town, as was recently achieved in Godalming. Certainly not! Much research is dull, and undoubtedly some of the illustrious names just mentioned spent similarly long hours seemingly achieving little whilst yearning for stimulation and "eureka" moments in pursuit of their scientific goals. So, and to borrow from my colleague's tongue, *voilà*! The longest week I have ever experienced has confirmed the generalised hypotheses that these ancient stones neither turn nor dance, and that they are not frequented by little people. Whether or not this will convince the local peasant stock remains to be seen, but it is our conclusion that the belief in the movement of the stones stems from an optical illusion probably associated with moonlight and the shadows cast. Furthermore, the idea that the dolmens are a gathering place for little people is probably a case of mistaken identity. As we have found, they make useful places for itinerant drunks and lunatics to find shelter. An ever exaggerated tale combined with the unyielding superstitions of a simple intelligence does the rest in both cases. The human mind often embellishes reality well beyond the point of merely converting it into fiction. Paradoxically, perhaps, the more limited the mind the greater, inadvertently, its invention. We thus have the birth and the existence of folklore. As for the poor man we discovered in the dolmen, he provides us with a case in point. His terrified rantings about a marsh man have been, unsurprisingly, heard by others who are now further disseminating ungodly nonsense about this spectre. Only this morning on our return to the village our hostess, the sturdy Madame Rontard, tried to dissuade us from undertaking the second part of our research in the marshland on the basis that our lives would be imperilled by the reappearance of this marsh man. It is astonishing how, in this century of enlightenment, mistaken identity, deceptions of the light, and drunken gibberish can all instil terrifying beliefs in those who become all the more susceptible collectively. Just why do people so easily believe in the supernaturally absurd? Perhaps never again will a century be as notable as this one for the comprehension, harnessing, and utilisation of the forces of nature. Until the dawn of this great century we had scarcely been more sophisticated than the unearthed Neander Valley brute, and yet here we are amongst a pocket of people resolved to fester in ignorance. De Menec may lack my understanding of social anthropology, but his contentions about these folk are not incorrect. Rural isolation is as much a breeding-ground for ignorance as it is a ground for inbreeding. A woebegone union of afflictions indeed! In more civilised communities many of these impoverished and deformed souls would be ushered into the care of lunatic asylums. I should thank God that He has blessed me with intellect, education and sanity. Of course, Monsieur de Menec reacted to Madame Rontard by once again shrugging his shoulders and smiling knowingly if politely. But then he would, because he is both a worldly scientist and also an exemplum of good breeding – his bewildering atheism excepted.

We have the night off to enjoy some conversation over dinner, and no doubt even more over some bottles of wine afterwards. I'd like to discuss the mysterious force of gravity. I am also hoping that de Menec will elaborate on his contention that all miracles are explainable by science already understood or yet to be so. He is certainly correct when he states that the photograph or the electric lamp would have been considered products of either wizardry or Divine intervention but a few years ago. Disconcertingly he seems intent on dismissing God's presence in the course of events, ignoring my enlightened counsel.

"You 'ave faith, monsieur. 'Ow can you 'ave faith in somesing when you 'ave no proof for zees? Zis eez not wiz my comprehension why peoples belief in somesing wiz no proof. Eet eez not wiz my comprehension zat eet eez a greater virtue to 'ave faith wizout questioning anysing. You, monsieur, are a scionteest. As a scionteest you look for ze evidence to support or deesagree wiz ze hypothesis. So your faith is not wiz my comprehension," de Menec stated.

While his logic, superficially, may seem sound, it is clear to me as a Christian that there is an enormous hole in his capacity for "comprehension". It is a void I intend to fill. I eagerly await greater debate and the pitting of my wits against his before the resumption of our responsibilities. Tomorrow night we head for the marshes in search of ball lightning and will o' the wisps. We have no united formal hypotheses, but wish to observe, collect data and learn enough to formulate hypotheses for future research. All measurable variables including atmospheric conditions will be recorded in a separate log along with any other relevant observations. My own supposition regarding ball lightning could well benefit from being subjected to some scrutiny. That in itself would be a useful examination of my wisdom on this phenomenon, and help to sharpen my focus. De Menec informs me that he has witnessed neither ball lightning nor will o' the wisps. His interest apparently stems from some sightings in these parts many years ago by his grandfather while exploring the secrets of the marshes. We are both relishing this stage of our expedition. It will be so much more interesting than solitary stone gazing that it can be scarcely stressed enough. We are to work together at all times. This is not only for the comparison and discussion of any interesting phenomena observed, but also for safety purposes. The marshes can be a treacherous place in broad daylight. The bogs and the steep-banked dikes and rivulets can be death traps at night. These wetlands will become even more menacing during a thunderstorm, and electric storm clouds are surely needed if we are to observe any ball lightning.

13th October 1883

It was a miserable night. Incessant rain was hurled against our waning flesh throughout by angry winds. We saw nothing of interest. Instead we trod around in syrupy mud, boots sucked down or slipping and sliding hither and thither. Fortunately the plexus of water-channels – lethally sprung snares after sundown – were avoided in the dense darkness. It was a blessing too that we had each other for company and also that we were able to negotiate our path back to where we had tied the cowering horses. The ride back was less grim in the knowledge that we could soon change out of our dripping clothes, towel ourselves dry, take some nourishment, and be soothed by the hospitality of sleep. It was a series of incidents prior to our departure that proffered the only excitement worth recording. Once again this marsh man has impinged upon our routine, although more in my musings than in any other respect. Certainly Monsieur de Menec seems quite unruffled by a nonsensical hocus pocus that seems to be afflicting the locals like a religious mania. *Haxpax max Deus adiflax*! Methinks it takes considerably less than this for these people to conjure up phantoms from nothing! Firstly, Madame Rontard once more tried to dissuade us from visiting the marshes. This was followed, as we were untethering our horses, by the appearance of a weather-beaten man who approached to warn us against conducting any further research. He said that he was a fisherman who knew the marshes better than any place on this earth. I had no difficulty in believing this. However, he also claimed to have seen this marsh man character a couple of nights earlier, in the early hours as dawn was breaking. Despite his grave demeanour and sombre tone, it was infinitely harder to afford this assertion any credence. My colleague gave it none at all, shaking his imposing head whilst smiling at me. He courteously thanked the fisherman for his advice and concern before explaining,

"Zees is *typique* of zees peoples in zees places when zay 'ave zees superstisioos hideas in zer 'eads. *Typique!*"

15ᵗʰ October 1883

Arriving back after a barren night of toil, myself weary, cold and wretched, and de Menec resembling a fortress unimpaired by so much as a scratch on the masonry, we first strode past a surly gathering of men of all ages before entering the auberge. The men had stared at us with unmistakable malice in their eyes. They had muttered to one another as their eyes followed our path into the hostelry. Inside, Madame Rontard accosted de Menec and spoke earnestly to him. De Menec remained calm as ever. He responded to our hostess with words accompanied by the characteristic smile, and Madame Rontard eventually relaxed into an even broader smile before the lines of anxiety exploded back across her face. By then de Menec was already beckoning me to proceed ahead of him up the stairs to our rooms. On reaching the landing I asked de Menec to enlighten me about the exchange.

"I am weary, Monsieur. Contrary to my usual disposition I have begun struggling to procure adequate slumber these last few days. I was unable to follow that conversation. Please afford me the details."

"Monsieur Nudd. It eez nussing," de Menec replied dismissively. "Madame once more asks me if we leave. If we don't leave she ask me can we *se depêcher*, 'urry it up. She say to me there are too much bad rumours about zis marsh man. I tell her zat it iz like preparing good cuisine: good scientific work takes ze time and ze good attention to ze details. I tell her it must be good quality like her cuisine. Zat eez all. Monsieur. Hanyway, some rumours have truth, and some do not."

"Yes, indeed. That may be. But people act on rumours whether they have a basis of truth or not," I retorted.

"Oh please, Monsieur Nudd. Do not you forget zat while zis is sometimes true, rational peoples like you and me act ze best because we 'ave more control," de Menec argued as if there was not a single reason in the whole world to cause him consternation. While he was speaking it occurred to me that people like de Menec are products of such comfortable and privileged upbringings that they fail to fully engage with the real world. By contrast, a product of slightly more modest blood, my achievements have been hard won through perseverance and keen wit. Nonetheless I entered my room with my head swirling with afflictions. I concede it is possible that my developing fatigue is distorting my judgement and exaggerating my concerns. It is difficult to be sure. Queer and threatening notions are bubbling to the surface. In addition to the supposedly witnessed manifestations of this marsh man, here is a short list of other events that have occurred nearby during the previous two days, fomenting restlessness amongst the natives: three men, returning along the narrow causeway ridge from the nearby Isle of Noirmoutier, were swept to their deaths by some monster waves; the death of a sheep, correctly identified by de Menec as having first perished of natural causes and subsequently been scavenged by semi-feral dogs and wild boar, has been attributed to this marsh man; the local bishop has been unsuccessfully petitioned by a delegation of villagers to find a priest willing to locate and exorcise this marsh man, dispatching him back whence he came. Something decidedly odd is gathering momentum.

Equally curious are my feelings towards de Menec. I am beginning to wonder if, screened behind a façade of scientific investigation, he is harbouring an undisclosed reason for our presence here. I can even report that during a dream I experienced amongst my last batch of disrupted slumber, I was alone with de Menec in the ghastly night-time marshes when he held up the lantern to his face, and grinned as he revealed through reptilian teeth that his real name was not de Menec but de Monic. Almost instantly I awoke with my heart pounding and sweat trickling down my face. This should not come as a complete surprise since only common idiots, heathens, lunatics and Satanists for some unfathomable reason reject God's existence. Sometimes I even wonder whether de Menec is suffering from insanity like many of these ill-bred villagers. I can imagine him being committed to a lunatic asylum now, and where the clergy had failed, having his demons cast out and into a passing herd of swine by a complement of physicians. In addition to that sourced from my faith, my powers of reason, and my marriage, I can draw further strength from knowing that I will never be committed to such an establishment – and I look forward to throwing the full weight of my intellect at de Menec's atheism in due course. De Menec is intelligent and well-read. Therein lies the difficulty in grasping how he could possibly dismiss God who created us, watches over each and every one of us, and who hears all our individual prayers. It seems nonetheless a step too far to construe Monsieur as demonic. I might have been a little uncharitable. Perhaps lately fatigue and unamiable encounters have agitated my imagination. Ambivalence is a tricky customer with which to deal: de

Menec disturbs me, I confess, and yet inconguously the more he does so the more secure I feel in the man's company.

16th October 1883

Last night the weather was again dry. This should not hinder any prospects of witnessing will o' the wisps, though we have seen none yet. The likelihood of seeing any ball lightning, however, remains as remote as the chances of man building a machine to fly him to the moon. On the one hand it is considerably more comfortable to spend a dry night on the cold marshes, although a blanket of cloud is wont to render the cold less hostile. On the other, our prospects of furthering the scientific knowledge of our chosen subjects means that we should be disappointed. Perhaps I am missing the comforts provided by my dear Emily to possess the enthusiasm for a task befitting a committed scientist. I must remain positive. Last night de Menec and I were discussing the unhelpful atmospheric conditions and he assured me that thunderstorms were due soon. We proceeded to spend an agreeable few hours discussing ball lightning, or "boules de feu" as they are known here, in which I outlined the difference between ball lightning and St Elmo's fire. De Menec was interested in my conclusions that the latter, often seen on ships during storms, should hover around metallic structures either as a function of magnetism or conductivity. This, I asserted, was clearly a different phenomenon from ball lightning that typically descends from thunderclouds, moves laterally for a few seconds, and then abruptly disappears with a fizz or a bang. I was pleased that my colleague concurred with my rationale. We did disagree on one thing, however. We have hardly encountered a soul near the marshes, and certainly not at all after dark. This is unusual for an area where so many make their living, even during the night hours. I wondered whether or not this was due to this strange affair of the marsh man. De Menec insisted otherwise. He did his best to assure me that that only a few foolish individuals might be deterred, but also insisted that the chances of encountering another fellow out there were as unlikely as finding a leaf of rolled tobacco in a muddy barnyard. I was not entirely convinced. I hope I can be forgiven for stating at this juncture that I don't know who de Menec thinks he is. Nor do I believe that I am going to find out. He has some sort of genuine aristocratic roots – of that I am sure. Yet for all my hunger to learn more about his background, his offerings on the silver platter only ever consist of a morsel or two about his grandfather. Perhaps I am unreasonably curious. Though I doubt it.

This morning delivered another dead sheep, a torn and bloodspattered specimen of carrion, left on display undoubtedly for our benefit. We encountered it in the middle of the road, halfway along our route from the village extremity to our hostelry. De Menec's jocular remark did little to reassure me.

"Don't worry, Monsieur Nudd," he laughed, "Ze *mouton* was not killed by a panther." In response to my raised eyebrows, he merely enthused about the sweet and salty quality of the mutton from the local marsh-grazing sheep while we were closely watched by a gathering of hostile eyes. Shortly after returning to the auberge, I was alarmed by hearing what I thought were thunderclaps. It transpired that these noises were, after all, only the sounds of gunshot nearby. I was, I confess, rather relieved that the shooting of ducks was not a reason for a weary soul to have to get out of bed and trample back out into the miserable expanses during an electric storm. We shall see what the next sortie offers.

In the meantime, and most disagreeably, my slumber was disturbed by an infernal row. At least it curtailed an unpleasant dream where yet again I was back on the night marshes when Emily appeared out of the darkness like a spectre calling out to me to return home. She wandered straight past me and away without noticing my presence, but hard though I tried, I was unable to free my feet from the mud and move towards her. As Emily disappeared into the darkness, I was quite unable to call out to her or engineer any sound other than stifled grunts. These were soon overwhelmed by some male voices I heard shouting behind me. It was at this point that I awoke. The noisy parties, if my ears were functioning properly, were Madame Rontard and at least three men whom I could not identify. The dreadful shouting must have continued for at least half an hour. People really ought to be more considerate. Having got back to sleep I awoke with a start by the noise of the door to my room, which I swear I had earlier locked, being pulled shut. As I sat up in the bed, I detected the sound of footsteps moving away along the creaking corridor. I went over to check the door and relocked it. Fortunately I was able to swiftly return to sleep. De Menec was to later dismiss the episode as nothing more than the contrivance of a dream within a dream. Despite being alarmed, the fact that I returned to sleep so easily supports this explanation. On the other hand, a physician might argue that my overwhelming fatigue had inescapably plunged me back to slumber, whatever the disturbances. I concede that in this instance I am baffled for now in my quest for the truth. I admit without a qualm that a table and chair will henceforth be repositioned behind the door to barricade my room from uninvited intrusions when asleep.

After I finally got up and was eating with de Menec, I was aware that Madame Rontard was on occasions staring suspiciously – even frostily – at us with arms folded from the corner of the salon. When serving our refreshments she seemed to have mislaid her usual courtesy. Her attitude towards us has distinctly chilled. I have noticed too that other locals are giving us a wide berth while still casting disconcerting looks in our direction. I articulated my concerns to de Menec, adding that I nonetheless have faith in God's protection. I further added that it was time that de Menec embraced Jesus Christ if he was to be afforded the same grace now and forever by God.

"Monsieur, why are you Protestant and not *Catholique*? Why a *Chretien* and not Hindi or Buddhist or *Juif* or *Musselman*?" he asked.

"Because I was fortunate enough to have been born into a family who introduced me to the teachings of the one true son and principal prophet of God," I answered.

"Hmph," was de Menec's irksome response complete with his shoulder shrug, followed by his suggestion that I should, "Theenk about zis."

This I naturally don't need to do. And any further promptings on de Menec's part were interrupted by yet more commotion emanating from Madame Rontard's restaurant bar.

"What are they saying?" I asked my fellow researcher. "I heard the word *prêtre* mentioned, and something about quitting the village. The voices were obviously angry."

"Eez nussing," de Menec predictably revealed with his usual grinning nonchalance. "Some foolish peoples say to Madame Rontard that ze *evêque* priest 'e will still not come here to repel ze marsh man of zeir imaginations. Zay say zat if no *evêque* priest comes, then zay want us to leave. Madame she says we are *honête* peoples, you and me, and zat she don't want to take back our rooms. But she say she will counsel us again, nussing more. We 'ave, Monsieur Nudd, *le droit*, ze legal right, to stay here. What do you sink zat zees stupide peoples zay can do to us? Kill us? *Il faut les ignorer.*"

The marshes tonight, whatever the weather, will be more welcoming than la Chapelle-sur-le-Marais.

17th October 1883

I shall commence this entry by listing the principal conclusions I have formulated. These conclusions are based on the information at my disposal, the observation and logic of a keen mind, and the benefit of many solitary hours' consideration. Firstly it is clear that it is exclusively de Menec's presence that the villagers find so objectionable. My misfortune is that I am here as his colleague. I am condemned by association. Secondly the perception of the phantom marsh man's appearance is linked to our – or rather de Menec's – arrival. Thirdly, de Menec's field research is likely to be a cover for some ulterior and possibly diabolical motive. Fourthly, and paradoxically, I reaffirm that I feel safer in his company than when alone here. In this, I still lack a firm conclusion as to why it should be. However, our research, like de Menec's knowledge, is still of some interest. Further, I cannot complain about de Menec's approach to our tasks. Despite possessing the narrow and corrupted mind of an atheist, de Menec's scientific capacity seems surprisingly undiminished. Having a more robust scientific mind than my colleague, he at least knows that I can offer a great deal more than support as required. With all of this acknowledged, it is now apt to return to the entries fundamental to this diary.

It has once more been a fruitless night although the clouds have been gathering and the air thickening. Finding our way back and forth to de Menec's favoured position has not been too difficult, whatever the weather God sees fit to deliver us. Along the route three windmills serve as markers. Nearer the spot, a peasant salt harvester's hovel indicates that we are less than fifteen minutes' ride and trudge from our destination. Even if the hut cannot be perceived in the gloom, the raked-up heaps of salt glow in the dark like piles of swept snow reflecting the light of a streetlamp. On this occasion, however, even the pristine salt had been struggling to reveal itself. We could hear our poor horses during the night with their whinnies of anxiety. Not such good tidings for them but perhaps better for science. De Menec and I turned our attention to the subject of will o' the wisps. I reiterate that it is interesting how the locals reliably permit superstitious nonsense to interfere with reason. Note this, however. I am not dissuaded from admitting that, both during this night and the last, I have perceived hungry beasts and companies of malevolent men creeping towards us in the darkness. On one such occasion I swung around my lantern to witness the red, glaring eyes and white, bared enamel of the largest wolf ever known to science. But my point is this: I was tricked on each occasion by shadows, cast by lanterns or blinks of moonlight, and the rustling actuated by wind. Distorted further by fatigue and a mind fouled with concerns for our safety, my imagination was prone to becoming confused with reality. I know this, as would de Menec should I divulge these incidents to him. The ability to rationalize prevents me from nurturing a false belief that these marshes are infested with throat-tearers and throat-cutters. Likewise I know, however unrelentingly my imagination is stoked, that there is no Marsh Man, no little people, nor evil spectres. According to de Menec, it is strongly believed that will o' the wisps are lanterns carried by either mischievous sprites or diabolical sirens to lure travellers to their death. I have heard that similar notions abound in the British Isles. We also once more analysed the diverse opinions of their origin and had little difficulty again in agreeing on two candidates. The ignited marsh gas theory is our best, but we didn't preclude the possibility of two gases of volatile nature coming together to produce a chemical reaction. De Menec continues, of course, to bring his mercury barometer, mercury thermometer, binocular field glasses as well as a variety of portable contraptions that he says can detect methane, the marsh gases. Further, the latter instruments yielded yet more positive results last night. This continues to be promising because the "feu follet" is reported to be active here – in the context of their general scarcity, at least. We attempted for the first time, with limited success, to ignite small discharges of marsh gas and will be keen to make any comparisons with the bona fide phenomenon. Colour of flame, brightness, form, duration and mobility are all to be noted. It must be said that our own igniting of marsh gas produced brief and rather static pyrotechnics. This is unlike the established notion of the will o' the wisp darting around although they are sometimes said to flicker and vanish, only to reappear and so on. This could indicate a series of independent gas emissions being successively ignited by the same catalyst. Hopefully, we will see for ourselves.

De Menec has also now brought several long iron rods which he hopes might serve as a luring device, when erected, for a "feu Saint-Elme." We shall stand away from this at a distance of at least twenty running paces in the event of an electric storm. I have no desire to attract a lightning bolt onto myself or my colleague, and indeed suffer the fate of the Russian scientist Richmann who was electrocuted whilst studying ball lightning in the middle of the last century.

"I have no desire to be transported in the blink of an eye to the next life just yet!" I remarked.

"And I 'ave no desire to see you transported into ze oblivion yet, Monsieur," de Menec quibbled, and I shook my head in astonishment.

"Genuinely you are utterly bereft of belief in God, Monsieur de Menec. And you give no credence to an afterlife or anything else taught to us by Jesus Christ. Is that not so?"

"As I say to you many times, I don't beleef in anysing of ze supernature, Monsieur Nudd. I don't beleef in ze little peoples, or in ze moving monoleet stones, or in God, ze hangels, or in ze Devil. Ze 'uman mind eez a strange and *fantastique* place, Monsieur. Inside eez ze ability to create and recreate. Peoples often recreate zings into ze supernature when eet eez not zis. Peoples want to beleef. Inside ze 'uman mind eez ze conscious. Wiz zis we 'ave fears, many imaginations, and very big, big problems wiz our mortality. But I say you zis, Monsieur. If I hever meet wiz somesink of ze supernature, and I am 'appy wiz ze evidence for zis, zen I will be 'appy. Maybe I will die 'appy man because of zees. But until zees time if it 'appen, non – I don't beleef," de Menec answered solemnly. This response, although disappointing, was not unexpected. At length with a smile he added,

"*Au minimum*, monsieur Nudd, you are not of zee Catholique faith and 'ave no reason, zerefore, of being sheepwrecked on ze desert ile of purgatory like Defoe's meester Crusoe. Alzough you could make a *changement* of faith to be Catholique if you become a reech man so you can pay ze *Pape* many monies to *reduire* ze time in purgatory."

I wish to make it clear that, despite their blasphemous, unreasoned and generally shocking nature, I have persevered with recording de Menec's comments. I have never heard anything like them, and I hope not to ever again. However I am of the opinion that they are so extraordinary that de Menec's comments warrant documentation even if they merit absolutely nothing else. In the meanwhile it is my Christian duty to do my best to remedy this Monsieur de Menec's sinister lunacy. For example, until I can enlighten my colleague to the contrary, we shall have to disagree on issues such as an afterlife. To be sure though, I have no desire to be returned to Emily as a pile of ashes in a casket. I doubt it would be to her fancy either – and all three of us could surely agree on that!

I have just slept slightly better, and that despite the prospects of an uninvited guest trying to enter my room, in addition to Madame Rontard persisting with her performance of reluctant hostess. On awakening, de Menec has managed to replenish my head with more of his pseudo-scientific gabbling of last night without being present in the same room! Once more I heard his voice suggesting that what the more rational and enlightened perceive as supernatural might be the harnessing of the laws of physics in various manners as yet undetermined by most of us. I heard him speculate about future discoveries, about travel to the moon and beyond, about distortions and tears in the fabric of time and space, and so on and on with ever and ever increasing absurdity. Inevitably, all this leads to his denial of

God and his reverence for his grandfather. Incredibly, so he has now revealed, it transpires that de Menec had only met his "granfarzer" as a small infant scarcely old enough to remember him. Yet he refers to him as if he were his mentor. He expanded upon his grandfather's odyssey to discover the truth about the supernatural, and the role played by chicanery in all of this. Once again much of de Menec's ideas eluded me, doubtless due to their effusive weakness. When less blunted by fatigue my sharper intellect will be able to more roundly refute de Menec's notions. I confess to not being blameless. Too often I provoke de Menec's imagination by querying his knowledge and by dismissing his lack of theism. Though oft subsequently regretted, it is difficult to resist.

De Menec's thoughts were wearying me and I hadn't been awake long. Hence I took a stroll in the village alone. In any case there were other issues to consider. I was curious, rather than eager, to see what reactions my presence might provoke in the locals. Monsieur de Menec as usual appears to be quite unperturbed by these things. He continues to laugh, mock, and shrug them off. I am less convinced and have been proven correct. I encountered two villagers whilst walking. A young woman glanced slyly at me before hurrying away. Then a middle-aged man approached shaking his head, wagging his finger, and muttering. I responded with a smile and the greeting "bonjour". At this he began to get rather irate, jabbing his finger in my direction. An unpleasant incident might have occurred had not the village priest come scuttling over to us from a doorway, holding his hat to his head, to intervene. He eventually placated the unruly man and beckoned me to follow him inside the chapel. This fellow then proceeded to look gravely into my eyes before calmly stating in a mixture of French and English,

"Your life is in danger here, Monsieur. It is best that you leave soon."

I asked him why this should be, as my agitation swelled into tangible anxiety.

"The older people who have memories do not trust you or your partner," he said enigmatically. "Something terrible happened here forty years ago. People do not like to talk about it but they are doing so now because the man of the marshes has returned," he continued. Unsure of what to make of this, though nonetheless disconcerted, I thanked the priest for his consternation and decided to return to the auberge forthwith to relate his words to de Menec. I arrived back without, fortunately, I have determined, further incident. For a second, crossing the road, I thought I detected a rifle barrel pointing at me from between the open shutters of a window. On closer inspection it seems I was mistaken, if not on the issue of hostility towards us. Yet again de Menec was unconcerned. Had I misinterpreted the French language uttered by the priest, he had wondered. Perhaps my insecurity of being in a lonely foreign place distorted my perception of things, he had suggested, after I had mentioned the faint possibility of being the target of a sniper's rifle.

"Wiz a bayonette, monsieur?" he had asked, before I reminded him that I had almost certainly been mistaken.

"Maybe zis eez a *Chassepot* you 'ave seen. Zee *Prusses* would *certainement* say you zat zees eez a *superieur* rifle, monsieur. *Rapide* for ze loading, and a very long distance."

I confess that de Menec's blasé attitude, his know-all smugness, and even his arrogance are all beginning to take their toll on our relationship. At the same time he does continue to exude a certain calmness and authority that still provides some comfort. At length he persuaded me to take little notice. Madame Rontard has become disturbed by the rumours about this marsh man, and that would strengthen my interpretation that she has become hostile towards us, he explained. De Menec is right, though, that all outsiders become targets of some enmity in small communities that are in the grip of some plague or superstitious mania. I shall certainly be all the more pleased to escape to the marshes tonight. They are becoming more benign by the day in comparison.

18th October 1883

After the events of last night and this morning I am already heading home. I have failed to snatch any sleep having arrived at Nantes early afternoon. I will make a detailed entry about what occurred last night and morn in a subsequent entry after I have had further rest, gathered my thoughts, and put a greater distance between my traumatised self and the Breton Marshes. God willing, I will be able to sleep. God willing, I won't be further savaged by an ambush of nightmares.

19th October 1883

As I make this entry I am now safely on a train heading for the port of Saint Nazaire. There I can sail on a 'paquebot' steamer that is bound for Southampton early tomorrow morning. I have decided to describe the events of my final night on the marshes as they unfolded. I can then at some easier time in the future reconsider them with a sober mind to see if any reappraisal is merited. As for any other reader of my journals, make of this what you will. All I would say, for guidance, is that I am a scientist not prone to either the imagination or the superstitions of simple folk. I would prefer not to relive this. Nonetheless the sequence of events was as follows:

De Menec and I strode to the stable to untether the horses. De Menec strode, to be sure, although I walked with nervous haste because, unlike my colleague, I was not unaffected by the hostility our presence was arousing.

"Monsieur, zee mood of zees peoples eez not a problem for hus," he declared, sensing my unease. "It will, az you Breetish say, soon blow eet over. But a good zing eez that a beautiful *tempête*, a thunserstorm, will blow over us zis night."

Having trotted to our preferred site and tied our restless mounts, we ventured again into the chasmic darkness carrying de Menec's assorted contraptions. The wind had been swirling and gusting for a while, bearing salvos of heavy rain showers. We waited in this inclement weather, in this pitiless terrain, in the blackest of nights for something to happen. I took a few sips from a miniature bottle of brandy Madame Rontard had slipped into my hand. Though eager for us to depart, this motherly woman retained her decency. De Menec, however, scoffed at my behaviour.

"I ham surprised, Monsieur Nudd. A scionteest should avoid ze *alcool* when working to keep ze clear head at all ze times."

I had so far endured long nights and been deprived sufficient sleep. I had tolerated de Menec's blasphemies, and also his Gallic shrugs while the local mood had become ever more menacing towards us. I was furious, and responded accordingly.

"Your impertinence astonishes me, sir. Would you rather I abstained from some medicinal liquor that will warm my blood in this vilest of weather? Would you prefer me to be struck down with a fatal attack of pneumonia?"

Of course there was little de Menec could do other than apologise. This, being the good Christian that I am, was accepted. And more suitable converstion between us, being the dedicated scientist that I am, was permitted to continue, even if de Menec deserved less.

We tarried throughout several lengthy, shivering hours for the arrival of lightning whilst scouring the murk for will o' the wisps. We felt the rain hit our faces like twelve-bore pellets. We could hear the distressed equine clamour amongst the growls of the wind trying to rip off our hats. Yet for a long period we saw nothing, nothing until the demons broke loose from hell all at once. Rumbling portents of thunder became canon fire before exploding yet louder into the terrifying whip cracks of a furious Mars. The heavens would fleetingly illuminate as if the Devil's own photographer was igniting his massif of flash-powder. Then, with irregular discharge, great bolts of jagged lightning flared like the forked-tongue flicking of serpent-headed clouds.

"Look around ze efferywhere for ze *boule* lightning, Monsieur, and I weel watch for ze Saint-Elme," shouted my encouraged colleague, although I was rather more occupied with the small matter of our safety. Shortly, with daybreak little more than a countdown away, the raging atmosphere began to calm. It was not totally pacified, though, but still saturated with moisture and less vicious electrical charge. It was in these conditions, after only a few minutes during which the first seeds of dawn were scattered, that I scrambled spellbound over to Monsieur and tugged hard on his shoulder.

"Look to my left, about five metres up and descending," I urged, but not too loudly for daft fear I might scare the object away. De Menec followed my instructions without hesitation. He instantly knew from the tone of my voice that I had espied ball lightning. It was a truly astonishing vision. Perfectly spherical and of a flaming red hue, it was the size of a standard Christmas pudding and yet lighter than a feather as it drifted down. At a height of about two feet from the ground it stopped descending and instead floated across us, no more than about four yards away, accompanied by a vile sulphurous odour like rotting eggs. De Menec and I watched in entranced silence until this ball of mystery abruptly exploded and was no more.

"Did you notice the colour and the smell?" I asked. "Sulphur dioxide, perhaps?"

"Ah yes, Monsieur, *soufre* per'aps. Magnifique! Magnifique!" de Menec enthused. "I am zinking zat ze speerit of my granfarzer it is with us."

"You never told me what became of him," I shouted as a strong gust rattled us like the defiant last words of a dying storm.

"He deesappeared. He didn't come 'ome from a field study *précisément* like zis," replied de Menec, scouring the marshes for more unusual phenomena. "Zis is *absolument magnifique,*" resumed my collegue's eulogies when I suddenly witnessed another extraordinary apparition. I had detected a wispy, flickering light flitting haphazardly roughly thirty yards or so to our right. I immediately drew Monsieur's attention to it lest it vanish before he had beheld it. It did vanish though before seemingly reappearing a little further to the right. At the same instance I heard the sound of splashing. This was probably the sound of an overweight boar that had fallen into a dyke and was trying to break free, I had initially concluded. I was mistaken, but could be more than excused for this as it transpired. De Menec and I stood still to listen. The will o' the wisp had extinguished, and then it struck me that the entire marsh had stopped to listen. The splashing noise had stopped, like de Menec and I and everything else. The marshland animals and birds that occasionally called out in the darkness or the break of day had gone silent. The wild boar that strayed from the woodland could sometimes be heard rumbling past – though not during this hiatus. In the distance the horses were mute, and the wind had dropped to nothing. We continued to listen to absolutely nothing save the inhalations and exhalations of our breath. Despite the flatness of a land lacking branches and foliage, the wind here had demonstrated its ability to mimic a repertoire of voices: from the cooing of sirens, the dirges of Scots pipers, the whistling of idlers, and the howling of wolves, to the toppling of mountainous ocean waves. Though not during this moment when the entire marsh was suspended in silence while it was watching and listening and awaiting I didn't know what. If only I had guessed. Then we heard another brief splash, and I couldn't decide whether this interruption was yet worse than the silence.

"What do you think it is?" I whispered.

"I do not know," replied de Menec.

"Is it man or beast?" I asked in a low voice. I saw de Menec shrug his shoulders. Eventually he answered,

"P'raps eez neizer, monsieur. P'raps eez both."

I waited for de Menec to say or do something else and, as if reading my mind, he moved a few paces towards the source of the disturbance. This wasn't, perhaps, the action of my choice. Don't go there, hold back, stay put, I recall myself thinking. Perhaps he could hear my thoughts. De Menec stopped, and I was unable to stifle my heavy breathing and the thumping of my heart that would have reverberated across the ground from my feet had it not been so soft. Otherwise all was silent yet again. Don't move forward another inch, I then heard myself urging de Menec in my head, and belligerently – or recklessly – he took another step forward. A split second later, and from a position yards closer, the noise resurfaced like a whale bursting through the waterline from the deep. The water settled back into inertia as the silence hung heavily. And so things tarried for half a minute – until the water was re-awoken. As the seconds slowly elapsed I could now be certain that whatever was approaching us was categorically not any animal known to science. Somebody, it seemed, having slipped into the water was now wading through it. This was no mortal. For out of the wet darkness emerged the most gruesome beast of my worst childhood nightmares, brightly illuminated only spasmodically by the re-ignited will o' the wisp that was, so it seemed, displaying sufficient intent to serve as a torch for this appalling monstrosity. At other times the beast radiated eerily with the green-tinged phosphorescence of a jaded glow-worm. It is true, I concede, that visibility was only of modest or staccato nature, but I swear upon the Good Book of the Lord that this creature bore the appearance that I shall now describe. It was human-like, only immense in stature and foulness – a veritable Homeric monster. With a jaw of exploding bushy whiskers like a chimney-boy's brush, the scalp was as hairless as that of the bald-headed vulture. This head had no ears that I could see, and the eye sockets were cavernous. Within, its eyes were open wide and stared like those of the possessed. It was altogether too terrible to hold any fascination whatsoever. Then there was the body that was covered in dripping mud and an ectoplasmic slime, similar to basted smotherings of goose fat, that was indistinguishable from its flesh. Certainly slime and flesh seemed imperceptible to an even greater extent than the skin and viscous secretions of a threatened toad. This was evident all over – for it was as naked as Adam except for a loin-cloth and the drapings of water weeds that clung about its body like ivy and dropped off the slime. Even worse and even more unfathomable, and I can only report what my eyes saw, it was swarming with eels that slithered, writhed, and fell from all parts of its body into the boggy undergrowth. These eels even seemed to emerge from inside the body like maggots erupting out of a rotting corpse. This thing, I instantly knew, had to be the dreaded marsh man. This thing I now knew to exist. Even still worse, it was lumbering straight towards us with the will o' the wisp still intermittently dancing in attendance.

"Oh my God," I muttered, glancing quickly towards de Menec and retreating backwards. My colleague, however, stood motionless. He did not return my glance but merely gazed, as if enchanted by sorcery, at this grotesque apparition that stomped ever closer. "Extraordinaire! Vraiment extraordinaire!" at length uttered de Menec, his eyes still fixed on the terrible monster.

De Menec's words, though not without validity, were hardly satisfactory in the circumstances. I fumbled about in my breast pocket with quivering fingers until I had grasped and extracted the locket containing Emily's hair which I clutched tightly. I crossed myself. I raised the lantern, summoned all my internal strength, and (I confess now), desperately hoping to perform some sort of exorcism, shouted,

"In the name of God and His son Jesus Christ leave us. Ungodly abomination, return to the place from whence you came."

Perhaps deservedly my presumption was unproductive. I knew not what to do and had an overwhelming feeling that anything I could attempt would prove futile. And the marsh man with his glow, his wispy flares, his mud, slime, weed, eels, and hell-hole wide eyes was almost upon us. With de Menec standing awestruck I had to try something. While further retreating, and without taking my eyes off the spectre, I began reciting the Paternoster but soon faltered somewhere around "Hallowed be Thy name". Then, this mad-eyed creature came to a halt. Ignoring me as if I didn't exist, it looked with unchanging dispassion into de Menec's eyes, and then perversely nodded its head like a gesture of courtesy – or even of confirmation of some esoteric pact. To my horror I saw de Menec's gaze convert into that all-knowing smile, and from his lips at first spilled out laughter that quickly developed into roars of hilarity clattering from a gaping mouth like musket shot. He seemed to be appreciating some joke between the two of them – either that, or he was possessed by demons of lunacy.

"Hallowed be Thy name," I repeated, attempting to continue my prayers before failing once more under the barrage of de Menec's deranged and blasphemous laughter whilst confronted by a grotesque smile gradually forming on the monster's face. "Hallowed be Thy name," I shouted, "Hallowed be Thy name." This was more than I could bear. With my heart already pounding I turned and ran through the hazardous quagmires back towards the horses. As I did so I could still just about hear de Menec's laughter continue to inundate the marshes without inhibition. I then slipped badly, dropping both the lantern and my precious locket. Momentarily I groped for the locket in

306

vain. So I picked myself up and continued to flee. I only managed to locate the horses so quickly because they were now audibly unsettled. I mounted mine and found the way back onto the correct track without, I later realised, my hat. Speeding towards la Chapelle-sur-le-Marais I heard the sound of another horse galloping nearer from the rear.

"Monsieur, wait. Monsieur Nudd, ATTENDEZ-VOUS, PLEASE!" yelled de Menec after me. "Monsieur you are a scionteest and you know zat you 'ave to know ze truth about zees," he continued. And he was right. Despite my state of terrified confusion, de Menec had persuaded me to stop. He caught up with me, and, breathlessly, said,

"I swear I didn't know at ze beginning zis would 'appen. *Je jure*, Monsieur. Listen. I murst tell you ze story of my granfarzer. Zis was a great man, a scionteest like you and me, a conjureur who entertained me and my brozzer when very leetle boys. Eez all I can remember of 'eem. Also 'e entertained many other peoples. My granfarzer also was 'ere in zees marais for ze study of *boules de feu* and *feu follet* and 'e 'ad been to zis place one time before also but ze local peoples did not want 'im. Zay think zat to be in ze dark 'ere to be wiz zees things must make 'im a man who eez a friend of ze little peoples, a friend of ze bad spirits, a friend of ze devil. So ze local peoples chased 'im away. My granfarzer 'e came home and wrote about iz theories but 'e want to continue eez studies. So 'e came back 'ere but told my farzer 'e would pretend to be zis terreebla creature to scare away ze local peoples so zay leave 'im alone to study in ze nights. My granfarzer was strong man. Hevery year on ze first day of ze year 'e broke ze hice to swim in a lake in Alsace. Strong like zees and strong also wiz illusions. So 'e returned to zees marshes but 'e didn't come 'ome after. Anuzer man, a friend, came to look for 'im and 'e told my farzer zat 'e thinks ze peoples 'ere, in a mob, zay waited for 'im to come out of ze marshes because zay were frightened of zis marsh man who zay think is 'eez diabolique friend. Then, my Granfarzer's friend beleef, zay killed 'im like zay kill ze poor wolf. Your 'at, monsieur," he added, passing me my spilt headwear.

I didn't know what to say. It was as implausible as it made sense. What I had just seen in the marshes had not made sense either although I had unequivocally witnessed it.

"So you understand. Monsieur, you 'ave just seen my granfarzer who az returned 'ere to protect us," de Menec explained and then again thrust out his hand, unfurling his fingers to reveal my precious locket besmirched with mud. I snatched, inserted it into a leather poke, and thrust it deep into my coat pocket. Luck notwithstanding, de Menec must have the eyes of cat, I briefly considered before trying to grasp the full extent of all I had witnessed and all he had just told me. I simply did still not know what to say but requested that we rode, which we duly did in silence, back to the auberge. My head, alas, was far from tranquil. Along the way the rather silly words with de Menec's accent, "unfeenished family beezness", kept entering my head as the memory of that unearthly marsh man invaded my consciousness. My heartbeat raced as unrelentingly as the image of that creature striding closer in the mud, with those eyes gaping like the portals of death. "Unfeenished family beezness. Unfeenished family beezness".

Yet it is the living who are always more dangerous than the dead. De Menec was quite right about that. As we entered the village a gathering of primeval locals – sinister silhouettes in the eerie light – were waiting to greet us with hurled stones and verbal atrocities that I gladly failed to comprehend. In the square, outside the auberge, lay our baggage and effects in an untidy heap. De Menec dismounted and passed me up some smaller items of my baggage that he then helped to strap onto the back of the horse. As he was doing this the handful of aggressive locals had swollen into a large lynch-mob brandishing clubs and shotguns, throwing rocks at us, and encroaching closer step by step. My horse almost bolted and de Menec screamed at me to get away at once.

"I am French. I can speak to zem in zeir own language. Go now. Monsieur Nudd, take ze 'orse and *GO NOW*. My granfarzer will protect me. One cannot keell somebody who eez already dead. ALLEZ!"

De Menec then slapped my horse hard and it finally bolted. As I galloped away I looked back briefly to see the towering de Menec surrounded by the jostling horde, some brutes shoving him while another swung a heavy stick into his back. I also thought I could hear Madame Rontard's shrieks piercing the hubbub, pleading, I think, with the others to let my colleague go. What happened subsequently I do not know, save for my own escape by the munificent mercy of God alone.